# DENISE ROBERTSON

## The Winds of War

Published in the United Kingdom in 2009 by Little Books Ltd,
Notting Hill, London W11 3QW

10 9 8 7 6 5 4 3 2

Text copyright © 2009 by Denise Robertson
Design and layout copyright © by Little Books Ltd

A CIP catalogue record for this book is available from the British Library.

ISBN 978 1 906264 07 9

Printed and bound by Scandbook

# Prologue

'It's cold in here.'

'Here, come inside my coat. Is that better?'

'I can hear your heart beating. It's racing. Do I make it beat faster? I don't want you to go, I don't want you to leave me.'

'I have to go, but the war won't last. Wars never do. Did you see those Canadian troops arrive? In the paper? And there'll be others, Aussies and Kiwis – they've said they're coming. It'll soon be over, you'll see.'

'And then you'll come back to me?'

'I'll come back, but they won't let us be together, you know that. Anyroad, don't think about it. Are you warmer now?'

'Yes, a little bit. They *can't* stop us. This war will make a difference. I'm putting my hand inside your shirt. Your skin is warm.'

'I like it when you touch me. But nothing alters people, not even war. They fight side by side, but afterwards they go back to the old ways. And there's religion, Cathy. We've got two strikes against us. They'll part us, you'll see.'

'They won't . . . we won't let them. Give me your hand. I want to feel it on my heart. On my skin.'

'We shouldn't do this.'

'Hush. You're wasting time. The door's locked. No one knows we're here. Love me . . . I want you to love me.'

'We can't. Please – don't make it hard for me.'

'We only have one day. One day, and then you'll be gone. I

1

need to remember you. I want to make sure you remember me. Don't be afraid. There's only you and I now. Just you and I, wanting each other, loving each other. Not even war can change that.'

'I might not come back.'

'You will come back. There, see . . . you want me, I know you do.'

'I love you, Cathy. Oh God, I love you.'

# BOOK 1

# Chapter One

## March 1940

CATHERINE COULD HEAR VOICES IN the kitchen as she came downstairs. Her mother's voice, calm and measured, Maisie's excited and stumbling over words as usual, Cook's mournful as ever. They would be talking about the war. She reached the hall and turned towards the breakfast-room. War was all anyone talked about now, or thought about, for that matter. It was all she thought about.

Her father was buried behind his paper. She reached to kiss the top of his head and got a grunt for her pains. She longed to ask about the Western Front, but it wouldn't do to look too eager. That could lead to questions. Instead she helped herself to eggs from the sideboard and sat down in her chair.

Her father lowered his paper as her mother appeared, looking slightly flustered.

'Not our usual bacon?' Her father's tone was not angry, merely curious.

'Oh dear.' Her mother put up a hand and fingered an earring. 'I hoped . . . well, we did think . . .'

'Think? Think what? For heaven's sake, finish a sentence!' Catherine chewed her toast as noiselessly as possible. Her father had been quite ratty lately. It must be the war.

'We only get four ounces now.' Her mother sounded incredulous. 'Four ounces each. Hardly two rashers. Cook got us some extra through a friend who works at the Maypole. But it's not like Mr Harrison's. I knew you'd see the difference; she thought you might not.'

The conversation about bacon went on but Catherine shut her ears. She was itching to get her hands on the newspaper and turn to the war news. He was '*somewhere in France*' – that was how his last letter had been headed. In the trenches along the Belgian border, probably. She knew that was where British soldiers were, trying to close the gap between the Maginot Line and the Channel coast. It had said so in the paper after the King had visited the troops.

There was a clatter in the hall, and Pamela erupted into the room. 'She hasn't stitched my hem, Mummy. You know I need it for tonight. I will be mortified if I have to go in that green dress. She said – you promised – my white taffeta would be ready. We'll look like country cousins, I can see it. *She* may not care but I do.'

This last was directed at Catherine, who made no response. It was Henry Callingham's 21st birthday tonight, and a huge party, in spite of the war. In Catherine's opinion, it wasn't seemly that Henry should have a party when people were fighting and dying. As for going on about a dress! But as usual everyone would scurry to pacify Pamela.

Her father put down the paper and Catherine put out a stealthy hand to steal it. 'Not at the table, dear,' her mother said. 'It isn't ladylike.'

She would have to wait for news. All she could see was a headline: '*Plunging temperatures halt German plans to attack on the Western Front.*'

She felt a sudden wave of nausea. Perhaps she had eaten her egg too quickly. She reached for a piece of dry toast and waited for it to pass.

There was frost in the paddock as David turned his mare for the stable block. In spite of the cold, he had enjoyed the ride. The Durham countryside was beautiful at any time, but under frost it took on grandeur. Besides, it had been good to get out of the house and avoid the party preparations. He groaned at the thought that his own 21st was a mere two years away, and the whole rigmarole would have to be gone through again.

But looking on the peaceful landscape it was hard to believe England was at war. The dreaded air raids had not materialised, the strictness over black-out was slackening, the gas-masks no one had moved without last year were seldom seen nowadays. And yet his brother was in training to fight in the air, and perhaps to die.

David was in the courtyard now, swinging down from the horse, surrendering the saddle that allowed him to forget he was lame. 'The limping one' – that's what they'd said at Eton when they talked of the Callinghams. Henry had been 'Young Callingham'; he had been the other brother, the limping one.

As he let himself into the house by the side door, he could hear the chatter coming from every quarter, servants running here and there at his sister's bidding. 'Thank goodness it's his birthday now,' India had said yesterday. 'Another month, and they'll all be called up.' If the war lasted for two years, he thought suddenly, he might not have a birthday party at all. There would be no food, the cellar would be ransacked and no more wine from France ... Kynaston itself might even be taken over as a billet for officers, or a hospital. It was big enough.

He made his way up to his room to change, buoyed up by the thought of a possible reprieve – and by the fact that he would see Catherine Allerton tonight. Henry would sweep her off as soon as she appeared, but that was how it had always been. And at least he would see her.

7

'Well, I've never known a winter like it.' Hannah Chaffey looked around as though to detect disagreement.

'We're not supposed to talk about the weather.' Sarah McGuire looked up from the sink in surprise at the sombre tone of her father's voice. Normally he took no notice of their neighbour's visit. Or pretended he didn't notice.

'Why ever not?' Mrs Chaffey had folded her arms under her bosom, ready for an argument.

'They don't want Hitler knowing what the weather's like here. They can't put it out on the wireless, not for two weeks.'

'Well, you live and learn. But you're not telling me Hitler's listening to what I say about it?'

Her father shook a doubtful head. 'Fifth Column's everywhere. What do they say? Careless talk costs lives.'

'In your back kitchen? Get off with you!'

Behind the cover of a tea-towel, Sarah smiled. They were a music-hall act, those two. As good as anything on the wireless. If she was not mistaken, Mrs Chaffey was after her Dad, but she was wasting her time.

She felt a sudden flutter in her abdomen. Her baby was stirring. She put down the towel, and laid her hand on her belly, feeling the tiny thump that was a fist or an arm. Her baby was safe in her womb, but his father was God knew where. At least he was with Joe.

She smiled to herself again, remembering her brother. You could depend on Joe. '*I'll bring your Gerard back for you, Sal. You leave it to me.*' That was all she could do. What had Joe said in his letter? '*It's cold here but we are in good spirits. Take care of things, Sal. We'll be back before you know it.*' He had a reason of his own to come back – some girl he was keeping a secret even from his sister. Whoever she was, she would have to be good to measure up to Joe.

Sarah fingered the wedding ring on her third finger, smiled into space again, and went back to her dishes.

'Put it there! No, *there*!'

David hated the way his sister spoke to servants, as though they were idiots.

'Let me.' He took the huge cake-stand from the hands of a nervous maid and placed it on the sideboard. Three tiers, rather like a wedding cake, as befitted the heir to Kynaston. The smallest tier would be eaten tonight, and the other two cut up and sent in white and silver boxes to everyone who worked on the estate. Workers in the two coal mines would receive cake only if they were deputies or above.

He never understood the hierarchy of the pit. Datal hands were the lowest form of life, then putters . . . or was it hewers? No, they were big men, mostly, and quite lordly. He gave up trying to sort it out. The pits would be Henry's problem one day, not his, thank God. There were benefits to being a second son.

And it was Henry who had been needed to go to war. His twisted foot would keep him at home, twiddling his thumbs. That was not a blessing, but a curse.

'Watch what you're doing with that pan, our Sarah.'

Her father was all concern as Sarah lifted the pan of boiling water from one hob to another.

'I'm not an invalid, Dad.' Her father's expression said, 'Not yet, but carry on like that and you will be.' This would be his first grandchild.

His own children had come quickly: Sarah, then Joe, then Jim, then Terence. Four children in hardly more than five years. And yet her mother had been so desperate for a bairn in her arms again that she had fallen almost straight away, and had died in labour. Gerard had been firm: '*It's not what I want for you, Sal.*' They would enjoy this baby for a few years, two at least, and to hell with what the priest said.

'That party's on tonight, isn't it?' Young Terry sounded both curious and envious.

Sarah nodded, 'Yes, they've been getting ready for weeks. Sides of beef, pheasants. They've got Italian ice-cream coming from Darlington. I got it off Jenny. She says the bottles are six deep in the cellar.'

'No rationing there, then. I might have known. No smear of butter, spoonful of sugar for them.' Jim didn't like coal-owners at any time, especially not when they were giving parties.

'They won't escape everything, Jim. Not if there's air raids. And he's in the Air Force. He's doing his bit.'

'Who?'

'The birthday boy.'

'The other one'll get off, being a cripple,' her father said. 'The old man was a hero last time. Decorated. I remember me Dad going on about it. They all turned out to welcome him back.'

Sarah chuckled suddenly. 'They should call up that eldest one. The daughter, her with the silly name. She'd see Hitler off – Mussolini as well.'

The bedroom smelled of soap and scent, and, faintly, of moth-balls. That was the evening capes taken from her mother's wardrobe: sable for Pamela, and fox-fur for her. Left to her own devices, Catherine would have preferred a shawl . . . or not to have gone at all.

But an invitation from the Callinghams was not to be disregarded. '*A good family*' – how many times had her mother stressed the Callingham lineage? If she or Pamela could land a Callingham . . . Catherine realised she was grinning at a vision of her mother dancing round the drawing-room in exultation at the thought of a 'good' marriage. *'It's so important. It's all a woman has in the end, security. You've seen how Daddy has looked after us all . . . that's what I want for my girls.'*

Catherine thought Henry Callingham rather arrogant. David was nicer, but tongue-tied. Polio was such bad luck. She turned to look at her sister. Pamela was fiddling with her hair again, agitated because she was pinning her hopes on making a splash at the party and securing her future: marriage, and two or three nice children in a house exactly like this one.

What would her own fate be? Catherine let herself think of it for a moment, and then shut out dangerous thoughts. It wouldn't do for anyone to know. She didn't share Joe's fears for their future, but nor did she underestimate the lengths her parents would go to, to prevent what they would see as a mistake. She and Joe would have to run away probably, but none of that mattered as long as he came home safely. She folded her hands on her breast, thinking of how they had made love. She had wanted to give him that, a gift to take him safely through the war. But for now it must be her secret.

As they came down the stairs, Catherine in blue and Pamela in white as became a younger sister, their parents came into in the hall.

'Don't they look wonderful, Daddy?'

'Not bad. A credit to you, my dear.'

And then they were swirled into fur and into the back seat of the Morris, and its wheels were crunching over the frosty drive. Outside the sky was inky and spattered with stars. Beside her, Pamela was trembling.

'Buck up. It's only a party.'

'The last party there'll be for a while,' her father said from the front seat. 'You should do your best to enjoy it.'

'I can hardly believe there is a war on,' Pamela said. 'They're calling it a phoney war.'

'Tell that to the men dying in France,' was her father's reply. And suddenly the war seemed very, very real indeed.

## Chapter Two

February 1940

LIGHT WAS STREAMING THROUGH a split in the curtains. Catherine had left them a little open last night, so that she could see the stars. She and Joe had made that pact: look at the stars wherever they were, and each would know that the other was looking, too. She had done that last night, never mind how late it was. She had stood in her bare feet, the events of the evening skittering around her mind, and thought of Joe. Outside, the night had been cold and clear and utterly silent. Where he was, there would be the sound of gunfire, the thud of falling shells, perhaps the screams of the dying –

She had leaped into bed and buried her face in the pillow, reviewing the events of the last few hours to blot out that thought.

They had eaten in the huge dining-room, a salmon mousse, guinea fowl, and something creamy called Le Petit Henri, in honour of the birthday boy.

After that there had been speeches from Sir Gervase and a funny riposte from Henry, and then the ladies had escaped to the drawing-room for coffee, leaving the men to their port. She had caught David's eye as she passed him, but he had blushed and looked away.

It had been Henry who sought her out when it was time for

dancing. That had upset Pamela, and India Callingham too, especially when he came back to her time after time. Dancing had made her head swim, or perhaps it had been the unaccustomed wine. They had wine at home on special occasions, but in very small quantities. At the Hall it had flowed, waiters at your elbow every few minutes to top up your glass so that you didn't know how many glasses you had drunk. Had she had three or four – or more? However many, she had felt distinctly queasy. Now, as she swung her legs to the floor and sat on the edge of the bed, she still had a feeling of nausea. She had slept eventually last night, but she did not feel refreshed now.

She felt a little better when she was washed and dressed and on her way down to breakfast. Surprisingly, Cook was in the dining-room, bustling between sideboard and table. Her mother pre-empted her question. 'Maisie has had to go home. Her cousin has been killed in France.'

Catherine concentrated on buttering her toast. Maisie probably had lots of cousins – it wouldn't be Joe. He had laughed a little uneasily when he told her a cousin of his worked for her family, but all the colliery families were related. It couldn't, it mustn't, be him. Her mother was bemoaning the fact that Pamela wasn't down yet; her father was invisible behind his newspaper.

'Well, tell us what happened last night.' Her mother's face was eager.

'It was good . . . lovely.' She felt sick again, but this time it was the sickness of fear.

'Good? Lovely? Really, the way you girls speak. What happened?'

Catherine sought desperately for something, anything to say in reply. 'Henry said he was glad he'd joined the RAF, and everyone cheered.'

Her mother's face fell. 'Is that all? Did he dance with you and Pamela? I didn't think he was old enough to join up. I

13

thought – but of course he's 21 now.'

Her father lowered his paper. 'The boy was in the University Air Squadron at Oxford. They enlisted as soon as war broke out. Anyway, all the boys will have to go before this is finished. Hitler is sweeping everything before him.'

'Herbert! You're always so defeatist. All those Canadians and Australians are coming over. It'll be all right. Don't scare the children.'

The newspaper shook and went back into place, but her father continued to speak from behind it. 'Tell that to that girl in the kitchen.'

Catherine found her voice then. 'What was her cousin's name?' She had tried to sound disinterested, but even to her own ears she sounded keen.

'I don't know, dear. Some Catholic name, quite common. Joseph, I think. Something like that.'

Her father lowered his paper. 'I thought your grandpapa was a Joseph. The one who had the ale house?' Her mother turned her face away to show her contempt for such a remark, but Catherine was pushing back her chair.

'If you don't mind', she was standing up, and there was singing in her ears, 'I think I'll go back to bed for a little while.' And then she was in the hall, and the fear that was engulfing her could be allowed to show in her face.

The telegram had come at seven o'clock, the boy's face full of curiosity as he handed it over. Sarah had felt a surge of relief when she saw it was addressed to her father. It wasn't for her! It wasn't Gerard, father of the child kicking inside her. But the relief was short-lived. If it wasn't Gerard, it must be Joe.

She watched as her father tore it open, and suddenly reached behind him for something, anything, to hold on to. 'What is it,

Dad?' Her father did not speak, just handed her the paper. '*Killed in action*': the words jumped out. Joe was dead, killed in action. Joe, who was always laughing, and liked tomato fried with his bacon, and had carried her to school on his back when her knee was bad, was dead.

The phrase rolled round and round in her mind all the while she went from house to house, summoning aunts to her father, finding someone to fetch her brothers out of the pit. Aunty Jessie clutched the sink when she heard, and then fetched her coat from the back of the door.

'The first in the village,' she said. 'But he won't be the last. Have you told our Helen? Good.' She picked up her big leather purse and fetched the front-door key from the mantelpiece. Her fingers were swollen at the knuckles, and looked red raw. It was funny how you could notice things like that when something a thousand times bigger was happening.

'I want to cry,' Sarah thought, 'but I can't. It's too big to cry about.'

'You leave your father to me,' Aunty Jessie said, arming her over the step and locking the door. 'Fetch your Jim and Terry. Go to the overman's house in Lady Maureen Terrace. It's the end one. You might catch him still up – he was on night shift. If not, wake him up, he won't mind. He's got a telephone, and he'll likely ring the colliery office. Then come home, lass. You look half-frozen, out in this with no coat, and you five months gone.'

Sarah had not felt the cold till then, never realised that goosebumps were apparent on her bare arms. When she had roused the overman from a sound sleep and got his promise to fix everything, she sat down on the wall of the churchyard and cried for her brother.

'There's been a death in the village. A casualty somewhere in France.' India announced it as though death in war was a normal occurrence. David looked across at his brother and saw his own impression mirrored there.

'Who was it?' Henry asked.

'I don't know – some relative of Cook's. She's taken it very well. I said we'd manage breakfast if she wanted to go home, but she said she'd rather work. They say work's a solace, don't they?' India was smearing marmalade on to her toast. 'They're used to death in the pit. I don't think they have the same reactions . . .'

'. . . as decent people?' Henry's voice was tart, and David was torn between wishing he had had the courage to say it and anxiety that it would provoke a row.

'That's not what India meant at all.' His father was rebuking Henry, but without much conviction. 'Anyway, it's very sad, but we can't let it interfere when there's so much to do.'

At midnight last night Henry, in party mood, had declared his eagerness to go to war. 'You should be toasting the RAF, not me. So raise your glasses, everyone. Here's to licking the Hun!' Everyone had cheered, but his father had looked apprehensive, though proud. David had put his hand on his brother's shoulder to show support, and Henry had smiled at him. 'I'm escaping, old chap, and leaving it all to you. Take care of everyone, especially Catherine Allerton. I mean to marry her, David. If Jerry doesn't get me.' And David had done his very best to look pleased at the news.

India had finished her toast now and was looking across at Henry. 'Did you really have to behave in that theatrical way last night? On the stroke of midnight! Like a bad play.'

'I thought it would annoy you, dear sister. What better reason could there be?'

'Father? You tell him . . . he's such a show-off. And dancing with those dreadful Allerton girls. I said we shouldn't have asked them.'

'Is it because their father's in trade? Or perhaps it's because their house has a number?' Henry turned to David now. 'Whatever you do, David, don't marry into trade. Of course, everything we have came from someone who found coal in his one field and dug it out with his bare hands, but that's lost in the mists of time. We, you see, have arrived.'

David felt a sense of despair. Henry and India would be at it all day now, sniping at one another, and all the while the world was at war. He put down his napkin, excused himself from the table, and made his way as quickly as his limp allowed to the stables.

Catherine had racked her brains for excuses to go to the village and find out the facts. Inside her, hope flared up – and was as quickly extinguished. There were thousands of Josephs, probably a dozen just in the village. But most of the villagers worked in the pit. Joe had enlisted in 1938 as soon as he was 18. '*Four years in the hole was enough for me, Cathy. Down in the dark, mice at your back, cockroaches in your clays. I wanted to see the sun and the stars at night.*' He had always loved the stars. She realised then that she was talking about him in the past tense, and quickly converted: 'He is somewhere now, smiling, writing to me!' He'd be laughing at her now if he knew.

Except that he was dead, lying somewhere in a foreign field. She told herself that, repeating it over and over again, as though it were a spell. She was still wondering how she could find out when she heard the phone ring in the hall, and then Cook's telephone voice: 'Belgate 237.' Her mother was in the hall, but Cook was speaking again. 'It's for Miss Catherine, Madam. Shall I fetch her?'

For a fleeting, crazy moment, Catherine thought it might be Joe, ringing to laugh with her and put her mind at rest. But they had never spoken on the telephone. There had been only covert messages whispered from sides of mouths, until they could be alone and mouths were not for talking.

The voice on the phone was Henry Callingham's. 'Will you come to tea? Or let me take you out somewhere? You can't say no. I only have a few days left.'

In the end she said yes. He might know something; he might take her somewhere where she could find out. When she put down the phone, her mother's face was suffused with satisfaction. Pamela, in the background, looked anything but pleased that a Callingham would be having tea with her sister instead of her.

---

'There can't be a funeral, of course, although I'm certain Joe would have been laid to rest with great respect where he fell.' The priest had been a chaplain in the last war. Now his face was troubled, and Sarah was glad of that. It had to matter that Joe had died. When she had a bairn safely in the world, she would tell him about his Uncle Joe. Every little detail. She thought of the letter he had sent her after his embarkation leave. '*Give the folks my love, Sal. When I come home I'll bring something for you, very French. And tell that bairn his uncle's going to spoil him something rotten. We'll all be OK when we get this lot over.*'

They had prayed when the priest came. Prayers for Joe, for those he had left behind, for his comrades in arms, and for a swift end to a just war. 'It is a just war.' The priest had patted her father's arm to emphasise the point.

But her father had remained stony-faced, Jim, too. He was still black from the pit, except for a soapy flannel taken across his face. No one had liked to drag out the tin bath in a room full of comings and goings. Terry would be back before long, and then something would have to be done. Life couldn't stop, not even for death, certainly not the life of the pit.

'A remembrance service,' the priest was saying. 'The Monsignor will approve of that, I'm sure. Next week, perhaps. Would that comfort you?'

McGuire had nodded fervently as he nodded to everything a priest or nun suggested. But after the priest had gone he rose to his feet and moved to the fire. 'He'll be drunk tonight,' Sarah thought. That was how he dealt with grief: he drowned it. Her Gerard drank, too, but he had promised her, '*The odd pint, Sally. That's all there'll be when this is over and we have our own place*'. Like Joe he had turned away from the pit. '*I hate the bitch. She'll have you if she gets half a chance. I'd rather face a bullet than be trapped in the hole.*'

He had been in the Army three years when they married. They had never had a home of their own. There were only colliery houses in Belgate, except for a handful of council houses and they were for the chosen few Protestants. Still, something would turn up. A bairn gave you priority – or Gerard might get Army accommodation. For now, she had a roof over her head and a brother to mourn.

They gathered in the library before dinner. Somehow, meals had taken on an extra importance for David since Henry had joined up. One day there might be an empty chair at the table. Permanently empty. There had been one death in the village already.

He couldn't imagine life without his brother. Henry had been there, peering into the pram, from the first moment David's eyes had focused. They had bathed together, played together, fought rarely, and laughed often. And when he was ill, Henry had goaded him back to life, made him move again when he had thought his wasted leg would not hold him up. They had been together at school, David seeking a vocation, Henry knowing he was heir to Kynaston. But Henry had gone off to Oxford alone – no pressure had been put on David to follow him there, and for that he was grateful. He had stayed at home and buried himself in books.

That had been his sanctuary, the world of books. It was all that remained for a cripple. He forced the word to the forefront of his mind: no need to shirk it, and no need to be ashamed of it, either. His sister might be ashamed of it, but he wasn't and nor was Henry. Nor his father – his father had never made David feel an outcast. A terrible thought struck him then. If Henry died the weight of Kynaston would fall upon him, and he wasn't up to it. He looked across the library at his father. The consumption that had dogged him for years showed in his face now. He had been an important man, almost a great one. Now he was frail, a shadow of his former self. If he went, too . . . It was a relief when India's voice cut across his thoughts.

'We'll have to close off some of the rooms. They're enforcing the black-out now, and we can't deal with all the windows. Barrass says he can get frames made, but they'll have to be put in place each night, and with staff going off to this awful war . . . I suggested heavy curtains, but he says even a chink of light is forbidden.'

They talked of the war, then, of rationing, and the rounding-up of Germans and Italians. 'Some poor little pork butcher has had his windows put in in Darlesden. Been there a lifetime, but the name above the shop condemned him. Schmeling – it's in the *Advertiser*.' That was his father.

'What else do they expect?' India sounded furious as usual, and not for the first time David wondered what drove her to such rage with life.

'They shouldn't have been here in the first place – they have their own country. Now it's causing havoc. They have to go.'

If Henry had been home, there would have been another

argument. But he was off somewhere with Catherine Allerton. David tried not to dwell on that, and instead stood up and moved to the sideboard to replenish his glass.

≈

It was cold in the summer house but Catherine could see faint stars appearing through the frosted panes. She couldn't stay there for long, She had persuaded Henry Callingham to drop her at the gate instead of the front door, and then she had picked her way across the lawn, the grass soft underfoot, until she reached the path that led round the house to the place where she and Joe had met and loved and talked of a future together.

She knew now that Joe was dead. She felt it, and acceptance had brought her a kind of peace. She had nodded and smiled at Henry today, and appeared to hang on every word, when in fact her thoughts had been elsewhere. What had Joe said? '*They'll never let us be together, Cathy.*' In the end, though, it wasn't class or religion that had parted them.

She laid her cheek against a window pane that let in moonlight through a cobweb of frost, and wept at the futility of war.

# Chapter Three

## March 1940

'AT LEAST THE FRENCH ARE suffering, too.' Her mother's tone was resigned as she surveyed the comparatively meagre breakfast table, but a little smile of satisfaction was hovering round her lips. 'It says in the *Express* that everything is going to be rationed there, and there'll be limits on restaurants, too.'

Catherine looked across the table. Her father was sure to have some comment. He hated the French. Sure enough, he was lowering his paper.

'They'll find a way round it. Weasely lot, the French.'

'It won't matter soon, Daddy,' said Pamela. 'The Germans'll swallow them all up. Anthea Norris's father says the Maginot Line's made of paper.'

Her mother was looking apprehensive, her father's face was colouring up, and the paper was put aside. 'Anthea Norris's father's an idiot, then.'

Catherine felt herself relax. There was going to be an argument, which meant no one would notice that she couldn't face breakfast. She felt sickly again, but even worse was the heavy weight inside her. He was dead. And she daren't even cry.

Her father was leaning over the table. 'The Maginot Line is built into the ground. All the way from Belgium to Switzerland. Paper, indeed! It's full of tank traps and gun posts, all along the border with Germany.' Pamela looked suitably impressed and her father was mollified.

Maisie, still a little tearful around the eyes, came in then, with the post on the silver hall tray. Catherine was seized with envy. Maisie could cry, get sympathy, bewail her loss, and she had only lost a cousin. But she, Catherine, must keep her grief to herself. Her father seized the post and riffled through it. 'Bills,' he said. 'Bills, bills . . . one for you, Catherine.'

The envelope was cream, the paper inside it matching. 'Who's it from?' Her mother's eyes were bright with curiosity, and any hope Catherine of keeping the letter for later faded. She opened it. 'It's from Henry Callingham,' she said, feeling her cheeks redden.

'Henry Callingham!' Her mother was looking meaningfully at her husband, but he had gone back to his paper.

'Please may I leave the table?' Pamela almost spat out the words, and was halfway into the hall before any permission could be given. Catherine was about to make her own excuses, when her father looked up.

'There's going to be a memorial service for that boy in the village. Joseph whatever his name was.'

'The boy who died in France? Maisie's cousin?' Her mother's hand had gone up to finger her pearls as it always did when emotional matters were under discussion, but it didn't divert her attention from the letter. 'Come on, Catherine, what does he say? Is he coming home?'

'No mother, he's at the Air Centre in Oxford. But he says it's all right, and he's having basic training.' She turned to her father, trying to make her voice nonchalant. 'When is that service? The one for that poor boy?'

'Today, I think.' He was checking the pages. 'Yes, today, at two o'clock.'

'I might go.' Surely they would hear the grief and terror in her voice?

'There's no need, dear. It's very sad, and I expect the whole village will turn out to show respect. But we don't know them. And they're not really our people, are they?' Her mother's eyes were still fixed on the cream envelope.

'I'd still like to go. Just to show respect. And to back up Maisie.' That was a master stroke. Her mother was fond of the term '*noblesse oblige*' and prided herself on her attitude to servants.

'Well, if you can spare the time. And it is the first war death. You won't be able to go to them all, I'm afraid. Not unless Mr Chamberlain finds a way out.'

---

'One of us should go.' There were only two of them in the morning-room, he and India. 'I wish Henry were here,' David thought. He would have understood, would probably have gone himself. India was unmoved.

'He didn't work on the estate any more, David. He was a soldier. Not our responsibility.'

'I still think we should show our face. I'll do it. It needn't concern you.'

India had taken to weaving her hair round into a coil at the back of her head, which made her gestures seem even more extravagant. Now she tossed her head as though to dismiss the subject, and leaned forward to reach the marmalade.

'You must do as you please. But once you start something you may find yourself overwhelmed. Don't say I didn't warn you.'

David didn't answer. You couldn't discuss things with India. When they were children, Henry had christened her the Dominatrix and received a dressing-down from his father. But it was true. Ever since their mother had died, she had taken over Kynaston. Simply assumed the role of mistress of the house. Of their lives, come to that.

Anyway he was going to the funeral. Partly because it was the least he could do, in the absence of a proper role in the war, to show respect to the dead. And partly because Catherine Allerton might be there. She lived quite near to the village, and she cared about people. Yes, she might very well be there.

⸺

They had planned out the garden as soon as war was declared. 'We won't starve,' Sarah's father had said, as he turned over the shabby grass to reveal the rich, black earth beneath. When news came of Joe's death he had seemed to lose interest, but today he was attacking the sods like a man possessed.

'Summer cabbage,' he told Sarah. 'Carrots, early crop, cauliflowers and parsley. We'll likely still get fish from the harbour, if they don't block it off.' Later would come leeks and broad beans and crunchy radishes. 'And there'll be pigeons.' He had nodded towards the cree in the yard as he said that, and Sarah had shuddered. She would starve before she ate pigeon pie, knowing that once the meat it contained had fluttered, warm and feathered, beneath her window.

Then she thought of the child she was carrying and rested a hand on her swollen belly. She would have to eat something. She had promised Gerard she would take care of herself and his child. But not pigeon. That was a step too far.

She watched as her father dibbed and sowed, pushing seedlings into the earth with a huge hand. A pitman's hand, flecked with blue marks that were really coal dust under the skin. Gerard, like Joe, had preferred to work above ground, and so they had both gone for soldiers. She would rather have had them safe in the pit. There was death there, too, but it was rare, thank God.

Far off she heard the church clock chime. 'You should be getting ready now, Dad.' For a moment he didn't look up or cease his planting. Surely he was not going to say he wasn't going to the service, not when Father Lavery had arranged it specially? But, no, the dibber was being laid aside, and he was rising from his knees to dust soil from his trousers.

＝＝＝

Catherine had tried to slip from the house unnoticed, but her mother was passing through the hall as she descended the stairs. 'You've put a hat on, I hope? Good.' She was fiddling with the narcissi in the vase on the hall-stand. 'Come straight back, and be careful not to sit too close to anyone. So many colds and sneezes about at this time of year.' Catherine had reached the door and was almost over the step. 'Straight back, remember. There could be an air raid. All those deaths at Scapa Flow last Saturday.'

'Only one civilian.' That was Pamela, hanging over the banister. 'Besides, they won't bomb here. There's nothing worth bombing in a dump like this.'

Her mother's wail of protest followed Catherine down the drive, her gas-mask case banging against her hip as she walked. She could feel tears at the back of her eyes, treacherous tears that would give her away if she wasn't careful. Joe had been so afraid of anyone finding out. *'They'll separate us if they do, Cathy. They'll never let us be.'*

He was the only person who had ever called her Cathy. 'What's your name?' he had asked that first day, as they struggled to free her dog's paw from the snare that held it.

'Cathy,' she had said, and then wondered why. She was always Catherine, but Cathy had just popped into her head. He had nodded. 'I'm Joe.' And then, a moment later, when the dog was free, 'There you are, Cathy. He'll need a vet, but he'll be all right. Tough, aren't you, old son?' And Jet had licked his hand. She had been 14 then to Joe's 16, and somehow they had just melded into one. But always in secret. '*We're different you and me, Cathy. They'll never let us be.*'

He had underestimated how strong she was. If he had lived, she would have made it happen. Made her family accept it, or else gone off with him and left her old life behind. She had written to him while she was away at school, and signed the letters with kisses. For a moment a wild desire to stalk up to the front of the church and lay claim to him occurred, but it was swiftly beaten down. Joe had loved her, had loved with her, so what did it matter who walked behind his coffin?

Except that there wasn't a coffin. He was dead somewhere in France, and she could never tell the world that he had mattered. She let the tears run unchecked down her cheeks until the church came into view, and she saw the villagers lining the way.

David parked the Wolseley a little way from the church and walked the last few hundred yards. He had never been in a Catholic church before, but according to his father it was simply a more extreme version of the established church.

'Lots of smells and candles,' India had contributed.

He had not bargained for the curious stares of the villagers clustered outside the church wall. One or two he knew, as they worked on the estate. Men took off their caps and bobbed their heads as he passed, and he nodded in return. The women's gaze was more curious, their eyes meeting his briefly then dropping to his limping foot. He tried not to hurry. When he hurried he was inclined to trip, and that wouldn't do. It was a relief when he passed through the doorway, and the scent and colour of the church engulfed him.

She was there at the side, towards the back. He knew he should go nearer the front, indeed the verger was already leading him down the aisle, but the temptation to sit beside

Catherine was too great. He slipped into the pew beside her, seeing her smile in the flickering light of what seemed a dozen candled shrines, and buried his head in prayer.

He prayed for the family of the dead man. Boy, really – someone had said he was only 20. He prayed for his mother, then *'Bring Henry back.'* He was afraid of the responsibility that would fall upon him if his brother died. Their father was not in good health, but he would surely live long enough for Henry to marry and produce an heir? David redoubled his efforts to pray, jumbling in everything: an end to war, an easing of his gammy leg, a job, something useful to do, and then, crazily, that Catherine might hold out a hand to him and smile again.

When he opened his eyes, it was time to stand up as the mourners entered the church, and the priest began to intone the opening words of the service. He wondered why Catherine Allerton was weeping for a dead soldier whom she couldn't have known – but she had a kind heart, so that explained it.

'You can't do away with the tennis court!' Pamela felt outrage swell up in her. 'We won't be able to have tennis parties any more. And how can we accept invitations if we can't invite people back?'

Her father was rolling his eyes in exasperation, but it was her mother who answered her. 'Everyone will be doing the same, darling. The Wentworth-Evanses have already turned theirs over, *and* their rose garden. We have to "Dig for Victory", or we shan't get any vegetables.'

'We can still buy them. Farmers will still grow them.'

''Fraid not.' Her father's moustache was bristling, but Pamela didn't care if he was annoyed.

'You're ruining my life. You don't seem to mind.'

'You won't be here to have your life ruined. You'll be called up, unless we can find you a reserved occupation.'

They were expecting her to work! Pamela felt fear clutch at her chest. Everything was crumbling, everything she wanted and needed to make the right marriage and be able to hold her head high. She had always been ashamed of their being in trade; girls at school had talked of being 'in trade' as little better than being working class. She had always been careful not to tarnish her reputation, because a good marriage was her way out, her only way out. And now war was engulfing them, and destroying her plans.

She was seeking another argument in favour of the tennis parties when Catherine came in, casting off her hat and roughing up her hair.

'They're going to dig up the tennis court!'

She might have expected Catherine to go against her, so her 'Good!' came as no surprise. 'I've just been talking to David – he gave me a lift home – he says they're ploughing up everything at the Hall. And they're turning the wine cellar into an air-raid shelter.'

'Have you been crying?' Her mother sounded surprised, and Pamela turned to stare at her sister. Catherine's eyes were red, and so was her nose. She muttered something about its being cold outside, and the service being sad, but it didn't sound convincing.

'Did you say David Callingham was there? I wouldn't have thought he'd come down from the Hall, not when the dead man wasn't an estate worker.' She felt a twinge of jealousy. Trust Catherine to get a ride with a Callingham! 'Was it the Bentley?'

'How would I know? It was a car, quite big. David says they've heard from Henry, and he's been flying already.

Inside Pamela, an idea was growing. If the worst came to the worst, there was always David Callingham. No one would want him with that twisted leg, and even a second son in that family would be wealthy. She had never really thought of him before, but he was good-looking. If it hadn't been for the limp . . . It was a comfort to know he would be there, if nothing better offered.

$\approx$

They had made the best of an evening meal, talking all the while of the service, and Father Lavery, who had done them proud. Sarah had found comfort as his soft Irish voice praised her brother, and the sacrifices men made in war. The priest was hardly more than a bairn himself, but he had put his heart and soul into that service. It had been good, all of it. You could see it in the quiet contentment on her father's face, which had replaced the anguish of the past two weeks. Now he had a pint of stout at his side, his boots cast off, and his socked feet to the fire, and soon he would be asleep.

There had been so many people in the church today, more than she had bargained for. The one with the limp from the big house, and the dark-haired girl from the houses in the Dene, the one who had gone away to school. Her sister was a snobby bitch, but this one had cried during the service. Crying over someone she never even knew, because he had died for his country. It comforted Sarah to think that people cared that much.

$\approx$

The evening dragged interminably. At dinner Catherine toyed with her food until her father lost patience with her. 'For goodness sake, stop mauling your food and eat it. Your mother and Cook have put effort into this meal, and you don't seem interested.'

Her eyes had filled with tears, and her mother had made

faces at her father to tell him enough was enough. She had managed to swallow a few more mouthfuls, and to make it through to coffee, and then she had pleaded a headache and been excused.

Now, in her bedroom, she waited as the house gradually grew silent. Bedroom and bathroom doors opened and closed. Cook first, then Pamela, then her parents, then Maisie scampering up to the attic bedroom. When all was quiet, she sat on for 20 minutes before wrapping up warmly and picking her way down the dark staircase, across the hall and kitchen, unbolting the back door and easing it shut behind her.

The cold seized at her breath, and the frosted grass crackled so loudly beneath her feet that she looked back at the house, certain a light would spring up in a window. But the house stayed dark until she was safe in the summerhouse with the door shut on the world.

She cried then, remembering love, the feel of his arms around her as they had lain there that last night. He had been afraid, but she had known it was the right thing to do. It had been painful for her, but he had cried at the wonder of it, and smothered her face with kisses. '*There'll never be anyone else, Cathy. Never has been, never will be. Only you.*' And she had vowed the same.

But now he was gone, and life was over before it had even begun.

# Chapter Four

## April 1940

THE WINTER HAD BEEN ONE of the hardest David could remember. Traffic had been marooned on icy roads, pipes had frozen, skies had been leaden for weeks on end. Which meant that spring had never been more welcome. He stood by the window as he finished dressing. The parkland rolled away from the house, dotted here and there with yellow spots of daffodils. Beyond the trees, the farms on the estate would be sprouting green. Thank God something was untouched by war.

His father was already at the breakfast table when he reached it, *The Times* open in front of him. David helped himself to eggs, and sat opposite him. 'Anything special?'

His father shook his head. 'Bader's back with the RAF.'

David put down his knife and fork. 'Flying?'

'Yes. They've obviously modified the aircraft to accommodate the fact that he has no legs. Huge morale boost, of course: "Legless flyer fights the Hun", that sort of thing. Not that it'll do much good. You can't rely on the French to hold. Hitler will take the Low Countries against little or no resistance. After that, France – and he's at the Channel.'

David didn't respond. His father was always gloomy when it came to the war. Best not to encourage him. But as he ate his breakfast he thought about Douglas Bader. If they could modify a plane for a man with no legs, why not for a man with one good leg? He shifted his heavy boot under the table, and gave way to a reverie about heroism and whether or not Catherine would then notice that he was on the earth.

Catherine feigned sleep until she heard Pamela come out of her room and go clattering down to breakfast. These mornings she avoided her sister's curious gaze. Things were bad enough without prying eyes. When she awoke each day she felt calm and happy, and then she would remember. She would never see Joe again. Never again feel his touch, his breath on her cheek, his hand on her arm. They would never laugh together, or kiss, or lie quietly on the grass, each content that the other was there. He was dead. This morning, as in previous mornings, she poked that fact like a sore tooth. Dead, dead, dead.

She sat up suddenly in the bed as a wave of nausea overcame her. She folded her arms across her chest, seeking comfort. Her breasts felt tender and seemed to loom large under the cotton nightie. She felt a sudden fear, and then dismissed it. You couldn't be pregnant after the first time you made love. Everyone at school had said that, so it was true. It had been a brief, painful moment, which had given her the most intense satisfaction – not what she had felt physically, which was little but discomfort, but Joe's sigh of relief and pleasure. That had made it worth while. He was going away to war and she had given him a gift.

Now she threw back the cover, swung her feet to the floor and got to her feet. She would have to go down to breakfast or questions would be asked.

She was coming down stairs when she heard the hubbub in the kitchen. 'Hitler's invaded Denmark and Norway. It's on the wireless.' Her mother's face was twisted with anxiety as she looked up at her daughter.

'Don't worry,' Catherine said with a calm she was far from feeling. 'They won't get through France, not with the Maginot Line.'

<hr>

'Remember to keep them earthed up.' Her father stood up, dusting his hands together as he looked down at the potatoes he had just planted.

'Thank you,' Sarah said. 'Yes, I will look after them, I promise.'

They were continuing to clear the rubbish from the back garden and plant vegetables. At the bottom of the garden there were hens now, scratching in a pen. 'It'll be up to the women,' her father had said flatly when Mrs Chaffey had declared that food would have to come from somewhere once rationing began to bite. 'I can't do a day's work down the hole and then dig all night.'

'I'll do it,' Sarah had said hastily, in order to cut off a row.

He had muttered about bringing on an early labour, but he hadn't stopped her. And then Joe had died, and suddenly her father had seized on the garden, as though making something grow would fill the hole left in his life by the death of his son.

She was putting the spade and the dibber back in the shed when she saw the telegraph boy. Her heart stopped for a second, and then restarted. Gerard was in England somewhere. He couldn't be dead. A spitfire and a Heinkel had shot one another down over the Yorkshire coast a few days ago, but Gerard was nowhere near the coast, and nothing else had happened.

The telegram was brief: '*Home today 48 hrs*'. Embarkation leave. She knew what '48 hrs' meant even without its being written down. She shrugged into her coat and made her way into the street.

'Gerard's got leave, 48 hours.'

Her aunt was making bread in her kitchen, kneading the dough with her knuckles, folding, turning it over with a slap, and riddling flour over it. 'You can have the bedroom to yourselves. Your Dad can go in with the boys for two nights.' Neither woman mentioned the word 'embarkation': there was no need.

Now Aunty Jessie turned to the dresser, reaching for her fat leather purse. 'Away to the butcher's and see what you can get. We can give him one good meal while he's here.'

Sarah knew better than to hug her aunt, so the tears which pricked her eyes were blinked back and she accepted the money. 'Tell them he's going overseas,' her aunt called out, as Sarah let herself out of the door. 'That should be good for a bit extra.'

They were talking about evacuation in the shop. 'Well, no bairn of mine's going,' a woman was saying. 'If we go we'll go together.'

'There's half of them gone back home.' That was the butcher.

It was true, Sarah thought, as she waited her turn. According to the newspaper, three million people had evacuated the cities in the first months of the war. Now, in the absence of the nightly bombings everyone had expected, many of them had gone home.

She left the shop with a pound of stewing steak and a pound and a half of pork sausages. 'Give the lad my best,' the butcher said as she exited, and there was a murmured agreement from the customers. Everyone had sympathy with a woman whose man was about to go off to war.

She was still contemplating the thought of letting her own child be evacuated when she heard the voice behind her. 'It's Sarah, isn't it? Sarah McGuire?' It was Catherine Allerton, the girl from the Dene who had come to Joe's funeral. 'Well, I'm Sarah Foxton, now.' She smiled as Catherine fell into step beside her and said: 'How are your family? It must be very difficult for you all.'

Sarah tried to think of something to say. A nod and smile wouldn't do. 'Did you know our Joe?'

She knew it was a silly question even before it left her lips. How could a girl from the Dene know a lad from a colliery house? But to her amazement the other girl was nodding her head. 'He helped with my dog once. I thought he was very kind.'

They stood there, one clutching the precious meat to her chest, the other with gloved hands clasped over her handbag, drawn together by a death.

≈

'You'd never know there was a war on, not in Harrods, anyway.' Henry had been home for half an hour, fresh from two days in London to have his uniforms fitted. 'The place is full of women buying hats. If it wasn't for gas masks – and everyone's got a fancy cover for them. They say the whores in Piccadilly have them. Of course, all anyone can talk about is Haw-Haw. They say he was a Mosleyite.'

David had listened to the seductive tones of the traitor, William Joyce, known to everyone now as Lord Haw-Haw because of his nasal voice. Listened, and been appalled at his attempts to persuade everyone that resistance was futile and that Hitler was a saviour rather than a threat. 'If he's a fan of Mosley, that would explain it,' he said. 'He's still a traitor though.'

'Drink your tea.' India was in the wing chair that had been her mother's, one well-shod foot tapping the air as she sat with legs crossed.

'She's still taking charge,' David thought again.

'Dinner is at 7.30. Be prompt, Henry. You know Pa hates it if anyone is late.'

'Actually,' Henry drained his cup and set it back in the saucer, 'I thought I might pop out tonight, see friends, catch up, that sort of thing. I've got four more days, sister dear. You'll get your turn here.'

'He's mocking her,' David thought ruefully. 'She doesn't cut any ice with him.'

There were two round pink patches high on India's pale cheeks, so she, too, knew she was being brushed aside. David's heart sank. Someone would pay for it, and it could only be him.

⸻

'Catherine! Catherine!' her mother's voice was agitated as she half-ran into the room. 'Quickly – on the phone. It's Henry Callingham.'

Catherine put aside her book, and got to her feet. 'What does he want?'

'How should I know? Be quick.' Her mother was propelling her into the hall.

'Hello?'

'Catherine? It's Henry, Henry Callingham. I told you I was coming home on leave, just for a few days. I was wondering . . .'

When she put the phone down, she felt bemused. She had never gone out to dinner with a man. Not on her own. And now she was. He had rushed her into it.

'Well?' Her mother's eyes were pools of enquiry.

'He wants to take me out to dinner. At the Grand Hotel. Is it all right?'

'All right?' Her mother's euphoria propelled them both upstairs in search of a suitable outfit.

⸻

David perched on the window seat as Henry moved around his

bedroom, getting ready for the evening ahead. He sensed a change in his brother. He was just as boisterous, as swift, as decisive in his movements, but something was different. 'He has grown up,' David thought. Henry had been gone for only a few weeks, but in that time he had become a man.

'It's amazing being up there,' he had told David that afternoon. 'They gave us all a practice flight, to see if we were scared, I suppose, but of course we'd already had air time. I'm looking forward to the actual thing – combat, I mean. But you do think about how it might end. That's why I want to see Catherine tonight. I feel . . . well, I suppose I want someone to remember me if I go.'

'We'd all remember you.' David wished he had found better words, but Henry was rushing on, not really listening.

'I know I would matter to the family, to the estate too, but I mean – well, I suppose I don't want to die without knowing . . . you know. The others are going to whores, but I want something more.'

The implications of what Henry was saying loosened David's reluctant tongue. 'You don't mean – Catherine?'

Henry was shaking his head. 'Of course I don't mean that, not with her. I love her, David. I think it's love, anyway. You'll understand what I mean eventually. India will be an old maid and drive poor Pa to distraction, but you'll fall in love one day. It's a good feeling.'

———

Around them the hotel tinkled and bubbled with conversation and laughter, and the occasional chink of crystal. 'It was good of your parents to let you dine with me.' Across the table Henry looked handsome and kind, and unbelievably grown up.

'I'm sure they were happy to say yes,' Catherine said. It wouldn't do to tell him that her mother had danced a jig at the news, and her father had chewed on his moustache with satisfaction.

He was reaching out to her hand where it rested on the table, covering it with his own. 'I'm very fond of you Catherine. Oh, come on, you must have realised I was keen.'

She knew what she ought to do: simper and say she'd had no such idea. But the words wouldn't come. She felt uncomfortable and out of her depth. Which was odd, since she had felt no such reluctance with Joe. From that first moment when their eyes met above the dog's heaving flanks, she had felt at ease with him.

Tears pricked her eyes, and she removed her hand from Henry's grasp. Seeing her discomfort, he put down his napkin and leaned towards her. 'I'm sorry. I don't want to frighten you.' He was smiling now, an indulgent loving smile. 'You look like a scared little girl.'

For a moment she contemplated telling him that she was a woman and might even be carrying another man's child – but that would never do. She was enough her mother's daughter to understand the game. Girls were supposed to be gentle creatures who needed protection. You assumed an aura of vulnerability until the ring was on your finger, and thus you secured the life you wanted and lived happily ever after. She would never marry now, but it couldn't do any harm to play the game for a while. If she didn't, they might know something was wrong.

'It's all right,' she said. 'I'm flattered. Now tell me more about flying.' Her voice sounded quite calm, which was amazing when she was so afraid of what might lie ahead. She had been sick again this morning, which everyone knew was a sign. She closed her mind to her thoughts and tried to concentrate on what Henry was saying.

'Well, I'm one of the lucky ones because I did my initial flying with the university's Air Squadron, when I was up at Oxford. That means I'm commissioned on the strength of my Oxford Proficiency Certificate, and could skip the initial training and move straight on to a flying training-school. I've been excused the rudimentaries, but we all received numerous needles, inoculations, vaccinations – and we had tests to work out pilot fitness. I'm A1, thank God.

'We were also kitted out. Of course I'm getting my dress uniforms from my tailor, but the RAF doesn't seem to care about things like that. It's regulation, regulation, regulation. "If it's on the list, you gets it," one man said to me. So I took it. Some of the other chaps will be glad of the kit, no doubt. One or two have that awful under-nourished look about them. But they're all good chaps, picked for pilot training. We're known as UTPs, under-training pilots, and are seen as the *crème de la crème*. But we still have drills and marching.'

Catherine widened her eyes, and tried to look impressed, as he continued.

'At first we went over the basic precepts. Straight and level flying, climbing, gliding, gentle turns, that sort of thing. Then it was taking off into the wind and flying circuits. Oh, and glide-approach landings. I'd done it before, but I still botched it. I came over the boundary far too high the first time, and when I tried to correct it I just pushed down the nose and raised my airspeed. *Quel horreur*! When I straightened out, my kite – that's a plane – just floated on and on, until the instructor seized his controls and lifted us clear. Actually, he said that in spite of that foul-up he thought I was a natural flyer, so it looks as though I'll get my wish and fly fighter planes.

'Soon I do cross-country flying, together with another trainee, one at the controls, the other map-reading. We fly at every opportunity, because we must be finished on time to let the next draft come in. And my instructor tells me that I'm now to master formation flying. Thank God the unremitting square-bashing of those first days is a dim memory. I swear all that stuff is to break your spirit – I can't see another reason for it. We're going to fly, not march, on Berchtesgaden.

'Anyway, after that it's Spitfires, and God help the Hun.'

≈≈≈

Sarah and Gerard had made love as soon as they were alone in the bedroom her brothers shared. Her father had agreed to sharing his bed, but had drawn the line at moving out of his own room. The boys must move in with him. They made love gingerly, partly because the bed was narrow and partly because of the baby. Gerard had demurred at first. 'You're too far gone, Sarah. It's not right.'

But she had stilled his objections, and drawn him into her. 'I love you, Gerard. I love you.' It was soon over, and it was a relief when he rolled off her, but what they had had was sweet. She wanted to block out all thought of war. Surely Gerard must be afraid of what lay ahead?

After supper they had listened to the news on the old wireless Jim had swapped for a mangle and some old clothes, and the news had been stark. '*German troops are in occupation of all of Denmark. King Christian the Tenth ordered a ceasefire at 6 this morning.*' The newsreader's tone was sombre as he went on to give further details.

'It'll be Norway next,' Gerard said.

'You can't know that. There's a sea between them, isn't there?' She had sought desperately for soothing words. 'The Royal Navy'll stop them, you'll see. Mr Churchill's in charge of the Navy. He won't let them through.' But they both knew her words were merely spitting into the wind.

Now she took his hand and placed it on her belly. 'Feel that? That's your son kicking, cheeky little devil.'

'It might be a girl.' She smiled in the darkness. He wanted a girl, she knew that. What had Catherine Allerton said to her on the street this afternoon, after asking what Sarah was hoping for? '*They're a blessing anyway, aren't they?*' They were supposed to be snobs, the Allertons, but Catherine was all right.

She turned on her side, putting her arm across her husband's chest. 'Go to sleep, Gerard. If you're a good boy there might be something nice for you in the morning.'

Catherine had recounted every detail of her trip to the Grand, told it over and over again to make her mother happy. Well, almost every detail. The journey home in the car she had kept to herself. It was a relief when at last she could make her excuses and escape to her own room.

She got ready for bed, and then retrieved the book from its hiding-place. She had hunted for it this morning, and when she discovered it at the back of her mother's handkerchief drawer, she had found a hiding-place of her own, between mattress and bedsprings. *Everyman's Medical Directory*. She turned to the P section, and put her finger on 'Pregnancy'. As she read, she felt a sudden heat envelop her, a prickling heat that made her heart race. It was all there, the things she felt, experienced, dreaded.

'What've you got there?' Pamela had slipped into the room and was gazing at the book with undisguised curiosity. 'Just a book. About health and things. I've got a sore throat.' She ruffled the pages quickly to get away from the P section.

'You never said.' Pamela was still probing.

'It's just come on. Anyway, I'm going to sleep it off. Put the light out as you go.'

Alone in the dark, fear threatened to overwhelm her. There would be no help for her at home, that much was sure. It would kill her mother, and she would be driven out. She tried to remember what she had heard about abortions, but how did you obtain them? Everyone said they happened in back streets, but which back street? She was still fretting when merciful sleep overtook her.

# Chapter Five

## April 1940

CATHERINE HAD USED THE EXCUSE of going to see an old school-friend who lived in Stokesley. 'You've never mentioned her, dear,' her mother said, but without real curiosity. Nowadays she wasn't interested in anything that didn't centre on Henry Callingham. Catherine murmured something about a promise to celebrate a birthday, and that excuse was accepted. Now she was on a train bound for the smoky blur of Middlesbrough. 'Don't leave it too late to get home,' her father had said, 'and ring me from the station when you get into Sunderland.'

She looked from the window, seeing the countryside coming to life after the long winter, thinking over the past few days. Henry had spent some part of every day of his leave with her, much to her mother's delight. Only Pamela had been irritated by it: 'He's bored back here after being away. And everyone else is in the Forces. He wouldn't bother with us – with you – if it wasn't for that,' she had said.

Catherine had not told them about Henry's proposal, repeated twice since. 'Marry me, Catherine. Before I get sent to some god-damned awful place. We could get a special licence. Pa can usually swing these things. You could come down to wherever I'm posted – we could get digs.' And he kissed her –

on the cheek, because she always managed to slide her mouth away from his lips. She had smiled non-committally until her cheeks ached, feeling as though what was happening was some sort of show. Any moment the cinema lights would go up and they would play 'God Save the King'. And all the while there was the ache in her for Joe, and the fear, increasing every day.

Now, she sat, hands folded neatly over her handbag, and tried not to think of the ordeal ahead.

The doctor's house was in a leafy street on the outskirts of the town. She had seen his name in a daily paper, an article about a new method of caring for premature babies which had named him as one of the North's premier obstetricians. She had obtained his number from directory enquiries, and she was due to see him at 2 p. m. this very day. Her own doctor would have been kind and familiar. He had seen her through every child-hood disease, and an ankle sprained while playing hockey – but there was no way she could have faced him. She would have seen the disgust in his eyes, and felt ashamed. He would have told her parent, too, with the best of intentions.

As she rang the doctor's bell she almost lost her nerve, but then a maid in black and white was opening the door, and it was too late.

He seemed surprised when she said she had no letter from her own doctor. At first he had frowned at this breach of protocol, and then his gaze dropped to her ringless fingers. 'Ah,' he said, 'I see.' She was eight weeks pregnant. 'If you have given me the correct dates, that is. But it looks about right. You need attention, my dear. I can't take you under my wing without your doctor's approval. It's not done. But you need someone to oversee this pregnancy and birth. With a first baby that's essential'.

She promised to confide in her own doctor, and got up to leave. He had waved aside the money she had proffered earlier, money drawn secretly from the savings account into which her allowance was paid. 'This is not an official visit. Take it as advice from a friend.'

He came with her to the door and walked her down the path. 'Take care of yourself,' he called as she reached the gate, and she felt moved by his kindness.

Safe in the train once more, she took out Henry's letter, which had arrived that morning. *'Say yes, Catherine, and I promise I will make you happy.'* In the opposite seat, people were talking about British troops landing in Norway, but it was hard to take the war seriously. That, too, was a story played out in celluloid, somewhere far away. Except that it had robbed her of the one man she would ever love.

Lunch was simple today: an *omelette aux fines herbes* and garden peas followed by bottled plums. 'The last of the summer's fruit, Cook tells me. And probably the last we shall see of cream. It's getting harder and harder. We have farms on the estate but we can't have first choice of what they produce.' India's brow was furrowed more in annoyance at the new regulations than regret at vanishing luxury.

'Yes.' David turned to his father as the older man's sombre tones rang out. 'Yes, it will get worse, I fear. And this Norwegian débâcle won't help.'

'Why have the troops gone in?' David asked.

'The key ports. They need Narvik and Trondheim if they're to have any hope of holding the Germans. But I fear it won't work. Dietl, the German commander in Norway, is a superb tactitian. His troops are Alpine-trained; ours are, for the most part, only half trained, and have no mountain-warfare experience. The French Chasseurs Alpins are there, and they know what they're doing, but they'll be overwhelmed. We'll have to withdraw, mark my words.'

He turned to his daughter now. 'They'll mobilise women eventually, for war work if not actual combat. I think you should consider your options now, my dear, while you still have a chance.'

'What are *my* options?' David tried not to speak in angry tones. Why would no one give him a role? Did they expect him to sit contemplating his boot while his peers fought and died?

His father was ready with his answer. 'Your job is to run the estate, David, in your brother's absence. You'd have had no difficulty in getting deferment for that, even without your misfortune. The land will have to play its part in this war. Once the U-boats get cracking, this island will be beleaguered. Every field must yield the maximum.'

'I know nothing about farming, father.'

'Then learn. Talk to the estate office. Don't sit and wallow in self-pity – make it your business to understand your responsibilities. For my sake and for your brother's, whose inheritance Kynaston is. You can start with the moors. Partridge were scarce last year, and as for grouse – we used to take 3,000 brace out of Meringill, and last year it was down to 1,900. That's food, David, not sport. Not while there's a war on. Talk to Renwick, take his advice, particularly about the pheasant. And see if we can get more from our kitchen garden. Men don't work, in my experience, unless you manage them.'

David nodded, but he couldn't help thinking about the gardens of the villages on the estate, each packed with neatly sown rows. No management needed there.

When his father had left the dining-room, India sat back in her chair. 'I loved the exhortation to care for Henry's inheritance, when Henry is so keen to throw it away on a disastrous marriage.'

'If you mean Catherine, I think he'll be lucky to get her.'

'Oh, of course. Bags of breeding, oodles of cash, Mother is Mama Bennett straight out of *Pride and Prejudice*. Still, there's nothing we can do about his madness, I suppose. Jump to it, brother dear. Let's both go and whip on the peasantry.'

Sarah tried to concentrate on the garden. Everything was sprouting now in the April sunshine. She put a hand to her belly, aware of the life beneath. Not long now. The oft-imagined labour came into her mind – all the stories she had heard of untold agonies, biting on towels to stem the screams, blood everywhere, and then the thing that all mothers spoke of, the first indignant cry. If only Gerard could be there with her, but he was God knows where by now. She had scoured the papers and listened to the wireless. He might be anywhere; they seemed to be sending men to all four corners of the globe.

Not for the first time, Sarah rued the scant attention she had paid to her lessons. They were using all sorts of names now, places around the globe that she should have been able to recognise. But she had never listened in geography lessons. Her world had been bordered by the Cleveland Hills on one side, the Pennines on another. Even the Scottish Borders had seemed as far away as the moon. And now Norway and France were in her living-room nightly, and she could not place them.

India had not reacted to her father's suggestion that she should get some sort of job to help the war effort. Partly that was because the thought scared her, but more importantly because she was needed here. She was the only one who understood Kynaston. Without her to watch over it, it would go to rack and ruin.

Besides, she had never really believed in this war. If Halifax had headed the government instead of that weak fool Chamberlain, it would never have happened. As for David looking after the estate, she wanted to laugh at the very thought, but there was no mirth in her. Not when the subject was so serious.

She went to her window and looked out on the park: Callingham land, stretching away to the horizon and beyond, unbelievably beautiful and productive, farmland and woodland and underneath, coal. Callinghams had been here since Charles II. They would always be here, unless some fool let it all slip away. She moved back into the room, and sat down on the ottoman that stood at the foot of her bed. She could marry of course. Have children. If something happened to Henry, Kynaston would need a male heir, and David would never marry. But India had never seen a man who measured up, who was fit to live in this house.

She had been almost three when her mother brought her back from India in 1915. The house they had lived in in Delhi had been imposing, as befitted an *aide de camp* to the Viceroy, but she had never seen anything to match the splendour of Kynaston. They had lifted her from the carriage, and she had gasped at the sight. It had looked like a fairy palace out of her story books, the stone a warm cream in the afternoon sun, light reflected from its myriad windows. She had fallen in love then, and her love had never wavered. Ayah had held her aloft, the better to see it.

Dear Ayah, asleep now in the churchyard. Not in the Callingham vault – that would not have done – but not far away. She placed flowers there on holy days, trying not to dwell on the fact that Ayah had been Hindu and not Christian at all. She had cried when Ayah died, more tears than she had shed for her mother. Her mother had been the cousin of a duke, an aristocrat to her fingertips, beautiful but remote. India had not inherited her beauty: that had gone to the boys. But she had inherited her hands. She looked down at them now with satisfaction. Ayah had been small and brown, and always smelled faintly of spice.

India found she was weeping a little, and brushed the tears away. She couldn't afford to be weak; she had never had that luxury. When her father came back from the war in 1919, and the boys were born, she had realised the hard fact that Kynaston was now more theirs than hers. But while this war lasted she was all the Hall had. Her father seemed not to care. As for her brothers . . .

She got to her feet and went resolutely about the business of the day.

━━━

They were talking about *Gone with the Wind* as they tidied away the remnants of dinner.

'They're queuing six deep in London,' Pamela said, awestruck. 'They set the studios on fire to film the sacking of Atlanta – it said so in the *Express*.'

Privately, Catherine doubted that any studio would be so foolish as to burn itself down for a single film, but she kept her thoughts to herself. Pamela would fight with a feather nowadays. As soon as she could, she escaped to her room and took out the writing paper she had stolen from her father's study. She had thought and thought on the train journey home, and now she knew what she must do.

'*Dear Henry* –' She was sucking her pen and seeking the right words when Pamela came in without knocking.

'What are you doing?'

'Writing a letter.'

'To Henry, I suppose. You can write all you like, it won't make any difference. They tolerate us, Catherine, because their titled friends are too far away, but we're not their sort and we never will be.'

The fury on her sister's face roused something in Catherine. 'Who says I'm writing to Henry?'

'Well, aren't you? Mother is practically writing the place cards for the reception. It's pathetic. He took you to dinner because there was no one else. The Palmer-Jones are in London and the Whitworths have gone to the country for the duration. Face it: you were a substitute.'

'I'm going to marry him, Pamela.' That was it then, matter settled.

When her sister had crashed out of the room, Catherine took up her pen and began to write. '*If it's what you really want. . .*'

# Chapter Six

## May 1940

A T TIMES CATHERINE FELT QUITE detached from the hubbub in the house. Even the war news failed to diminish the wedding fever that now gripped her mother. 'A special licence . . . so little time . . . we must do it well, the Callinghams will expect it . . . thank goodness it's the right time of year for flowers.' It went on and on. Even her father had been impressed by Henry's summoning-up of the special licence that would cut short the waiting time before the wedding could take place.

But most of the time, except when he was at the factory, her father was glued to the wireless, or locked in his study going through papers. Catherine read the sombre words of the new Prime Minister, the man everyone said would sort out all problems: *'I have nothing to offer but blood, toil, tears and sweat. We have before us an ordeal of the most grievous kind . . .'*

Somehow those words seemed meant for her. She could feel no joy at the prospect of a wedding. She was using a good man to hide her own misdeeds, and she would surely pay for it. But she would be a good wife. 'I will, I will, I will,' – she vowed it over and over again in a desperate attempt to ease her conscience.

This morning a dressmaker was coming to fit her white watered-silk dress and Pamela's peach taffeta. 'Shop bought,' her mother had wailed. 'We could have gone to a couturier if there'd been time. As it is, we'll have to do our best.' She bright-ened then. 'I have my eau-de-nil. Never worn, thank goodness. It's still in the Selfridge's box.' Catherine suppressed the urge to scream a halt to the chatter and tried to look interested. No one must suspect that she was not the impatient bride.

And then Henry was arriving with a screech of tyres on gravel and a honking on the horn as he leapt from the car. They went to the door to greet him, alerted by the noise.

'Catherine!' He was seizing her by the arms and then turning, laughing, towards her mother. 'I am allowed, aren't I?' Catherine was holding up her cheek for his kiss when she saw Pamela standing at her mother's shoulder. 'She's jealous,' Catherine thought, and felt guilty. This should be happening to Pamela, not to her. But it was too late to draw back now. He was leading her into the house and sweeping her mother up with his other arm, and the terrible round of celebration was in full swing.

---

It was becoming hard to bend now, with the bulk of her belly in the way, but Sarah persevered, pulling out weeds that threat-ened her precious lettuces. They were round and firm, pale hearts hidden in rich green leaves. She felt a sudden movement within her and a sour taste in her mouth. Water brash. The little rascal was playing merry hell with her innards.

They would need to grow all the food they could, for things looked black. Everyone said it would be better now that Churchill was back, but what difference could one man make? She had not understood all the hounding of Mr Chamberlain, but according to her father it was Clement Attlee and Arthur Greenwood, good Labour men, who had put Churchill in Downing Street, so he must have a bit about him. She was struggling to water the seedlings in the cold frame when the uniformed figure appeared at the fence. For a second she thought it was Gerard, and her heart skipped a beat, but the man was a total stranger.

'Are you Sarah?' he asked, and she nodded. 'Sarah McGuire?' She nodded again. and put down the bucket.

'I was. I'm Sarah Foxton now.' The man looked odd, half-embarrassed, half-upset. 'Do you want something?'

He was holding out an envelope. 'These are for you. They're from your brother. I was his mate, and we swopped letters – not the Army ones, other ones, more private, like.'

She took the envelope, seeing then that his other arm was in plaster. He saw her start of surprise.

'Bone shattered,' he said. 'Bullet wound. That's why I didn't come sooner. I just got out of the Emergency Hospital, and I'm on my way home now. Our lass is expecting, too.' He nodded towards her belly.

'Will you have some tea?' But he was already turning away. He paused at the end of the fence, and looked back. 'He was all right, your brother. Died like a man.'

It was a while before her eyes were dry enough to look at the envelope she held in her hand. She sat down on the wooden bench and opened it. There were two brown envelopes, and a folded sheet. Her heart lurched at the sight of the familiar writing. He had had a lovely hand, ever since infant school.

'*Dear Sal,*' it began. '*I am sending this to you instead of Dad because I want you to do something for me. There is a letter here for Catherine Allerton. She lives in that big house in the Dene, the one with wrought-iron gates. No one must see you give it to her. Don't try to understand now. If you get this, it means I'm a goner, so what's the point? But I need her to get it, and I'm trusting you. The other is for Dad, and comes with my love to you and the others. If I've bought it, it was to keep you lot safe and keep life the way it is, only better, I hope. I can't be sloppy, Sal, but you know what I feel. I'm with Mam now. Your loving brother, Joe.*

*    P.S. There are five Josephs in this platoon, so it's a common name, but like they say, if it was good enough for Jesus's dad, it's good enough for me.'*

It was a long time before she tucked one letter inside the bodice of her blouse, and composed herself enough to carry the other into the house.

There were spring flowers in a blue-and-white vase in the hall, and David felt a shaft of foreboding. There would be flowers in the church next week, and that indefinable smell of dust and incense, and he would have to stand at his brother's side as he married Catherine. 'Catherine' – he let the name echo around his head, realising the pain of it, probing it like an aching tooth. 'Hurry up, David, Mrs Earnshaw wants to clear early today. She's laying down eggs.' India was standing in the doorway of the dining-room, looking flustered. He had a vague idea what 'laying down eggs' was – some ghastly way of preserving them. All everyone thought about now was the war and food. And placating Mrs Earnshaw, called out of retirement now that they were bereft of pantry maids who had gone off to munitions.

France had been discussed over breakfast. According to his father, France had been betrayed by a Fifth Column working within. 'But Germany had so many tanks,' David offered.

This had been brushed aside. 'It was air-power,' India said dismissively. Since Henry had entered the Royal Air Force she had been reading up on air warfare. 'Heinkels, Stukas, Messerschmitts– they just rained down fire on everything that moved. They'll do that here when the Germans have finished with France. We can't match them.'

'Where is Henry, anyway?' David asked now.

India's frown deepened. 'If he intends to go through

this ridiculous wedding, he'll be here some time today, unless he goes straight to the Allertons. I'm still hoping he'll see sense. He's always been impossible, but this last – '

Her father entered the room now, looking a little flustered, as though he had lost something. 'Pa, couldn't you stop it, even now? She's not part of our set. We only ever invited them here out of pity.'

'I don't remember you inviting them at all,' David said. 'Henry and I met them playing tennis, and we invited them. You haven't offered them common courtesy, as far as I can see. As for pity, I don't think it's in your nature.' Being stung to Catherine's defence made him more eloquent than usual – he saw that in the widening of India's eyes.

But it was his father who answered him. 'Whatever we may think, whatever may or may not have obtained in the past, we're talking about a young woman who will soon be part of this family. We'd all do well to remember that. And as we now have guests, I suggest this conversation ceases. They'll appear at any moment, and we hardly want them privy to our squabbles.'

Twin spots of colour appeared on India's cheeks. They remained there long after her father had left the room and Mrs Earnshaw was hurrying to clear and reset.

'Thank you, Mr David,' she said, as he passed her a plate.

'What with one thing and another . . . one pair of hands . . . and your aunts coming for the wedding. I'll never forgive that Adolf Hitler! What a carry-on.' She was still burbling grievance as he excused himself, and went upstairs to change for riding, which now was the only thing saving his reason.

He could hear chatter from the other rooms as he came out onto the landing. The round of arrivals had begun yesterday: aunts and uncles, cousins. Odds and ends. People they never saw from one year's end to another. David smiled and nodded incessantly, was courteous to 14-year-olds and informal with the children.

'God, collectively they're a fearsome sight,' India said, coming behind him and looking down into the hall as a wave of talk rose up from below. Her arms were full of towels and her hair had straggled on to her brow.

'I'm sorry about earlier,' David said, trying to relieve her of her burden.

She shook him off. 'It doesn't matter. It's all so ghastly that words can't make it any worse. If only we hadn't lost the maids.'

'Can't you get help from the village?'

'I suppose we'll have to but employing married women is always difficult.'

'Mrs Earnshaw's all right.'

'She's a widow – no ties. But she's hardly competent. She wouldn't have lasted five minutes in Mother's day.'

David felt a pang of sympathy. 'It isn't fair on you, old girl. If you want to go . . .'

She was looking at him with scorn. 'Leave Kynaston to your tender mercies? I'll never do that, David. The family matters to me, even if it matters to no one else.'

Sarah waited in the shadow of the hedge at the bottom of the front garden until she saw the lights of a car flare up and heard the rumble of an engine. Now it was coming down the drive. Sarah shrank back, and then it was off down the road with a roar. A figure was still standing in the lighted doorway, and then the light was cut off as the door closed.

Could she simply walk up the drive and ask for Catherine Allerton, make some excuse to get her alone? But she could hardly knock at this time of night. Should she just drop the letter through the letter box? The name on the envelope was clear enough. But Joe had asked her to deliver it – '*and no one must know*'. What if someone else opened it? She would have broken faith with her dead brother. She was about to retreat and come back another day, when she saw light stream across the dark garden from a door at the side, and then a woman's figure flitting across the lawn. She would have to take a chance that it was Catherine and not the other one.

She moved as quickly as she could, but the woman had almost reached a little hut thing with windows by the time she caught up with her. 'It is Catherine, isn't it? I've got a letter for you – from our Joe.'

'A letter!' She was surprised, but not surprised enough.

'I didn't know you knew him that well?' Sarah said. The letter hung between them for a second, and then Sarah let it go.

'I did know him, as I told you the other day. We – we kept it secret. He wanted it that way.'

'I didn't realise you meant really know him.' Sarah tried to keep her tone even. If anyone had wanted to keep it quiet it would have been Catherine, not their Joe. He had been as open as the living day. 'Anyway, I've done what he asked.'

She was turning on her heel when Catherine touched her arm. 'Please, I would like it if we could be friends.'

'Some other time,' Sarah said, and walked away. She had a sudden desire to laugh out loud. What a bloody silly thing to say in a dark garden, talking to a stranger, with a war on. She turned back at the gate, but Catherine Allerton had vanished, and the garden was empty.

She had to go back into the house before she could read the letter. There was not enough light in the summerhouse, even with a full moon. When she was safe in her room, she opened it. '*Dear Cathy,*' it began. It was written on thin paper with some sort of official crest on it, but it was hard to make out the words because her hand was shaking. '*Dear Cathy, if you're reading this it means I've bought it. Oh Cathy, I hope you never do and that I come home, and you are brave enough to love me.'*

She welled up when she had finished, but she did not cry. She had Joe's child to consider. They said a mother's sorrow could upset the baby in the womb.

Instead, she crossed to the window and stared out on the moonlit garden. Would she have been brave enough to love him openly before the whole world? Was she brave enough to protect his child now, and go through with the wedding? And if those who had died could look down from Heaven, what would he be thinking of what she was about to do?

# Chapter Seven

## May 1940

HANNAH CHAFFEY HAD GIVEN HER the sheet of newspaper. 'Mind you, I want it back. I've promised it to Meggie after you, and then to our Gran.'

Spreading it out on the kitchen table, Sarah leaned closer to read. '*Paratroops in uniform will come down in bunches and be dealt with by the authorities. However, men in disguise may come down in ones or twos. It is important to inspect footwear which may conflict with the rest of their garb.*' Well, that bit was true. Everyone knew about the spy disguised as a nun and given away by his regulation Army boots. She read on. '*Each man is armed with a revolver and one in five has a machine pistol with a maximum range of 200 yards. They may also carry egg-shaped grenades.*'

She read to the end, feeling uneasy, thinking constantly of her baby. God help a paratrooper that threatened her bairn. But even as she thought defiance, she acknowledged that a German would not think twice about bayoneting a woman, baby or no baby. The pot was still warm from breakfast, and she poured herself a yellowing cup.

Last night had been strange. There had been tears in the Allerton girl's eyes as soon as she had mentioned Joe. Theirs must have been more than just a chance meeting if he was writing to her, and yet he had never breathed a word. Sarah had always thought they were closer than brother and sister usually were, but he had gone off to war without saying a thing.

She was trying to think ahead to the morning and what must be done when Hannah knocked and entered. 'Have you read it? I'm off to see Meggie now. We want to catch sight of the bride.'

Sarah sat up. She should have noticed that Hannah had her Sunday coat and hat on. 'The bride?'

'Yes, Allerton's girl. The oldest one. She's marrying young Henry from the Hall. Rush job! Special licence! We know what that means.'

Sarah tried to keep her voice steady. 'Fancy. I didn't know. He's likely off to the Army or something. There's plenty getting wed quick for that reason.'

Hannah was folding the cutting and putting it carefully into her handbag. 'Well, time will tell. That's for sure.'

When she had gone, Sarah sat down at the table. A wedding? There had been no mention of a wedding last night. Not that they had talked much but still – She was suddenly seized by anger. Perhaps Catherine Allerton had been leading Joe up the garden path, and now he was dead in a war he hadn't sought, protecting the likes of her. Some of the gentry did things like that, played with people they wouldn't dream of wedding. Her baby gave a vigorous kick, and then another, gentler one. She rose to her feet and went in search of potatoes to peel. Anything rather than struggle with the mysteries of life.

---

There was an overpowering smell of flowers in the air, until the hairdresser's tongs singed Pamela's fringe and the smell of burnt hair prevailed. 'Oh dear,' her mother wailed. 'So much mess, and I can't do everything.' Maisie had now gone off to work in a munitions factory, and the woman from the village who had replaced her was less than capable. The room did indeed resemble a jumble sale – but what did it matter? Catherine longed to slip away, to find a quiet place where she could pretend none of all this was happening. But there was no escape. She was the bride, the centre of the whole teeming edifice, the cause of all the scurrying back and forth, the ringing doorbells, the jangling telephone.

'All right?' Her father was quieter than the rest, his face anxious as he slipped into her room when Pamela had departed in a flurry of long skirts and ill-will. Catherine nodded, and he cleared his throat. 'This is what you want, isn't it? If not, you must say so. Pay no attention to all this – if you go ahead, it's for life, Catherine. You do realise that?'

For a moment she was tempted to tell him the truth, that she was doing something horribly, horribly wrong. But there could be no confession. She knew how his face would crumple at the news, how he would tell her mother and Pamela, how the world would fall round her ears and nothing ever be the same again. So she smiled. 'I'm sure, Daddy.'

Then, silently as so as to stem the guilt, she murmured the words that had become her mantra: '*I'll make him happy. I will. I will be a good wife.*' She had repeated it for the third time when she realised that she could not remember what Henry looked like. It was Joe's face in her mind's eye, Joe to whom she was making her vow – and he was dead in a field in France, perhaps not even a wooden cross to mark his presence.

———

For reasons they could not voice to one another, the brothers had gravitated towards their old nursery. Henry, half dressed in his wedding finery, sat astride the old rocking-horse, his long legs bent at the knees, his feet on the floor. David was curled in the window seat, one arm around the giant bear that had sat there for as long as they could remember. Henry was telling a joke. 'So this kid says to his friend, "The Germans have landed," and the other says, "How d'you know?" and he says, "Heard mum tell dad there was a Jerry under the bed."'

They both laughed but neither thought it funny. 'Seriously,' Henry said at last, 'it's true what Dad said. The Germans are closing in on what's left of the French and Belgians, and the bulk of the BEF. They'll squeeze them tighter and tighter until they run out of supplies. Then it's *kaput*.'

'They could be supplied by sea, they've got the sea at their back. We still hold Calais and Dunkirk, and the lines of communication are open to the coast.'

But Henry was shaking his head. 'There's no holding the Germans, brother. A week ago they were south of Douai, now they're racing through France, and coming down through Belgium. Their raids on England are sporadic at the moment, but wait until the Luftwaffe get going – they'll not stop at the North Riding and East Anglia, you'll feel it here. Unless the RAF can really move. My fear is that it will be over before I get in there.'

It was hard to think of anything to say in the face of such gloom, but David tried. 'Men are flocking to join the LDF, and I'm going to see if they'll take me.' He wanted Henry to reassure him, or tell him he had a part to play, but Henry was moving on.

'The Emergency Powers Act gives the Government unlimited powers to mobilise. India will have to work – one of the services, or the FANYS, or in a factory. She won't like that, soiling her hands. The estate'll be up to you, then, David. And if I cop it –'

'Don't talk like that!' The words burst from David's lips, in horror both at the idea of Henry's death and at the responsibility that would fall upon him.

'Sorry, old son, but it's true. If I go, there's only you. Unless

I live long enough to sire a sprog.' He blushed suddenly. 'My God, I'm getting married today.' His voice dropped now, and his face softened. 'I rather love her, you know. Quite suddenly. It's amazing how the possibility of death speeds up your thought-processes.'

He chuckled softly. 'Don't look so glum, David. It's a celebration, not a wake.' And then, as though his own turn of phrase had chilled him, he slapped the horse's wooden flank and whipped it, creaking, into a bucking ride.

It was a relief when the car containing the bridesmaids had departed, and the house was quiet. Her father was refilling his glass at the sideboard, and when he bent to kiss her Catherine could smell the whisky on his breath. 'As I said before, if you're not sure . . . ?' There were lines on his face that she had not noticed before, and his kind eyes were tired.

'I'm fine, Daddy. Honestly.' For a second or two, Catherine pondered the lie. She was far from fine. She was drowning in waters far deeper than she could ever have imagined.

'Time to go,' her father said, glancing at his watch. And she was walking out to the bedecked wedding car, hearing the tinkling of coins as her father threw coppers to the waiting children, hearing the people at the gate – 'Ah, she's a bonny bride!' 'Lovely dress!' – and then she was safe in the car and could relax for a little while.

Pamela was waiting in the porch to adjust her train and draw the veil down over her face. 'Take this,' she said, thrusting the bouquet into her sister's hands. White roses and stephanotis, surprisingly heavy, the bound stems pressing into her stomach, hidden now by white slipper satin. Perhaps she had only dreamed there was a baby? That could happen: overwhelming desire for, or fear of, pregnancy could do that. She had read it in her mother's book. Perhaps there was no need to marry an almost stranger, and commit a sin before an altar? Perhaps someone would stand up in the church and denounce her when it came to the bit about anyone here present?

And then the 'Wedding March' was pealing out, and she was walking, dragging the heavy train behind her, towards the man who now turned to face her, looking so nervous that she felt a sudden compassion for him. '*I will make him happy,*' she vowed again, fixing her eyes on the blues and reds of the round window as the vicar called upon everyone present to join in the celebration.

Sarah was in the garden inspecting her vegetables when she saw the telegram boy. He was pedalling quite fast, half-standing up on the pedals. No one ever got telegrams unless it was bad news. And in that moment she knew it was coming to her. As he drew nearer she heard the squeak of his bicycle wheels. He was dismounting, peering at the numbers on the gates. 'Mrs Sarah Foxton?'

It was there, the narrow paper with the black type. '*We regret to inform you . . .*' Gerard was missing, believed killed.

The wheels were squeaking again, the boy anxious to get away from the sight of a woman squatting on the bare earth and rocking backwards and forwards, the telegram pressed against her heart.

The reception had passed in a haze of congratulation and sentiment, everyone fingering her dress, patting her hands, commenting on what a lovely couple they made and what a lucky girl she was. Only India, seeming to despise the whole affair, stayed aloof. In their official visit to the Hall, so that her parents could meet Sir Gervase, her mother had asked if India would like to be a bridesmaid. The look on India's face had said more than her curt refusal, and the subject had not been raised again.

'If the wind changes, she'll stick like that,' her mother hissed, as the feeble jokes of the speeches left her new sister-in-law unmoved. Catherine didn't care about India. In an hour or two she would be alone with Henry. In a bedroom. They would share a bedroom for the rest of their lives. The terror that thought inspired stayed with her throughout the rest of the reception.

'Welcome to the family,' David had said as he helped her out of the bridal carriage. She had seen genuine kindness in his eyes – and something else, a sadness perhaps? Henry's eyes, in contrast, were sparkling. Now he squeezed her hands or hugged her to him at every opportunity, and when he stood to speak he said, 'My wife', and paused so that everyone could drink in the wonder of it.

When at last they were alone, in the lofty bedroom of the Callinghams' country retreat, he was oddly shy, however. 'I'm sorry that this is all I can offer you,' he said, taking her hands in his. 'When this war is over I'll take you to Paris. Venice, if you prefer? All of Europe. You deserve a wonderful honeymoon.'

He went into the adjoining bathroom to prepare for bed, allowing her to undress alone and climb beneath the sheets. She wondered if he would put out the light, or insist it be on. If he did that, how would she school her face to indicate lost virginity? What had she done that time with Joe? Whimpered at sudden pain, so that he had stopped thrusting and raised his head to see her face. 'All right?' he had asked, and she had urged him on, and cried aloud at the wonder of it when it came.

Now, she must enter into a terrible re-enactment of that moment, and give Henry what every man was entitled to, a virgin bride. He was far more inexperienced than Joe had been, so that, in the end, she guided him into her, and it was over in seconds. 'Oh Catherine, Catherine,' he said, and she shushed him, all the while repeating silently, '*I will be good. I will make him happy.*'

⁓

David got out of bed as dawn broke, and limped to the stable. The horses were whinnying gently, hoping for a feed, and he moved along the stalls, patting each one in turn. Only when he was mounted did he let himself think of Catherine, asleep now in his brother's arms. How would he cope with the sight of them together, after the war when Henry was here all the time? He would go away. The Empire, Europe – anywhere where he need not acknowledge their union.

A flock of birds rose up suddenly from a field, wheeling and turning against the dawn sky, looking for all the world like seed thrown skywards by someone casting crops. He urged his mount to a canter then a gallop, seeing the fence ahead, clearing it, feeling the wind on his face, blotting out everything from his mind except the freedom of a mount between his legs and a thousand acres before him. Until he remembered that only his brother's survival would prevent those same acres from being a millstone round his neck.

# Chapter Eight

## May 1940

CATHERINE STILL FOUND IT STRANGE to wake up in the bedroom that had been Henry's and was now hers. In the Dene, there had been the sound of traffic on the road, the rattle of milk bottles on steps, the voices of children. Here, with acres of parkland around the Hall, there was deep silence, except for the twittering of birds.

She had been married for four weeks now. The ring on the third finger of her left hand told her so, but there was still a dreamlike quality about it, as though it was happening to someone else. She felt tears prick her eyes and blinked them away. Mustn't cry here in this strange house, with India's prying eyes upon her. She stared up at the ornate ceiling, beautiful but somehow alien. She belonged in the Dene, in her room with its pretty little dressing-table and flower-sprigged curtains, and the back numbers of the *Girls' Crystal* filed neatly in the bookcase. If it hadn't been for the war, she would still be there.

Except that there was a baby growing inside her. She would have had to leave the Dene anyway – but then Joe would have been there to protect her, to tell her what to do, to take her somewhere where they could live happily ever after, alone with their baby. 'I want to be a girl again,' she said aloud, but the words made no impression in the huge room.

She shuffled up on her pillows and reached for Henry's letter. It had arrived yesterday, and been opened by India. 'I do apologise, I opened it inadvertently.' She had said it as though she were apologising to a servant for dropping a crumb from the dinner-table. 'She doesn't want me here,' Catherine thought. But, then, India didn't want either of her brothers at Kynaston, either. 'She thinks she *is* the Callingham family,' Catherine realised.

A picture of India came into her mind. The boys were beautiful, Henry with a face straight out of an Italian painting, and hair that curled about his forehead; David, even handsomer, if it were not for the air of anxiety he wore, as though feeling bound to apologise for his game leg. But India was plain – except for her hands, the long slender hands with their perfect oval nails which she examined constantly, as though terrified there was a speck upon them. Catherine shuddered at the memory of those hands as she opened the letter, and read once more the now familiar greeting.

'*My darling wife*'. He had called her that on their honeymoon, saying it over and over as if it were something wonderful he had just stumbled upon. She closed her eyes, remembering his hunger for sex. '*It's wonderful Catherine. Wonderful, so much more than they say. It's mind-splitting.*' And then he would begin again, loving her as though both their lives depended on it. She had been glad of his eagerness because it made her feel less guilty about her deception. He had wanted her. She had not set out to get a father for her child, for Joe's child – Henry had wanted her. And if that need in him had been the product of war and his fear of death, that was not Catherine's fault.

She started to read again, to blot out uncomfortable thoughts. '*Life here is hectic, but would be fun if I wasn't missing you so much. I've had to cram RAF law and aircraft recognition, because the Varsity course didn't cover that. One useful thing I've learned: no airman can be arrested or compelled to appear before the courts for any debt less than £30. How's that for privilege? I wish I were with you now, my darling wife. It makes such a difference to have your photo by my bed. It makes me feel ... complete, I suppose, and I pity the men who seem to have no one. I wish there wasn't a war, darling, and we could be together, but otherwise I'm rather enjoying this. I hope India and David are looking after you. They say we get a 48 soon, so we'll soon be together, my darling wife. I love that phrase.'*

She put the letter back in its envelope. How could he love her so completely and so suddenly? It had taken her months to love Joe – but, then, they had had only stolen meetings. Henry had simply taken over her life. But he was a Callingham, and there was the war. Soon she must work out how to make everyone believe that a baby conceived in late February hadn't been conceived until April.

———

There was dandruff on the priest's shoulders and a speck of dried egg yolk on his vest. Sarah concentrated on these details so that she did not have to listen to what he was saying. He had assured her that Gerard was with God, but she knew better. He was lying somewhere, in mud probably. Rain might be spattering his face. His lovely face. When he was making love to her he always closed his eyes, but she had kept her eyes open just for the joy of seeing him, face screwed up with the effort, and then relaxing as he came, a smile spreading slowly across his mouth.

She realised she had moaned aloud. Father Lavery was shushing her and babbling on about God and Heaven. What had she said out loud, and what the hell did he know, with his soft priest's hands that had never done a day's work? A wave of shame came over her, then – thinking such thoughts of a priest!

She would surely be damned. Was damned already, with no man to care for her, and a child to bring into the world.

<hr/>

Breakfast was over, a somewhat sparser meal than hitherto. Rationing was biting now, and India's moans had intensified. 'It's so stupid. Of course one's prepared to make sacrifices, but they're enjoying it, these little dictators with their coupons and their regulations. It's all got to be accounted for. So much feed goes in, so much food must come out, and be shipped to strangers.'

'There's a war on,' David said savagely. He couldn't stand it when she talked like that. His father remained behind the paper, his hand snaking out now and again to search for his cup. Sun was streaming into the morning-room, lightening its sombre panelling. Outside the window roses were coming into bud. Hard to believe men were out there, dying.

'One knows there's a war on, dear brother. One knows that all too well. I'm just protesting at bureaucracy, petty bureaucracy. Anyway, I can't sit and argue. Someone must run this house.'

That was directed at him, at his uselessness. His father put down his paper, seeming to sense his son's disquiet, and not for the first time David wondered whether the newspaper was a defence against India and her eternal grumbling. Surely not.

'Things are not good over in France.' Sir Gervase was reaching for toast, spreading butter thinly over it, and then the thin-cut marmalade he preferred.

'I heard you talking to Uncle Bertie last night. Is he up with the latest news?' Sir Gervase's cousin was an adviser to Beaverbrook, the fiery newspaper proprietor who now headed the new ministry for aircraft production.

His father nodded. 'The troops are on the beaches near Dunkirk or Gravelines – no one seems quite sure. Churchill has ordered in the Navy, but what can they do without landing craft?'

As he listened, David saw that his father's shirts, usually immaculate, now seemed too large for his neck. 'He's getting old,' David thought, and was afraid. He needed Sir Gervase's calm presence. How would they all cope if it was gone? But his father's mind was as alert as ever, his grasp of the war situation as acute as it had been in the Great War when he had been a brigadier. 'Gort is using his BEF well, and the French have thrown everything into holding the line at Lille. All they can do is buy time, of course, but given time – and a miracle – we may salvage something.'

'The Germans have air superiority.'

His father was frowning at such despondency. 'For now, David, for now. We've been slow off the mark, but with Churchill back and Eden at the War Office, things will pick up.' There was quiet authority in his tone and David dared essay a joke.

'And there's Henry, Papa. Once he gets there.' He had meant to lighten the atmosphere, but when he looked more closely he saw a tear had formed in his father's eye at the mention of his absent son.

---

'I was wondering –' Pamela paused, the teapot aloft in her hand. 'I was wondering,' she went on pouring, 'if I could possibly have Catherine's room? It's bigger than mine, and she doesn't need it.'

'But her things are there!' Her mother sounded shocked. 'And she chose those curtains and that bedspread herself.'

'I know, that's why they're so drab. I'd need new ones, of course, and the wallpaper would have to be changed. I thought a nice pale beech for the furnishings.'

Her mother was looking helpless, as she always did when decisions were to be made.

'I can do it, Daddy, can't I? I could go into Durham today, or Newcastle – yes, Newcastle. I'd bring swatches so we could choose together. Say yes, Daddy, pleeeeeeese – for your poor, unmarried daughter who is destined to be a sad old maid.'

'Don't be silly, Pamela.' Her mother had come to life at the thought of a daughter of hers left on the shelf. 'And we can't make poor Catherine feel she doesn't belong here any more. I'll ask Mrs Hemmings to spring-clean your room, and we might look for something in the July sales.'

That was too much! A titled marriage for one and the July sales for the other. 'That's right, humiliate me, Mummy, why don't you? You spent hundreds on Catherine and the wedding! Hundreds! And I'm to wait for something from the bargain basement. Why are you doing this? Why don't I matter?'

She was working up to a crescendo when there was a sudden crash that halted her, mouth open in mid-flow. Her father had swept his arm across the table, pushing food, china and cutlery to the floor. 'Shut up!' he cried. 'For Christ's sake, shut up!'

She had never before heard her father raise his voice, let alone seen him do anything so violent. Shaking, Pamela fell to her knees and began to pick up the debris. She was aware of Mrs Hemmings opened-mouthed in the doorway, and her mother sobbing quietly in the background, and she was lost for words. Something bad was happening, that was sure.

Catherine could see the swelling of her belly now, only a little mound and easily concealed at the moment, but what of the future? She was fearful of the moment when she would bring forth a full-term child and questions would be asked. Everyone would look at her and know that she was a liar. Henry might even repudiate her. Send her packing. She would deserve it. Alone in the enormous bedroom, Catherine rocked back and forth, wishing she had simply run away, found work and lodgings, and not needed to face up to anyone.

She could already feel India's eyes on her, full of contempt and something else that might be curiosity. Her father-in-law smiled vaguely at her at times, and called her 'my dear', but hardly seemed to notice she was there. Only David was kind. She went in search of him now, moving down the wide staircase, past the portraits of dead Callinghams, all seeming to stare at the woman who was about to place a cuckoo in the nest.

She had not thought of that when she married Henry – that the child she was carrying would one day inherit Kynaston – but it was true. That was theft, though she had not done it deliberately. All she had thought of was hiding her shame. And Henry had been so insistently in love, he had almost convinced her that she was doing it for him, to make him happy as he went off to war. In fact, she was a cheat and a liar, and would confirm it when she wrote to tell him she was pregnant. That letter would have to be written soon.

Catherine crossed the hall, patting her hair into place as though the action could tidy away her uncomfortable thoughts, and found David in the library, the table before him littered with atlases. 'They're there, Catherine,' he said, jabbing at a map. 'Between Gravelines and Nieuwport, but mainly in the Dunkirk area. It's about 30 miles, cutting into Belgium, a long coastal strip. But the Germans are coming at them from all sides – France, Belgium, the whole damn Continent's over-run.'

Catherine sat down in a chintz armchair. 'Will they invade here?' If the Germans came, if she died, a problem would be solved.

But David was rushing to reassure her. 'There's the Channel between them and us, and the Navy will never let them cross the Channel.'

Catherine felt an urge to laugh, and suppressed it with difficulty. To David, the Royal Navy was a saviour, to her a nemesis.

'Have you had breakfast?' David asked kindly. 'I should

have had something sent up.'

She was less nauseous in the mornings now but her appetite had left her. 'I'm fine,' she said. He was snapping shut his books and reaching for the satchel slung on the back of his chair. 'I'm going riding. I could find you a nice gentle mare if you fancied it?'

She had never ridden, despite her mother's insistence that anybody who was anybody learned to sit astride a horse. If she mounted a horse, if it threw her, there might be a solution to her problem.

She got to her feet. 'You'll have to show me how but, yes, I'd like that.' She felt his arm at her back, guiding her towards the side door that led to the stables. The gesture moved her. If she got out of this somehow, she would not only be a good wife, she would be the best-ever sister-in-law. And not only to David but to India, too, however difficult that might be.

⸻

'Forgive me, Father, for I have sinned.' The words came easily to her lips, although she was not in the confessional. How could you tell a priest you had had bad thoughts about him, called him stupid even if only in your head? She sat now in the darkened church, subject to the black-out like every other building, with only flickering candles at the feet of the statues and on the altar. Was Gerard in Heaven now or hell? Or the dreaded Limbo? A part of her said none of them: he was in a field in France. She thought of rats and other night creatures, and clutched her rosary beads until her fingers hurt. The priest had assured her he'd have had a Christian burial – but how could you dig a grave in the middle of a war, with the Germans advancing everywhere?

They would hold a memorial service here in this church, as they had done for Joe. People would come, some out of friendship, others out of respect for a man dead in battle. But there would be no body, no flowers, no solid coffin to touch. If only she could have seen him, just once. Kissed his cold face. She had a sudden vision of bringing him back to life with a kiss, as had happened in *Snow White*.

Opening her eyes, she fixed them on the blue and crimson of the window behind the altar. There was a sky behind it, darkening now, but sprinkled with stars and a crescent moon. Somewhere that same sky was over Gerard. She was contemplating that marvellous fact when she felt a pain, small at first, and then rippling through her. She gripped the edge of the pew in front and clung on till it subsided. The baby wasn't due for another month, but this wasn't wind or indigestion.

She was rising to her feet when she felt a sudden wetness between her legs. If the baby came here, in church, it would be blessed – but then again, with no one to help her it might die. She was turning to the door, forgetting the all-important bob to the altar, when she heard feet on the stone flags.

'Sarah? Is that you? God Almighty!' And then Father Lavery's arms were round her, and she knew she was going to be all right.

Catherine still found the custom of dressing for dinner strange, but India had made clear that it was mandatory. 'We need to keep up standards, even when we're *en famille*.' Tonight she was wearing plum velvet with a décolleté neck, and looked rather splendid. During the *hors d'oeuvres*, Catherine tried to imagine India in a man's arms. That was just possible, but not even the strongest degree of concentration could let her envisage her in a man's bed. She felt a dangerous chuckle brewing, and tried to concentrate on her plate.

At the head of the table, Sir Gervase was toying with his food. Now that Catherine came to think about it, he seldom ate and never heartily. He was talking to David about the new Home Guard. She had heard Anthony Eden on the wireless, talking in that lovely film star way he had: '*We are going to ask you to help us. We want large numbers of men aged 17 to 65 to come forward and offer their services . . .*'

India was interfering now. 'It's ridiculous. All the able-bodied men will be in the armed forces. They'll leave callow youths and old men and . . .' She paused, looking down at her plate.

'And cripples, India. Don't forget cripples. I can hold a gun, and they tell me I'm quite a shot!' Colour had appeared in David's cheeks.

'I didn't mean –' India said, but David cut across her, talking directly to Catherine.

'I meant to tell you earlier, that since we went to that funeral in the village – McGuire, the first casualty –'

'Joe McGuire,' Catherine said. Perhaps he was going to say there had been a terrible mistake, and Joe was alive? Those things happened in war. She fixed her eyes on her brother-in-law's face.

'Well, now his brother-in-law has bought it, too. I think you talked to the sister, his wife? She's pregnant, poor girl. We'll have to see what can be done for her.'

India threw down her napkin. 'We can't "do something" for everyone. There'll be dozens dying, perhaps hundreds. The estate is not a bottomless pit, David.'

'We can try.' This was Sir Gervase. 'We can show them some respect.'

'I'll go and see her,' Catherine said. 'Perhaps she'd rather see another woman.'

'Yes.' David and his father spoke together. 'Tell her we're very sorry . . .' They were still talking but Catherine was thinking of Sarah the night she had crept through the garden with Joe's letter. They had something in common, now. They had each lost the man they loved, and they were each carrying that man's child.

# Chapter Nine

## June 1940

SARAH COULD SEE THE DARK fluff of the baby's hair peeping above the shawl in which he was swaddled. She wanted to reach out and touch it, but a terrible fatigue had overcome her, so she contented herself with looking. Her labour had been long and painful. The midwife had soaked a towel and then knotted it at one end and hooked the other over the bedpost. 'When the pains come, bite on that,' she had said, but Sarah had simply clung on to the damp knot and kept her moaning behind closed teeth.

And the baby had come forth, screaming from the sharp slap the midwife had given him. 'It's a boy,' she'd said, holding the red, squirming bundle aloft while she wiped blood from him. When he had been wrapped and placed in her arms, she had felt a surge of such pleasure that it scared her. 'I would kill for this child,' she thought and knew that she meant it.

After it was over and the midwife had gone, she cried for Gerard, who would never see his son. 'You'll likely call him after his Dad,' her father had said, and she had nodded. 'Joseph Gerard,' she had said, and saw her father's lip tremble at his dead son's name.

There was a commotion on the stairs, and Hannah Chaffey was erupting into the room, eyes popping, sweat beading her upper lip. 'You'll have to excuse the room, miss, It's tidy, usually. Not now, of course, not while the babby – well. . .' She was brushing clothes off the room's one chair, and Catherine Allerton – now Catherine Callingham – was coming through the door, making soothing noises and saying everything was fine.

'I don't know what to say to her,' Sarah thought, panicking, but then saw her own confusion mirrored in the other face.

'I came to say how sorry I was to hear about your husband.' Catherine turned to make sure they were alone. 'And to thank you for bringing me Joseph's letter.' It was out, and they both relaxed. 'Are you all right? The baby looks beautiful. It's a boy, I hear. Your neighbour told me.'

Sarah raised herself on one elbow to peer into the crib. 'Yes, it's a boy. Joseph Gerard.' There was silence for a moment, and then Catherine spoke softly.

'I was fond of your brother. Did he tell you that?'

Sarah shook her head. 'No. That letter, that was the only thing I knew – that he wanted you to have it.'

'Have you told anyone about it?'

'No!' Sarah's voice rose. 'I haven't told a soul and I won't.'

'Thank you. If Joe had lived, if he had come back, things would have been different. But now I have to go on – as you do.' She put her hand on Sarah's where it lay on the coverlet. 'I want to be friends, if you're willing. You're my link with Joe.'

For a moment Sarah wondered whether this was a ploy to keep her quiet about the letter, because it wouldn't do for the family at the Hall to know about it. But the eyes that met hers were steady, and there was no guile there.

'Yes,' Sarah said. 'I'd like that.'

There was silence at the lunch table. Sir Gervase again toyed with his food, David seemed abstracted, India put down her knife and fork occasionally to make notes on a pad beside her plate. Eventually David spoke, irritation with his sister apparent in the glance he gave her before turning his attention to his sister-in-law. 'Did Henry have much to say in his letter?'

'I thought I told you,' Catherine said. 'He's excited about his first solo cross-country flight, and he says Oxford men are known as "the long-haired boys" and everyone wants to bring them down a peg.'

'That was yesterday,' David interrupted. 'I meant this morning's letter.'

Everyone's eyes turned to India, now. Her habit was to have the post delivered to her at the breakfast table, and then to take an interminable time sorting it and handing it to the proper recipients. A faint flush was now mottling her pale cheeks. 'Yes, there was a letter. I'd placed it with mine, inadvertently. I meant to give it to you earlier.'

'Now will do.' David was glaring at her as she fished in the pocket of her loose jacket.

'There it is. I wouldn't have forgotten it.'

'They want to take the railings from the park,' Sir Gervase said suddenly. They all looked at him, struggling to make a connection with the letter.

'The railings? They can't do that!' India seized on the change of subject.

'They say we should set an example. Robert Darcy's written to me. He says it's up to our class to give a lead.'

'It's all very well for the Darcys. They don't have parkland. What do they expect us to do with the deer? Bring them into the house?'

Catherine stayed silent, anxious to get away and read Henry's letter in peace, but afraid to make a move just yet. She knew about railings: Londoners were sacrificing the iron railings of their houses to the drive for scrap metal. Bandstands were going, too – only Buckingham Palace was to be spared.

'We need to show willing, India.' That was David.

'He feels guilty,' Catherine thought. 'He wants to go to war, and he can't, and he can't bear it.' Somehow the thought gave her the courage to make her excuses and scurry upstairs to her room to read her letter.

'*Well, my darling, Spiff Howard and I had a day off, so we motored to the coast to see the effects of Dunkirk for ourselves. Tired, ragged men returning to England defeated, and without their equipment. They can't understand why the rest of us see it as a victory, and I don't blame them. In Brighton the streets, beaches and pubs were just a mass of troops, all nationalities – the boats picked up anyone. I found myself interpreting for some of them – God bless my schoolboy French. Anyway, they couldn't understand why our planes hadn't done more to defend them. I tried to explain that we were there, attacking the Hun for all we were worth, but I could see they didn't believe me.*

'*But they all talked about the little boats, not much more than dinghies, that went in again and again. God, pride nearly choked me and I swear Spiff had tears in his eyes, although he threatened to punch me when I said so.*

'*I hope to have leave soon, and then I will spend my every waking hour making love to my wife. And every sleeping hour, too, if she permits. You don't know what a difference it makes to know you are there, waiting for me. I love Papa and David – India too, in small doses – but to have a wife! I keep dropping your name into the conversation. My wife this and my wife that. Few of the other men are married, so I'm one of the privileged.*'

Catherine folded the letter, and put it back in the envelope. She was making him happy. Relaxing in that comforting thought, she heard a knock at her door. It was David, looking somewhat embarrassed.

'Your sister has been on the telephone, Catherine. You're needed at home. I asked what was wrong, but she wouldn't say.

She seemed upset. I've asked Bates to bring the Bentley round, and I'll drive you.'

———

Pamela had been still in her nightdress that morning when she heard the knocking at the door. She had peeped from the landing and seen two men in shabby raincoats. One of them had seated himself on the carved hall chair, the other was arguing with her mother, who was beginning to weep. Of her father there was no sign.

She turned back into her bedroom and found a dressing-gown. 'What's wrong?' She asked the question twice as she ran downstairs, but no one answered. The second man was making notes, moving from hall table to the grandfather clock in the alcove, turning towards the drawing-room. Her mother was letting out a thin, continuous wail now, and Pamela pushed her aside. 'Who are you?'

The man looked her up and down. 'Who are you?'

She drew herself up and tried to keep her voice steady. 'I'm Pamela Allerton, and this is my house. My parents' house. What are you doing in it?'

He was waving a piece of paper. 'Court order, miss. We're here to distrain on your father's goods in settlement of debts owing to Messrs Cursor and Cursor.' It was insane, it was crazy, but somehow Pamela knew it was true. She didn't speak again to the man; instead she went in search of her father.

The door to his study was locked, and when she kneeled to put her eye to the keyhole, it was blocked by the key.

'Daddy! I'm frightened, Daddy. You must come out and deal with this.'

But he did not come out, not even when the men announced their intention of removing the choicest pieces of furniture from the house. That was when Pamela had telephoned Catherine.

Why should she get off scot free? If the world was to tumble around their ears, Catherine too must feel the pain.

And now she was here, looking anxious, with David Callingham hovering behind her. 'What's happening?' Catherine's hands were clasped in front of her, her diamond engagement ring huge and brilliant.

'What's happening?' Pamela tried not to sound shrill. 'We've got the bailiffs in, sister dear. Bills for your wedding, I shouldn't wonder. They're taking everything. Everything! Do you understand?' Her mother's thin wailing deepened and grew louder, so that if Catherine said anything in reply no one could hear her.

⚊⚊⚊

Hannah Chaffey had admired the baby, and was settled in a chair with a cup of tea. She was obviously there for a long chat, and Sarah tried hard not to let her tiredness show.

'Well, they were on last night about some marshalling yards at a German place called Ham something. Ten big targets were hit, according to the BBC man. I hope it's true, and not just made up to keep our spirits up. Your sweet peas looked well on as I came up the garden. Just think, this time last year we never thought there'd be a war, did we?'

Sarah nodded agreement and tried to concentrate on what the other woman was saying, although her mind kept wandering off.

'We had a man round from the ARP. Looked just like Max Miller, he did. Round the eyes. Sort of cheeky. I love Max Miller, he gives you a good laugh even if he is rude. Talking of rude, Edie Wilson says her lad told her the beach at Dunkirk was like an abattoir. Blood everywhere, and running into the sea till it turned red with it.'

Sarah was moved to protest. 'I don't think that's true, Hannah. Anyway, if it is we shouldn't spread it. Folks don't need to hear stuff like that.'

'Well, I'm only telling you. Speaking of gossip, have you heard about the goings on in the Dene?'

Sarah shook her head, hardly interested until she remembered that the Dene was where Catherine lived. Where she had taken Joe's letter on that night only weeks ago. When she had been a wife, and not a widow.

'You know those stuck-up Allertons? The ones with the two daughters? He's got a factory somewhere. Drives a big car. Anyway, they've got the bums in. Jenny Harding chars next door, and she says they were carrying stuff out, and then the older girl arrived, her that married young Callingham. She had her brother-in-law with her, and he stopped them. But Allerton's factory's closed, and the workers sent home. Well, I won't cry for them. Toffee-nosed, if you ask me.'

'She's not,' Sarah said stoutly. 'The one who wed young Henry. She came here to see the baby.' Too late she realised she would have to give an explanation. 'Well, she heard about Gerard. She came to pay her respects on account of us losing him and Joe as well.' She rose to her feet then, beginning to unbutton her blouse. 'Anyroad, I'll have to get on. He needs a feed, and me sitting here as though I had corn growing.'

She saw her neighbour off, and settled in a chair with her son at her breast. It was soothing to feel the vigorous pull on her nipple, but her mind still raced. So the Allertons were bankrupt and the bums were in. What was going to happen next?

⸻

'I expected something like this.' Inside India, cold fury was erupting. 'We should have done more to stop that wedding, Pa. It was madness.'

Opposite, Sir Gervase sat in his wing chair, hands curved around the arm rests.

'Well?'

She wanted him to agree with her, but he sat as though carved from stone. 'You must have an opinion. For Heaven's sake, Pa! David has some quixotic idea that we can get them out of this mess. It's lunacy, and you just sit there pretending it isn't happening.'

He shook his head slightly, but no words left his lips.

'She's common, and her wretched father is in trade. I could weep. What the county must make of it, I can't imagine. Henry will come charging home, and he and David will pour money in, good money after bad. Take notice, Pa!'

Now he did speak, drawing himself up in the chair. 'No, my dear. I'm trying not to notice that my daughter has grown into an ungracious woman.'

<hr />

Catherine had stayed in her room ever since David had brought her back from her parents' home.

'Don't worry,' he had said, as they drove back to the Hall. 'I'm sure we can sort it out. I've bought them off for the time being, and I'll speak to Papa.'

Shame had engulfed her as David had pulled notes from his wallet, but at least the house she had left behind was quiet now, and her mother allowed into her father's study. 'I'll come back tomorrow,' she had reassured Pamela – but what could she do then, especially if it was true that bailiffs were in at the factory, too? Was it really the cost of her wedding, as Pamela had said?

She rose to her feet as there came a knock at the door. It was David, staggering under the weight of a radio. 'I wasn't sure you'd be coming down for dinner, so I've asked them to bring you something on a tray. I'll share it with you, if I may? And this . . .' he was plugging in the radio, 'this is for Churchill. He's repeating the speech he made in the House today, about

Dunkirk. They say France will surrender in days, but getting so much of the BEF back is bound to help us.'

They sat together, picking at an omelette as the sonorous tones of the Prime Minister rang out: '*We shall go on to the end. We shall fight on the beaches, we shall fight on the landing grounds, we shall fight in the fields and in the streets, we shall fight in the hills; we shall never surrender.*'

'He sounds so certain,' David said, his voice choked with the emotion of the moment. Catherine nodded, but she felt far from certain that Churchill could be as confident as he sounded. How could you be confident when the whole world was falling about your ears?

She did not realise she was crying until David proffered a handkerchief and put a comforting arm around her shoulders. 'There, there,' he said. 'We'll win, Catherine. Right always triumphs in the end.'

No use telling him that her tears were for her own fate, and not for the possible downfall of the British Empire.

THE LETTER WAS EUPHORIC. '*I can't believe I'm going to have a son. Or a daughter – either welcome. You clever girl! It's so strange to think that only weeks ago I hadn't ever thought of children. Or even a wife. And now you and this baby mean the whole world to me.*'

There were two pages of Henry's delight and plans for the future, and then he turned to his life as a pilot. '*It's so good to be in the air. The rasping note of the engine, the blast of wind on your face, and that overwhelming sense of freedom as you soar upward. I'm so glad I flew at Oxford. If not, I'd've had to go to Nova Scotia for 11 weeks of intensive training. As it is, I'm here and ready, but I've heard tales from some of the boys here now. They go to Iceland first, and then join a convoy.*'

Catherine had read about convoys, which were sitting ducks for U-boats that hunted in packs, however heavily protected by destroyers and minesweepers the convoy might be. She read on:

'*You, little darling, must eat all your greens. I told the MO, who's an Oxford man, and he said to be sure to eat your greens. Must close now, as it's up with the lark tomorrow. I love you, love you, love you, little Catherine. See you in five days' time for 72 glorious hours, and then it's back to some real flying.*'

He was glad about the baby – but how glad would he be if

he knew it was not his child? She looked down. The pregnancy was showing. She was four months gone now, almost five. If the baby came on time, everyone would know it was full-term. Not for the first time, she wished fervently that she had run away instead of marrying Henry. Then she would have been condemned for having loose morals; now she was not only a harlot, she was a liar and a cheat.

She went to the mirror and checked her face for signs of distress. Wouldn't do to show her fears, not with India about. Besides, she must thank David for his endless kindness to her parents. 'I've found them a house on the estate, Catherine,' he had told her. 'Not the greatest place, but we can sort it out for them.'

And when she had stammered out her thanks, he had held up a hand to silence her. 'It's nothing. Nothing at all.'

———

Now that the garden was full of vegetables, Sarah missed the flowers. There were still sweet peas on the trellis, this year a better show than ever, and the hollyhocks were still hard up against the fence, but now, in the middle of summer, there should have been a blaze of colour everywhere you looked. Still, considering what people were suffering in air raids, the loss of a flower plot was nothing.

She straightened up from earthing up celery as Hannah Chaffey appeared at the gate. 'They got Norwich last night. Razed to the ground, Billy Herman says.'

Billy Herman was given to exaggeration, so Sarah merely shook her head in wonderment. 'Still,' Hannah was in full flow now, 'the RAF are giving as good as they get. Churchill says it will be a long hard war, but I think that's rubbish. If Hitler was going to invade us he'd have done it before we got ourselves sorted. He'll never do it now, not with over a million in the LDV. I mean, the Home Guard – not that a name matters.

'Anyroad, I'm off to see if there's any offal going. I can't go a day without meat, no matter what Lord Woolton says. Mind you, they say they want pans now for turning into Spitfires. We have to give them to the WVS. Fancy them planes being made of aluminium. You learn something every day. Though how we're expected to cook without pans, I do not know.'

She went on her way, still spouting news and opinions on that news, and Sarah went back into the house. It was dark and still after the sunlit garden, and she shivered slightly as she bent over the crib. The baby was sleeping soundly. If it weren't for the baby, she could have joined up, or at least done something useful. The Government was asking women to play a larger part in the war effort, not just working in munitions or on the land, but even becoming soldiers. She would have liked to do something to pay Hitler back for the loss of a husband and a brother.

And then the baby opened its blue eyes, and contorted its little face at a spasm of wind, and she knew she was in the right place. All the same, as she lifted her son from his crib and put him against her shoulder so he could bring up the wind, she knew she needed a purpose to her life. Tomorrow she would go to see Catherine Callingham, and commiserate with her about her family's troubles, which people were now saying were owing to the war and no one needing furniture making any more. That wouldn't help the war effort, but it would ease her conscience.

―――

Around him the countryside rippled gold and green. A skein of geese swooped low across the sky, heading seawards. David rested forward in the saddle, and felt a satisfaction at the scene before him. It was normal. A normal English summer. No sign of war, or whisper of the fear and discontent he sometimes felt as he moved around the estate. He thought ahead to the evening. Henry should be home by then, installed in his seat at the table.

David dug his heels into the horse's flanks to urge it forward, and turned its head for home. He had had Catherine to himself for several weeks. Now he must make way for his brother, her husband. The thought of them together, tonight, was suddenly unbearable. But perhaps there could be no lovemaking when there was a baby on the way? It was not the thought of sex that upset him, though. It was the thought of someone, anyone, even his brother, having her attention.

He provoked the horse to a gallop, and took fences and hedges in its stride as they made their way home as the crow flies. As he unsaddled his mare and handed her to the elderly groom, called out of retirement to lend a hand, the man told him he was wanted in the house.

He found his father in his study. 'You wanted to see me, Papa?'

Sir Gervase looked somehow shrunken, sitting behind the massive desk. 'Yes, David. I've spoken to Hartley Lewis.' Hartley Lewis was the county's Lord Lieutenant, and the man in charge of the LDV. His father's face was impassive, but there was just the hint of a smile around his lips, so it wasn't trouble. 'He says there's a place for you in this new Home Guard, if you want it.'

'If I want it? Papa, that's wonderful. I've felt so useless with Henry away.'

'And India in charge at home?' His father didn't wait for a reply. 'She tells me you've been helping Catherine's family?'

So India had told tales on him. 'I've told them they can have temporary use of the old keeper's house at Styles. They've nowhere else to go, and it's been empty since Gibbs was called up.'

'Good. We must do what we can. Apparently the war is to blame for their plight. The emphasis is all on necessities now, rather than luxuries like furniture. And they'd been living beyond their means, by all accounts.'

David nodded. '*The Times* says the Government is putting

24 per cent tax on luxuries.'

His father was nodding. 'And an extra shilling on income tax. Eight shillings and sixpence in the pound. Unheard of! Still, we must all do what we can.' He put up a hand suddenly and pressed his chest.

'Something wrong?'

But his father was shaking his head again. 'Nothing – it's nothing. A touch of indigestion.'

Pamela had pinned up her hair, and put one of Mrs Hemming's pinafores over her dress. She and Cook were long gone, scarpering without wages at the first sign of trouble. 'I can earn more in a factory. I was going anyway.' That had been Cook. It was all up to her now.

In a way, nothing had changed. She had always been taken for granted; now she wore the uniform of a servant. She was piling books into boxes, but what use books would be in a keeper's cottage God alone knew. After that there would be china to shroud in paper, and pack – and all for nothing. Tears pricked her eyes. One sister up at the Hall with everything, the other living in a hovel with no future at all. She had reproached her father last night: 'How could you let it happen?' She had wanted to say: 'Why didn't you make provision for me, your daughter?' but she had bitten back the words. It was true, though: Catherine's wedding had brought them to their knees. Her father must have known disaster was coming, and yet nothing had been spared. For her there would be no wedding, no lady's life, not even a roof over her head except a borrowed one.

She was still crying when Catherine arrived. 'Oh Pam, Pammy, don't cry. It's going to be all right. I'm here now, I'll help. And I've got some news for you, lovely news. You're going to be an aunt. I'm having a baby.'

For Pamela it was the last straw. She sobbed in her sister's arms, all the while wishing that sister dead and gone, instead of always, always being in first place.

═══════

India found her father in his study, sitting behind his desk. 'Have you spoken to David?'

Sir Gervase nodded. 'Yes, I saw him an hour ago.'

'So you told him?'

'Told him what?'

The old fool was going to drive her mad with his stonewalling. 'Told him he can't give out houses as though they were soup for the needy. If the Allertons are in trouble, that's not our fault. And before you call me hard or ungracious again, Pa, I have to be all those things. Someone has to be realistic, and it can't be David with his head in the clouds. Henry's gallivanting on an airfield somewhere, and you behave as though the estate runs itself.'

'David says the keeper's cottage is superfluous to our needs, India, with so many men away. Why are you making this ridiculous fuss? If I didn't know better I'd say you were enjoying your sister-in-law's discomfort. The Germans have a nasty word for that: *Schadenfreude*.'

India felt rage boiling up in her at the sanctimonious tone of his voice. 'You silly old fool!' she said at last, hissing the words.

Sir Gervase didn't speak for a moment, and then made a small noise that might or might not have been a word. Then his hand was moving to his chest, and he was slumping backwards in the chair, his eyes rolling upwards as though in search of something beyond his sight.

═══════

Catherine had arrived back at Kynaston to a scene of confusion. David was attempting to find out what had happened. The doctor had banished everyone from the bedroom, and he and his nurse were in there labouring to revive Sir Gervase.

India was red-eyed, and strangely defiant. 'Nothing happened, I keep telling you. He just collapsed.'

Turning, David saw Catherine's stricken face, and ordered her to sit in the library, and wait until someone could bring her some tea. 'There's nothing you can do, Catherine, except keep calm for the baby's sake.'

So she sat in the book-lined room, and tried to work out what was going on beyond the door. It was the doctor who came to find her. 'My dear, I'm sorry to have to tell you that your father-in-law passed away half an hour ago. Quite peacefully. A coronary thrombosis. Nothing to be done. He hadn't been well for some time.'

'He never said anything,' Catherine said woodenly.

'No, it wasn't his way. He didn't like displays of emotion. But I saw him yesterday, just by chance, and he did tell me your news. He was very happy at the thought of a grandchild. An heir.'

Catherine felt her cheeks flush as Dr Cunningham continued. 'You haven't been to see me.'

'No. I thought. . . Well, I wanted to tell Henry.'

'And now you have family problems. I've heard about that. But the baby is the important thing. How far on are you?'

He was staring at her with a practised eye. Could she lie?

'I'm not sure.'

'You were married in April?'

'Yes. April.'

'Then are you sure it's a pregnancy? It's very early days.'

The blush had turned into a forest fire, now. He was going to find out and he would tell. But he was leaning forward suddenly to pat her hand.

'Don't worry. I understand. I wondered, when I heard about the sudden wedding. I'm fond of young Henry – a little impetuous, but a good chap.'

At first Catherine didn't understand his meaning, and then it dawned. He thought that the baby was Henry's, conceived too early, and that the wedding had been a hasty attempt to make it all proper.

'No one knows,' she said at last.

'And no one shall. You leave it to me. In due course I shall say it's a premature birth, and no one will be any the wiser. But you must let me examine you properly when all this sadness is over. Now, get some more tea, and get ready for young Henry's home-coming. He'll have no trouble getting compassionate leave – and he'll need you, Catherine. He loved his father.'

She felt relief flood over her as Dr Cunningham made his goodbyes. He would cover for her, even to India. She was happy for a moment – until she remembered there was one person who could not be fooled and that was her husband.

＝＝＝＝

The old man's death was the chief topic of conversation in the house that night.

'Old bugger won't be missed,' was Mr McGuire's pronouncement. 'Made his millions from his pits and his farms, and never set foot there. It'll be different after the war. Men won't stand for being worked to death.'

Sarah was standing at the stove, clasping the teapot to her chest as she waited for the kettle to boil.

'All the same, it's hard on the lad that's away. The other one's a cripple, so he won't be much good.' That was her brother Jim, warming his backside at the fire.

Her father shook his head. 'They'll likely let the older lad out. Jammy bugger. Get home, and mind your millions – other lads'll do the fighting.'

Sarah again felt an urge to defend Catherine's husband. 'He joined up of his own accord. At least, that's what I heard. So he may decide he's not coming back. And he might not get the chance: there's a war on.'

'I know there's a war on, miss, because I'm eating sausage instead of a good bit of beef. And your Aunty Jessie has to cadge baccy for me. I know there's a bloody war on! But I still say it won't be as hard on that lot as it is on us. They'll have their game on the table, and their port in the cellar, while we have to lick arses to get anything eatable. It's an unfair world, Sal, and your Gerard was the first one to say so.'

It was true, Gerard had often rued the unfairness of life. All the same, Sarah would have to go to Catherine now, and offer what comfort she could. As she looked round the table her face softened. They worked hard, the men in her family, going down the hole, and living close to death, for it was never far from the pit. She leaned forward and put her elbows on the table. 'Tell you what, Dad, I'll go for your baccy the next time, and see whether a lass can do better with Baccy Ward than an old woman.'

Her brother's howl of laughter followed her up the stairs as she went to check on Gerard's son.

---

Catherine had waited in the hall till she heard the car approaching, and then she stepped out on to the steps of the portico. Henry knew already, from the set look on his face. David must have told him at the station, although they had agreed that she should break the news to him.

'I couldn't help it,' David said as he passed her, carrying his brother's bags. 'He asked outright how the old man was. I couldn't lie.'

'Of course not.' Catherine was turning to her husband, but he was moving past her, taking the stairs three at a time in his haste to reach his father's room. She found him there, standing at the foot of the bed. Sir Gervase looked serene now, all strain gone from his face, the white hair carefully brushed above his brow.

'I can't believe it, Catherine. Not Papa. I thought he was indestructible.'

'I know,' She leaned her head against his shoulder, anxious to give comfort.

'Did he know about the baby? Had you told him?'

'Yes. He knew and he was pleased. He said so to me, but apparently he spoke to Dr Cunningham, too, and told him how happy he was.'

She was compounding the lie, but what else could she do? It would be hard enough to face him with the truth when the time came. She couldn't tell him now, when the illusion of an heir was the only thing the new Sir Henry could cling to. She was in their own room when the enormity of the phrase 'son and heir' struck her. If the baby was a boy it would inherit Kynaston one day, and thereby disinherit whoever was rightfully entitled to it.

# Chapter Eleven

## August 1940

AFTER THE BRILLIANT SUNSHINE, THE cathedral seemed dark and cold as the stone from which it was built. It looked to Catherine as if every pew was filled to bursting, and she tried not to meet the curious, if surreptitious, stares of those come to mourn. As heir, and now Sir Henry, her husband walked behind his father's coffin with Catherine, now Lady Callingham, at his side. Behind them David walked with India, her face stony beneath the brim of her hat.

They had not talked in the limousine that had driven them from Kynaston Hall across the county and into the peninsula that contained the city of Durham. Estate workers had lined the route when they set out, but eventually the onlookers were gone, and the cortège had speeded up, passing through fields and villages until at last the towers of the cathedral and the turrets of Durham Castle came into view.

Catherine bowed her head in prayer, opening her eyes occasionally to look at the blaze of the rose window behind the altar. She loved the cathedral, with its stone pillars and marble effigies. She especially loved the quiet corner where the tomb of the Venerable Bede stood. She had learned about Bede as a child – the boy who grew up in the North East to become a great scholar. Somehow he had come alive for her, not as a distant figure of history but a real person. As a girl she had kneeled at his tomb to pray for her own future happiness. Now she prayed for the stranger sitting beside her who, by some strange trick of fate, was her husband. 'Let him be safe,' she prayed, squeezing shut her eyelids in an effort to stress her need. 'Bring him home when the war is over.' But even as she prayed for his return, she knew she was praying that her own disgrace should not be uncovered.

The service was over, and she was following in the coffin's wake, nearing the great door, when a face sprang out at her from the sea of other faces. It was Sarah Foxton, dressed in black, a hat sitting oddly on her abundant hair and looking what it undoubtedly was, borrowed for the occasion. What was Joe's sister doing here, so far from Belgate? How kind of her to come! They exchanged a half-smile of acknowledgement, and then she was passing through the door, and sunlight was depriving her of the sight of anything or anyone.

—————

Back at Kynaston after the interment, India moved among the mourners, accepting condolences, patting the arms of distant cousins upset by remembering a childhood shared with her father. Yes, he had been a wonderful man; yes, he had contributed so much to national life; yes, he would be missed. She schooled her face to a degree of quiet grieving she did not feel. She felt angry. He had died, and with his death she had lost her place as first lady of the family.

She tried not to glance at Catherine Allerton standing at Henry's side. She would never call her Catherine Callingham, Lady Callingham, not to herself at least. She was an interloper, an accident of war, nothing more. If it had not been for Germany, Henry would have stayed unmarried for years, and she, India, would have continued to ensure the smooth running of Kynaston. But now her father was no longer there, it was she, not Catherine, who was the cuckoo in the nest. She felt her nails biting into her palms and enjoyed the pain. 'Thank you so much,' she mouthed to people she hardly knew, and who she heartily wished would disappear. She was trying to play her proper part, as mistress of Kynaston, but, in truth, the part was gone from her, and all she wanted was to see these people leave.

When she caught sight of Pamela Allerton talking with the Bishop, for all the world as though she belonged at Kynaston, it was too much. India threaded her way through the throng towards the conservatory, to hide her fury among the greenery.

The crowd was thinning now, and David felt relieved. He had been proud of such an overwhelming tribute to his father, and anxious to support Henry, but he ached to get away. He would have liked to saddle a horse and ride off in search of peace, but in two hours' time Henry must leave and return to his duties, and he was driving him in the Bentley.

Soon there would be no freedom to get behind the wheel, as petrol supplies were rationed and Britain girded itself for war. Sea-fronts were no-go areas now, and beaches protected by gun emplacements, barbed wire and pill-boxes. Stories abounded of the latter being disguised as pubs and guest-houses, but he couldn't see the sense in such dissembling. If the Fifth Column was as deeply embedded in Britain as it was supposed to be, that cover would be blown in the first wireless message smuggled out.

The preparations did not end at the coast. Open spaces, unless under cultivation, were being strewn with old cars and buses, carts and timber, anything to render them unsuitable as landing sites where gliders could disgorge German troops. No bells had been rung at his father's service, because they were to be rung only in the event of an invasion. And for the past week, the Luftwaffe had been pounding the South Coast, presumably to soften it up, ready for invasion.

Across the room he could see his brother, with Catherine at his side. Henry was smiling as he talked with friends. No sign now of the tears he had shed at news of his father's death. 'He's brave,' David thought. 'Braver than me.' He knew that Henry was thirsting to get into the air and join the fight. 'I'd go today if they'd let me,' he had said yesterday, reading of the carnage the German planes were wreaking on Britain. But an untrained pilot was worse than useless: he must finish his training before he could take to the skies.

A waiter passed David with a tray of glasses, and he took one. He didn't like wine normally, but today he needed something. Please God Henry, would come through the war unscathed, and continue standing between him and the weight of Kynaston. Well, their baby would be born in the New Year, another buffer between him and a long-term responsibility he felt himself incapable of carrying out.

He sipped his wine, noticing as he did so that his sister was not to be seen anywhere. Not like India to leave centre stage. He put down his glass and went in search of her.

Sarah had begged a lift into Durham on the Co-op van, but her homeward journey had to be made by bus. It was hot inside the shuddering vehicle, and the air was heavy with the smell of sweat and bodies. She wrinkled her nose and turned her face to the window, all the while thinking how sweet it would be to see the baby again. It was the first time they had been apart, and if she had her way it would be the last. 'He's all I've got,' she thought, and then felt ashamed because her family were giving her shelter, and what support they could. 'I'm better off than most,' she told herself, and tried to relax into her seat.

Around her, the bus hummed with gossip about the Duke of

Windsor. He and the Duchess had left Europe aboard a US liner, bound for God knew where. They had fled to Spain when the Germans invaded France, the country that had given them sanctuary after the abdication. According to half the bus, however, the Duke was in league with Hitler, and would take over the English throne once Germany had won the war.

At last a man spoke up from the back of the bus. 'You lot sound like the bloody Fifth Column. There'll be no taking over, because there'll be no German victory. And before Churchill lets that bugger back in, he'll sink the bloody country.' There was a murmur of agreement and no dissent except for one woman who said Mrs Simpson had been von Ribbentrop's fancy woman, and that there was definitely a Nazi plot. But she was told to pipe down by her embarrassed husband, and a comfortable silence ensued.

Sarah wiped sweat from her eyes, and tried to keep her arms off her breasts, engorged now with milk. Her father had thought her mad to go to the funeral, but she had felt impelled to be there. Not for the old man – he had been a distant figure. But somehow she felt a bond with Catherine. If Joe had been alive, he would have gone . . . except that, if Joe had been alive, Catherine might never have become a Callingham. No, that was silly. She could never have married Joe and come down to living in a pit village. Things like that didn't happen.

She had looked sad in the church. Tired and eye-y, the way Sarah herself had looked when she had fallen with little Joe. Perhaps Catherine was pregnant? She had been married since April, and some women fell straight away. Sarah started counting weeks and days as the Durham countryside sped by.

⁓

They sat in the window of their bedroom, close together but not embracing, conscious of the minutes ticking away till they must part. 'I wish I could stay longer – for you, mostly, but for David, too. He'll have to take on Kynaston and the estate till the war's over, and I know he'll hate it.'

'How do you feel, now that it's yours?'

'I don't know. I haven't taken it in, I suppose. It feels rather like a jape, not like real life. It will be different when I'm home for good. I think I might actually enjoy it.'

He kissed her then, moving his hand to cup her belly. 'I love you, Catherine. I sometimes think of how short a time I've known you, and how much I have to learn, and I feel as though four lifetimes won't be long enough. Take care of yourself, and my son – or daughter. A girl would be nice, a little Catherine.'

His lips came down on hers again, and then he looked towards the bed. 'I wish there was time to show you how much I love you. You've made a difference to this past week – I would have felt such desolation at my father's death, but now I have you, and the sprog. And Papa knew he had a grandchild.'

She kissed him then, half out of a kind of affectionate feeling, but also to stem his words before she gave way, and told him he was the victim of a terrible lie.

---

Pamela took off the dark clothes she had worn to the funeral, and then lay down on her bed, pulling the coverlet up to her breast. The house was quiet. There were no servants, her mother seemed permanently to take to her bed; her father sat in the study pretending to sort out his papers but in fact doing nothing at all.

It would not be quiet up at the Hall. They would still be drinking wine and eating their fill. She had seen no sign of rationing in the funeral meats. And Catherine queening it over the whole thing, glued to Henry's side. It wasn't fair! Once they moved to the poky little house David Callingham had found them, she would be buried there. Buried alive. You couldn't swing a cat in the rooms; there was a garden hardly bigger than a window box; and no tennis court. She knew well what an asset a court was: it meant a constant stream of young people coming and going. 'I'll be left on the shelf,' she thought bitterly, and turned her face into her pillow.

But only for a moment. She would not, *not* let her life come to an end because she had a fool for a father. All the Callinghams had money, and David had looked very presentable in the cathedral, and afterwards moving among the guests at the Hall. If you discounted the dipping walk, he was quite a fine man. A good catch. She closed her eyes and began to make plans.

It was a relief when the goodbyes were over, and he and Henry were in the car and speeding down the drive. David listened as his brother rhapsodised about his wife. 'You will take care of her, old man? Keep her from India's clutches – you know what she can be like.'

David vowed to prevent even dew from falling upon his sister-in-law, all the while giving thanks that Henry had not heard India's diatribe against his marriage at the funeral gathering. He had followed her out of the gathering and into the conservatory. 'All right?' he had said, coming up behind her as she stared out on to the garden.

'All right?' She had turned on him. 'You do say the most stupid things, David. How can I be all right, with my father gone to his grave and my brother in a disastrous marriage? Don't give me that shocked look of yours. You know it will be a disaster. Did you see the sister? Prowling round evaluating the furniture? They're common, David, irredeemably common, and we're stuck with them, you and I.'

He had turned on his heel, then, and left her to her rant.

Now he kept his eyes on the road, and promised to do all in his power to keep the peace. It was the least he could do for a man off to war. After that, he tried to make conversation, anything to take their minds off family affairs. 'Beaverbrook's joining the Cabinet is a good move. They say he's done wonders for aircraft production.'

Henry, too, was enthusiastic. 'He turned a short-fall in February into a surplus in May. Not bad. With planes being downed all the time, we need that kind of drive.'

'You won't take risks, will you? You know what you're like – a bit . . .'

'Impetuous?' Henry finished for him.

David turned to look at him, a little shamefaced. 'I didn't mean . . .'

'You did, and I have been a bit of a fool at times. But pranging a car in peace-time is one thing, David. Pranging a plane in wartime is quite another. I will be sober, sensible, and deadly to the enemy, and the war will be over by Christmas. Now, put your foot down and there'll be time for a swift half before I have to leave you.'

<hr/>

Catherine went up to her room after she had waved Henry off in the car. She was half-way up the stairs when India appeared in the hall. 'Only you and me for dinner, I fear, but I've told them to serve as usual, so we'll change, I think. Although of course it's up to you to decide these things now. I mustn't presume.'

'Please, India. I've no wish to decide anything. It's very kind of you to suggest I might, but. . .' She didn't get a chance to finish.

'It's not kind at all.' India's tone exhibited abhorrence at the idea that she might wish to be kind to Catherine. 'It's not kind, it's merely your due as mistress of the house.'

Catherine shook her head but didn't speak, anxious to reach the refuge of her room. That India resented her was not in doubt. The painful thing was that she had every right to resent Catherine's place in her home because it was based on a falsehood.

They made polite conversation as they ate at opposite ends of the long table. India wore peacock-blue taffeta, and had jet at ears and neck. The colour did nothing for her sallow skin, but she had presence in a regal way. Around them light gleamed from silver and crystal, as a servant moved about, placing and removing courses to the huge sideboard. There was less food under the covers now, but the embellishment was undiminished.

'I see a contingent of airmen has arrived from Southern Rhodesia,' Catherine said, quoting an article she had seen in *The Times* over breakfast. 'One never thinks of Rhodesia as having airmen.'

India nodded gravely. 'Yes, the colonies are behaving well, with notable exceptions. And so many Irish citizens have flocked to enlist. Quite amazing, considering Eire is neutral and its government anti-British. But I'm disappointed in India. My father served that country well. I'm glad he didn't live to see how they're dragging their heels.'

'They have sent some men, or at least they have men under arms already,' Catherine offered.

But India was shaking her head vehemently. 'The Hindus and the Congress Party seem determined to pretend there is no war. It's shameful. England has made India what she is, and there should be repayment at a time like this.'

Privately, Catherine thought the English had exploited India rather than 'made' it, but she feigned agreement. That was what she would do: tread water with India until Henry came home and there was a return to normality. If life could ever be normal again.

She thought of her family, sitting now in the midst of their belongings, waiting for a removal van to take them away from all they knew. David had been kind to find them a cottage, but it could not replace the house in which she had grown up. She closed her eyes briefly, remembering the summerhouse. That had been her place with Joe. Thinking of Joe reminded her of

Sarah, his sister. She must have made her way to Durham today simply to show respect. 'For Sir Gervase undoubtedly, but also out of friendship for me,' Catherine thought, and was comforted. It was always good to have a friend, and the fact that that friend was Joe's sister made it all the more precious.

# Chapter Twelve

## August 1940

THIS TIME, INDIA HANDED HENRY'S letter to Catherine without a word, and David tried not to let his satisfaction show. He had taken her to task over withholding the last letter. *'It's not up to you, India. Face it, it's addressed to Catherine, his wife. What is it to do with you in even the smallest part? And I have to wonder if you ever intended to give it to her. Perhaps you were going to quietly lose it?'* That had stung. Her eyes had glittered fury in a way he had not seen since childhood but all she said was, *'You can be so silly, David. You really should grow up.'* All the same, she had obviously taken his words to heart, and it gave him a degree of satisfaction.

They had all taken to reading newspapers at the breakfast table. 'A bad habit,' their mother had always called it, and had forbidden any reading till breakfast was cleared away. After her death his father had retreated behind his paper at every opportunity; and with the news so bad at the moment it was now accepted that any conversation at the breakfast table would be muttered from behind newsprint.

'It says here that we have over a million men in arms, and half a million in the Home Guard. What a joke.' This was India from behind the *Telegraph*.

Catherine had not taken a paper but sat, cup in both hands,

staring out of the window into the garden and occasionally at the letter by her plate. Now, though, she was stung to words. 'It sounds quite formidable. Almost two million soldiers.'

'Half of them still shell-shocked from Dunkirk, no doubt. As for the Home Guard – senile or fluffy-chinned, and armed with broomsticks. Some protection!'

'Honestly, to hear you is to wonder which side you're on,' said David, sharply. 'For your information, we're all training hard. You may be very glad of us one day.'

'I'm on the side of realism, David. The German army is formidable. And as far as I can see, all we have is a lot of hot air from Churchill, and a rag, tag and bobtail of amateurs.'

'That's precious near sedition, dear sister. I've half a mind to report you.'

'Oh do, do! At least it would mean you were doing something other than playing soldiers.'

There it was again the suggestion that he was useless. Catherine was remonstrating on his behalf; but David had had enough. He rose to his feet, made his excuses, and set off for the stables.

It was a relief to Catherine when she was safe in her room and could put the conflict at the breakfast table behind her. She and Pamela had bickered, but what she had witnessed below was not bickering. It was – or seemed to be – hatred. She curled up on the window seat, carefully, to accommodate her thickened waist, and began to read her letter.

'*My darling wife,*' it began, and she smiled at his obvious love of those words, '*I thought I'd be afraid when it came to combat, but now that I'm up there I feel no fear at all, just a kind of euphoria. You look down and see wave after wave of undulating cloud, white cloud, stretching for miles in every direction. Sometimes you find yourself in a canyon with walls of white cloud on either side, and the plane's shadow on them. Awesome!*

'*Now I've got spring to look forward to, and you and the sprog. Shall we put him down for Eton – or Cheltenham if he's a girl? Well, you know what I mean. Oh Catherine, how much I'm looking forward to peace, and you and me with time to get to know one another. We had so little time, but I know this, that I love you with all my heart, you funny, shy little thing. And I mean to make you happy. I truly do.*

'*Everyone here is whistling and humming the same song. It's French and is called "J'Attendrai" which, if I remember my ghastly French lessons, means "I will wait". I'll take you to Paris one day for a proper honeymoon, and serenade you on the Champs Elysées with that dratted tune.*'

Catherine's tears were falling on to the letter now, and she blinked them away and tried to continue. '*Take care of yourself, and don't worry about me. Must close now, or miss the collection. Take care, my darling wife, Your loving husband, Henry.*'

She folded it, trying not to picture him flying above white clouds in a flimsy plane. Then she realised she was crumpling the letter, and laid it on her knee to straighten it, aware suddenly that she did care for Henry. She didn't love him as she had loved Joe, but she cared for him, and wanted him to come safely home.

---

Hannah Chaffey was holding forth as usual, and Sarah tried to shush her baby so as not to interfere with the conversation. If she had had a bedroom to go to, she would have retreated to it now, but Jim was dead to the world in there at the end of a long shift.

'I seen it, I tell you. *Daily Mirror*, front page. Our boys shot down 144 Jerries, although they say there was thousands of them. Sky was black with them. We lost 27 planes and 19 pilots. Just boys, most of them. They got some of our aerodromes with their dratted bombs, but our boys were fearless. It said so in the paper. Flying within inches of the Jerries. There was something about the Duke of Windsor in there as well. Off to the Bahamas for a rest. I'd give him rest, running off and leaving his poor brother with a war on his hands.'

Hannah would have gone on had not Sarah's father proffered more tea. Sarah sat back, grateful for the lull, and wiped sweat from her eye-sockets. If she could find work, she could maybe rent a room somewhere, even a little place. This wasn't fair on everyone – five of them in a two-up one-down miner's cottage. And they were always calling for women to do their bit now, even mothers.

Hannah was on to Ernest Bevin now. The Minister for Labour had banned strikes and lock-outs, and imposed seven-day working in arms factories. Miners must stay in their jobs, and all labour was controlled. 'My brother says they'll go along with it till Jerry's done for, but not a day longer. Give them an inch, he says –'

She was interrupted by a knock at the door. Sarah would have struggled up, but Hannah was ahead of her. Sarah was subsiding into her chair when she heard Catherine's voice. She mustn't come in here, Sarah thought urgently, not with washing hung round the fire and the sickly smell of soaking pit clays in the air.

'I'm coming, Hannah!' She held the baby in one arm and ushered Catherine back into the garden. 'It's hot inside, Lady Callingham.'

'Catherine,' the other said firmly. 'Now, let me see this baby again. My, he's grown.'

'Not long now for you,' Sarah ventured. As she saw confusion in the other woman's face she regretted her impertinence.

'No. Not long. Well – several months.'

Sarah nodded but her mind was working furiously. Like most women, she herself had known to the day how long she had to go. Catherine Callingham must know, so why be so shy about telling? She struggled to think of a change of subject.

'It's his christening next week. Joseph Gerard. Would you be a godmother?' It was out before it even occurred to her. But Catherine was nodding and smiling. There would be hell to pay when the priest heard that she was a Protestant. Still it was done, and the more she thought about it the better Sarah liked the idea.

⸻

They had unloaded the boxes and decanted the furniture into the tiny house. Pamela persisted in calling it tiny, although it had two reception rooms and four bedrooms. In the Dene there had been five lofty-ceilinged rooms downstairs, and four spacious bedrooms above plus two bedrooms for staff. This house had been built for a worker, and that in itself was a comedown. 'We're grateful,' her mother had said to David Callingham when he handed over the keys, but Pamela didn't feel grateful. She felt enraged by the sheer bloody unfairness of life. She was prettier than Catherine, everyone said so. And more talented. And a better tennis-player by half.

'There are stains on the bowl in the WC,' she told her mother gleefully. 'And a wooden draining-board in the scullery.' She emphasised the word 'scullery' because it was a common word. She could not recollect ever having used it in her life before, but standing in the galley-like room with its distempered walls and drab linoleum, she rolled the word round in her mind, using it to sum up the huge burden of grievance that now oppressed her.

'We must do something about curtains,' her mother said, but her tone was dispirited.

'You mean I must do something, I suppose. What do you suggest?' The curtains at the Dene had been cream brocade with a flower pattern of turquoise woven in. They were in a bundle somewhere in the mêlée of boxes and tea-chests that surrounded them, but they would look ridiculous hanging at these narrow windows with their tiny leaded panes.

Pamela was about to suggest putting them up, just so everyone could see how far they had sunk in the world, when she heard the doorbell. For a split second she waited to hear Maisie's step in the hall as she hurried to answer. But there was no Maisie – answering the door would be up to her now, like everything else in the nightmare. She was half-way to tears as she pulled open the door, ready to bite the head off a caller, no matter who it might be, especially if it was Catherine.

But the man standing apologetically below the step was David Callingham. 'How lovely,' she said, extending a hand. 'We're in a terrible muddle, I'm afraid, but do come in for a cup of tea. You can help us christen our new house.'

～～～

Catherine lay on her bed, listening to the birdsong outside her window. Heat lay heavy upon her, and it had been a relief to cast off confining clothes and lie down after the long walk back from the McGuires' cottage. She was to be a godmother. She smiled at the ceiling, thinking how Joe would have laughed. '*A godmother? To our Sarah's bairn?*' But he would have loved it all the same. How would she break the news to India? Perhaps she needn't tell her – she could just slip quietly away to the church. David would help her. And he would understand.

She closed her eyes, remembering the baby, its blue eyes fixed on her face, and yet not quite seeing her. It had looked wise, and yet it was less than six weeks old – which made it all the more extraordinary that Sarah had journeyed to the cathedral for Sir Gervase's funeral.

Thinking of the funeral reminded her of Henry. What had he said in the letter. '*I will take you to Paris.*' That was because of that song he had written about, and that everyone was singing. She hummed it to herself, uncertainly at first and then more confidently.

> '*J'attendrai, le jour et la nuit,*
> *J'attendrai toujours ton retour,*
> *J'attendrai car l'oiseau qui s'enfuit*
> *Vient chercher l'oubli dans son nid,*
> *Le temps passe et court, en battant tristement*
> *Dans mon coeur si lourd . . .*'

Suddenly she thought of Henry returning, bending over the crib, allowing a baby's fingers to close around his own forefinger. He would smile at his son – except it would not be his son. It would be the child of another man. 'What have I done?' she said aloud, and turned her face into the pillow.

<p style="text-align:center">~~~~~</p>

As India mounted the stairs she could hear someone humming. She paused outside Henry's (she refused to call it Catherine's) room. The tune was that dreadful French thing everyone was humming or whistling, even errand boys. She moved on, working out how she could return the letter to Catherine's dressing-case if her sister-in-law stayed in her room until dinner. She would just have to bluff it out. Unless – she took it from the pocket of her silk jacket and gazed down on it. No need to read it again, the words were imprinted on her mind. '*My darling wife. My dear little wife.*' Henry was becoming maudlin, dragged down by the insipid little cow he had married in the fever of war.

'I can't bear it,' India thought. In the mirror her face stared back at her. She was not beautiful like her brothers, but she was a Callingham. Good bones. Their line had good bones. Now Henry's child would be born of a union with a – she sought for a word. Not plebeian. Not common slut. How much easier it would have been to understand if Catherine Allerton had been a guttersnipe. All men were foolish sometimes.

But she was simply middle class, and Henry had elevated her to the status of Lady Callingham. There was a pain in India's heart, and she pressed the letter to her breast as though to subdue it. And then she took the flimsy airmail between her long fingers, and slowly and methodically ripped it to shreds.

~~~~~

They settled in the library after dinner. 'It should be on in a moment.' David said, leaning back in his chair. Catherine and India sat side by side on the sofa. The chair that had been Sir Gervase's remained unoccupied. Churchill was to comment on the war that had raged in the air without ceasing over the past few months.

Then the great voice was booming out. 'Almost a year has passed since the war began, and it is natural for us, I think, to pause on our journey at this milestone and survey the dark, wide field.' That sounded ominous. 'The British casualties in the first 12 months of the Great War amounted to 365,000. In this war, I am thankful to say, British killed, wounded, prisoners, and missing, including civilians, do not exceed 92,000, and of these a large proportion are alive as prisoners of war.'

Catherine had hardly thought about prisoners of war. If Henry was shot down, it might be months, years even, before he came home. The relief this thought brought made her feel ashamed, and she turned her attention back to Churchill.

'Hitler is now sprawled over Europe. Our offensive springs are being slowly compressed, and we must resolutely and methodically prepare ourselves for the campaigns of 1941 and 1942. The road to victory may not be so long as we expect. But we have no right to count upon this. Be it long or short, rough or smooth, we mean to reach our journey's end. The whole Western seaboard of Europe from the North Cape to the Spanish frontier is in German hands; all the ports, all the airfields on this immense front, employed against us as potential springboards of invasion. Moreover, the German air power, numerically so far outstripping ours, has been brought so close to our island that what we used to dread greatly has come to pass, and the hostile bombers not only reach our shores in a few minutes and from many directions, but can be escorted by their fighting aircraft.

'The British nation and the British Empire, finding themselves alone, stood undismayed against disaster. No one flinched or wavered; nay, some who formerly thought of peace, now think only of war. Our people are united and resolved, as they have never been before. Death and ruin have become small things compared with the shame of defeat or failure in duty.

'We cannot tell what lies ahead. It may be that even greater ordeals lie before us. We shall face whatever is coming to us. The whole British Army is at home. More than two million determined men have rifles and bayonets in their hands tonight, and three-quarters of them are in regular military formations. We have never had armies like this in our island in time of war. The whole island bristles against invaders, from the sea or from the air.'

David was sitting forward now, a half smile on his face. He caught Catherine's eye. 'My God, he's good, Catherine.'

She nodded, 'Yes,' she said. 'He's what we need.'

Only India was silent as the speech continued.

'The gratitude of every home in our island, in our Empire, and indeed throughout the world, except in the abodes of the guilty, goes out to the British airmen who, undaunted by odds, unwearied in their constant challenge and mortal danger, are turning the tide of the world war by their prowess and by their devotion. Never in the field of human conflict was so much owed by so many to so few.'

They sat on as Churchill outlined the strategy for winning the war.

'I don't know why I'm crying,' Catherine said, when at last he ended.

David was rising to his feet. 'Don't worry, sister-in-law. I expect half the nation is blubbing by now. Or cheering. Or giving thanks.'

# Chapter Thirteen

September 1940

'ONLY ONE EGG, I'M AFRAID.' India spoke in tones of doom. 'And that is the last of the marmalade.'

David tried to look concerned, but, with details of the war in the air on the page in front of him, the lack of another egg for breakfast failed to impress.

India went on: 'I'm certain we're losing produce from Home Farm. How can we be without eggs when there seem to be thousands of hens there? And feed bills to match?'

Catherine made sympathetic noises. 'She's scared to stand up to India,' David thought, 'and yet she's mistress of the house now, if she cared to put down her foot.'

He shook out his paper. 'Farmers have to turn over most of the output, India. There's a War Ag. Committee, you know, and rationing. We must all make sacrifices.'

Catherine had raised her eyebrows at the unfamiliar name and David smiled at her. 'War Agricultural Committee. The farmers loathe them.'

India merely scowled at this remark, so at least he had shut her up. David turned back to the headlines. Since the beginning of the month, the Luftwaffe had mounted increasingly ferocious attacks on Britain. The Air Chief Marshal in charge of RAF tactics was said to be short of pilots, and there were rumours that half-trained men were being thrown into the thick of the fight and shot down on their first sortie. It was a thought too terrible to contemplate, and yet India was wittering on about missing eggs.

There were details of the massive daylight raid on London that had taken place a week ago. Over 400 dead, and more than 1,000 injured. One fire-fighter was quoted as saying: 'The whole bloody world's on fire,' as bombed warehouses blazed along the Thames. The Germans had obviously switched their attacks from the airfields to the capital, which was good news for the RAF but a death sentence for Londoners.

In the Letters column there was some grumbling about civil servants receiving a sixpenny rise a month, before it was given to soldiers. A sixpenny rise – how could that be a matter of import? But even as he thought that, David acknowledged his own remoteness from real life. Life at Kynaston Hall had changed comparatively little, except for the odd egg or two. He had not been plucked from his home and his workplace, and forced to fly a plane or fire a gun. 'I've never had a workplace,' he thought ruefully.

Catherine was clearing her throat. 'I'm going to the village this morning.'

David lowered his paper, glad of diversion from his thoughts. 'Can I drive you?'

India put down her cup with a clatter. 'It's less than a mile, David. Besides, as you were so keen to point out earlier, there's a war on and petrol is rationed.'

'Please, I'm quite happy to walk.' Catherine was sounding more agitated than usual. Something was up.

India must have noticed it too. 'Do you have to go? Is there a reason?'

There was silence for a moment, and then Catherine's chin came up. 'I'm going to be godmother to Sarah Foxton's baby.'

David dared not look at India as he spoke. 'That's good.

They've had more than their share of tragedy, that family.'

'They're Catholics.' India was controlling her words with an effort. 'They won't have you as a god-parent.'

'The priest's given a special dispensation,' Catherine said quietly. And then more firmly. 'Anyway, I'm doing it.'

The tension was relieved when a servant brought in the post. There were two letters addressed in Henry's hand, one for Catherine and one for David. Looking at his sister, David felt sudden sympathy. She cared so much for her brother, and Henry seemed not to remember she was alive.

———

Sarah ladled out mash to the chickens, the sour smell of it almost making her retch. But at least it was cooler, now that September was here. She was going back into the house when she saw Terry coming up the lane, trudging as men did at the end of a shift. He smiled as he reached the gate, teeth white in his coal-blackened face.

'Got the water ready, Sal? I'll need to get a move on if I'm to get to the church on time.' He was going to be a god-father to little Joe. Now, though, Sarah was concerned for the weariness she could see in his face.

'Get in, and get some breakfast down you. And straight up to bed when we get back.'

He was rolling his eyes as he came through the gate. 'Ooh no, I'm hoping for high jinks with Lady Muck when we get back.' His name for Catherine was Lady Muck of Vinegar Hill, but she would kill him if he came out with it today.

'They're putting shelters in up Marlborough Street,' he said as he sat, newly washed, at the kitchen table wolfing down fried bread. 'Andersons. We'll get them next. Six foot deep. Sammy Otterson's seen them down in the Midlands. He says they're muck-damp, and kids that sleep in them are getting croup.'

'Better croup than being blown to smithereens,' Sarah said, moving the brown sauce bottle out of his reach. It was the last one, and he used it like soup if he got the chance.

'Where's me Dad?' he said, suddenly noticing his father was not in his usual chair. 'And where's Hannah Chaffey? They haven't done a runner together, have they?'

'Me Dad's at the shop and she's at church. She went for early mass, and said she might as well stay till we got there.'

He was pushing back his chair. 'Let's get on with it then. Let the dog see the rabbit!'

'Never mind the dog and the rabbit, Terry McGuire. One wrong word from you in front of Lady Callingham, and I'll dog your rabbit, all right.'

As she looked at him, she realised how much she loved him. Sixteen years old and already two years down the pit!

But even the pit was safer than going to war. She thought of the ceremony ahead: a baby being baptised, and its father dead and lying in a foreign field.

---

After lunch, David retreated to his room and took out Henry's letter again. There were comments about life at home, and taking care of everything in his absence, but then Henry's enthusiasm for what he was doing broke through.

'*Good old Beaverbrook, churning out the planes. I hated Lysanders, which Spiff termed "flying coffins", but my Spit is amazing, sweeter to handle than any other I have flown. Push it too far, and it gets temperamental, but it truly feels like wings. Up there at 12,000 feet you're in a vast and peaceful land which seems a million miles away from war. And then you remember the Hun may be lurking above you ready to finish things. That sobers your thinking.*

'*Speaking of thinking, I think of you all a lot. You're all putting up with so much and I'm not there to help. Still, it's a means to an end. You won't believe it, David, but I am one of the oldest here. Some of the boys are 18 or 19, wet behind the ears, but brave as tigers. They say the average age of a crew can 21 or 22. Scarcely out of school. Still, that's the way it has to be. I can't wait to be home to Catherine. A baby, David. You get this feeling that, if you buy it, you want a part of you to go on. Looking back, I can't really remember how Catherine and I wound up married, and soon to be parents into the bargain. And now Papa's gone – I keep asking myself if I said goodbye to him properly that last time I went off. Can you remember? If so, be a good chap and put my mind at rest.*

'*I'm off soon, night flying. The moon seems very bright and full. And my CO tells me that pilots from the occupied countries are joining the RAF in droves: Czechs, Poles, Yugoslavs, Norwegians, Danes, all good fliers, especially the Poles. Apparently they have a burning hatred of Jerry because their families are left behind in Europe. The gen here is that it's Bomber Command's turn now. The RAF have pretty well sewn up the Luftwaffe at home. Now we carry the war to the people who started it.*

'*Take care of my family, David – Catherine and the sprog, and even India. She will have to join something or other soon, when women are mobilised, but it's good that you are "reserved", and can care for Kynaston. Your loving brother – well, some of the time. I was a swine to you at others. Sorry. And love, Henry.*'

David folded the flimsy paper and put it back into his desk drawer; then he brushed his eyes with the back of his hand and got ready to attend to his duties.

Catherine fixed her eyes on the face of the Virgin, lit as it was by flickering candles. Her baby would come into a troubled world, just as Mary's baby had. She let her hand creep down to her belly. She had not felt the baby stir today. Or yesterday, come to that. Or had she? She struggled to remember as the words of a hymn rose into the incense-scented air.

The service was strange to her but beautiful. A piece of theatre, certainly, but full of joy at the coming of a new life.

'You'll stay for a cup of tea?' Sarah asked, as they emerged into the sunlight.

The McGuire family was celebrating the baptism in high style, or as high as wartime restrictions would permit. The church hall was packed, and almost every guest had con- tributed – pies, cakes, sausage rolls, and floury baps. Women scurried about with huge aluminium teapots, and in a corner men held pint glasses.

'To wet the baby's head,' Sarah's father said apologetically when he saw her looking. He waited on Catherine, obviously grateful, if a little abashed at her presence. 'By, that's sad,' he said lifting the top from a bap and eyeing the filling. 'A great chunk of ham with a little drop of pease pudden – that's what it used to be. Now look! I could read the *Echo* through that slice of ham. Hitler's got a lot to answer for.'

Catherine laughed as he delicately replaced the lid of the sandwich with huge, blue-flecked fingers. She knew what those blue flecks were. Joe had explained that to her when she had queried the same mark on him. She remembered the feel of his mouth on hers, his tongue against hers . . .

Suddenly she realised Joe's father was staring at her, obvi- ously waiting for an answer. 'I'm sorry – I didn't hear what you said?'

He was telling her about Sarah, what a good daughter she had been, and what a good wife she would have made if Gerard had lived. 'It's hard for her now, living in with us, but she'll have no chance of a house without a man.'

Catherine knew enough about Belgate to know this was true. Colliery houses were for men who worked in the pit – 'stables for workhorses', Joe had called them once. Perhaps she could speak to David – except that even he did not have an endless supply of roofs, and he had already found a place for her family.

'Perhaps they'll make provision for war widows,' she said lamely, and saw derision in Mr McGuire's eyes.

All morning India had found it impossible to think of anything but the notion of a Callingham taking part in a ceremony in a Catholic church. Catherine was not Callingham by blood, but, like it or not, she now bore the name, and should conduct herself accordingly. Sir Gervase had dealt evenly with Catholic and Protestant alike, but India had always known there was a difference. 'They breed like rabbits,' her mother had said once. Quite lightly, in the way she spoke lightly of everything, but India had known she meant it. Uneducated people bred like rabbits.

She had seen that for herself in India. The people they mixed with there, people of rank, had two or three children, four at the most. Down in the sink that was the inner city, or out in the rural areas, every house teemed with ill-clad, moon-eyed children clinging to their mother's skirts, or even to their sagging breasts.

India shuddered at the memory, and turned her attention back to the linen cupboard. Once upon a time, a servant would have done this job, discarding any napkin or cloth with the least fraying at the edge and ordering replacements from Heal's. Now there was only her, and if the wretched Bevin had his way, she too would be off to some factory or menial task, propping up the war effort. Effort for a war which should never have happened. Chamberlain had been weak. If he had been elbowed aside for Halifax – except that Attlee and Bevin, upstarts both of them, would not have allowed that to happen.

'We are being governed by fools,' India thought, and went back to counting damask, thinking as she did so how elegant her hands were. Patrician – the word popped into her mind, and it pleased her so much she let it roll on and on as she counted.

———

Catherine walked the mile and a half from the church hall to her parents' new home. She pushed open the green-painted gate, seeing flowers in the garden which she had not noticed the first time David had taken her there. The house looked lived-in now, and she felt her heart lift as she walked up the path.

Inside, her spirits quickly sank. Unpacked boxes were everywhere, piles of linen and rugs piled up on them, higgledy-piggledy. 'Everything has been dumped here,' she thought despairingly, 'and no one has had the heart to sort it out.'

She found her parents in the small room that led to the kitchen. This room, at least, had a semblance of tidiness. There was tea on a tray, and china cups, so an effort was being made. But her father sat staring into space, scarcely responding when she kissed his cheek. Her mother's eyes were puffy from weeping, and she pulled a lace-edged hankie hither and thither between her fingers. Catherine was unfastening her coat and wondering where to make a start when she heard Pamela's heels on the bare boards of the hall.

'You've come!' Pamela's voice was almost hysterical. 'I hope you've brought beef tea. That's what the gentry take to the peasantry, isn't it? Or have you come to gloat? As well you may! Look around you, and then remember where we used to live – our home, my home, swallowed up by your over-priced wedding. That's what brought us down in the end – spooning you into a soft sitting-down, while I . . .'

She would have carried on, but her father was levering himself from his chair. 'Shut up! Shut up! Catherine's wedding had nothing to do with it. The business had been losing money for years. I borrowed, I gambled in the end – anything to keep afloat. The wedding didn't make a bit of difference because the bills for it aren't paid!'

———

It was all Sarah could do to cover her emotions through a day that seemed to last forever. So many people had helped, the priest had fallen over himself to make it memorable, Catherine had come down from the Hall – but what did it matter when the one person who should have been present was not? She had looked at her baby, sleeping peacefully until the holy water fell on him, and pictured Gerard there, holding his son.

The party was over in the church hall, but seemed to have migrated home with her. In the safety of the water closet, the only place she could get privacy with the house still thronged with people, she gave way to tears and allowed her long-suppressed fears to surface. How was she going to manage? Where would she live? How would she cope with a growing boy as he became a man? The nonsense of this did bring a smile to her face: he was hardly out of the womb, and she was worrying about his coming to manhood. After a while she pulled the chain to cover the noise of a hearty blow of her nose, and girded herself to go back into the fray.

'They're set here for the neet,' her father muttered, looking round. And then – 'She's all right, that lass from the Hall. Nee side to her. I thought you had a tile off, asking her to stand up for the bairn, but she's all right.'

Sarah couldn't resist it. 'She knew our Joe,' she said as casually as she could.

'Get away?' her father said, but his eye was wandering across the room to the interloper sitting in his chair. 'Haway,' he said. 'Let's see if we can get rid of this lot and get a bit of peace.' And then, as he was turning away: 'I was proud of you today, our lass. Keeping your chin up. It can't have been easy. He'd've been proud of you too, your man.'

It was too much. She fled back to the lavatory, and sobbed until there were no tears left to cry.

≈

Catherine felt weary as she descended the stairs for dinner. What was troubling her was the memory of Pamela's face that afternoon. Had she really ruined her sister's life? Her brain said a wedding couldn't bring down a thriving business: the factory must have been in trouble for years, and indeed her father had said as much. But had her selfish action to solve her own dilemma been the straw that broke the camel's back? If that was so, she must do what she could to make reparation. She could do nothing now till the baby was born, but when that time came she would have some thinking to do. As she crossed the hall, she tilted her chin and tried to look forward to the meal.

David was there in the library, rising from his seat to pour her sherry. 'You look tired, Catherine. Come and sit down. I heard from my brother, your husband, today. I'm under orders to watch over you.'

India was sitting on the chaise, one silk-shod leg over the other, a buckled patent shoe dangling from the foot that swung up and down. 'She does that when she's annoyed,' Catherine thought, and tried to remember when she had seen it before. It was impossible to dismiss the afternoon's events from her mind. Her family was disintegrating – and if the wedding had not been paid for, as her father had said, would it come to India's notice? Thoughts chased round and round her mind as she kept her face impassive and sipped her sherry.

They made conversation until it was time to go in to dinner. David asked her about the christening, and seemed genuinely interested. India was disapproving: 'I know you mean well, Catherine. And of course the McGuires have had a terrible misfortune. Two wage-earners dead in the first months of the war –'

David's tone was harsh as he interrupted her. 'Wage-earners, India? You make them sound like machines. They were men, they had people who loved them – for more than their ability to bring in a wage, I hope. Catherine was absolutely right to show support. The mother of the baby came to Papa's funeral service: I saw her there. She was in the last months of her pregnancy, and I remember being touched by the thought of how hard it must have been for her to get to the cathedral.'

India threw up her hands, hands that were almost assuming a life of their own in Catherine's eyes. 'Have it your way, David. I'm simply warning. This war is unsettling everyone, breaking down barriers that were there for very good reasons. I don't think members of this family should add to the confusion.'

Suddenly Catherine heard her own voice, a little shaky but quite loud. 'I'm not confused, India. It's good of you to worry, but I know what I'm doing.'

She didn't catch what India said in reply – it might even have been no more than a grunt. A pain that had appeared, low down in her belly, as a tiny flicker at first, was now blossoming into something more. A servant had appeared in the doorway to announce dinner, and David was offering her his arm. She rose to her feet, feeling as though she wanted to pass water, but afraid to admit it now. They moved into the dining-room, the table glittering with silver and crystal as it always did, and she subsided into the chair David pulled out for her. The pain had gone now. It was going to be all right.

She was halfway through her soup when it came again. This time it was more demanding than before.

India had fumed all day about the wretched christening, and Catherine had compounded her crime by being away for almost the whole day, as if a brief visit to the church would not have been enough. She had looked exhausted when she got back, which indicated how little consideration she was showing for Henry's child. India had confronted her in the hall – 'Where have you been all this time?' – looking pointedly at her wristwatch; but Catherine had chosen to ignore what she had said. Instead she had muttered something about going upstairs to change, and hurried away.

Watching her mount the stairs. India could see she was labouring, clinging to the banister as though hauling her body upwards. The baby was not due until January. Unless Henry had been foolish? That might explain the hurried wedding.

She looked at Catherine across the glittering display of silver and crystal. Was that how she had done it? Trapped him into marriage? If so, she was a harlot and Henry a fool. India looked down and saw that she had torn her bread into small pieces so that it covered her plate. Mustn't say anything now, or give anything away – not until the child was safe. After that. . . well, her sort didn't stick. She would be off, and Henry would have the child. 'I will be there to help him,' India vowed and tried not to let her exultation show in her face.

She was thinking of the old nursery, and what they could do to keep its atmosphere while refreshing it for the newcomer, when she heard Catherine groan suddenly, and saw her put her napkin to her mouth. David was looking, too – then he was pushing back his chair and moving to Catherine's side, asking what was wrong, and generally wringing his hands in the way men always did when things went awry.

India said nothing. Instead she lifted her glass to her lips. It didn't do to waste a good wine, not when a future supply could not be guaranteed.

'I'm very sorry, my dear.' Dr Cunningham's eyes were kind, his touch on her arm gentle. He – it was a boy – had probably died some days ago.'

Catherine nodded. 'I haven't felt him move . . . not since yesterday.' Or was it before? She was still hazy from whatever the doctor had given her, but she had known it was useless even while he and the nurse had laboured over her. Now he was patting her arm again. 'And you're not to worry – I'll deal with any discrepancy. No one will know. Now you must rest, and build yourself up for young Henry's return. There'll be more babies, no need to worry about that.'

She had felt the baby slither into the world and tried to think of Henry and how disappointed he would be. But she could only see Joe's face, feel Joe's body against hers, making that baby. His baby. That was wrong of her – she was married to Henry. What had he said in his letter? '*I know I will be coming home to a land of black-outs and rationing, but you will be there, and our baby.*'

Across the room, the nurse was holding a towel-wrapped bundle. 'I want to see him,' Catherine said. The doctor was shaking his head, but the nurse moved forward and placed the bundle on Catherine's breast. 'One peep,' she said, 'just one peep.' The little face was serene, the tiny nose and mouth as perfect as any cherub's. Did he look like his father? She couldn't remember Joe's face, hard as she tried.

'Little Joe,' Catherine said and felt tears roll down her cheeks.

'He's not a Joe,' the nurse said, gently removing the baby from Catherine's arms. 'That's no name for a baby.'

Dr Cunningham cleared his throat. 'That will do, I think, nurse.'

They were moving away, and Catherine closed her eyes.

What did she feel? Sorrow, certainly, but also relief. No one would know, now. The doctor would say the baby had been conceived in April. She was safe. But the Callinghams would mourn the loss of Henry's heir, and she was saddled with her lie forever.

~~~

David would have liked to pace the hall until the doctor appeared with news, but India forced him to sit opposite her and wait. 'I knew she'd be trouble,' she said at last. 'A hasty wedding, and now this. But if the baby can just survive . . . It's too soon, though, not even six months.'

'Then you do care,' David said.

She looked at him, her eyes glittering. 'Of course I care. The child is a Callingham. Kynaston will be his one day. A girl would mean nothing, just as I mean nothing. And yet I care for all this much more than you or Henry.'

David would have argued with her, not least over her callous disregard of what might be happening to Catherine. All she cared for was that the child should live. But somehow it seemed not to matter. He kept thinking of Henry's letter: '*A baby, David. You get the feeling that, if you buy it, you want a part of you to go on . . .*' He sat there, willing life to the woman and the baby above him. He went on willing it, until Dr Cunningham appeared in the doorway and he knew that it was too late.

# Chapter Fourteen

## December 1940

Mrs Earnshaw had laid a fire in the grate in Catherine's bedroom and put a match to it. It blazed up the chimney, cheering the room. The woman had gone out of her way to be kind in the past few months, and so had David, as though they were trying to make up for her loss. Only India was unyielding. She had looked down at Catherine as she lay, newly washed and propped up to receive visitors, and had shaken her head. 'Poor Henry,' she had said, quite softly so that the doctor and nurse could not hear but more than audibly to Catherine, for whom it was intended.

That had been September, and now it was Christmas, or would be in two days' time. Downstairs in the hall they were erecting a tree, and hanging holly from every ledge, all to welcome the master of the house. '*I'll be home for Christmas, I'll swing it somehow,*' Henry had said in his last letter. He had been granted a brief compassionate leave after the baby's death, and had done his best to console her. '*We'll always love him, Catherine. Our first son. But there'll be others. And we still have each other.*'

His optimistic letter had been written in the middle of the month, and David had looked rueful when she told him of the promise it contained. 'I don't know if he'll be able do it. I hope he will, but Jerry won't let up for Christmas, you can be sure of that. So will they be able to spare pilots?' But the mood of Henry's letter had been deliberately designed to lift her spirits. He had not mentioned the dead baby in that letter, although he had been more than consoling in other letters. This time he had contented himself with saying '*ETA Christmas Eve, my darling wife. Oh, how I long to see Kynaston, and you there in the hall. I hope there's a tree – David will see to that, I know. So wait for me, my darling, until I can kiss away the pain of the last few months, and point us both to a bright New Year.*'

Now she forced herself out of the chair and began to lay out clothes for the day. She had to make herself go downstairs each day, for with the world outside frozen there was nothing to do but share the house with her sister-in-law's disapproval. 'I am nothing to her now,' Catherine thought. 'While there was a baby, an heir, she could tolerate me. Now there is nothing.'

When David was around, it was easier not to think of the baby, walled up in the Callingham vault in its handsome coffin. At least it had not been consigned to some anonymous grave, as other unbaptised stillborns were. She had wanted to cry out when she saw the name on the brass plate: *Henry Alexander Joseph Callingham*. Except that her baby's name had been McGuire. And she could tell no one, not even Sarah.

Sarah had been to see her twice, the first time without her own boy. When Catherine had asked why she hadn't brought little Joe, Sarah had coloured and been lost for words. 'It wouldn't have upset me,' Catherine had said gently. 'I don't hate other children because I lost my own.' So Sarah had returned with her baby in her arms, and Catherine had breathed in the sweetness of him, and wished to be a girl again in the summerhouse with nothing to think about except being in love.

But there was no going back. She was here, childless, in a huge and echoing house which boasted two nurseries, one for day and one for night. And Sarah was raising her own child in a huddled one-up, two-down with more people in it than it could hold.

⟆⟆⟆

The tree was eight feet tall and stood in the angle of the sweeping staircase. In previous years, there had been servants to climb ladders and deck it head to foot. Now there was only David and an elderly kitchen-hand to pass him the baubles. He had had to borrow labourers from the Home Farm to lug the tree up from the copse where it had grown, and make it firm in its huge tub. For Catherine's sake, he hoped Henry would get home in time. Since the stillbirth she had been a ghost of the girl who had welcomed them to the Dene in those long-gone peace-time summers.

India had not helped. Was it wrong to hate your own flesh and blood? If so, God would have to forgive him, for at times he did hate his sister. She had some sort of a job now, doing 'good works' with the WVS, and that got her out of the way sometimes; but the atmosphere at Kynaston was dreadful, especially for someone coming to terms with the loss of a child. At times he yearned to take Catherine in his arms, smooth the hair from her forehead, and kiss the doleful mouth . . . He winced suddenly, and looked down to see blood on his palm where he had crushed an emerald globe until it splintered in his hand.

⟆⟆⟆

Hannah Chaffey had come round in the hope of a cup of tea. Now she sat across the table, cup held in both hands, and gave Sarah the news of the day. 'Scott's lad was there at that Sidi Barrani.' She paused to see if Sarah was impressed that a Belgate lad had been present at a great victory.

'Fancy,' Sarah said.

Hannah nodded. The British Army had scored the victory over the Italians ten days earlier, taking thousands of black-shirted Italians prisoner and capturing two more forts in the aftermath. Papers and radio broadcasts had trumpeted a triumph sorely needed to lighten the winter gloom. Although, Sarah conceded privately, everyone knew you could fight off the Italians with a feather duster.

'He saw it all his mother says. But he's sick of sand. He says it's red, not yellow, and not a bit of green anywhere.'

'Fancy,' Sarah said again. There was a mound of dirty dishes in the sink and clothes to press, but you couldn't be inhospitable to a neighbour, even one who talked as though there was no tomorrow.

'The other lad's in London. Fire Service. He's told his mam they put notices on bombed shops: "Open for business" – and then go right on selling from the rubble. He says it's morale, whatever that is.'

'Fighting spirit,' Sarah said absently, still thinking of the piled crockery.

'Sheffield's had a pasting, according to the postman. His sister's man comes from there. Still, if they're getting it now, somewhere else is getting a bit of peace. You've got to look at it that way. Have you heard about the Hall? Eight foot tree. Disgusting with a war on, but when have they ever gone short? Two men had to go up from the farm to lend a hand. Scandalous! Since when was a Christmas tree vital war work?'

'They've had their troubles,' Sarah said, defensively. 'Sir Henry's wife lost her baby, and her man's in Canada, training.'

Hannah was not to be mollified. 'Every family's got someone away, Sarah. Look what your lot have lost. Anyroad, it'll likely be over soon, now Anthony Eden's in charge.'

'In charge?' Sarah was genuinely surprised by this. The last she had heard of Eden, he had resigned in protest over

Chamberlain's appeasement. And surely Churchill was in charge?

The other woman's eyes lit up with satisfaction at having imparted surprising news. 'Yes, back in the Foreign Office. Churchill's right-hand man. They've packed that Halifax off to America, and good riddance.'

Sarah knew Lord Halifax had been on the side of the appeasers, so he was no loss. She was seeking for something to say when there was a wail from above.

'Oh, there's the bairn,' she said, feigning regret as she rose to her feet. 'If he's awake, he'll need his feed.' As she ushered her neighbour over the step and mounted the narrow stairs to fetch her baby, she thought of Catherine, up in that huge and comfortable house, even if it did have an eight-foot tree. She would pick some holly for the mantelpiece, and see if there were still some paper chains at the back of the cupboard. It was Christmas, after all.

---

'He's gorgeous, Catherine, simply gorgeous. His father's an architect, very posh. We've been to the flicks twice. You must see *Rebecca*. Laurence Olivier is divine. Divine! Quite like Roger, actually – very stiff upper lip, and all that. Mother says he's the perfect officer type. He's a lieutenant already, and that's after six months.'

Since the death of Catherine's baby, Pamela had mellowed towards her sister. It was almost as though Catherine's loss reduced her crime in Pamela's eyes. But the advent of an army camp near to the new house had acted like a magic wand. Now there were eligible men around, lonely men who didn't demand a tennis court as a prerequisite to a courtship.

'Disgusting,' India had said. 'Throwing themselves at boys still wet behind the ears. Tricking them, no doubt.' She had looked hard at Catherine as she said this, and Catherine had squirmed inwardly. Could India know? Had the doctor broken his promise?

Now she looked at her sister. Pamela seldom visited without a purpose. What did she want this time?

As if she had intercepted Catherine's thoughts, Pamela spoke. 'The thing is, well, tonight we're going into Durham. To a nice place, he says. Quite posh. And I have simply nothing to wear. And as you got all those things in your trousseau, and you already had a lot of clothes. . .'

'Help yourself,' Catherine said. 'Everything I have is here. You're welcome.' She sat on the bed, legs tucked under her as Pamela rifled through the two huge wardrobes, holding things against her before discarding them and foraging again.

'I know it's early days, Catherine, but the thing is, they're sure to call women up before long. Everyone says so. If I was married – well, it makes a difference. I mean, I could be preg . . .' She stopped in mid-sentence, remembering. 'We're going to see the Chaplin film next week.' She turned back to the wardrobe, humming as she searched.

Catherine knew the tune, 'A Nightingale Sang in Berkeley Square'. Somewhere there were lovers dancing cheek to cheek, looking forward to a tomorrow when the world had ceased to rock on its axis. She stood up. 'I should look something out for myself. Henry's coming home.'

———

India heard girlish voices as she crossed the landing to her room. The odious sister, probably, who was never away nowadays. In her room she shed the hated green uniform and changed into a housecoat. Her WVS job might keep her out of a munitions factory, but she didn't have to like it. Today she had listened to women whingeing about ration books. Idiots!

They were worried about bananas, of all things. The Ministry of Food had announced that after Christmas no more bananas would be imported, because shipping space must be saved for essentials.

She rinsed hands and face in the basin on her chest of drawers, and sat down at her dressing-table to smooth lotion on to her hands, enjoying the sensation of cupping her long fingers. The Allerton girls were rounded and stubby, with dimpled little chins and hands to match.

Perhaps it had been as well that Catherine's baby had not lived. Who knew what could happen with a war on? The marriage might not last. Catherine might get her head turned by one of the uniformed idiots careering round the roads in Army vehicles. Henry might come back at the end of the war and find her gone, and life would go back to normal.

As she creamed her hands and arms, she thought about tomorrow. She would have to talk to the police about the van. In several villages they had told her of a mysterious van, and there had been a number of poultry thefts in the area. For the black market, no doubt. Since there had to be rules, they must be obeyed. She had a certain amount of power, now, over food supplies in the area, and she meant to use it. There had been a lot of grumbling about taxes, especially the new tax on luxuries – 'It isn't fair,' a woman had said of the rise in the price of things like furs and silk stockings and cosmetics. But their class had never been able to afford those things in peace-time, so why were they whingeing now?

She would wear her mauve cloque tonight, and save the burgundy velvet for Christmas when Henry would be here and in his rightful place at the head of the table, she opposite him at the foot. If only they had been able to keep all the servants, it would feel quite like old times.

Sarah had been working in the pub for a week now, but she still hadn't got used to leaving the baby. Perhaps Mr Fisk would let her bring him with her and leave him in the parlour? Once she had learned how to pull a pint and get the change right, she might ask him. Her war widow's pension of 32 shillings for her and 11 shillings for the baby was enough to manage on while she lived at home, but sooner or later she must find somewhere to rent.

There was a lull in the clamour for drinks, and she leaned her back against a cupboard. Around her noise throbbed – the customers were men from the camp, tie-less and bare headed, their battle-dress jackets loosened at the neck, not at all like the disciplined fighting machines she sometimes saw out marching. A group of young miners were in the corner, keeping themselves to themselves. The soldiers looked down on the miners, thinking them shirkers. That was because they didn't know the pit.

A man was coming through the door, and she saw that it was her brother, Jim. 'What'll it be?' she said, as he approached the counter, glad that she sounded quite professional. But he had not come in for a drink, he had come in search of her.

'Molly's fallen wrong,' he said desperately. 'She's just told me. I'm standing by her, Sarah, so don't argue.'

Her eyes widened. 'Of course you're standing by her.' He and Molly had been sweethearts since junior school.

'Where are we going to live, though, Sal? I've got to find somewhere. Molly says her dad won't let her stay once he knows. Besides, we want to get wed before – well, before. . .'

She tried to calm him with a reassurance she was far from feeling. The family home was bursting at the seams. Already she was fearful of what would happen when her baby grew. And Jim had as much right to its shelter as she had. More – he paid his way far more than she did.

He moved off to be with his mates as she went on serving, trying not to let anxiety distract her. She handed one man his change, but instead of taking it he caught hold of her hand.

'How about a bit of the other when you finish, Sally? Come on, I know you're up for it.'

She felt her mouth dry. If Jim heard him, there would be a row. 'Let go, please,' she said. 'Let me get on.' But instead he was reaching over the bar with his other hand, trying to draw her forward.

'Is he bothering you, miss?' The voice was deep and Scottish. Or Irish. She could never tell them apart. It belonged to a tall man with reddish hair and stripes on his arm, and the other man was releasing her. 'Only a bit of fun, Sarge.'

The Scottish man said something half under his breath, and the other soldier sloped off. 'Thank you,' Sarah said, and turned away to hide her flushed cheeks.

They gathered, as usual, in the library. 'Thank God we had some wine laid down,' David said. 'The sherry's getting low. Now that you're the real *gauleiter*, dear sister, can we get hold of some more?' He was joking but India didn't smile.

'I'm there to uphold the rules, David, not break them.'

They moved into the dining-room. 'I see Halifax is to be Ambassador to Washington.' said India, taking her place at the head of the table. 'Pa was fond of Lord Halifax; he said he had a brilliant grasp of foreign affairs.'

'He didn't grasp the significance of Herr Hitler.' David was unfolding his napkin, and Catherine saw India draw herself up for a riposte. But just then Mrs Earnshaw appeared in the doorway to the hall.

'I'm sorry, sir, but there's someone on the telephone.'

'Does he want me?' David was already rising to his feet.

'Yes, sir, he most particularly said you and no one else.'

'So annoying, just as we're sitting down,' India said. 'People are so inconsiderate.' She looked across to where a maid stood at the sideboard. 'Go ahead and serve. Mr David won't be long.'

'And too bad if he is, as far as you're concerned,' Catherine thought, but kept the thought to herself.

They had finished their soup when David came back into the room.

'What's wrong?' India asked, seeing his face. He moved forward until he stood by Catherine. 'I'm so sorry,' he said to her. 'I'm so very, very sorry . . .'

'What is it, for God's sake? Who was that?'

Catherine was glad India spoke, for she couldn't find her voice.

'It was Michael Illingworth. We were at school together, and now he's at the War Office. He says we'll get official conformation but it's definite. Henry's plane was shot down this morning, over the Channel. There were no survivors.'

'No!' It was a wail of protest as India's hands went up to her throat.

'How can they be certain?' Catherine said. 'He could be in the sea, in a life raft.' She realised suddenly that her teeth were chattering.

'It happened yesterday.' David said. 'They've been searching all day. There's no doubt now.'

Catherine turned towards the other woman, sensing that her agony was the greater. 'I'm so sorry, India. I know what he meant to you.'

'Know? *Know*? What do you know of this family's loss?'

'India!' David's voice was a whiplash. 'Henry is . . . was . . . Catherine's husband.'

India's face was contorting now and Catherine felt afraid, but before anyone could speak there was a sudden burst of singing from somewhere outside. '*Beneath thy deep and dreamless sleep the silent stars go by . . .*'

'It's the church choir,' David said. 'I forgot they were coming.'

Catherine knew that carol, had sung it in church a dozen or more Christmases. She felt a sudden urge to laugh. This was some sort of ghastly dream. In a minute she would wake up, sweating but safe in her own bed.

'Get rid of them. Get rid of them!' India had sat down at the table, clenched fists in front of her, her face white except for two black coals of eyes.

'I'll go,' Catherine said, glad of a chance to escape. In the library she took a note from her purse and gave it to the wide-eyed maid. 'Thank them, please, but explain that there has been a death, and would they please go away.' She felt suddenly calm, as though she could control the situation.

She was about to re-enter the dining-room when she heard India's voice, more composed now but cold with fury. 'Tragedy? Oh, you're so right, David. It's tragic for this family that the wrong brother has died.'

If David replied, Catherine didn't hear. She stepped back, into the shelter of a night-watchman's chair that stood at one side of the door. 'I've got to get away from this hateful house,' she thought – and then felt ashamed that she was thinking of herself when a young life had been swallowed up by swirling ocean waters.

# Chapter Fifteen

## January 1941

'It won't matter what you say, David, nothing will change my mind. I still think she has no place here. If there'd been a child – but she couldn't even do that successfully. If she stays, it will be awkward when you marry. A house can't have two mistresses, not even a house like Kynaston.'

David wanted to bury his face in his hands, such was his weariness. India had talked like this almost from the moment they heard of Henry's death, and he knew why. She cared more for the future of the damned house than anything else. He was all that was left, the estate would come, with the title, to him, and she was expecting him to marry and bring forth an heir. He had to suppress a wry smile, then, thinking of what she had said about no house having two mistresses: when had she ever allowed Catherine to be mistress of Kynaston? It would be no different when he married. If he married. Damn the laws of inheritance – he was the master now, with all the worry and responsibility that involved. But Catherine belonged here at Kynaston, and he was damned if India would interfere with that.

Aloud, he said, 'It's pointless to argue, India.'

'She wasn't worthy of him!' The words sprang from India's lips, and he saw that her hands were twined together at her breast. 'She trapped him, David. That lovely boy.'

He couldn't help himself. 'For God's sake, you talk as though he was your child – or your lover.' Even as he said it he regretted it, regretted it even more when he saw his words had struck home. He tried to keep his voice steady as he continued: 'As you say, I am the heir. I decide what happens here, and Catherine stays. Now, for God's sake, let's compose ourselves. In case you've forgotten, we're burying our dead brother today.'

Catherine stood at the window, looking out on the land that made up the estate. Below her was the formal garden, beyond that kitchen gardens, and hothouses, beyond them the high wall that surrounded Kynaston Hall, and beyond that again the fields and farms and villages that made up the estate. If her baby had lived, and inherited, it would have been theft on a grand scale. Yet she had gone ahead – had she been a knave or a little fool? She mourned Joe's baby, but thank God she had been spared the crisis of conscience that would have followed Henry's death and the realisation that all that was Kynaston would belong to a child who had no place there. If Henry hadn't died, and he and she had had another child, the rightful heir, could she have stood by and seen that child robbed?

She turned away and moved to the mirror. Her black dress intensified the pallor of her face. 'I look old,' she thought. 'I am old.' Widows in stories were always old. She was 19, and her life was over. The thought of years spent living in India's presence was unbearable. 'I must get away,' she said aloud. But how? And where to?

She stood for a moment, contemplating her reflection, then she squared her shoulders and lifted her chin. She had wronged Henry Callingham in life; she must make sure she honoured him in death.

India kept her eyes fixed on the altar as they walked down the aisle. At least Henry's body had been plucked from the sea eventually, and had been returned to his home. That was some consolation. At the prick of tears, she bit her lip hard. Mustn't cry in front of the tenants. In front of her, she saw Catherine's shoulders were shaking . . . she had no idea of how to behave. 'It should have been me with David. Henry's sister. I should have walked there.'

For a second, her gaze flickered left and right in case she had spoken aloud. And then the Bishop was in front of her, smiling sympathy, and an attendant was ushering her into the pew, David and Catherine standing to one side to let her in, to push her away, to the far end of the pew, while they sat by the aisle. She should have been near to Henry's body . . . his beautiful body!

She knelt to pray, and was glad that all other eyes in the cathedral would be closed, preventing anyone from seeing the tears she could no longer restrain.

On the way back from the cathedral, Sarah's thoughts alternated between reliving the service and worrying about her brother. She would have to get out of the small house somehow, and make room for him and Molly. She could stay on till the baby came, but then Jim and Molly must be together. Anger flared as she thought of the rows of colliery houses, built with just enough room for miners to multiply and bring forth more workers for the Callingham pits.

Up at the hall there was stabling for horses more spacious – her father had told her that once, and it had stuck in her mind. He was pinning his hopes on change after the war. 'We'll own the pits then, Sarah. You'll see.' But the war had to be won first. Who would be left standing to enjoy the new Utopia?

She and Catherine were united in widowhood, both victims of a war neither of them had wanted or, in her own case certainly, completely understood. She had cried when they sang, 'I vow to thee, my country', without really knowing why. But the choir had done young Callingham proud. And the Bishop. Father Lavery had been kind, but all Gerard had had was a special prayer at the end of mass.

Too many men were dying now for there to be many elaborate services. Everyone was saying Mr Roosevelt would bring America into the war, and it would soon be over, but she had scoured the papers and seen no mention of it. He had gone on about freedom, certainly. Freedom of speech and religion, and freedom from hunger and fear. But the Yanks were not putting their money behind their words, not according to gossip in the pub. They were going to lend money to buy weapons, but they wanted their money back with interest.

Last night in the pub someone had called Mr Roosevelt 'nothing but a bloody moneylender', and the Scottish sergeant had told him to shut his mouth. She liked it when the Scotsman was there. He made her feel safe. But his lot was supposed to be shipping out soon, so he would likely die like the rest. As the house came into view, she quickened her pace. War or no war, it didn't solve the problem of Jim, and where he and his bairn were going to lay their heads.

———

'It's gloomy, but rather grand,' Roger said, looking round. Pamela could see he was impressed. As well he might be. They stood in the post-funeral throng on one side of the huge hall, sipping the wine they had been handed on arrival. Her parents should have been here, taking their rightful place – after all, it all belonged to Catherine now, so they were entitled. As it was, India was gliding around doing her Lady Muck act.

'That's Henry's sister,' she whispered to Roger. 'She's plain, isn't she? Such a pity for a girl. Henry was so handsome. That's the other brother over there. He had polio, so he doesn't do much.' She looked to see if Roger was impressed by his surroundings, but his eyes were fixed on the people milling round. They were all laughing and talking, which was odd considering it was a funeral. 'That's the Lord Lieutenant,' she said, pointing to a grey-haired man in a striking uniform. And that's Sir Richard and Lady Anstruther. He's Anstruther chemicals.' Roger didn't seem too interested. Not coming from round here, he didn't really know who was who, or realise that everyone who was anyone was here today.

She caught sight of Catherine, looking pale and sad, which was proper in the circumstances, and lifted a hand in greeting. She was glad when her sister began to move towards her. 'Catherine, this is Roger.' Catherine was holding out her hand and smiling, and Pamela felt a little glow. He looked good in uniform with his one pip. He didn't have a tennis court at his family home, but they lived in Alderley Edge, which her mother said was a good area. She stood sipping her wine, as Catherine questioned him about life at the camp and how he felt about the Army. Let them get to know one another. After all, they could well be related one day.

She looked across to where India was holding court with a group of men in uniform. Perhaps she would move out now that the Hall was Catherine's? For a glorious moment Pamela pondered the possibility of Catherine letting her family move in here. If she did –! She indulged in a wild fantasy of going down the long drive in a horse-drawn carriage, on her way to her wedding.

Her daydream was interrupted by Catherine's voice. 'You didn't tell me Roger's sister was a nurse. She's with a marvellous

145

surgeon called McIndoe who is doing skin grafts on burned pilots. His sister says it's miraculous. Some of the men he's treating would have died, not so long ago.'

'How interesting, but I couldn't do it. No!' Pamela shuddered and put a proprietary hand on her boyfriend's arm. She was about to ask her sister what was going to happen to India and David now, when Catherine murmured excuses and moved away to talk to someone else. But not before she had said, 'We'll meet again,' and Roger had replied, 'I hope so.'

Catherine went to her room as soon as the last guest had departed. She had accepted condolences, smiled, and promised to be brave a thousand times, or so it seemed, all the while feeling guilty. Now she curled up in the window seat and looked out on the garden again. It would be easier when she got away from here, away from reminders of her brief marriage. 'You made him happy,' she told herself as fiercely as she could. 'You sent him away happy. He believed we would have another child.' It hadn't all been wasted, but that did not excuse her. 'I was a coward,' she realised.

She was composing herself for the ordeal of dinner, when there was a tap at her door. 'Sir David would be grateful if you would come down to the library, Lady . . .' The girl hesitated, uncertain what Catherine's title was now.

'Thank you,' Catherine said.

David was waiting in the library, but he was not alone. India sat in a wing chair by the fireplace, and a young man, a stranger, had leapt to his feet when she entered. 'Catherine, this is Jeremy Holborrow. He was at the service today but he – well, I'll let him tell you himself.'

Catherine held out her hand and the young man took it between his own. 'I'm so glad we could meet. Hal talked so much about you. That's why he wanted to be home for Christmas: "our first Christmas together", he called it. He was going to set off home as soon as we landed, he had it all arranged. 'I'll walk in and take them all by surprise,' was what he said as we walked out on to the tarmac. I saw him go down – it was over in seconds, if that's a help. I just felt I wanted you to know how much you all meant to him – especially you, Lady Callingham.

'And this place, too – not that he ever said anything about it being as grand as this. He was just Hal – no side to him. I was coming up this way, anyway, as I live in Northumberland, and I heard about the service at the pub. So I went to the church.

'That's all I wanted to say, really.'

He refused their invitation to dinner, obviously anxious to get away now that his duty was done. David arranged a car to take him to the station, and saw him off at the door, Catherine at his side.

When they came back into the library, India was standing at the fireplace, her back to the door, her hands either side on the mantelpiece above her. She turned at the sound of her entrance. 'Has he gone?'

'Yes.' David's voice was sombre. 'It was kind of him to come, wasn't it? And now he's off again, to God knows what.'

'I was thinking that,' Catherine said. 'They're all so brave.'

'Brave? Or stupid? This pointless war has made people lose sight of what matters.' India was sharp.

'It's not pointless.' Catherine was stung into a reply.

'How would you know – and how dare you speak in this room? Did you hear what he said: Henry could have been safe if he'd kept his mind on the danger. But no, he had to get back to you, to the love affair that wouldn't have lasted a week in peace-time.'

'India!' David was moving across the room, his haste making him clumsier than usual. He stopped, his face inches

147

from that of his sister. 'Be quiet! I will have no more of your vileness. I won't say aloud why you do this, because I don't want Catherine to hear. But you know that I know. I order you to leave this room now. Now, India! And please consider whether or not you have a place here any more.'

For a moment Catherine feared India would strike him. Instead she looked down at her hands, turning them slightly until they were palm up. And then she pushed past him and crossed the room without glancing at its other occupant.

'Don't go, Catherine. I wanted to talk to you, anyway. Come and sit down.' David's voice was still shaking, and she turned obediently to sit in the wing chair that India had vacated. David stood at the fire, one arm on the mantel, his gammy foot on the massive fender that surrounded the hearth.

'I wish it could be postponed, but it can't, I'm afraid.' His voice faltered, and then he continued. 'My father's will was made, as Callingham wills have always been made: the house and core estate to whoever inherits the baronetcy, and the rest of the assets to others, such as India and me. When Henry came home for my father's funeral, he didn't have much time, but he asked for his will to be drawn up in the usual pattern, house and estate going to the male heir, and he signed it after the funeral. He believed, of course, that the male heir would be the son that you and he would have together. As it is now, the title comes to me, and the estate comes with it. I wish it didn't, but I can't change it.'

He looked so anguished that Catherine butted in. 'I know. Henry explained it all to me once. It doesn't matter, David.'

'It matters to me. We can challenge the disposition of the estate . . .'

Terror was overcoming Catherine. He was trying to make her profit from her lie, and she must stop him. 'David, you mustn't do that – unless you wish to make me unhappy. I have no wish to stay here. I want to work. I can make my own way in the world.'

He was smiling now. 'It won't quite come to that, Catherine. The assets you inherit, sometimes called the dower, are not inconsiderable. As well as that, Henry had money of his own, from my mother and her side of the family. That also comes to you. The dower includes a house, but I hope you will stay here at Kynaston.'

'I can't David. For a lot of reasons, I have to get away.'

'I wish you'd stay, Catherine. Like you, I'm not fond of this great echoing house. And I know I'm not up to running the estate.'

'Hush.' She rose to her feet and moved towards him. 'I won't let you say that. Henry trusted you, and he admired you, admired the way you coped when you were ill. You can do it, David, I know you can. I would stay and help you, but I can't. I have to go – don't ask me why. I need to get away.'

'To your parents?'

'No. But I would like to know –'

'If they can stay in the estate cottage? Of course. For as long as they like.'

Her hands were resting on his arms, and now she stretched up and put her lips against his cheek. When she moved away, she saw that he was trying to smile, but his face was set and his eyes sad.

Her mother, as usual, was huddled by the radio in the small back room. Of her father there was no sign. Pamela unpinned the hat that mourning had decreed she should wear to church, and stuck the pins back in it. 'Honestly, Mummy, I don't think you've moved since I went out, and it's been ages. Why don't you sort something, put some things away? I expect the breakfast dishes are still out there.'

'Your father did them.' Her mother's voice was flat.

'Did he? Well, speaking of Daddy, where is he?'

'Upstairs somewhere. I think he said something about lying down.'

Pamela pulled a face, trying not to put her irritation into words. Not today. 'Well, I'm going to make some tea, and then we'll all jolly well get cracking. I know we're not going to be here for ever, but we can't live as though we were passing through. What will Roger think when I bring him home? His father's an architect.'

Her mother seemed to perk up a little then. 'Yes, you must bring him home. At least this house is detached. That's one blessing.'

Pamela went through to the kitchen and filled the kettle, then she went into the hall and mounted the first three stairs. 'Daddy! Daddy, I'm making some tea.'

On an impulse she rooted through boxes until she found a tray and an embroidered tray-cloth and even a cosy for the teapot. She felt virtuous, empowered even. It was going to be all right, and all she had to do was get her parents moving.

Her father came into the room as she began to pour. 'Good,' she said. 'Now sit down, and I'll tell you about the service. Although you should both have been there. Henry was your son-in-law, after all.'

'We're not seeing anyone at the moment,' her mother said defensively. 'And your father's not well. Anyway, how did it go?'

Pamela told them about the stirring hymns and the bevy of aristocracy – 'even the Lord Lieutenant, *and* he came back afterwards' – and the stirring address from the pulpit. 'Afterwards there was wine flowing like water. Up from the cellars. Vintage stuff. And gorgeous canapés. How they did it, I don't know.

'Anyway, Catherine has really fallen on her feet, now that

it's all hers. I'm not counting my chickens, but it's a relief that she'll pay for my wedding if Roger – well, anyone – pops the question. And she's sure to find us a better place than this. I mean, there's money swishing about like water there. I knew they were wealthy, but when you really see it . . .'

Her father put his cup down, and she noticed that his hand was shaking. 'It's none of it Catherine's,' he said.

Pamela felt a giggle rise up in her throat. 'Don't be silly, Daddy. She's Henry's heir.'

'The estate will be entailed. All these great houses are entailed, they pass straight to the next male heir. That's Henry's brother, David. Sir David, now. Even if it's not entailed, they'll have seen to the continuing of the line. That's what matters to their sort.'

'No!' But even as Pamela, protested she knew it had to be true. She never had any luck. And even when it seemed she had, it was snatched from her.

〰〰

The men had come home, bathed in the tin bath in front of the fire, and been fed. Sarah had baled out the sullen contents until they could carry the bath into the garden and tip the remaining water over the leek bed. Now the men were either side of the fire, stockinged feet held out to the blaze, alternately dozing and pretending to read the newspaper.

Sarah sat sipping her tea, enjoying the lull before she got ready for the pub. They had switched off the radio now, and she was glad. There was never anything but war news, and not all of that was good. Tonight they had been talking about the death of Amy Johnson who had flown round the world ten years before, and made history. She had been flying a plane for the RAF, and crashed, and another man, a Navy man, had lost his life trying to save her. Nothing but death.

She got to her feet and crossed to the crib. Her son was sleeping soundly, and she felt her mouth curve into a smile at the sight of him. He was life. Please God he would have a life. She could certainly tell him that his father and his uncle had died for him.

Unless the Germans invaded! God help them all, then. Still, the Australians were taking the Italians prisoner in North Africa. That had been on tonight. Hordes of them were just giving up, apparently, so it wasn't all doom and gloom. Apart from that, she had a nice plump pigeon for the men tomorrow. The man two doors down had dropped it off earlier. And Lord Woolton was putting price controls on 21 foodstuffs to stop the toffs buying them all up, so that was another good thing.

She was turning back to her seat and her cup of tea when her father lowered his paper 'Old Gibbs's lad's gone. Shot down. Only child. They say his mam's in a bad way. Still, I told them, it's come to every house. War's like that.'

It was true, Sarah thought. Last week she had gone to see Greer Garson in *Mrs Miniver*. It had been lovely, but a bit unreal. One thing had stuck in her mind, however. Greer Garson had said, '*This is the people's war. It is our war. We are the fighters. Fight it then. Fight it with all that is in us. And may God defend the right.*'

It had been a bit stagey, but it was still true. This was the peoples's war, and the people were suffering.

---

Already the light was beginning to fade. It was three o'clock. Another hour of daylight, no more. Catherine wrapped up warmly and let herself out of the house. She would have liked to take one of the dogs, even all three, but they went berserk at the hint of an expedition, so she left well alone. She skirted the kitchen garden, and let herself out of the door in the wall. The grass beneath her feet was crisp with frost, the trees stark and bare. She shivered a little and quickened her pace.

In the distance she could see the huddle of houses that was Belgate. She had seen Sarah Foxton in the cathedral, looking careworn and shabby. What did army widows get? Not much, she imagined. At least she herself would have money in her pocket. Was she justified in taking Henry's money? She had given him something to hope for, Jeremy Holborrow's visit had convinced her of that. So she would take the money, but she must leave Kynaston. She shuddered slightly at the memory of India's face. Why does she hate me so much, Catherine wondered.

She came to a stile and climbed it cautiously, her feet slipping on the frosted wood. She would go to see Sarah tomorrow. Surely the country would do something for the widows of serving men? Except that no one knew how many of them there would be. And how many men would be crippled by war, unable to fend for their families.

As she skirted a beck she thought of what Pamela's boyfriend had said that morning. Pamela had shuddered at the very thought of nursing a wounded man, but what greater calling could there be?

She paused for a moment on the breast of a small hill, and looked back at the smoky blur of Belgate. She felt a sudden longing to go there now, to tell Sarah the truth about her brother's baby. But it couldn't be: a secret was something only one person knew. She would have to keep her secret forever. Too many people would be hurt if she told.

She had returned to the road when she heard an engine behind her. It was David behind the wheel of the Bentley. 'Get in,' he said, opening the passenger door.

'What is it?' she asked, sinking into the seat. 'Is everything all right? Where's India?'

He revved the engine and the car shot forward. 'I neither

know nor care. I want to show you something. We'll have to be quick, the light is going.'

She sat in silence as they flashed through the lanes. At last he turned into a gateway and slowed as they drove up a curved drive. The house that lay before them was low and rambling, its windows glinting in the dying sun. 'Whose is it?' Catherine asked, but she already knew what he was going to say.

'It's yours. Take it Catherine – if you like it, that is. If not, we'll look at others. I told you there was a dower house, but actually it's a bit decrepit now. This one is – a little grander. It's called Mellows, I don't know why. It's been empty for a year or two. A distant relative of my father's took refuge here for a while, but she's long gone. The agent was going to sell it, but I want you to have it. It's close to Kynaston, but not too close. I feel bad enough that I'm there and Henry is dead. Let me at least do this for his widow.'

Catherine opened the door and stepped out of the car. The house looked friendly, even in the fading light. David had climbed out, too, and stood now, looking at her with apprehensive eyes.

'It's lovely, David. And very generous of you.' He thought she was going to say 'but', and she saw his lips part in protest, so she hurried on. 'I know what I'm going to do with my life, in the near future, anyway. It'll mean my going away for a while, but I'll come home eventually, and this house feels . . . welcoming.'

'You're going away?'

'Only for a while. But I'll come here often. I know what I want to do with Mellows. I want to make it a home.'

# BOOK 2

# Chapter Sixteen

## May 1941

CATHERINE'S UNIFORM HUNG ON THE wardrobe. Looking at it now, there seemed to be an awful lot of it. For outdoors, a navy serge overcoat, jacket and skirt, to wear with white shirt and black tie. The grey-blue dresses were neatly folded on the chest of drawers alongside the white aprons with their big red cross, and the six pairs of black stockings, the white half-sleeves, and the caps that finished off the ward uniforms. The clumpy, black rubber-soled shoes, two pairs, in shoe-bags, were already packed in her trunk. The hideous pudding-basin hat leered at her from the dressing-table. She hated the look of it and the feel of it on her head, but without it she would be improperly dressed, and liable to discipline.

After a moment she turned to look at the clock on the bedside table. It was ten minutes past six. Five more minutes, and she must get up and prepare for her last day in training. She closed her eyes and thought back over the three months that had brought her to this day. The time following Henry's funeral had been painful. There had been a certain relief that the tie which had bound her to that great echoing house was broken, but at the same time she felt adrift. She could not go home to her parents, and her initial enthusiasm for Mellows had waned when she realised it was too big for one woman to fill.

It was not until she realised that it enabled her to do something for Sarah Foxton that life began to make sense again. She smiled now, remembering the moment when she had asked if Sarah would move into Mellows as caretaker. 'With the baby?' Sarah had said, and when Catherine nodded, incredulity had replaced doubt on the other woman's face. Together they had explored the house, opening shutters here and there, sending up clouds of dust that dissolved in shafts of sunshine, tutting over grimy sinks and water-closets, before finally declaring that the house was wonderful.

She had installed Sarah there on a small wage, but had not moved in herself. There was no point. She was due at the Sutton and Cheam Hospital to begin a three-month training as a Red Cross VAD. She had filled in forms at an office in Grosvenor Square and answered a great number of questions. They had frowned at her lack of experience, but perked up when she remembered the First Aid exam she had passed at her boarding-school. After that, there had been a furious round of medical examinations and shopping for uniform at Garroulds, and the packing up of everything she had taken to Kynaston when she married.

'It looks as though you're never coming back,' David had said, miserably, and she had put out a hand to console him. 'You know I'll be back, David, and we'll keep in touch, I promise, wherever they send me.'

Her training had passed in a blur of hospital corners perfect in her eyes and ripped apart by a sister tutor because they were 'horrible', of washing bedpans in echoing sluices, being bombarded with medical terminology and pharmaceutical terms, and run off her feet, at the beck and call of anyone with a claim to being trained. Above all, she was conscious of the smell of hospitals, antiseptic but with a faint, underlying odour of death. She had not exactly enjoyed it, but she had experienced a huge satisfaction, a feeling that she was doing right at last.

It was a pity, though, that she had had to leave David behind in that bleak place, with only India for company. 'God help him,' she thought now, before throwing back the covers and swinging her legs to the floor.

━━━

There was a letter from Catherine among his post, and David felt a thrill of pleasure at the sight. But he did not rush to open it. That was a pleasure to be saved for later, when he was alone.

'Good God!' India's face appeared on the other aside of the breakfast table as she lowered her paper. 'It says here that Rudolph Hess has parachuted into a field in Scotland.'

David nodded. 'I heard it on the wireless last night. Parachuted from a crashing Messerschmitt, apparently.'

'But he's Hitler's deputy! Does this mean the Germans are beginning to crack?'

'I think it's more a case of his deciding that he was about to fall out of favour, and jumping before he was pushed. He told the ploughman who captured him – with a pitchfork, I believe – that he'd come to make peace. But, seeing what the Luftwaffe has done to Liverpool in the past ten days, I doubt that peace is what they have in mind.'

'Four thousand dead,' India said of the Liverpool raid, as coolly as if she were quoting share prices in the Stock Exchange. David felt words bubbling up inside him, but did not let them escape his lips. His sister was what she was, and trying to change her was futile. Besides, she was on to the estate again now.

'I cannot believe what it says here, that there's a shortage of eggs everywhere. I know it's happening on the estate. We have the same number of hens, more even. And ducks, but do we ever see a duck egg? I mean to find out what the estate hands are doing with them.'

'You told us this yesterday, India. And the week before. Are you sure you aren't becoming obsessed with the damn things?'

'Oh, how easy for you to criticise, David. If only we still had an agent, or servants. I can't be everywhere. . .'

'Here it comes,' David thought.

'Honestly, you must begin to concern yourself with the estate. And with our interests.'

'I do, India. I spend a major part of my day in the estate office, which still functions, I might add, even if Gareth Renwick has gone off to war. I spend whole days going round, asking about their problems and trying to sort them out. But if you mean I should hunt for purloined hens' eggs, I tell you now, I won't do it. They've probably gone off in that van you're always complaining about. And good luck to whoever drives it.'

After that there was silence for a while, except for the chomping of toast or the turning of pages.

'I see Herbert Hoover is urging America to stay out of the war,' India said at last. 'He says it's the best way to help Britain. I don't suppose for a moment that's his real motive. Self-interest is the hallmark of the American.'

'I would hardly say that. But as you're always saying this war is a mistake, I fail to see why you should expect the Americans to do anything but hang back.'

'You're impossible to talk to, David. Puerile. We used to have good discussions at this table. Now –'

'You're stuck with me. Well, hard cheese, sister. I wish for your sake it could be different, but it's not. However, I can relieve you of my presence, and I will.'

As he made his way to his room, David wondered why India could enrage but never hurt him. Even on the night they had learned of Henry's death and she had wept that the wrong brother was gone, he had felt no resentment towards her for the remark. What he did resent were her constant pessimism, and her snobbery. If only Catherine were still here, lifting the atmosphere and laughing whenever he uttered the slightest witticism.

He closed the door behind him and tore at the envelope as he crossed to the window seat. '*Well,*' she began, '*your sister-in-law is now a fully qualified mobile VAD. This means I can be sent anywhere, but first I'm going to a hospital on the outskirts of London. They tell me it's an Emergency Hospital, which means it has been hastily assembled from matchsticks. I will receive 39 shillings a week, but I have to pay a pound for mess, and buy my own clothes out of the 19 shillings left to me. No spare cash for high jinks, but if you can get up to London you can treat me to a wonderful night out . . . or weekend, if indeed I get weekends off. I have oodles of uniform, grey-blue dresses and pinafores with red crosses on them. Oh, and a cap. You'll like the cap. Très chic!*'

He smiled, imagining her with a cap on her head. But going to London – that was a thought! He crossed to the desk and took up his pen to reply.

―――

David had not opened his letter at the breakfast table, India thought, and he had done it deliberately. He was shutting her out. Still, what did she care what a silly girl had to say, except in so far as she held sway over David. He was a fool and a weakling, but he was all that was left upholding the family. As she put on her WVS uniform and got ready for the day, settling the green hat on her head and skewering it with hat-pins, she thought of her brother's folly. He had obviously not thought about death duties: they would be levied on the estate for her father's death, and again for Henry's. And he had given Catherine a particularly valuable house that could have been sold to defray the drain on the estate, as well as allowing her feckless family to occupy another. The old dower house would have done well enough, too well! She jabbed even more fiercely with the pin, and winced as it scratched her scalp. Still, she would get Kynaston one day, that was what really mattered.

Hat secure, she put her arms by her side and examined herself in the mirror. She looked as a Callingham should, dignified. It was up to her, really. Tomorrow she would go to see Gerald Rowbarrow, their solicitor, and ask him to consult her on all estate matters. Satisfied with her decision, she picked up her leather shoulder bag and her gas-mask case, and went downstairs to take up her duties.

Sarah lay in bed most mornings, glorying in the silence. In her father's house there had always been noise, someone coming off shift or setting out, milk bottles rattling on steps, traffic on the street. Here at Mellows there was only peace. The road was far off, and passing vehicles were few and far between, and there was no one but her and little Joe in the house. The whole house.

She opened her eyes and surveyed her bedroom. It was the size of a football pitch, or felt like that. High ceilings and tall windows, light and space, carpets beneath her feet, and warmth. Not the heat of a fire, but all-over warmth from radiators, and hot water at the turn of a tap. Sometimes, in the morning, she would take a moment or two to convince herself she hadn't dreamed it.

Today, though, she struggled up on her pillows and luxuriated in her luck. When Catherine had first asked her to move in to Mellows and take care of the house she had been disbelieving. In real life, things like that didn't happen. There was no such thing as a magic solution. Especially not one that came with a wage. Even when she had stood in the hall, her baby in her arms, her possessions in bags and boxes around her, she could hardly believe it.

That had been two months ago. Since then, she had cleaned and scrubbed, and washed and rehung curtains, till her back felt as though it would snap. But it had all been worth it. Now, as she moved around the house, she exulted in the freedom it gave her. And when thoughts of the future intruded, the moment when the war ended and Catherine came home to reclaim her house, she resolutely suppressed them. Living a day at a time was all she could manage.

In the kitchen with its tiled floor and fruit-patterned wallpaper, she set the kettle to boil and switched on the big brown wireless. There had been a bomber's moon last night, and London had endured the heaviest raid of the war. The city was in flames, and the House of Commons had been evacuated to another place. The House of Commons! What next? She thought of the newspaper pictures she had seen, of homes destroyed, people's possessions peeping from the rubble of their homes, ambulances ferrying bodies to crowded mortuaries.

When she had brewed her tea she sat down at the pine table, and acknowledged the one drawback of living at Mellows. There was no one with whom she could gossip. Back in Belgate she had seen Hannah Chaffey's visits as a cross to be borne. Now she would have welcomed the sight of the other woman across the table, pouring out a stream of gossip and information, giving her views on the air raids, and what the bloody Nazis would do next.

As if on cue, there was the sound of a horn outside. Sarah crossed to the window and saw the Co-op van in the courtyard and Hannah descending from the passenger seat. 'I got the chance of a lift. The lass'll likely be lonely up there, I thought, so I took it. I hope you've got the kettle on.'

After she had oohed and aahed over the house, and declared that Sarah had fallen on her feet, Hannah was a mine of information. 'Henry's lass's fallen wrong, and that bairn of Crossthwaite's is in trouble again. Pinching coal. And they're missing you at the pub. Two or three have told me that.'

The gossip out of the way, the conversation took a more

serious turn. Thirty-nine thousand people had died in the Blitz.

'I can't believe that,' Sarah said, putting down her cup – 39,000 was the population of a town.

'It's true,' Hannah said 'Official. And more than that are injured. Harry Prosser's daughter's in the Ministry of Information. She told her dad they're using cardboard coffins. I mean, there's 20,000 dead in London alone. The undertakers can't cope, and there's millions homeless. She says they're in rest centres, sleeping on floors. Nowt but bread and tea, bairns crying, not enough lavvies. She says they're getting it sorted, but it makes you think. Looking round here, you'd never think there was a war on at all. In Belgate neither, if it wasn't for rationing.'

Her face lit up, then. 'But they've got that Hess in the Tower. That's one bugger less to deal with. Our Harry says they should string him up from Tower Bridge. And speaking of Harry –' She broke off to reach into her oilcloth bag. 'There's a couple of duck eggs for you and the bairn.'

⸻

Pamela had spent hours trying to work out a reason for going to Kynaston. At last she had decided to say that something of hers that Catherine had borrowed was urgently needed. Could it possibly still be in Catherine's room? It wouldn't do to go when India was about: she would get short shift from that hard-faced madam. Everyone was talking about her throwing her weight about in the WVS, as though she was the police. Instead she lurked about the main street till she saw India's black car pass, with the erect, green-clad figure in the driving seat. So far so good. She checked her appearance in a shop window and set out to walk up to the Hall.

She had her green suede court shoes on, and before long she could feel a blister burning on her left heel. She kept grimly on.

Since she had dropped Roger – well, he had dropped her, but she would have done it anyway, if he hadn't – she had thought again of David Callingham. He had been quite masterly that day when he had seen off the bailiffs. And he was now Sir David. And polio could not be passed on to your children, so that was all right.

Once she got beyond the village, the sun seemed even fiercer and she felt sweat collecting under her breasts. She made sure there was no one around, and then lifted the front of her broderie anglais blouse to let air in. She looked good in that blouse, especially since she had coloured up a little with the sun. David was sure to ask her in for a drink. After that it was up to her to draw him out. He was shy, that was all.

As she turned at the bend in the drive and saw the house, she marvelled once more at the scope of it. Kings lived in lesser places. Once in there, she would make the county sit up. And pay for a few slights inflicted since her father's downfall.

It was a long while before anyone answered the bell, and then, disappointingly, it was a harassed- looking woman in an overall, not what she had been expecting at all.

'Sir David, please. It's his sister-in-law.' She wasn't quite sure of her relationship to David Callingham, but sister-in-law would do.

'He's out.' The woman was already closing the door.

'Just a moment!' Should she go in and wait? But if she did that he might be ages, and India might return instead. 'Where is he?' she asked firmly.

The woman shrugged. 'He's off somewhere. Went at crack of dawn, they say. He could be anywhere on the estate.'

Disconsolate, Pamela turned away. All that way, and a sore foot, and all for nothing. She felt tears prick her eyes as she started back down the drive. It wasn't fair. Catherine had waltzed in there. Literally waltzed. And now she was queening it in London, being wined and dined by Spitfire pilots, no doubt. Any moment she would arrive back with another ring on her finger while she herself, just as deserving, was walled up here in a dump.

She was wiping her nose on the back of her hand, when a car turned in at the gates. It was him.

'It's Pamela, isn't it?' Framed in the window of the car, David looked handsome, dashing even, his shirt open on a brown neck, the bare arm resting on the ledge of the door tanned and muscled and covered in fine black hairs.

'I've just been at the house – Hall – your place.' He was looking enquiring. 'I was wondering if my tennis racquet was there. Catherine borrowed it ages ago.'

He was shaking his head ''Fraid not. She emptied her room when she left. It could be at her new house.' He was getting out now, dipping as the weight went on his gammy leg. 'Hop in. I can't let you walk back into Belgate.'

She let him fold her into the car, making sure he saw that her legs were brown and slim. He seemed not to notice, but men were like that. Always hiding it when they were impressed. She talked animatedly as they drove back into Belgate.

But 'I'd take you over to Mellows, only I'm due at Home Farm, so I'm afraid I can't,' he explained, as he slowed the car. And 'Goodbye' was all he said when she got out. Not even a 'Nice to see you,' or 'You must come up for tennis some time.' But of course he was a cripple, so he couldn't play tennis even if he'd wanted to. He asked her to give his compliments to her parents, and was off in a swirl of dust.

She stood there, lifting her bleeding heel out of her shoe and feeling a fool.

---

Catherine caught a train at Waterloo. There were lots of uniforms on the platform, many of them worn by women, but no one was wearing the same uniform as her. A soldier winked at her, and she felt herself blush. 'Wouldn't mind being nursed by you,' he said. She was glad that the train was puffing into the station, but what would she do if he got in beside her?

Suddenly a sergeant appeared, a group of soldiers behind him. 'Need a hand, miss?' And then to the men, 'Oi, you lot! Get fell in here.' In seconds she and her bags were hoisted on to the train, she was installed in a seat, and the sergeant was giving a mock salute and leaving, closing the carriage door behind him. Catherine heaved a sigh of relief that the other seats were occupied by middle-aged passengers and settled back for the journey.

As the train rattled out of the station, she thought about her mother's letter, received that morning. Pamela's romance with Roger was over because he had been a brute and Pamela had given him his marching orders. Her father did nothing all day but brood, and they were living hand to mouth. Catherine looked out of the window but nothing in the landscape distracted her from her worries. She would have to do something for them. David had told her that when probate was completed she would have a sizeable amount of money of her own. He had offered her an unlimited advance, and she had accepted £500, so as to pay Sarah a small amount. The remainder had seen her through her training, bought all she needed for her new job, and there was still £100 or so left. She would write a cheque tonight and put it in the post.

Above her on the rack were her suitcases containing the new uniforms. 'I'm going to try hard,' she thought. 'I'm going to make a difference.' If she could do that, if she could help a bit, perhaps she could forgive herself for stealing the name, 'C. Callingham', that was stencilled on the sides of her cases. At least in the hospital she would be plain 'Nurse Callingham', and no nonsense about titles.

Sarah parked the pram outside the butcher's and went inside, watching over her baby through the window all the while. There were no sausages today, and only scrag end or pork chops. She handed over her ration books, hoping she had the points for a chop. She was still breastfeeding, so it was important to eat. She would start to wean him soon, but for the moment it was a comfort to them both to have him at her breast. The chop was bought and paid for, and she had thanked the butcher, when she saw the figure of a man looming over the pram. She almost fell over in her haste to get outside, ready to defend her offspring, but the man was straightening up and smiling at her. 'I thought it was you in there, so I guessed this would be your bairn. He's a bonny little lad.'

It was the Scottish sergeant from the pub, and she smiled at him. He nodded towards the newspaper-wrapped bundle she was clutching to her chest. 'Got some fillet steak in there?' He was letting off the brake on the pram and turning it, and she found herself slipping into step beside him. 'We've missed you at the pub. Your brother said you'd had a stroke of luck, got a house?'

'Yes. Well, I haven't got it – I'm minding it for a friend.'

They walked on for a while in silence. It felt good, somehow, to have a man at her side again. He was a big man. Gerard had been a big man.

'There's a British Restaurant over there,' he said. 'We could get a cup of tea.'

She thought of the lonely house to which she was returning. And there was no harm in a cup of tea, as long as it went no further. 'That'd be nice,' she said.

# Chapter Seventeen

## May 1941

CATHERINE HAD BEEN AFRAID SHE would sleep in, but she was awake long before dawn. Across the room, in another single bed, her roommate slept soundly. The even sound of her breathing reminded Catherine of the time when she and Pamela had shared a bedroom. They had been such good friends then. It was only as they had grown up that they had also grown apart. For a moment she was consumed with homesickness, until she remembered the gulf that now existed between them, and how difficult relationships had become recently.

Her thoughts turned to the previous evening, when she had been bombarded with information and instructions. Too much to remember. The hospital itself was a large old building that might have been a private home once, or even an hotel. Behind it there were rows of timbered huts which seemed to radiate out: these were the wards. She wriggled a little, trying to find a comfortable position on the mattress. It was not like any mattress she had ever known, being thin and firm and, according to her roommate, known as a biscuit. In addition to that, the bed was not only narrow, it was short. She was only five feet six, and her feet, when she lay down, had poked over the edge.

Still, that was the least of her problems. When she arrived, she had been directed to a hall where other VADs, all in impressively new uniforms, were grouped round a tea urn. She had sipped her cup of sweet, yellow tea until Matron appeared with a Queen Alexandra sister in tow. Catherine had encountered QAs during her training, all immaculate, all beautiful, and all tyrants of the first order. Matron had explained that QAs really ran the hospital. They were assisted by Regulars, who were Army-trained, and Reserves, civilian-trained but fully qualified. Then there were VADs. They were there, Matron emphasised, to back up the proper nurses.

'To fetch and carry,' someone had whispered in Catherine's ear. She had turned to see a girl who looked no more than 16, with a beautifully lipsticked mouth and eyes dancing with amusement. That had been Tilly. 'I wish we could share a room,' Tilly had said over supper. 'We could have some fun.' But Tilly was paired with a bespectacled girl called Maude, and Catherine had Maureen, who seemed nice but not nearly as interesting as Tilly. 'We'll find a way to swap,' Tilly said, winking. 'Pretend to snore, then Maureen'll want out.'

When Matron had finished, an Army sergeant had reeled off rules like times tables, and then they were dismissed.

Today they would all begin their duties, but not before 'medicals', which, according to Tilly, were designed to rob you of your last vestige of modesty. 'I shall close my eyes and think of England, if the doc's a woman. If it's a man I can't do that. You need your eyes wide open when there's a man around.'

I like her, Catherine thought. She's a bit outrageous but I like her.

They wore their ordinary clothes for the medicals, which were not nearly as bad as Tilly had suggested. And then it was time to don her uniform. The dress and apron were easy, and so were the half-sleeves. The cap, though, defied all her efforts to sit it straight on her head. Catherine laid it flat on the bed, and folded it, as she had been shown, a dozen times, but it wouldn't fold to order. At last it looked as though two dogs had fought over it. 'Give it here,' Maureen said, her own cap squarely on her head. Within seconds she had twirled the white rectangle into the correct shape and shoved it firmly in place on Catherine's head.

'Right,' she said. 'Let's go forth and heal the world.' They were both laughing as they descended the broad stairs.

———

India was shown straight into Gerald Rowbarrow's office. 'India!' He rose from his seat and moved towards her.

'Gerald.' For a horrid moment she thought he was going to embrace her, as though he were a friend. People never knew their place. But he merely extended a hand to shake her gloved one. 'Do sit here. Can I get you some coffee? Or tea, perhaps?' She declined refreshment, anxious to get on with her task.

'I'll come straight to the point.' He was sitting back in his chair now, hands clasped in front of him, eyes on her face, as she began. 'You know my brother, David. He's an excellent fellow in every way, but as you know, he has his drawbacks. Since my father's death and Henry's, I've had to take over the running of the estate. It's not that David is unwilling, he's just – '

She allowed herself a small smile of encouragement, but the solicitor didn't speak. Instead he put his finger-tips together and lifted them to his lips. To her annoyance, he started to tap them against his pursed mouth as if he were weighing something.

'It's quite simple,' India said. 'If you'll communicate directly with me in future, we can consider the question of death duties. Two deaths in such a short time – we'll suffer for that.'

He still wasn't responding, and she felt her irritation grow. 'Do you understand what I'm asking for?'

He put his hands down now, one clutching each arm of his chair. 'I understand perfectly. What I'm having difficulty with is believing my own ears.'

'I don't understand.' Inside India unease was growing. Was

he going to defy her? If so, they would simply dispense with his petty little firm.

'What you're asking me to do is bypass the rightful owner of the estate and deal with someone who has no – I repeat, no – right to interfere in estate affairs. For your information, your brother has impressed me with his grasp of the complexities of estate management, his willingness to learn, and his commitment to his duty.'

India quelled her mounting agitation and stood up. 'Then there's no need to prolong this meeting.'

'No,' he said, reaching to ring for someone to show her out. 'No need at all.'

It was imagination, of course, but she could have sworn the cheap little tarts at their desks in the outer office were sniggering as she walked past them and out into the main street.

---

At first David had been wary of the estate workers. Until Gareth Renwick, the agent, had gone off to war, there had been little need for communication with them. His father had attended ceremonial occasions, and sometimes Henry, as the heir, had accompanied him. But there had been no need for David even to see them, and so he had stayed away. His limp had played a part, too, if he was honest. On a horse he felt complete; forced to limp his way into a meeting or a tenant's house he had felt at a disadvantage. Now, though, there was no agent, no father, no elder brother, there was only him and the clerks in the estate office; and since the war affected the people around him he felt the need to show his face.

Today he had gone from house to house in Belgate, hearing here of a son dead or prisoner, a daughter in some far off munitions factory, or the Wrens or the WRAC. He had met with tears sometimes, always the offer of hospitality, and an incredible amount of pride in families and country.

But the thing that tickled him was their attitude to Churchill. Before the war the old man had been their *bête noire*, the politician who had called them vermin. Sir Gervase had regaled him with tales of the working man's detestation of the politician. Now that same politician stood between the workers and annihilation, and they struggled uneasily between the old enmity and a new admiration that bordered on reverence. So he had agreed that Winston was a wonder, had drunk tea, looked at family photographs, and, above all, listened, until finally he made his last farewell and drove carefully out of the village, skirting puddles and stray dogs as he went.

The unmade state of some of the streets troubled him. When he could get hold of some labour, which would not be until the war was won, he would see to the make-up of the streets, do something about the earth-closets and the sewers. The day he discovered that some of the houses did not have electricity laid on to the upper floor and that children went to bed by candlelight, he had felt ashamed. The gulf between the classes was too wide. If men could fight and die side by side in war, they deserved equal conditions in peace.

As the last house fell away, he put down his foot and gunned the car towards Kynaston.

Pamela was still smarting from her encounter with David Callingham. He had been perfectly polite, but the fact was that he had not even noticed her. And yet when he had spoken of Catherine there had been a special note in his voice – of admiration, affection, even. 'She is important to him, but I don't exist,' Pamela thought. For a second or two she was angry but then came curiosity. Why the difference?

She sat up in bed. The clock on the bedside table said ten to eleven. Somewhere Catherine was working as a nurse, had probably been up since six or seven o'clock. Last night she had learned that Johnny Briggs, who had been her partner in mixed doubles, had been shot down over the Channel, and was missing, presumed dead, at 21 years of age. And he was an only child.

After a moment Pamela crossed to the dressing-table and sat down on the needlepoint stool. The face that stared back at her was still puffy with sleep, the hair was unkempt, but she was certainly pretty. That wasn't her being bumptious – it was fact. She was prettier than Catherine, always had been. She had a better backhand, she was faster getting to the net, she danced better, she had been everyone's favourite at school. And yet . . . and yet! She leaned closer to the mirror and stared into her own eyes. 'I am pretty,' she thought, 'but I am also selfish and petty and always wanting something.'

She put up her hands to cheeks that were suddenly hot to the touch. David Callingham was a good man, and yet she had thought of him as nothing but a means to an end. And he had seen her for what she was, although he had been too polite to show it. Inside her, heart and head fought a battle. 'I've been a bitch,' she said aloud.

Suddenly she leapt back into bed and drew the bedclothes over her head. She hid there for a while, thinking furiously. She could go on like this, or she could turn over a new leaf, become a better person, be nice. But could she keep it up? She had had good intentions before but never kept them. 'I want to be good,' her heart said. 'You'll never do it,' said her head.

In the end Pamela got up and dressed and went down to the small room where her parents sat silent, each pretending to doze but not sleeping. 'I'm going to make a start on this house,' she said firmly. 'And I'll have to get a move on, because when it's finished I'm going to get a job.'

Since she had said that fatal 'Yes, thank you,' to the Scottish sergeant, Sarah had regretted it a thousand times. But she had said it, and now she must pay for it. This afternoon she was meeting him. To the men he was Jock, but now she knew his name was Hamish Carlyle. He was 29 and unmarried, and he was taking her and the baby out to tea again. She had spent a feverish evening working out what to wear, even though, with one decent outfit to her name, she was not spoiled for choice.

Now, with an hour to go, she had put two metal curlers in her fringe and was trying to take her mind off what lay ahead by thinking about food. Or more specifically, about how to make the food they had at her father's house satisfy three healthy males and a pregnant woman. Molly was sweet but what she knew about spinning out rations could have been hidden under a sixpence. Sarah went as often as she could to give advice, but Molly was out of her depth, and that was a fact.

Not that it was easy. Dried eggs, which were shipped over from America, or so people said, were no substitute for a good hen's egg, and dried milk was no better. Even the bread was unappetising: the national loaf was a muddy colour that made you yearn for the soft white springiness of pre-war bread. But even if you made your own, the flour was rubbish. All that you could lay hands on were potatoes, and you weren't supposed to turn them into fluffy white mash. A poem about it had been put out by the Ministry of Food:

> *Those who have the will to win*
> *Cook potatoes in their skin,*
> *Knowing that the sight of peelings*
> *Deeply hurts Lord Woolton's feelings.*

Reciting it to herself, Sarah scowled. Lord Woolton, the Minister of Food, was full of good ideas, but not for anything you could put in front of a working man. If she'd offered her dad 'Woolton soup', the water in which vegetables had been boiled, flavoured with an Oxo cube, he would have told her what to do with it. And sandwiches with potato as a filling could not, in her opinion, be fed to a dog. What everyone was yearning for was meat, juicy steak, shin beef, liver and kidneys – her mouth watered at the thought.

She shook herself, and looked ahead to the coming meeting with Hamish. It was less painful to think of that than to remember pre-war steak-and-kidney pie.

≈

The ward contained two long rows of beds, one down each side of the room. There were screens beside each bed to pull round when privacy was needed. 'The poorly ones are at the top of the ward, so Sister can keep an eye on them,' the nurse who was showing Catherine the ropes explained. Those beds contained inert figures, frighteningly still. Further down, men were sitting up, bowls of water and shaving foam in front of them. One or two of them were seated in chairs in the centre of the ward, wearing 'hospital blues', the shapeless blue suits all wounded men were given.

Catherine turned to see Sister bearing down on her. She wore the uniform of the QAs and the face under the flowing cap was thunderous. 'Another VAD,' she said, when she reached Catherine, and in tones of resignation. 'Well you'd better make yourself useful. Show her where the cleaning materials are kept, Nurse.' And then, to Catherine, 'We have our own way of doing things on this ward, Nurse. See that you keep to it.'

Behind her back, the Regular was parroting her words. When Sister moved away, she continued to mimic her. 'I hate dust. Dust is dirty and spreads disease. I will not tolerate dust, Nurse. I will not tolerate untidiness. Untidiness is dirty and spreads disease.' It seemed she could continue this monologue indefinitely, but Catherine interrupted her.

'I'd better get on,' she said. 'Where do I begin?'

An hour later her arms felt heavy as lead and her back ached with scrubbing lockers and floors, polishing every scrap of brass, even keyholes, and making up every empty bed to look as though no patient had ever lain on it.

'Is it always like this?' she asked, as they tipped dirty water into the sluice.

'Not always.' To Catherine's horror, the other nurse was lighting the stub of a cigarette and puffing with gusto. 'Oh, that's better. No, there's a lot of this, but sometimes you can see why you're doing it. We had men in here two weeks ago off a ship that was bombed in the Thames. A tanker. They were burns, flash burns, all the fronts of their bodies, skin clean gone. We just bathed them, day and night with saline solution. Some of them, their eyelids were so burned they couldn't open them. "Am I blind?" one kept asking. Another lad had caught the steam when the boiler exploded. He was like a boiled lobster, poor lad. We bathed him, and put acriflavine on, but he was too far gone.

'And the heat and the steam and the gases off the petrol burning had affected their air passages and breathing. Nasty. But we had to treat them for shock first, then pain, then we could get to the burns. I earned my corn that night, I tell you.'

She drew on her cigarette again before carefully flushing it down the sluice and blowing to rid her breath of the smell of tobacco. 'And you know what, when they came round, lying there like skinned rabbits, all they were worried about was their wedding tackle.'

She smoothed down her pinafore and adjusted her cap. 'Come on, kid. MO's rounds next.'

It was strange to be alone with a man again, a man who was not a family member. He had asked her out to tea, but they wound up in a pub, making her glad she had decided to leave the baby with Hannah Chaffey. She would never have taken him into a public house. Now she listened as Hamish described his home. It was a place called Lochearnhead which was near another place called Crianlarich, which he seemed to think was the meeting-point of every road in Scotland. He talked a lot about the Trossachs, which she had never heard of, and Loch Lomond, which everyone had heard of. He didn't talk much about the Army or the war, except to say he would soon be posted; but his love of Scotland was clear, and she liked that.

'He makes me feel safe,' she thought. 'Like I felt with Gerard.' They were both big men, but there the resemblance ended. Gerard's hair had been black and his eyes blue. This man's hair was red and his eyes a greeny-grey. Once he reached out and covered her hand with his own, and she felt her skin prickle. If they went on meeting, he would expect her to go to bed with him. Men always did, if you'd been married. She'd heard them in the pub: 'She knows it all, that one.' Or, 'She's been round the track.' They had a certain respect for an unmarried girl, unless she was no better than she should be, and complete respect for other men's wives. But widows were fair game.

Except that this man seemed different. She let him take her elbow as they left the pub, but when he would have held her arm in the street she moved away from him. Gerard had been dead a mere few months. She must go on living and she would – but in her own time.

It seemed ridiculous to dress for dinner when there were only two of them, but David couldn't be bothered to face more of

India's disapproval than could be helped. Tonight she was resplendent in black lace with his mother's pearls at her neck. He smiled, remembering the pearls and how his mother would let him twine his fingers into them when he sat upon her knee. India was in full flow about the black market. 'They're doing it in public houses. Blatant trading in illegal foodstuffs. Everyone knows who the culprits are but no one will tell. They're like the Mafia.'

'*Omerta*,' David said, squinting at the wine in his crystal glass.

'What?'

'*Omerta*. It's the Italian vow of silence. They cut your throat if you tell.'

'Really, David, what a grasshopper mind you have.' She sighed, then, and he knew she was thinking how different Henry had been. It would have been easier to bear if he could have hated his brother, but Henry had been wonderful, so he couldn't even kick against India's pricks. Instead he tried to change the subject.

'Pity about *HMS Hood*.' The *Hood* had been the world's biggest battle cruiser, but two days ago it had been sunk by the *Bismarck*, Germany's biggest vessel.

'Yes,' India said absently. She was dissecting the food on her plate with her knife and fork rather like someone performing a post mortem. He felt his gorge rise at the sight of her hands hovering over the food, and tried another conversational gambit. 'Hess is in the Tower now. I expect they're grilling him.'

'I should hope so. The man is obviously a coward who's run away.'

'Really? I thought he was someone who'd decided to join a just cause.'

'You would think that. He's a German, David. He should be true to his own people.'

'Even when they're blackguards?'

'I expect that's what they say of us.'

'You're not suggesting that there is anything righteous about the Nazis, I hope?' That had gone home. Faint colour surged up in her cheeks. He would pay for it sooner or later, but scoring a hit was worth it.

'You know that isn't what I meant. And I don't want to discuss it. We should be talking about our plans for Kynaston, now and after the war.'

David put down his glass. 'I had a letter from Catherine today.' Another hit. 'She's enjoying her nursing. Says it's really worth while. Thank goodness one Callingham is doing something for the war effort. I do what I can with the Home Guard, but it hardly compares with saving lives.'

'I know what you're trying to do, David.' India's eyes glittered in the light from the candelabra on the table between them. 'You want me to say she isn't a Callingham. Well, I'll oblige you. She isn't, and she never will be. And I thank God for that.'

***

It was heaven to sink into bed and close weary eyes. Today had been – Catherine sought for a word – amazing. Amazing! And funny. She had been doing the floor with a bumper when a patient had told her he needed a bed-bath. 'It's not time,' she'd said, not mentioning that the thought of bathing a man head to foot terrified her. Where did you put your eyes, let alone your hands?

'I've peed me pants, miss. I need changing.' She put the bumper aside, and was pulling the heavy screens round the bed when she heard sniggering. 'Can I be next?' a voice called. Realising she was being teased, she had had to struggle not to smile at her own naivety. 'Of course you can have a bath,' she told the man sweetly. 'I'll just get a scrubbing brush and some

Lysol from the sluice.'

'She got you there, Sid,' someone said, and then the man who had asked for a bath winked at her. 'You'll do, Nurse,' he said, 'you'll do.'

She smiled with satisfaction at the memory, but didn't remember anything else. She was sound asleep, and the ward a million miles away.

# Chapter Eighteen

## July 1941

CATHERINE WAS WASHED AND DRESSED in plenty of time, leaving Tilly still in bed. She lay on her back, one slim arm flung out, eyes closed. Catherine sighed. 'I know you're awake, but I haven't got time to coax you.' Since they had managed to room together, getting Tilly out of bed had been her first duty of the day, but this was the day of the Colonel's inspection and she would get hell from Sister if everything wasn't 100 per cent perfect for his visit.

'No tea?' Tilly said plaintively. 'I could really do with a cup of tea. Weak. Milk. No sugar. My mouth is parched.'

Catherine was folding her cap, the last touch to her uniform. 'It's parched because you drank too much last night. I have no sympathy.'

'You do. You're just afraid to show your nice side. If you do make me a cup of tea I'll tell you what happened last night.' The blue eyes were open now in the cherub's face.

'I'll put the kettle on for you, but that's all I can do. And I know what happened last night. You got drunk. If there's more, I can't bear to hear it.' She lit the little camping-stove and placed the kettle on the ring. 'It's on. Now get up.'

As she left the room she heard a sigh from the bed. 'If I die of thirst because I'm too weak to reach the kettle, I don't want you to feel guilty. I forgive you freely, so if your conscience tortures you don't blame it on me.'

Catherine was still laughing when she reached the door that led to the open air and the pathway to the wards.

Sarah had fed the baby, several spoonfuls of ham-bone and vegetable broth and some nice, milky rice pudding. She settled him in his pram and sat down at the kitchen table to read the paper Catherine had insisted be delivered each day. She had jibbed at the expense of a paper bill, but Catherine had swept her objections aside. 'You'll be a little cut off there, Sarah. I won't have you going out of your mind with boredom. It will be different when Joseph is older, but for now you need to keep up with the news.'

So the paper came, and Catherine sent her money for the bill along with her wage. To be truthful, she relied on the wireless more than the paper when it came to news, but she liked the bits about stars and films, and she always read the headlines on the first few pages. Today they were all about Germany attacking Russia. That had been a shock, but no bad thing for the Allies, according to her father. 'You can't fight everyone, not even if you're Hitler. And don't underestimate the Russkies.'

The reporting was all about scorched earth. She read on, intrigued by a new phrase. Apparently Stalin, the Russian leader, had called on everyone to fight in the 'old Russian way', and that was by laying waste the land so that the invaders would find nothing, no crops, no livestock, no buildings, no bridges or roads. She thought of the countryside around her. How could you destroy the things you'd spent a lifetime creating? But apparently that was what they had done when Napoleon invaded, and it had defeated the French. She shuddered at details of how livestock that couldn't be moved would be slaughtered, fields set on fire. According to the paper, when the Russian winter came, the lack of shelter and the difficulty of getting supplies if the roads were blown up would leave the Germans defenceless. 'Serves the buggers right,' she thought, grinning to herself.

There was another headline: *First Briton Hanged for Treason*. He was a sailor, a ship's engineer called George Johnson Armstrong, who had offered to spy for the Nazis and been caught. He was to be hanged that morning in Wandsworth jail. She looked at the clock – five past nine. He had been due to die at eight, so he was gone by now. Somehow you couldn't imagine someone being hanged on this sunny morning.

A sudden impulse to get away from the paper took her into the hall. The phone stood mute on the hall table. She had picked it up once, to make sure there was a whirring sound, but she still fought shy of using it. She moved towards the front door and peered into the lobby. She did this every morning and there was never any post. There had been nothing there earlier, when she had picked up the paper. Now though, there was an envelope. She opened the inner door and picked it up. It bore the Army postmark, and it was in Hamish's writing. She carried it into the kitchen, excitement growing inside her, and sat down at the table to read it.

＝

They had hardly spoken at the breakfast table, both too busy thinking of their day ahead. However, David had to tell her of his trip to London.

'I'm going up to town later today,' he said.

India lifted her head from her post. 'Whatever for?'

'I'm going to take Catherine out to dinner.'

'All that way for a dinner?'

He longed to shout, 'Yes, and why bloody not?', but he restrained himself.

'I'm seeing Will Austin, too. He wants my views on our preparedness for upping food production.'

'How are you going to fit it all in? The last train is quite early, as I remember.'

'I shan't come home tonight.' He saw her lips tighten and ploughed on. 'I'm staying at the club. I'll ring you tonight to make sure everything's OK.'

'I wish you wouldn't use that expression. "OK" is so American!' She managed to invest that last word with overtones of utter degradation.

'I like the Americans,' David said cheerfully, not caring whether or not he riled her. 'Roosevelt is doing all he can to aid our war effort. What he's getting away with in Congress is amazing.'

India wrinkled her nose. 'Words are cheap. The Americans don't offer to fight.'

'Good God, India, Roosevelt has frozen Germany's assets in America, and he's seizing their ships when they arrive in US ports. If everyone was as supportive of Churchill as Roosevelt is being, I'd feel much better about things.' Last month Churchill had had to defend himself on the floor of the House after the Commons had forced a debate about the loss of Crete to the German onslaught. So much for loyalty from your own!

India was folding up letters and putting them back into their envelopes. 'Churchill, Churchill, that's all you hear nowadays, Well, I suppose I'd better get on. If you're determined to gallivant, one of us must do some work.'

'I haven't had a day off this year,' David said, but she was already retreating, tugging her green uniform into shape as she went. 'Have a good time, David,' he said sarcastically, but his words didn't interrupt her progress from the room.

Catherine was allowed to sterilise instruments now. Bandages and dressings were sterilised in the autoclave in the theatre suite, but the sterilisers for bowls and instruments were near to the sluice. First she scrubbed her hands, and then she lifted the lid of the steriliser and put in forceps, scissors, Cheatle forceps, scalpels, saying the names of each to herself to prove she could recognise them. Bowls went in the other steriliser. Once she had put them all in and switched it on, she rinsed her hands again, smoothed down her apron, and went to get ready for the inspection.

As she walked down the ward, her nostrils twitched. Smoke! She followed the smell to a corner bed. The boy who occupied it was gazing innocently into space. 'Where is it?' Catherine said. And then, more urgently, 'You'll get me into trouble!'

His hand came from under the cover, cupped round a smoking butt.

'I only wanted a drag' he said apologetically.

There was a sudden commotion at the end of the ward. The Colonel, escorted by Matron and a gaggle of doctors and senior nurses, was advancing on the first bed. Catherine seized the cigarette and stubbed it out in the kidney dish that stood on his locker. 'More of this later,' she said ominously, then she took the dish and slipped it into his locker. If anyone went in there during the inspection! She sniffed again. Could she still smell smoke?

The patients who had been sitting in chairs were standing to attention now, some trying to hobble to the foot of their bed. The Colonel was stopping beside each man, questioning, listening intently, seeming to pause for ages at beds where men were too ill even to care about his presence. There was another doctor with him, someone she hadn't seen before. With everyone else the Colonel was remote, even frosty, but he seemed almost to defer to this man. As they came abreast of Catherine, the Colonel ignored her, but the stranger met her eyes and smiled. It was only an acknowledgement, but courteous nevertheless.

'Who was that?' she asked the Staff Nurse when the inspection was over and they were making the morning medicine round.

'He's Jewish. Detweiler, I think they call him. American. He's a plastic surgeon, just here on loan.'

'Is he RAMC?' Catherine asked.

The Staff Nurse shook her head. 'No, he's just come to give a hand. Civilian. Not subject to army discipline. Couldn't you tell? He spent a long time with the phosphorus burn'. That boy was only 20 and much of his face was gone as the result of the phosphorus burns. 'They're moving him to McIndoe's place. We haven't got the technique here to sort that lot out. Maybe that's what the Yank is here to do, start up a plastic unit.'

As she doled out drugs, Catherine thought back to the day the boy, who name was Wilson, had been admitted. He was a sailor whose ship had been bombed as it came into port. They had cut away what remained of his clothing, revealing huge patches of flesh from which the skin had been burned away. Sister had worked with her to scrape the burning, ingrained phosphorus from his wounds. 'Will he die?' Catherine had whispered, and received a glare for her pains. She had wanted to say, 'How can a boy live with no face, and blind,' but she had not dared. Instead she had gone on removing the red-hot pieces of phosphorus from the scorched flesh because Sister had explained that it would continue to burn unless it was removed or immersed in water.

Once clean, the wounds were covered with bicarbonate of soda and copper sulphate, and all the while the boy had rambled, sometimes crying and in agony, at other times asking plaintively when 'mum' was coming. Three weeks on, he was now quiet. She crossed to his bed when she was free and straightened his sheets. 'What did that doctor have to say?' she asked. 'He seemed to spend ages here.'

The boy moved one of his bandaged hands towards his face. 'He says he can fix it – this.' The thing that had once been a mouth was widening in what could be a smile. 'I said, "You'll have to be a magician," and he said, "You'll see."'

There was silence for a moment, and then Wilson said, 'Do you think he can do something, Nurse?'

Catherine laid her hand gently on his arm, where there was an area of unburned, unbandaged skin. 'Everyone says he's clever, so I think he just might.'

'Know what? If I didn't have a girl, I'd ask you for a date.' She felt her eyes prick. His parents had been to visit him, but there'd been no sign of a girlfriend.

'You get well, and I'll ask you for a date, girlfriend or not.'

She was walking back to the nurses' desk when she saw Sister was watching her. 'Yes,' Sister said quietly, 'yes, it's not fair – but at least he's alive. The rest of his crew wasn't that lucky.'

Catherine nodded, and smiled with a certainty she was far from feeling.

———

As she cut and turned the casings, Pamela tried not look at her hands. They were rough and scarred, but it couldn't be helped. The moment they had explained the machines to her, she had felt a strange sense of power. The boy whose place she was taking had been called up. He seemed resentful of her at first, determined to prove she wasn't up to the job. In the end, though, he had come round.

When she was left on her own she had felt afraid of the huge machine, but then the noise of the shell shop seemed to recede, and all that mattered was her productivity. If she had a problem she went to one of the setters-up, but mostly she managed on her own. She was on piece work, and worked three shifts, six to two, two to ten and night shift. Her flat rate was 24 shillings a week, and she had to buy her own overalls and pay her bus fare; but in a good week she had money left over, and it gave her enormous satisfaction.

She tried whistling along to *Workers' Playtime*, but gave up when the woman at the next bench called out, 'We've got a bloody canary in here.' Instead she hummed under her breath. The charge-hand had praised her yesterday, and promised she could go on to boring next week.

She thought of Catherine's last letter, all the men being wounded and losing limbs. At least she would come out of the war intact. She winced as her finger end caught a whirring blade, sucked on it for a moment, and then went on with what she was doing. It was funny, but she couldn't remember what she had done with her time before the war. She put up a hand to wipe her brow. At least life now was never boring.

India picked at the keys with her forefingers. She had never envisaged having to act as a typist, but there was no one else. And now that she was in charge of the whole area, she had to fill in wherever needed. She had been promised more staff, but until they came it was her. She tried to count her blessings. At least she still had Kynaston. The Blatchfords had lost their home – the Army had simply walked in and commandeered it. Now the Blatchfords were living in a small rented house, and their horses had had to be farmed out to all and sundry.

Still, she hadn't got off scot-free, cooped up in this little office five days a week. It meant she wouldn't be called up, and that was a blessing, and she got a petrol allowance for the car; but she was doing the work of six people without being paid a penny.

Her area was divided into six now, and her workers were mostly housewives, and stupid into the bargain. She had arranged immediate first-aid lessons for them, so that they were prepared for air raids and casualties, and three of the little fools had fainted at the mention of blood. She had drawn up a rota for hot baths for the men at the camp in Horley Woods, where as yet there were no facilities. Each soldier was allocated a house and told that the housewife there would have hot water ready for him. India loved it when the women resisted – '*Have a strange man in my house?*' They looked horrified and thrilled at the same time. Idiots. It was the same when she was billeting evacuees in the west of the county. Flat refusals, until she explained her compulsory powers. That cooled them down.

She looked at her watch. She was due at the British Restaurant at twelve o'clock, but she meant to get there earlier, before they were on their guard. As she walked to the car she thought about David. He would be on the train now. He was an idiot, an irresponsible idiot, chasing off to London after Catherine Allerton when there was so much to do at Kynaston. It would end in tears, and she would have to sort it out. Which wasn't fair, but what else could she do but shoulder the burden?

<hr>

The train was terribly dirty. There was no paper in the WC, nor soap. No question of refreshments, and the corridors were crammed with people, mostly service-men and -women. In the comparative comfort of first class, envious faces looked in from the corridors. David spent most of his time looking out of the window and wondering if Catherine might have changed in the past few months. She had looked scared when he drove her to that first meeting with the VAD organisers. He had had to pull strings to push her through the induction course, but it was what she wanted. That was all that mattered.

Now he opened his *Telegraph* and tried to concentrate on the news. The Germans were heading for Leningrad, and sending in the SS, according to this account. Butchers! There was something noble about war, but that was not what the Nazis conducted. There were reports of Jews massacred in a place called Lwow, in the Ukraine, and in Kovno in Lithuania. The streets were running red with Jewish blood, and the world only watched. Once more he cursed his own inability to play a full part. He was active in the Home Guard now, and the estate was at full productivity; but he would have given anything to be in a tank somewhere, or up in the air, as his brother had been.

A headline caught his eye: '*V for victory*.' The BBC was urging occupied Europe to adopt the V sign as its symbol. '*The V sign is the symbol of the unconquerable will of the people of the occupied territories and a portent of the fate awaiting the Nazi tyranny.*' There was a musical clef to be chalked on walls; four notes to be known as the V sound. A Colonel Britton was in charge of the campaign. '*Tomorrow the V army, Europe's invisible army of many millions, will come into being. You are asked to do two things. Take a vow to continue this fight for your country's independence. Second, to demonstrate to the Germans by putting Vs on the wall and everywhere you can put them, and beating out the V sound wherever you get the chance.*' Fine words, David thought, but God help you if the Germans catch you.

As he alighted at King's Cross he was whistling what he thought would be the V sound. He went on whistling until he reached the club. There was a message waiting for him and for a second his heart sank. She wasn't coming! But the message read: '*Looking forward to seeing you. Unless you are desperate to eat, could we go to the flicks? Everyone is talking about* Target for Tonight *and I don't want to go on my own.*'

That meant there was no man in her life. David scorned the lift and, limping, took the stairs at a fine pace, anxious for the evening to begin.

Tonight the silence of the house was oppressive. Sarah walked from room to room, as though searching for someone. Even an intruder would be welcome. Eventually she settled in the kitchen, and took out the Scotsman's flimsy letter. '*Can't tell you where we are, but it's countryside, and no combat as yet. Not like home, though. One day I'll show you Scotland. You'll like it there, you and the wee-un.*' The words sent a shiver of delight and apprehension through her. Could she be with another man after Gerard? Would Hamish be good to little Joe? Would he want to live in Scotland – and if they stayed here instead could he find work?

In the end she filled the huge bath with the hot water that was such a luxury and climbed in, in the hope she could soak away her doubts.

The cinema seats were narrow, and the man on his left side was huge. David tried not to let his arm touch Catherine's, but it was impossible. He could feel her every movement, smell the faint smell of disinfectant that seemed to pervade her hair, sense her agitation as the film unfolded. It was an understated, unemotional account of a Wellington Bomber's mission over Germany. The plane was code-named F for Freddy, and the crew were airmen from Mildenhall in Suffolk, performing their real-life roles.

'They're so young,' Catherine murmured, turning her face to him. In the darkness David could see that her cheeks gleamed, as though they were wet. As the plane was hit by flak, and seemed destined to crash, he could feel her body vibrating. He longed to put an arm around her and comfort her by drawing her close – all around them other couples were doing just that. But Catherine was obviously thinking of Henry, and remembering how he had died. He himself was 'the other brother', just as he had been at school, and as he was destined to remain.

# Chapter Nineteen

## October 1941

'SO YOU SEE, I REALLY was terribly good last night, which is why I'm up bright and early and you're still lying in your bunk.'

'It's not a bunk,' Catherine said.

'Have it your own way, darling. Bed, bunk – it's not what you call it that counts. It's what you do in it!'

'Honestly!' Catherine tried to frown, but she couldn't resist smiling instead. Tilly reminded her of a little girl, or a puppy – something mischievous and young, and utterly untouched by life. Or war. 'It's all a wonderful game to you, isn't it?'

Tilly was standing sideways, holding in her stomach with one hand, her backside with the other. 'Do you think I'm fat?' she asked, serious for once.

'Obese, even blubbery.' Catherine delivered the verdict in flat tones.

'Pig!' A pillow was hurtling in her direction. It flew past her as she sat up in bed, and knocked the contents of her locker-top flying.

'See what you've done.' Catherine bent to retrieve things but Tilly was before her.

'Oh dear, I've knocked over your Patou's Joy. I'd just better check I haven't damaged it.' Tilly squeezed the bulb of the scent spray vigorously, directing it around her face and neck.

'Hoy! My brother-in-law gave me that for Christmas and you're emptying it.'

'I'm only doing it for the war effort, darling. Give the poor wounded a treat. I wouldn't touch it with a barge-pole normally, I prefer Je Reviens – but anything for our boys. You want to hang on to that brother-in-law if he buys you gifts like that. It's fearfully expensive. Now, are you getting up, or must I administer the enemas single-handed?'

Ten minutes later they walked across the quad together, cloaked against the October wind. 'At least Sister will know we're coming,' Catherine said drily. 'She'll smell you the length of the ward.'

Light was filtering through the curtains, now. It would soon be time to get up and get Joe dressed. Sarah felt beneath the pillow for the letter she had slipped there last night, and unfolded it. She knew the opening words by heart.

'*I miss you and think of you all the time in this hellhole. God knows what they call it, and I wouldn't be allowed to tell you, anyway. I'm not a man with a gift for words and you may think it a cheek of me to write like this when we've known each other a short time, but I know my own mind. I haven't got much to offer you and little Joseph, but Scotland is a bonny place and healthy for a wee-un.*

'*If I get back, I will ask you to share what I have, and I promise I'll work for you and you'll never want. If I don't make it back, I have put you down as my next of kin. There's no one else – no one who matters, anyway. I won't leave much, but what there is, is yours. I hope you'd care a bit. That's all I ask for now, that I matter a bit. If I come back I'll work at making that bit grow.*'

He talked of comrades, then, and food and the drudgery of

war. Then there was just his name and a row of crosses. She thought of his real kisses, warm and gentle, but passionate, none the less. Could she love him? Did she love him already? Did he love Joe, as he seemed to suggest. Would there be another dreadful telegram one day? Where was he now? It must be North Africa, the desert – there was no fighting anywhere else. Or was there? Too many questions.

She put the letter back in its hiding-place and turned her face into her pillow.

'I'm going into Darlesden this morning. There was a raid last night, a bad one. The Lord Lieutenant wants some moral support for the rest-centre workers. I said I'd go.'

David hadn't expected India's approval, but her venom took him by surprise. 'What can you do, David? You're not exactly able-bodied. You'll just get in the way. If you want to do something useful . . . '

He cut across her words '. . . I should see to the estate. To hell with the estate, India. I told you where I was going out of courtesy. I wasn't asking your permission, or your approval.'

She drummed on the table with the fingers of her right hand and then shrugged. 'Do as you please. It's utter lunacy, but who am I to argue?'

'Precisely,' he said, and left the table.

He was still seething as he drove through Belgate and on to the Darlesden road. As he drew near, he saw evidence of the raid. A pall of smoke still hung in the air, and as he drove through the outskirts of the town he could see windows blown out and roofs bereft of tiles. Incendiaries! Sure enough, there was evidence of scorching around the windows and doors and furniture and household goods piled in the pocket-hanky gardens, rescued from the blaze but probably too smoke- and water-damaged to be usable again.

The real destruction, however, was in the town centre. He had intended to drive to the church hall where people made homeless would be temporarily housed. But his way was blocked by rescue vehicles, fire engines, police cars, and, ominously, several ambulances. He turned off the engine and climbed out. A policeman barred his way. 'Sir David Callingham,' he said, using his title to gain access. 'The Lord Lieutenant asked me to come over.'

The policeman raised the barrier, and he moved through. There was an acrid smell in the air, a smell of burning, and somewhere he could hear water dripping.

'Watch it mate,' a man said, and handed him a tin hat. He put on, feeling a fool but anxious to obey the rules. A group of men were moving rubble, piece by arduous piece. He stood watching until suddenly there was a shout: 'There's someone under here!' At once there was a flurry of activity. He moved forward too, and began to tug at the rubble, feeling it sear his bare hands and not minding at all.

———

Pamela loved the moment when she emerged from the noise of the factory into daylight. Now she stood for a moment, face lifted to the sun, and breathed in air that did not smell of heat and engine oil. She would have liked to undo the scarf that bound up her hair, but it was sure to look a mess after a night at the lathe. Better leave it covered.

She was almost at the bus stop when she heard the bus coming up behind her. She started to run, but her legs were leaden from a night's standing. She saw it pull up, a passenger disembarked, the conductor rang the bell, and she slowed her pace momentarily. Then, thinking of a half-hour wait, she made one last spurt.

'Come on!' A blue-clad arm was reaching out from the platform. She put out a hand and felt herself almost lifted on to the step. 'OK, I've got you!'

She leaned against the uniformed figure and tried to slow her breathing.

'That's dangerous, miss, what you just done!' The conductor was eyeing them with disfavour.

'Sorry,' the airman grinned.

Pamela looked up into his face and smiled. 'Thank you,' she said. He was young, and good-looking rather than handsome; and his arm was still round her and not letting go. 'Thanks,' she said again. 'I was dreading the wait for another bus.'

He was looking at her, wrinkling his nose a little. 'Munitions?' he asked.

She felt herself blush. He must smell the oil on her clothes and hair. She tried to pull away but his grasp stayed firm. 'Can't have you falling off now, or I'll be in hot water again.' She could see his rank: sergeant pilot. Not really an officer, but almost.

'I don't expect you're scared of conductors,' she said. 'Not with what you do. And I do work at the munitions factory. Night shift, which is why I look deplorable.'

'All right from where I'm standing,' he said. The bus was slowing down and passengers were pushing past them to alight. 'Come on,' he said. 'Let's go up top and swap our wars.'

---

The ward was silent now, but half an hour earlier it had been abuzz. The great A. H. McIndoe had paid them a visit, accompanied by Mr Detweiler and Matron and another man Catherine didn't recognise. Even the QA had looked shaken. 'Any minute now she'll curtsey,' Staff Nurse had hissed to Catherine.

McIndoe was short and thickset, but his jaw was square, and the tired eyes behind the horn-rimmed glasses were kind. He didn't visit every bed, just those indicated by the other surgeon, but of those patients he made a thorough examination, lifting dressings and probing scars with fingers that were blunt and capable, but also gentle. 'He knows exactly what he's doing,' Catherine thought, and then winced in case he might not approve of what he found.

After he had gone, his retinue trailing in his wake, the QA said he had been 'very supportive'. 'That means we did OK,' Staff said. 'Watch Queenie for me, I'm off for a smoke.' The ward was strangely quiet after he had gone. Even Queenie had vanished, when Catherine heard a voice behind her. 'Excuse me?'

She turned. The airman was ridiculously young and looked scared. 'I'm looking for Arthur Mayhew?' he said apologetically.

Catherine smiled at him. 'Have you come to visit? That's nice, but I'll have to check with Sister first.' Sister was in her office and Catherine crossed her fingers under her apron. She could be such a dragon.

Today, though, she was in a good mood. 'A visitor? Do him good. Don't let him stay too long. No touching, and check the locker for booze afterwards.' Privately, Catherine wondered just how Mayhew would imbibe with his withered hands and wounded mouth, but she merely bobbed her thanks and backed out of the office. One thing she had learned was to keep QAs sweet. They ruled the roost in military hospitals, so a lowly VAD was not advised to get across them.

'It's OK,' she told the young airman when she reached the ward door. And then, as she conducted him down between the beds, 'I wouldn't stay too long. He –' She hesitated. 'He's pretty cut up, still, but he's getting wonderful treatment. Still, it might be a bit upsetting for you – try not to betray it in your voice.'

'So it's true, he's blind?' The young voice almost broke in the words.

'At the moment. We won't know if it's permanent until –' How did you explain that eyelids would have to be constructed before anyone tried to make sightless eyes see.

She felt apprehensive as they approached the bed, but the young pilot had steadied. 'Arthur? It's me, Jimmy Pendleton. How are you, you old shirker? Everybody's asking after you. They're calling you a jammy bastard, getting time off!'

And Mayhew's face, invisible behind the bandages, was surely relaxing into a smile. 'Jimmy? How are you, old son? I hoped you'd come.'

Sarah had bathed the baby and put him down for his nap, done her chores, and now she sat in the silent house, trying not to think about the letter. If she had still been at home there would have been the bustle of men home from the pit, perhaps Hannah Chaffey disgorging gossip, the crackle of pit coal on the fire, and the wireless blaring out news.

She seldom switched on the wireless in the kitchen at Mellows. There was nothing but gloom at the moment: a reported massacre in France; tales of suffering in the Warsaw ghetto; and endless reports of the Russian winter and how it was affecting the German advance. Thinking of all this, she tried to count her blessings. She wasn't being shot or penned in a ghetto without food, and no one belonging to her was trudging through snow, fighting for survival. 'I am lucky,' she told herself.

The impulse to take out Hamish's letter again came over her, but she resisted it. Instead she walked into the hall and looked at the telephone. Catherine had written: '*Here's my number in the nurses' home. Ring me if anything bothers you, anything at all.*' She had meant practical things like the house or the baby. Could Sarah ring about a personal dilemma? She opened the notebook at the C page and dialled. But Nurse Callingham was not in the nurses' home, nor did anyone know her whereabouts. Sarah put down the phone, and returned to her pondering.

———

Around India, stupid chatter ebbed and flowed. They had talked interminably of hay-boxes as a method of fuel conservation – apparently you could leave porridge in it to cook overnight, or produce stew in 16 hours. That was the level of their idiocy – that they talked of cooking meat when there was precious little meat to be found. Then they had moved on to fire-watching. More boredom.

She looked around her office. They had given her a poky little shop to start with, but now she had decent premises, and lots of hands to the wheel; and if those hands belonged to nincompoops that was not her fault. Now they were on to methods of raising morale when summer came round. Someone was suggesting 'holidays at home'. India stayed upright in her chair, her hands folded in front of her on the table, but her thoughts drifted off to holidays before the war. Before everyone who mattered had died. When she and Henry had swum in the blue waters off the Riviera and wandered hand-in-hand in the bazaars of Marrakesh. She had loved holidays, but had never minded coming home because she was coming back to Kynaston.

Kynaston must be kept safe, whatever happened. If it was bombed, she would rebuild it with her bare hands. But if it was left to David, it would be lost to the family, anyway. He would never marry, and it would pass, with the title, to some far-off cousin who did not even bear the Callingham name. It was up to her to protect Kynaston, and that meant marriage, and a son. She ran through the possibilities in her mind. Old men, and men too young to serve. The only eligible men were in the Army or the other services, or were over the age for military service.

There was nothing for it but to invite such men to the house, let them see the glory of it, and then select someone worthy of furnishing an heir.

≈≈≈

Catherine and the young airman, Jimmy Pendleton, had eaten in a smoky restaurant and then gone to a nearby pub, which was full of other young men and women in uniform. She had talked and laughed with him, and watched him get drunk, all the time aware of the fear behind his eyes. That afternoon he had come away from Mayhew's bed and stood in front of the nursing-station, shifting from foot to foot.

'I wonder – I was wondering. . .' She had kept on watching him, but did not speak. Important he should do it for himself. 'Are you married?'

She had smiled and shaken her head, and a look of relief had spread across his face. 'Will you come out with me tonight, when you come off duty? I'm back to ops tomorrow. So one last night . . .'

She knew they were both thinking the same thing: that this night might be the last night. That he might die in icy waters, or, like Mayhew, be burned beyond recognition. So she had said yes, and borrowed Tilly's mohair coat to make it special.

They ate an unidentifiable meat dish, and talked of war. 'And then the next day they're not there in the mess, being loud and throwing their weight about and you think, "It'll be me one day, wiped off the board" – that's what they do when you buy it – and everyone saying "good old Jimmy" and then never mentioning you again.'

'Come on,' she said, rising to her feet and leading him to the hotel opposite the pub. 'A room,' she said firmly to the receptionist, and pushed some notes across the counter. The receptionist hesitated, but only for a moment, before pushing her a key. He didn't ask her to sign in.

The boy came like a lamb, and let her undress him in a room lit only by the light from the moon outside the window. She kissed him rather as a mother might have done, and eased the way for him to enter her. She was doing it for Henry, and for all the men who were afraid of dying. Doing it because it was something she could do, and because to give herself like this assuaged her guilt.

As she felt him come, she thanked God that Tilly had given her a Volpar Gel. 'This'll work, Toots. Trust your Auntie Til. Shove it up, and then relax. They're better than French thingummys.'

---

David couldn't get the thought of the dead man in the rubble out of his head. He had looked serene, almost happy. But his wife's face had been filled with a terrible grief. 'She loved him,' he thought. Tonight he had listened to details of casualties, military and civilian. There were homes in mourning all over Britain, and there would be more before it was finished. At least they had died in a just cause: a Belgate woman had said that to him, when he had visited to console her on the death of her sailor son. 'He didn't die for nothing, Sir David, that's my comfort.' And the woman was right: what you died for made all the difference. He went up to his room and got ready for the night's patrol.

---

Before she put out the light, Sarah stood by the cot. In sleep the baby looked cherubic, but there was a hint of Gerard in the determined little chin. He would grow up to be a fighter like his dad, and she would tell him how strong his father had been and what a lover.

She smiled, then, at her own foolishness. You couldn't tell that to a boy, especially not your son. A tear ran down her cheek, and she brushed it away. Mustn't cry and wake with a sore nose in the morning. In the morning she had decisions to make, and for that you needed your sleep. She put out the light and climbed resolutely into bed.

# Chapter Twenty

## October 1941

'YOU'LL GET SLAUGHTERED IF MATRON sees that.' The 'that' in question was Tilly's anklet. It glittered through the sheer black nylons she was wearing and Catherine shook her head. 'She won't think much of the nylons, either. Where did you get them?'

Tilly tapped her nose to indicate secrecy. 'Never you mind. And I can hear the note of envy in your voice.' She lifted a leg and turned it this way and that to show off her ankle. 'Not bad, though I say it myself. Now let's get on. I'm famished, and the decent grub is always gone by the time I get there. Hurry up!'

Catherine was struggling to subdue her newly washed hair so that it would accept her cap. She took the hairpins from her mouth, 'You go ahead. I'll catch you up.' After Tilly had gone, she skewered a roving lock with the pins and set her cap in place. Much as she loved Tilly, she was glad of some time to herself before the rush and clatter of the ward. She wanted to think about last night, put it in order in her mind, so that she could move on.

She had actually taken a man by the hand and taken him to an hotel room for sex. Now she waited to be shocked, but no shock came. She had not enjoyed it, had almost, as he seemed insatiable, wished for it all to end. But at the same time she had felt relieved, serene almost. And when he had cried his fear of what might lie ahead, she had held him to her breast and felt proud that she could do it. She would do it all again. With him, if he came in search of her; with others, if they needed her. She had looked around the pub last night and heard, above the raucous laughter, a note almost of hysteria in their joviality.

'You never know,' the young man had said as they lay, limbs entwined, satiated by sex but too alive to sleep, 'you never know in the morning who will be in the mess that night. You say, "See you later," as you cross the tarmac, and you know, and he knows, there might not be a "later".'

Now, as she walked across the quad, the October wind made her shiver, even inside her cloak. It was true. You could never be sure of later. There was only now.

〜〜

It was heaven to turn over and close her eyes again. Pamela had a precious two days before she went back to day shift. Two lie-ins. Two leisurely breakfasts, if there was anything to breakfast on, and a chance to get to grips with the living-room. She was going to distemper the walls a nice shade of peach. There was good-quality embossed paper there already, but it was a grey-beige. Like school porridge, Pamela thought, and pulled a face. She was coming to like this house better. It was small, but cosy, and with a lick or two of paint it would be quite presentable, which was important if she was going to bring her pilot home.

The thought of him banished thought of more sleep. She swung her legs out of her bed and reached for her dressing-gown. They had had three dates, so it was going well. Sooner or later she would have to introduce him to her parents, and sooner would probably be better, because he could be posted any day.

She found her mother in the kitchen, and, amazingly, her father already at the breakfast table. Even more amazing, he was shaved, and his shirt, though tieless, was clean and buttoned. She slid on to her chair and reached for the toast. 'Anything in the paper?' At the Dene they had had three morning papers delivered. Now they had to share one – but what did it really matter? In fact, it made for better conversation.

Her father was grunting disapproval of the Germans. 'Fifty hostages shot in Nantes and 50 more to go if no one comes forward.'

'What did they do?'

He shook the paper irritably. 'Nothing. Hostages never have done anything. They pay the price for someone else.'

'What did he do?' She was scraping the last remnants of marmalade over her toast, remembering when there had been marmalade aplenty and you could ladle it on to your toast in golden heaps.

'He or she. Lots of the Resistance are women. They shot the local German commander. De Gaulle has asked the Resistance to stop what they're doing so as to save more hostages' lives, but I don't expect it will have any effect.'

Pamela licked in a crumb. 'Daddy, I was wondering if you would give me a hand today? I'm painting the walls.'

'There's nothing wrong with the walls as they are.'

Pamela perked up. They were grumpy words, but his tone was quite pleasant.

'I know, but a change would be nice. Please, Daddy.'

'I suppose so, but I can't rush about like a two-year-old.' He sat up suddenly. 'Good God, they're making Mountbatten Director of Combined Operations!'

'That's nice, dear.' Her mother was coming into the room carrying more toast. 'He's handsome, and she's elegant.'

'Elegant is as elegant does.' Inside Pamela a little knot of pleasure was forming. In a minute, she was going to spread a peach glow through the room, and her parents had managed two whole minutes of conversation without bemoaning the past.

It was nice to get home with thoughts of breakfast and bath ahead, but David didn't mind the nights he now spent on patrol. As he changed out of his Home Guard uniform, he smiled, thinking of the events of the night before, and of the enthusiasm of the men, most of whom had never seen a battlefield but who could now play at soldiers. They had chosen a password, 'Wendel Wilkie', the name of an American politician, because there was a belief, possibly apocryphal, that Germans were unable to pronounce the letter 'W' and, when challenged to repeat the password, would fail dismally. If, during patrols a suspicious figure was spotted flitting among the trees – and there were poachers about in plenty – there would be a good deal of 'halting' and 'who goes thereing', and a great deal of disappointment when it turned out to be Jim or Jack from next door, so the password needn't be invoked.

The main purpose of the patrols was to watch the night sky for the first sign of descending paratroops, whereupon the Home Guard would set upon the Hun as he landed and save England from the Nazi jackboot. That would have been difficult in the days of broom handles, but now they had the Lee Enfield rifle and five rounds apiece.

Sometimes, when there were clear skies, David found the night the perfect time and place to think and dream, although clear skies favoured night attacks by the Luftwaffe. He would look across to the nearby town, and see bright flashes as the bombs fell and the ground defences sent up a cascade of tracer bullets into the night sky. Afterwards there would be peace again. Moonlight would filter down through the trees, and occasionally the silence would be interrupted by the soulful hoot of an owl. He would think about Catherine, then, much more likely to be involved in air raids, and wish with all his heart that she might be safe.

The thought that there might be a letter took him downstairs two at a time but there was nothing. They stayed behind their newspapers throughout breakfast, but at last India folded hers neatly and cleared her throat.

'I'm giving a dinner party next week,' she announced. 'Tuesday evening, I think, if everyone's available.'

They hadn't entertained more than once or twice since the war had begun. David put his newspaper aside. Something was up. 'Do you want me there?'

'Of course I want you there. People will expect it.'

'People? Do I know them?'

'Lindsay Dane and Helen. The Nicholsons, and Valerie Graham-Poole. And Rupert Lindsay-Hogg. With you and me, that makes eight. God knows what we'll give them to eat, but at least there's some wine.'

'That's an odd bunch. I know the Danes and the Nicholsons, and the Graham-Poole girl a bit. But since when have we been thick with Rupert Lindsay-Hogg?'

'Thick? Must you use gutter language? He sits on one of my committees. And I like him. He's wonderful on a horse.'

'He looks good, mounted or on foot, but the man's a moron, India. He drives that Rolls like a man possessed. Is he bringing Valerie?'

'No. No, they're coming quite independently. I'm not even sure they know each other.'

Was he seeing things or was there a turkey-red flush around her neck. Blushing or not, she was being uncharacteristically vague.

'Well, I suppose I can put up with them for one night. I'll see to the wine.' India inclined her head in what was meant to be a thank-you and they went their separate ways.

━━━

'Cigarettes. They're another thing – scarcer than hen's teeth. Mary Croaker's Jim says you can't lay them down at work or they walk.'

Sarah transferred the child to her other arm. He was becoming quite a weight. 'You wouldn't think anyone'd pinch from workmates, would you?'

Hannah pursed her lips and shook her head. 'Smokers'll do anything for a fag. Beg, borrow or steal. I mean money's no object now, it's that the stuff's just not there to buy. Three pounds ten they're getting for firewatching. And that's on top of a wage.'

'I think it's just the AFS get that, Hannah.'

'No, every firewatcher gets it. Beats me where all the money comes from.'

Sarah didn't argue. When Hannah got her facts wrong, which happened regularly, you could no more shift her than a two-ton lorry.

'Anyroad, I reckon the AFS gets more than three pounds ten. So do the bodysnatchers.'

'I suppose you mean ambulance men,' Sarah said, trying not to laugh.

'That's what I said, bodysnatchers.' Hannah was looking round her. 'Boy, you've fallen on your feet here and no mistake. Why did she pick you?' She was leaning forward, her face full of curiosity. Sarah thought rapidly. Catherine had installed her here because of Joe. She knew that was the reason, but also couldn't quite believe it, not when her dad and Molly and the boys were cooped up in a house half the size of Mellows.

'She took a fancy to the bairn,' she said at last. 'She called in when Gerard died, well, when I had the bairn . . .'

She was saved from floundering when Hannah thought of another bit of news. 'The King's got a line round his bath.'

'What d'you mean? Muck, d'you mean?'

'No. Five inches. You know, no more than five inches of water in a bath. That wouldn't cover the arses on some women. Anyroad, they say he's painted them on every bath, and God help anyone who goes over them.'

'I don't believe it,' Sarah said absently, still thinking of Catherine and the house.

'That he's got a temper? It's a well-known fact.'

'No, about the five inches. If the royal family are going short of water, it'll be the only thing they are going short of. Have you seen the Queen's clothes? She's not doing them on coupons.'

'You're right there. And I bet they're not rationed to one roll of netty paper a week. Where will that go between a family of seven?'

Hannah was away, then, waxing lyrical about class difference and how the workers always came last, leaving Sarah free to pick away at the puzzle that was her friendship with Catherine, the woman who was also her employer. She was still puzzling when the doorbell rang, and she opened it to see the telegraph boy once more.

＝＝＝

They were short of staff in the ward, Sister had been called to a meeting with Matron, and the reserve nurse was accompanying a patient to another hospital. 'You'll have to do rounds if I'm not back,' she told Catherine. 'Keep your mouth shut, and don't miss a thing they say. I want it word for word when I get back.'

Catherine had spent an hour praying no surgeon would loom up before the QA's return, but she prayed in vain. Mr Detweiler and his house surgeon appeared on time, and she walked dutifully behind him as he moved from bed to bed. She had a lot of respect for him now that she had seen his handiwork. Mayhew was a fine example: patiently his face was being rebuilt, tissue replaced, and skin grafted over it, square by square. Now there was a semblance of a face there – a nose, a mouth – but it resembled a patchwork quilt. The first move had been to manufacture eyelids, essential if his sight was to be preserved. Then his hands. At first they had not only been devoid of skin and flesh, they had contracted into claws. There was still a long way to go, but now it was possible to believe that one day he would have something resembling human hands.

Mr Detweiler was bending over the bed, smiling and whispering, and the patched face was responding. 'He's a good man,' Catherine thought emotionally. She felt for all pilots, but especially those disfigured. 'They're not prepared for it,' the QA had told her. 'They're young gods, the girls flock round them – and then suddenly it's gone. They're no more than a burned cinder. No more dancing in nightclubs with the pick of the girls, no more the pick of the best job after the war – they can't see anything ahead. That's your job, Nurse, to convince them they have a future.'

She had tried that with Mayhew, but not got very far. 'He had a girlfriend,' Jimmy Pendleton had told her. 'A peach of a girl. He wrote to her – well, his sister wrote for him. But she never replied. She'd heard, you see, about his injuries.'

'But surely, if you love someone . . .' She had halted then, fearing she sounded too worthy. She could love the man within, however much he changed. If it had been Joe, nothing would have changed. And if it had been Henry – she found she was smiling foolishly, remembering how bright he had been and how kind – yes, she could have loved him if he had come back disfigured.

'Penny for them, Nurse?' Thank God Mr Detweiler was smiling. Another surgeon would have blasted her for inattention.

'I'm sorry sir. I didn't hear what you said.'

'He must be a special fella, to send you into a daydream. I want this patient prepared up for surgery tomorrow. And remind me I've promised to bring him in a brown ale after the op.' His brow was wrinkling. 'What is brown ale?'

'It's beer, sir. Strong beer.'

'Well, don't let Sister know. It's your secret and mine, Nurse –?' He was looking at her, eyebrows raised.

'Callingham, sir.'

'First name?'

'Catherine.'

'OK, Catherine Callingham. Thank you for doing my round – and keep shtum about the beer.'

It was her turn to look puzzled.

'Shtum' he said, lifting his hand sharply across his mouth. 'Keep it zipped to Sister. And put those eyes back in your head, or she'll think I've scared you.'

She could hear him laughing even after the ward doors had swung to behind him. He must think she was an idiot. All the same, he was a lot more human than the English surgeons, and seemed to care about the patients. If that was what Yanks were like, they were OK.

≈

India had rehearsed what to say, but her mouth dried as she dialled the number and she put the receiver back on the rest quickly. She had never asked a man for anything, or to do anything for that matter. In the old days, invitations had gone out in her mother's fine handwriting, and after that Henry had seen to social events.

She stood by the phone, thinking of what was at stake here. When David died, Kynaston and the estate would go to one of her father's distant cousins. She herself would be provided for: she already had her mother's money. But everything that mattered to her would go to a stranger. Unless – unless she had a child, and that child was a boy.

She picked up the phone again and dialled. 'Rupert? It's India Callingham here.' When she put down the phone she felt shaken but elated. The game was afoot.

David went upstairs to dress for dinner. He was tired after the adventures of the previous night. Lame though he was, he was by far the fittest of the group, so he had helped old men over stiles, and watched young men, little more than boys, slither under them. He had preached the importance of keeping their new equipment in order, and advised a young man on how to quell his girlfriend's fears that 'time spent 'on patrol' was a cover for carnal activity. Now he lay in a bath wickedly above the five-inch limit, and felt his tired limbs ease.

Catherine in a letter had bemoaned the fact that there were six nurses to a bathroom in the nurses' home, and one or two of them with no sense of time or fair play. He found he was smiling at the thought of her irate knocking on a locked door. If there had been no war, Henry would have ploughed his way through the local debutantes and finally made a good marriage. Then he, David, could have wooed Catherine, patiently, cunningly – and if he had won her, he would have made her happy. He knew that. She and Henry had not been well matched. She was a meadow flower, and Henry, lovable though he was, a hot-house bloom.

But such thoughts were idle. There had been a war, a hasty marriage, and then a death that had swept Catherine away from him forever. She would marry a doctor or a brigadier, and end her days tending a Home Counties garden, and embroidering kneelers for the local church.

Except . . . except . . . he began to plan. He had time and money and love enough to last the course. She was not a girl to care about a disability: what she had written about the injured pilots was proof of that. If the war ended in '43, she would come home, back to Mellows, and he would court her night and day. He lay back and closed his eyes at the pleasure of that thought, daydreaming until the cooling water drove him out in search of warm towels.

Catherine had a technique, now. She would enter the bar and make straight for the stools that surrounded it. The barman would avoid seeing her as long as he could, and that was OK. She would survey the crowd, picking out the clusters of khaki and blue, and the darker tones of naval personnel. These were fewer in number and were usually accompanied by girls. But the men in khaki and the men in blue would talk among themselves about her, and what she was doing here. Usually, and often before she had been served a drink, one of them would detach himself from the group and come across. 'Do I know you?' was the most frequent line. And she would say, 'I don't think so,' in a detached way while never breaking eye contact.

She never slept with the first one to approach her. Instead she would search his group for the man who looked apprehensive or subdued. Signs indicated the afraid – shadows under the eyes, a downturn to the mouth, fingernails chewed to the quick. Once she identified her mark, it was easy to split him, sheepdog like, from the rest of the herd. A few drinks, a lot of listening, and then she would take him to bed, and make sure that, for a while at least, thoughts of death in combat did not intrude.

# Chapter Twenty One

December 1941

'MY MOTHER SAYS ONLY BAD girls wear anklets, so I suppose that means I'm bad. Anyway, I'm not taking it off, bad or not.' Tilly was perched on her bed, clad only in peach satin cami-knickers, her hair tied out of the way on top of her head. She had just come off nights, and this morning had been her first chance to lie-in, but you could always count on Tilly to be contrary. Her uniform never conformed to the rules, dress 12 inches from the ground, aprons two inches from the hem of the dress. Her dresses tended to be two inches above her knee, and the apron pulled so tight around her tiny waist that it bunched in front like a pannier. The QAs raged, but Tilly sailed serenely on.

Today, however, she had been up with the lark and woken Catherine with a welcome cup of tea. 'Come on, lazybones. Some of us are disciplined.' She said 'disciplined' in the clipped tones Sister used, and the mimicry was perfect. Now she sat, slim legs tucked under her, and gave forth.

'Honestly, when this war is over, I'll be good, just like you want me to be. I'll wear tweed skirts, and twinsets with pearls, and blouses with Peter Pan collars, but for now I'm having such fun being bad! I'm living, Cath, I'm really living. I'm seeing my lovely Kiwi at the moment, and after that perhaps a Pole. They're quite small, Poles, but so –' She rolled her eyes to indicate sex, and then sat up straight. 'Don't put your little nun look on. I'm careful, you know I am. No babies, please God. Not yet. Just fun.'

Afterwards, as she walked across the courtyard, Catherine thought about Tilly's determination not to get pregnant. The Volpar Gels were said to be foolproof but was that true? Perhaps douching as well was the answer. It was not 100 per cent effective, but it was better than nothing. Some people said foreign troops carried French letters, probably to avoid infection rather than prevent a baby for a woman they would never see again. But the boys she had slept with up to now had been inexperienced, one at least a virgin. What would she do if she became pregnant? She shivered inside her cloak and quickened her pace.

Posters everywhere showed Churchill, smiling, giving the victory sign, urging them on. But news headlines belied the posters. Malta and Tobruk were under siege; tales of German atrocities everywhere; U-boats sinking ships; German tanks riding roughshod over Russian soil. Sarah had last listened to the radio three days before, to hear details of the call-up of women. Unmarried women aged between 20 and 30 could be called to serve in any of the services, and married women up to the age of 40 could be directed to industry. The baby would protect her from call-up, but otherwise she would have been proud to serve. And most women worth a light had already come forward, even Catherine's sister, who had been a stuck-up little bitch but who now worked hard at munitions, by all accounts.

Sarah heard the baby stir in his pram, but he went quiet again, and she let him lie. He had had her up since six, and then fallen asleep an hour ago when she put him in his pram to get herself a bit of peace. She looked at the clock. Time for his dinner, soon. She switched on the wireless and turned it down. Perhaps there would be a letter by the time she finished, telling her where Hamish was now, and when he might be sent home to convalesce. If he got a transfer to the Emergency Hospital at Ryhope, she could reach that by bus. Afterwards, maybe Catherine would let her bring him to Mellows.

She sat thinking of him, tall, his ginger head above the bright blue uniform and red tie of a wounded man. Perhaps . . . Half an hour later she woke with a start. Little Joe was still asleep. How had she dropped off like that, and what had woken her? It was a voice on the wireless, urgent, almost staccato. She couldn't disturb the baby to turn up the volume so she leaned closer to catch the words. It was something about America being bombed at a place called Pearl Harbor, and from the tone it wasn't good news.

～～

'India! India!' David took the stairs two at a time, his weak leg seeming to gain strength in his haste.

She came out on to the landing and looked down at him. 'What on earth is the matter?'

He halted to catch his breath, gazing up at her all the while. 'Japan has bombed the American fleet. In Hawaii. Smashed it to smithereens, by all accounts. And not a word of warning!'

'Is that all?' She was already turning away. 'From the noise you were making, I thought the Germans had landed in the paddock. Now, I must get on. I'm getting the linen ready for tonight.'

'Don't you see what this means? It means the Yanks are in the war now, bound to be. It's as good as over!'

But she had vanished to see to her ruddy dinner party, and he subsided on to a chair to get back his breath. It was true what he had said: this would shorten the war, and make victory certain. Roosevelt had been waiting for an excuse to throw America's weight behind the Allies. Now he had that excuse. It would be over in a year, maybe less. Life would get back to normal, there would be men and women to till the fields again and work on the farms. And Catherine would come home.

He was about to brush tears from his eyes when he remembered he had been mucking out the stables when he heard the news, and his hands were far from savoury. Instead, he wiped his sleeve across his face and went back to work.

Catherine looked forward to Mr Detweiler's coming into the ward now, particularly when she had to do his round. He treated nurses as though they had a brain. Other surgeons were respectful to the QAs but behaved as though ordinary nurses, even the trained ones, were vegetables. As for VADs, they were invisible. Mr Detweiler was different.

Today she had just walked away from Mayhew's bed, and he was writing up the patient notes and chatting as he did so.

'He's quite an exception. A fighter. Usually if more than a third of the body's surface is burned, chances of recovery are slim. But it's important not to give up. He was almost 50 per cent burned, but we got him early. The main problem is the enormous quantity of fluid lost through exudation from the burnt area. You can lose up to six litres that way. If you get the patients through the first 72 hours, you have a chance. Now we have to turn him back into something resembling a human being. He's a nice young chap.'

Catherine was making a mental note to look up the meaning of exudation when she heard a noise that smashed at her ears and then a terrifying roar. 'Bombs,' Mr Detweiler said, throwing down the notes.

Catherine felt rooted to the floor. 'There hasn't been a siren,' she said woodenly, but the surgeon was yanking at her arm.

'To hell with sirens, Nurse, snap to it!' And suddenly the drill came back, practised a dozen times and never fully appreciated. She saw Tilly run past her to help a patient out from and under his bed. What was Tilly doing here, out of uniform and not on duty?

And then she was helping the ambulant take cover, and yanking spare mattresses over men too ill to be moved. The noise was continuing, sometimes receding then suddenly louder, until the ward shook around her. There was a mist of dust in the air, and a sudden draught from a shattered window. That was when she remembered Mayhew. He must be terrified, there in the darkness, with the world exploding around him.

'I'm coming, I'm coming!' She was lugging a mattress, feeling it bend and twist away from her, and then Mr Detweiler was beside her, lifting his side of the mattress so that they could run together towards Mayhew's bed.

'We're covering you, to keep you safe,' Catherine said urgently. 'I'll stay with you . . .' And then there was a pain in her ears, and a flash, and she was falling into darkness, down and down . . .

'Thank God for that,' a girl said, wiping sweat from her forehead with the back of a greasy hand. The buzzer had sounded for the dinner break, and one by one the girls were switching off their lathes and reaching for fags and sweets. It was too cold to go outside, so they congregated round a table in the canteen.

'They say the Yanks'll be here by Christmas,' another girl said, carefully lighting a one-inch fag end. Pamela thanked God she didn't smoke. The eternal scrabbling for cigarettes was pitiful, and so was the smoking down to the last centimetre. She had even seen a girl stick a pin in one, when it burned down too short to be held by fingers. Horrid!

'We'll get nylons, then, and candy bars. Everyone says Yanks are generous.'

'Who says they'll come? It's Japan they're fighting, not Jerry.'

There was a chorus of dissent, and tortuous explanations of just who was on whose side and who would fight whom. Pamela let it all wash over her. Michael was coming on leave at the week-end, from his south-coast squadron, and her father had said he could stay in the spare room. She put up a hand to her turban and pushed stray hairs back into place. On Friday night she would wash her hair and get a long bath. There was nothing to be done about her damaged nails and scarred hands, but he had called them her war wounds, and insisted on kissing them before he went back last time.

She would have liked to take out his letter and read it again, but the girls would only scoff. Besides, she could almost remember it by heart, he wrote in such a lovely way. He had been elated about shooting down a German plane. '*I got right up close, and gave it a series of short bursts. It seemed to dart about a bit, and I was closing in again when it suddenly went into a spin and hit the sea about five miles off the coast. You asked me if I ever think about the Jerry pilots. The truthful answer is no. There isn't time, and, anyway, it wouldn't pay. But I'm not a butcher, Pammy. I wish we could win without anyone dying, their side or ours, but it's not like that. We must make sure we win. When the war is over, I am going to see what I can do to heal wounds and make things better. We'd make a good team, you and I, and I promise you'll have love and everything else I can give you.*'

'Wake up, Pam, your tea's going cold.' The speaker was middle-aged and kindly, curlers glinting from under her turban, cigarette dangling from her lips. 'She's mooning over her pilot again, girls. The sooner he gets his backside back here and gives her a good seeing-to, the better.'

The klaxon sounded, and there was a frenzied puffing on cigarettes and a careful stubbing out so that the fag end could be relit. 'Come on, lass.' The older woman's arm was round her, and they were moving back.

'Yes,' Pamela said, 'let's get the bloody war over.'

She had restarted her machine and fitted the next casing before she realised she had used a swear word. If her mother had heard that, there would have been hell to pay. Except that those rules had been left behind with the polished nails. She was grown up now, and could use whatever language she chose.

Suddenly, and for no reason, she thought about Catherine. It would be nice to see her again, and tell her about Michael. She was down where the bombing was going on, but they never bombed hospitals, everyone knew that.

———

There was a dull ache in her head, and her mouth was full of powder. She would have moved, but something was holding her down. Catherine opened her eyes. Light was coming through a space somewhere up above, high up above. She could hear water dripping, and then suddenly, somewhere to her left, electricity sparked across. She tried to free an arm but all that happened was that rubble shifted and bore down more heavily on her chest.

'Nurse?' The voice came from her left.

'Who's that?'

'It's Max Detweiler. Are you OK?' Someone, far off, was moaning.

'I'm all right. Have we been bombed?'

She heard a chuckle. 'Yes, I think you could safely say that. They'll be coming to find us soon. Can you work out where you're hit?'

'I'm not sure. There's no real pain anywhere, but my head hurts a bit, and I can't move. What about the patients?'

'I'm like you, I can't move. There's something across my legs, something wooden.'

There was silence for a moment, and then he raised his voice. 'Is there anyone there? Stevenson? Mayhew?' He was calling the patients' names, and Catherine joined in. 'Carter? Johnny Carter?'

There were one or two groans, and a muffled 'I'm OK,' but Catherine couldn't make out who was making the sounds. At least some of them had survived. Suddenly she felt movement at her side. Rats! There were always rats in rubble, she had seen them on bomb sites in London! But it was not a rat, it was a human hand, feeling its way along her arm, seeking her hand and finding it.

'Is that you?' The American voice was Max Detweiler's, but she couldn't see him.

'Yes.' Fingers touched and twined.

'It won't be long now?'

'I know.' She also knew that gas might be escaping or water reaching broken wires, or masonry shifting and bringing walls down. The sky above was bright and clear. Would she ever walk out there again?

'Are you scared?' he asked. She would have liked to be brave and say, 'No.' Instead she was truthful and said, 'Yes.'

They talked, then. He told her of his home in New York. Of his wife, Miriam, who was a neurologist, and his children Aaron and Rebecca, who were seven and five.

'How could you bear to leave them?'

'I'm a Jew. My grandparents lived in Poland, in a place called Bydgoszcz. In September 1939 the Germans rounded up 1000 civilians and shot them in the market-place. They said they'd been waging a guerrilla war. My grandfather was 82, my grandmother 79. They have this special squad now, the SS

Einsatzgruppen. It follows troops into Jewish areas and massacres the people there. Miriam's parents lived in Paris, and we begged them to get out, but they wanted to protect their home. We haven't heard from them since June last year.

'That was when we decided I should come and work here. I was tired of moulding rich ladies' faces. I wanted to make a difference.'

'Do you miss them, your family?'

'Very much, especially not seeing my children grow.'

'What will happen now that America is in the war?'

'I don't know. I'm a civilian at the moment, and I don't know what will happen if my country wants me to be somewhere else. I'll deal with that when it happens. Now, tell me about you . . .'

She was opening her mouth to speak when there was a sudden rush and crash of noise, and someone, somewhere, cried out.

'Poor devil,' Max's voice said, out of the dark. 'Something's come down. Over by the sluice I think.'

'Tilly was here,' Catherine said suddenly. 'I remember I saw her. She wasn't on duty, but she was in here.'

'She probably got out. We stayed with the patients, remember.'

'Yes,' she said.

His grip on her hand tightened. 'It's going to be all right. Now, where are you from?'

※

Her father was glued to the wireless when Pamela got home.

'It's official,' he said. 'Roosevelt has declared war, and called yesterday "a day that will live in infamy".' Her father sounded almost gleeful, and she saw that he had shaved.

They ate vegetable pie for their evening meal. Her mother

sighed apologetically. 'I tried for some meat, but it's no use. It's all under the counter unless you've still got coupons. And with points even for tinned food now, I don't know what we'll do. Still, that nice David Callingham brought us some apples this afternoon, so I've baked some. One each, and there's custard.'

Pamela moved the potato and pastry around her mouth and smiled warmly. 'It's delicious – well, good. You'll have to teach me to cook.' If her mother could take up the reins when Cook had gone, then she, Pamela, could learn to cook, too. And if – no, when – she married Michael, there would be no money for servants. Not at first, anyway.

'Will there be some hot water?' she asked hopefully. 'And have you any of that handcream left?' When she excused herself from the table, and went upstairs carrying not only handcream but a bath cube, she felt like a queen.

～～～

If he narrowed his eyes and squinted down the table, David could almost convince himself it was 1939 and that the war had never happened. Light glinted on china and glass, there were candles and flowers, women in beautiful dresses, and men in black tie and gleaming moiré lapels. It was only when you looked closely at the plates that you knew it was wartime. India had done her best, but the beef was cut wafer thin, the vegetables were sparse, and the gravy lacked the rich oiliness of more lavish times.

Tonight his sister was looking more girlish, quite pretty really. Most of her attention was going to the man on her right, Rupert Lindsay-Hogg. He was late 40s, even 50, which would explain why he wasn't in the services. There had been some tale about an affair years ago, but he seemed amiable enough now, making sure the woman on his right got a share of his attention, and laughing at everyone's jokes. The mood around the table was buoyant.

'Everyone thinks it's over now that America's in,' David thought. He had thought so himself at first, and had met with that mood on the estate today: 'The Yanks'll roll over Jerry,' one man had said. Another had been openly planning for his son's demobilisation, and his daughter's return from a Birmingham factory. By then David was having second thoughts about today's events being a magic solution, but he had kept his counsel. There had been so much bad news; if today was a holiday for some, who was he to spoil it? At least Churchill would be cock-a-hoop about it.

Thinking about soberly, after the first euphoria, David had realised Japan was a formidable enemy. How much manpower and armour would America have to spare for Europe, with the Japs advancing across the Thai isthmus, and their overwhelming air and sea superiority? They had almost wiped out the British Far East Fleet with the sinking of *Repulse* and *The Prince of Wales*, and 840 men had perished in the South China Sea. But there seemed little recognition of the Japanese menace here.

He was weighing up the difficulties for the Allies of running what was now a global war when the girl on his right put her hand on his arm.

'They tell me you're in the Home Guard?' She was Vanessa Graham-Poole, and she was small and dark with kind eyes. Rather like Catherine, in fact.

'Yes,' he said. 'Well, actually I'm a captain and nominally in charge, because I'm the only man fit enough to climb over fences.'

───≈≈≈───

There were pale stars in the patch of sky she could see above them, when rescue came. She had not heard voices for a while, except for Max Detweiler's, and he now spoke only occasionally.

'How long have we been here?' she asked once, and he had

answered, 'Hours. Three or four, I think. They'll have had a lot of places to attend to.'

But the rescuers were here now, flashing torches, probing, a dog suddenly above her, its nose wet and cold when it touched her face. Then it barked, and someone called, 'Here, Sarge.'

They lifted the rubble from her, piece by piece. At first she was afraid they would make things worse. She had grown almost used to her tomb, and was reluctant to leave it. But at last they were lifting her, gently. 'There's someone else there – Mr Detweiler.'

'We know, lass. Lie still. We'll get them all.'

She could smell the rescue workers, a strange odour of sweat and urine and something else, fear perhaps. They carried her to an ambulance, and she saw that there were giant floodlights everywhere, so that the work could go on. They paused while someone else was put into the ambulance, and she turned her head. There were things on the grass, long shapes under covers. Bodies. She tried to count – four, five, seven . . . They were lifting her in now, and she wasn't done. But she still saw the shape nearest to her – saw the shoeless foot escaping from the cover, and recognised the anklet, gleaming in the glaring lights.

Tilly had said this morning: '*I'm living, Cath. I'm really living.*' And now she was among the dead.

## Chapter Twenty Two
### December 1941

SARAH GLANCED FROM THE WINDOW as the train rattled through the countryside. It was the first time she had been on a train, and she sat bolt upright, feet together, gloved hands folded neatly over the handbag on her knee. She had not relaxed for a second since the train left Durham, nor would she. The sooner she was back home, the better. The carriage was dirty, filthy even, and packed with service-men and -women. She felt out of place in an ordinary coat and hat. Still, the behaviour of some of them was scandalous. Especially the girls, bold as brass!

There were hills on her left, low and seeming to stretch as far as the eye could see. Hannah Chaffey had told her to watch out for a white horse carved into the hillside, but it was probably another of Hannah's tales. 'She should take up embroidery,' her father had once said, 'the way she can dress things up.'

From time to time Sarah opened her bag, and re-read the letter containing her instructions. Hamish was in an Emergency Hospital in Leeds, and she was on her way there, with a travel warrant all stamped with a government seal. She closed her eyes, trying to remember what had brought her to this day. She had only known him for a few months, and now she was his next of kin and being treated like family. Like a wife! The thought made her hiccup suddenly, and she clapped her hand to her mouth in confusion.

'All right, love?' The soldier was young, with a cheeky face. Sarah turned her head away to indicate her indifference. But the boy persisted. 'I'm only asking if she's all right,' he told the rest of the carriage.

Sarah turned back and looked at him with what she hoped was a withering stare. 'I'm perfectly fine, thank you, and on my way to visit my husband, who is wounded and in hospital. So if you don't mind . . .'

A hush had fallen on the carriage. 'I didn't mean any harm,' the soldier said.

'None done,' Sarah said, more confident now, and turned back to the window. What had possessed her to say that? She could feel a red tide creeping up her neck and into her face. Her husband, Gerard Foxton, was dead, and here was his widow pretending to be married to a man she hardly knew. She stayed glued to the window for what seemed like ages and then tried a crafty peep back into the carriage. No one was looking at her, so she had got away with it. She straightened her hat and went back to her thoughts.

<hr>

'I'm going to go to London,' David said firmly. India finished putting margarine on her toast before she spoke. 'You'd only be in the way. Catherine's not seriously injured, just shaken. I expect she'll be back on duty tomorrow.'

'Don't be silly, India. If she's so unscathed, why did someone else have to ring her parents? Anyway, I'm not arguing. I'm going to ring the hospital this morning and find out exactly how things stand. I'll decide then – but if she needs me, I'm going.'

'Needs you! Oh forgive me, I didn't realise you'd become

medically qualified. Leave her to people who know what they're doing. And by the way, I shall be out tonight, so if you're not eating in tell Mrs Earnshaw.'

David shook out his paper and tried not to retaliate. Her being out tonight would be a blessing, except that he might not be at home himself. Pamela had known only the barest of details when she rang the night before. The hospital had been bombed; Catherine was not in danger; but she was hospitalised.

'If I find out more, I'll ring you,' she had said. But he wasn't waiting. He must find out for himself. India was pushing letters across the table. 'Your post.'

He opened a cream envelope and drew out a sheet of deckle-edged paper. '*Mr and Mrs Edward Graham-Poole invite you to a Christmas Dance at Hardwick House on December 23rd, 1941.*' Graham-Poole – the little girl who had sat next to him at India's dinner party. He wouldn't go, but he must reply. Right now, all he could think of was the need to get to Catherine's side.

---

'The Yanks have been hammered again.' Joyce was always a mine of war news. 'Half the US Air Force, they say. The Japs caught them on the ground, all laid out in rows. Boom, boom, boom, all gone.'

'Where d'you get all this? Hitler's bunker?' The speaker was a middle-aged woman who liked to think of herself as fore-woman, and resented Joyce's ability to provide constant head-lines.

Pamela kept her eyes fixed on the mug held in her cupped hands. She was in no mood to join in a row today, what with Michael gone back to the airfield, and Catherine in hospital. They had assured her it wasn't serious, but sometimes people lied. Her father had suggested she should go, but trains cost money and he had none. A ticket would mop up her savings, and she needed to save if she was to have even the simplest wedding. All the same, she felt guilty. Last night she had tossed and turned, remembering their childhood, Catherine holding her hand on the beach, Catherine showing her how to do French knitting, Catherine in those sunlit days when everything had been a party and there was nothing to worry about. She would ring up tonight, and if there was the least risk to Catherine she would go, even if it meant losing wages for the time off. Michael would want her to go, if he knew.

She thought of him as he had been on that 48 hours' leave – relaxed and happy, until it was time to go back and strain returned to his face.

'Are you afraid?' she had asked him on the station platform.

'We're all frightened,' he had answered. 'You know this could be it, that last trip, and your name wiped from the Ops board. And then you're gaining height, and the fields are below you, like a patchwork, and you have the controls in your hands, and you know what to do, and you forget fear – till you see Jerry spiralling down, and you think it could so easily have been him who got you, and not the other way around.' Pamela had made up her mind then. Next time, she would give in to him, even if she got pregnant and was ruined. She loved him enough for that.

'Wake up, Dolly Daydream. The buzzer's gone.'

She was walking back to her lathe when she remembered something. Her father had had tears in his eyes last night. She had noticed, but not really understood, then. It was because couldn't afford to go to his daughter when she needed him. He hardly had the price of a cigarette. Poor man! Tonight she would tell him that he could go, and she would pay. She would stay here and earn, and he could go to Catherine. That made sense. She put up a hand and switched on her machine.

'You've got a visitor,' the nurse said, hastily smoothing sheets and plumping pillows. The next moment Max Detweiler appeared at the foot of the bed. He was pale, there was a small, stitched wound above his left eye, and one hand was in a sling, but he was smiling.

'Well, then, Catherine,' he said. The nurse was swishing curtains into place around the bed, but Catherine could see her eyes were like saucers. He had called her Catherine! That would be all round the hospital by nightfall.

He sat down beside the bed and took a small bar of chocolate from his pocket. 'I know it should be grapes, but will this do?'

'Chocolate!' she said. 'Wonderful.' She felt suddenly embarrassed, remembering his hand on hers for those long hours.

'Don't worry,' he said, his smile deepening. 'I know all about hospital protocol, but being a foreigner I've never taken it too seriously, and frankly, several hours under rubble does tend to do away with the niceties.'

'I suppose so.' It was her turn to smile, but it soon faded. 'Do you know about Tilly? Nurse Levison? I've asked but they won't tell me.'

'She's dead, I'm afraid. Apparently she was on her way to the canteen when the raid started. She knew we'd need help moving the patients, so –'

'So she needn't have been there.' Catherine was remembering yesterday morning, and Tilly, alive and vibrant and in love with life.

'What about the patients?' she asked at last.

'We lost five, and two are pretty shaken, but alive, thank God.'

'Mayhew?'

Now he could smile again. 'Mayhew's OK, thanks to your mattress technique – plus it was the bottom of the ward that caught the worst of it.'

'It still seems like a dream. A nightmare. One minute we were doing rounds, and then there was a whistling noise and a kind of crump – and then I looked up and there was this hole in the sky.'

'Not in the sky, I hope. The roof maybe.'

'Now you're teasing. You know what I mean.'

'I do. All I remember is plaster and glass spraying all over the place. That's how I got this.' His hand went to his forehead. 'And then the dust, clouds of dust. It got in my mouth.'

'Yes,' she said, 'me too.'

'It didn't stop you talking!'

Catherine felt her cheeks flush. 'What do you mean?'

'Well, I know you're a widow, and titled. Lady Callingham, that has quite a ring to it. Staff Nurse told me – she was very impressed. And you told me you have a house called Mellows, and you'd like a dog when the war is over –'

'Oh Lord, don't tell me any more. I'm sorry.'

'Don't be sorry.' He leaned forward to pat her hand. 'You were very brave. And I talked too.' He chuckled. 'You could say we've been thrown together by Herr Hitler.'

She felt herself relax against her pillows. It was true; no use pretending that yesterday hadn't changed things. 'Tell me about Tilly,' she said. 'Do you know if someone's telling her parents?'

Hamish was clad in the rough blue serge of the wounded soldier, with a white shirt open at the neck. They sat in leatherette armchairs in a small room off the ward, with a nurse popping in from time to time to ask if everything was OK. Sarah had been shocked when she first saw his bandaged head.

'Jerry nearly did for me,' he said, seeing her consternation. She had brought him some home-baked scones and a small bar of chocolate cream. He thanked her, but seemed uninterested in them. What he was keen on, however, was the future.

'I meant what I said, Sarah.' He seemed agitated, and she leaned forward to soothe him.

'There, there,' she said and then, to divert him. 'How did it all happen?'

'It was like being in hell. I saw the bloke next to me go – blood spattering his face. He looked startled, that's all. Just startled, and then he fell on me. I pushed him off, I knew I had to get out of there. But the bastards got me. They say it was shrapnel.' He paused for a moment. 'I'll be all right. I'll be able to work for you.'

He was tearful, now, and she put down the bag and dropped to her knees. 'There, there,' she said again. 'We'll be all right. We'll get you out of here, get you home.' She was saying 'we'. Did she love him, or was it pity she felt? She couldn't decide. Instead she gathered him to her, and they rocked together, gently, to and fro.

***

'Hong Kong will go, of course – any day.' Rupert and India were in the bar of the theatre during the interval. Around them there was a buzz of conversation, the tinkling laughter of women, the deeper braying of men. More than half of the men were in uniform, and a handful of the women wore khaki or blue; but in the main, the women were dressed for the theatre. India approved of that. She had taken care with her own dress, and was using the last of her Worth. There would be no more perfume from France for a while, if ever.

'I thought the Governor had rejected the surrender call?'

'Oh, he did.' Rupert warmed to his subject. 'Of course he did, but they're hopelessly outnumbered. At least 40,000 Japs, and 6 or 7,000 of our troops. Remember there's only 500 yards of water separating Hong Kong from the mainland.'

'Of course, you were out there for a while.'

'ADC to the Governor. I know it well.'

The bell went then, and they went back into the theatre. The play was a Noel Coward revival, and funny enough, but India was glad of the darkness that hid her face as she thought of what she had to do. The silly Graham-Poole girl had set her cap at David: that was obvious. She had mooned over him at the dinner party, and then invited him to the supper dance. Now that India had really thought it through she had realised that it wouldn't do for David to provide the heir to Kynaston. The child would not only share his genes, he would oversee its upbringing. No, with luck he would drop the Graham-Poole girl, or she would get tired of chasing him, and it would all be up to her. It was a pity about the Callingham name but perhaps there could be some sort of compromise: a hyphen, perhaps. The important thing was to keep Kynaston as it was, as it was meant to be.

She glanced at the man sitting next to her. He was handsome, came of a good family, he was just too old to re-enlist, but was young enough to father a child. He would do. And if she had to pretend to be soft and foolish, if it meant staring at him wide-eyed and treating his every nondescript word as oracle, she would.

The journey home seemed to last forever. Sarah gazed from the bus that took her to the station at appalling bomb damage. Houses with their fronts blown off, staircases standing like toy bricks piled one on another, jagged walls with still vivid wallpaper peeling from them. It had been a relief to get on to the train and into open countryside.

What had she done? She tried to remember what she had

said. He had not proposed, he had simply behaved as though it was going to happen. But he had been a broken man, she knew that. She straightened her hat on her head and tried to think straight. She hardly knew him. They had kissed, but when his hand had strayed to her breast she had put it firmly away. There had been no promises. She could still back out.

But did she want to? Would Gerard have wanted her to marry again? If it had meant a better life for his son, he would have – of that she was sure. But what would people say? Hannah Chaffey would be waiting when she got home, the little boy on her hip. Her eyes would widen if she told her, and then she would be out of the house in a flash to put it all round Belgate.

'Squash up, love.' A woman's voice brought her back to earth. There were soldiers piling into the carriage, and she shuffled closer to the window. It was no good thinking about it now. She would deal with it tomorrow.

David had hoped to hear Catherine's voice, but she was in bed and couldn't come to the telephone. 'She's fine,' the Sister had assured him. 'Scratched and bruised but no fractures. She'll be up and about tomorrow, after doctor has seen her, and then she's going home for a week or so. She'll be back with you for Christmas. Now, isn't that lucky?'

He had agreed that it was, asked that his good wishes be given to his sister-in-law, and put down the phone. Now he was on patrol in pitch blackness, his fellow Home Guards panting and puffing behind him. The sky above was overcast – not much chance of a raid tonight, but you could never be sure. Tomorrow he would drive over to Mellows and make sure everything was ready for her homecoming. Unless he could persuade her to convalesce at Kynaston? India would bellyache, but he could deal with that.

Besides, India was a little preoccupied at the moment with her new beau. Her first beau, now that he came to think about it. She had always seemed to hold men in contempt. A wicked thought occurred: India in bed with a man. India naked – on top, obviously. He laughed aloud as the image of a praying mantis came to mind.

There was a splash, and a muffled oath from behind him. 'Never mind bloody laughing, mate. Lend a hand to get this old bugger out of the ditch.'

---

'Are you awake?'

Catherine turned her head on the pillow. 'Yes.'

It was Max again, silhouetted against the dim light of Sister's desk.

'I've just been in to see Mayhew. He sends his love. He calls you "little Cathy", which is odd, as he's never actually seen you. I told him you were fine. And I've made sure our condolences have been sent to Tilly's parents.'

'Thank you,' she said. 'Is Mayhew OK?'

'In surprisingly good form. Very anxious to know when I'll be back on duty and he can go on with his grafts.' There was silence for a moment. 'He's hoping his girl-friend will come to visit at Christmas.'

'Do you think she will?'

'She hasn't, up to now. No rush to the wounded hero's bedside. Still, you never know. You're going home for Christmas, Sister tells me?'

'Yes. What will you do? Can you go home?'

He was sitting down now, leaning closer so as not to disturb the other patients. 'I want to get back to work. There's so much to do here. So many men all desperate, all wondering how they'll face the world. And we're still a rare breed, those of us who can do this kind of work. McIndoe is training people all the while, but there are never enough. So I can wait. I'll stick around the hospital over the holiday. Or there's the Embassy – I dare say I could go there. I know one or two of its people.'

After she said it, Catherine she couldn't work out where the words had come from. Long after he'd left the ward she was still wondering why she had invited him to spend Christmas with her at Mellows.

'I have a friend there, a housekeeper really, so there'd be someone to look after us. It's just a house in quiet countryside but it's peaceful – and you'd be welcome.'

What was even harder to grasp was what could have possessed him to say 'Yes.'

# Chapter Twenty Three

Christmas 1941

CATHERINE WENT HOME TO MELLOWS five days before Christmas. She still felt shaken, and her various bruises were now a wonderful colour, but she felt in command of herself once more. She must have been out of her mind to invite Max Detweiler to stay, but it was done, and, unless he changed his mind, he was coming on the 22nd. His hand was still bandaged but he had discarded the sling, and the stitches were gone from his head wound. 'An English Christmas,' he had said when he last visited her. 'Wait till I tell them back home.'

She had gone to see Mayhew in his new ward before she left the hospital. 'Close shave,' was all he said about the bombing. And of course that's how a pilot would see it – a close shave, but nothing compared to the carnage in the air every day. She promised to come back as soon as she could, and he promised to be gentle with her replacement. He had even laughed a little, as far as she could see, and that was good.

Now she settled back in the railway carriage and thought ahead. She had completely overlooked the fact that Max was a Jew, so she had better keep Christmas trimmings discreet. Holly, perhaps, and a Yule log, nothing more. But the first thing she saw when she came into the hall at Mellows was a Christmas tree, towering to the ceiling, dripping with tinsel and baubles. 'Sir David did it,' Sarah said, beaming approval. 'He wanted everything nice for when you got home.'

David had wanted to meet her train, but she had pleaded uncertainty about times and had come in a cab from the station. She had stumbled through an explanation about Max's visit when they spoke on the phone, and she wasn't sure how he had taken it. There was nothing to it, of course: Max had a wife and children, and, anyway, there was nothing more between them than the bond between colleagues, two people working towards the same end.

Her escape from her troubled thoughts came at the sight of Sarah's son, standing unsteadily by her side. Joe was enchanting now, and the feel and the weight of him in her arms stirred feelings she had never experienced before. Her baby would have been a little boy like this if he had lived? She put her cheek against his head, and wondered. Guilt stirred, too: how long was it since she had last thought of that other Joe, her baby's father? He grew more shadowy in her memory with the passage of time, and yet he had changed the course of her life.

Her family arrived on the first day, her father shabby and older than when she had last seen him, but with a little of his old gravitas restored; her mother still pretty but jaded, and seeming very vague about everything. Pamela, however, was a revelation. Gone was the empty-headed girl who had stamped her foot at every attempt to thwart her. She seemed taller, more poised, not as pretty, and yet more beautiful. Her hands were work-scarred, her nails chipped, but she smiled readily, and seemed genuinely pleased to see Catherine home.

They were coming for Christmas Day, and Pamela was bringing her boyfriend. 'You'll love him, Catherine.' Pamela's speech had coarsened. It was no longer the clipped tones encouraged at their boarding-school, but her voice was animated and more attractive. 'He's a sergeant pilot, and so brave. I can't wait for you to meet him.'

Catherine drew breath, 'There'll be another guest. One of the doctors from the hospital. He's American, and before you ask he's not a boyfriend. He's a colleague with a wife and family back home in New York.'

———

'U-boats are the very devil, and we don't seem able to deal with them.'

David nodded. Across the desk, the solicitor, Gerald Rowbarrow, looked somehow older and greyer than he had been hitherto. He had a soldier son serving in Burma, and another son aboard a Royal Navy frigate. Of course, he looked worried.

'We're having some success, surely?' David said now. 'Combined air and sea power – that should work eventually.'

'I hope so. And if the Russian winter does its job . . .' In Russia the people of Leningrad were still holding out against the Germans, suffering terribly from starvation and cold, but hopeful that they could withstand a Russian winter better than the Germans.

'Apparently Goebbels has been appealing for people to donate their warm clothing, to be sent to the Russian front. So much for meticulous German planning.'

Both men laughed, but it was hollow laughter. They were still uncertain of the outcome of a war that showed no sign of a turning-point.

'How is Henry's widow?' asked Rowbarrow. 'I did hear that she was nursing?'

David tried not to sound too enthusiastic. 'Yes she's a VAD in an Emergency Hospital. It was bombed ten days ago, so she's coming back here to convalesce.'

'She was wounded?' The solicitor sat up in his chair.

'Not seriously. Shaken, I think, and several of her patients were killed.'

'Ah, that must have been distressing. Still, home for Christmas – whatever Christmas we can manage in these strait-ened times.'

'Don't talk of shortages. According to my sister it's all down to the black market. She spends her days hunting a mythical – well, I think it's mythical – van stuffed with illicit produce.'

'She's in the WVS of course. They seem to be running every-thing nowadays. All the same, I was in London last week and dined with a friend at his club. Salmon, freshwater trout – they don't go short there. There was game, too, if you fancied it. But speaking of India, do I scent a romance?'

David held up his hands in horror. 'Don't ask. I try to pretend I don't notice. But if it keeps her busy –' He did not need to say 'and out of my hair' – Rowbarrow knew all too well what India was like.

They completed their business regarding the estate, and David emerged into the winter sunshine, turning up his collar against an east wind and making for his car. Yes, Catherine was home for Christmas. How happy that would have made him, if it hadn't been for the man she was bringing with her.

<hr />

'If you've got a moment?' Sarah had carried coffee in on a tray, and was turning for the door, only to hesitate and turn back to ask her question.

'Of course I've got a moment. But bring another cup. There's enough here for two. We can drink as we talk.'

They sat on either side of the fireplace, sipping coffee until Catherine, impatient, said, 'Well?'

'I've got something to tell you. I hope – well, I hope you'll understand. It's not that I've forgotten Gerard, I'll never do that –' She was hanging her head now, a red flush colouring her neck. Catherine leaned forward to touch her arm.

'But you've met someone else? Well I'm delighted for you.' It all came out then: the pub and the pram outside the shop, the next of kin and the journey to Leeds.

'So you don't think I'm doing wrong?' Sarah's eyes were pleading.

'Of course I don't.'

For a moment Catherine contemplated telling Sarah that she, too, had married in the wake of a lover's death, but this was not the moment for revelation. 'We'll have the wedding here. When will he get out of hospital? I'll get leave, or come just for the day. This is good news, Sarah. And oh, how we need something to cheer us up!'

〰〰

Pamela had found it strange, seeing Catherine again. They were both changed. She could sense it in Catherine, could feel it in herself. She had felt at home here, in the factory, but seeing Catherine again had reminded her of that other world that had vanished with the war. Around her now the women were discussing the relative merits of *Citizen Kane* and *Pimpernel Smith*, two films that were filling the cinemas. 'What do you think, Pammy? Orson Welles or Leslie Howard for a bit of rumpy-pumpy?'

'I haven't seen either film yet. I like Leslie Howard, though. He's very – English.'

There was a roar of laughter. 'You're thinking about that boy of yours. "Very English".' This was said in a 'lah-de-dah' accent, and Pamela grinned.

'Yes, he does look like my Michael. So definitely Leslie for me.'

She let the conversation drift away from her then and thought of Michael's last letter. '*I like sorties at dusk and dawn.*

*Jerry stands out against the sun then, the first or the last of the light. But a moon is good for spotting movement in the Channel. It makes a path across the sea, and you can see a convoy for miles.'* He loved his flying, but a fighter pilot's life was precarious. She couldn't, mustn't lose him now, not when everything seemed to be going right. They said pilots couldn't get away with it, after a certain number of sorties. She didn't know what the exact figure was, nor did she want to know. All she could do was live from day to day. And pray.

As she operated her machine, she tried to banish fearful thoughts and look ahead to Christmas Day. They would all be together, just like before the war: Mummy and Daddy and she and Catherine. But it wasn't like before the war. Michael would be also there, and so would this doctor friend of Catherine's, who was bound to be a boyfriend, no matter what she said. But this time there would be no turkey with all the trimmings, no indulgent parents handing out expensive, gift-wrapped presents. And, besides, both she and Catherine had grown up.

≈≈≈

As the time for Max's arrival drew near, Catherine felt gripped by terror. What would happen if Matron found out? And how on earth would she occupy him for three whole days? Her agitation peaked as his arrival loomed. Despite her protestations, David was meeting him at the station, so she had elected to wait for him at home. Being there when he arrived, with David looking on, would have been too much to bear.

Her anxiety was allayed a little when young Joe awoke and began to cry. Sarah was off scouring the shops for whatever trappings of Christmas were available. No use looking for extra food: they would have to make do with their rations, and the odd tit-bit. She walked the floor with the child until his sobs turned to little moans of disgruntlement. 'There, there,' she said and then again 'there, there.' She had seldom handled a child. Now she was consumed with the wonder of it. She was still walking and rocking when a peal came at the door. No time to put down the boy or the teddy bear he clutched. She carried him into the hall to greet her guest.

David stood on the step, one of Max's bags in his hand. He shook his head at her invitation to come in. 'I must dash, I'm afraid. But Max and I have become acquainted on the drive here. I'll see you both tomorrow.'

'Well,' Max said, when the door was closed, 'have you been keeping something from me?' He was looking at the child, and his eyes were twinkling.

Catherine turned for the kitchen to hide her flaming cheeks. 'This is Joe. He belongs to Sarah, my housekeeper. But come in, let me put Joe down and get you some tea. How was the journey?'

Max had brought goodies: tinned fruit and ham, candied fruit and butter, a jar of caviar, brandy, and, best of all, a plum pudding adorned with holly.

'Where did you get them?' she said, eyes wide.

He tapped his nose with a forefinger. 'We're a resourceful nation, we Americans. Best not to ask.'

They carried them into the kitchen, and then ascended the stairs to his room. 'I think you have everything you need, but do shout if there's anything you want.'

Max had crossed to the window and was looking out at the quiet lane and the fields beyond. 'At last I feel I'm in England,' he said. 'Thank you for taking pity on a foreigner, even if he did keep up your morale under the direst circumstances.'

They both laughed then, remembering darkness and rubble and the electric feeling of seeking fingers finding other fingers to touch and hold.

They were sitting on either side of the sitting-room fire when Sarah returned. Her back was aching, her feet were frozen, and she would have liked nothing better than to put them up in the kitchen, but the formalities had to be observed. Catherine made the introductions, and she shook the surgeon's hand. He was older than she had imagined, a bit grizzled at the temples. But good-looking. A bit like Spencer Tracy, only handsomer. Perhaps Tyrone Power, but stockier. Anyway, he was nice about Joe, and Catherine seemed at ease with him.

She carried her son off to the kitchen, and goggled at the spoils piled on the table. They made her own poor scavenging pale into insignificance, but who cared! Pineapple chunks! She felt her mouth salivate at the very thought. All the same, there had been an atmosphere in the room she had just left. Catherine had told her that Mr Detweiler had a wife and children back in America, but if she, Sarah, was any judge those two were more than nurse and doctor. She would have to keep Hannah Chaffey well away from Mellows until he was safely gone, or Catherine's name would be dragged all round the neighbourhood.

---

'I don't intend to listen to the wireless any more.' India was looking at him, obviously expecting a reply.

David picked at the indeterminate fish on his plate, and obliged. 'Why not?'

'I can't take any more of that annoying Vera Lynn. Forces Sweetheart? She sounds like a cat calling its mate. And the songs! Drippy, nonsensical rubbish, all of them.'

'They say she's good for morale.' David didn't particularly care for Vera Lynn, but if India was against her that was reason enough to defend her.

'Oh, let's change the subject. I should know better than to try to talk sense with you. Let's talk about Christmas. If you can call it Christmas. When I think of the old days, and how good they were . . .'

'Good for some, India. I doubt the peasantry lived it up on turkey and truffles.' The minute he spoke he regretted it: he had risen to the bait. The glitter in his sister's eyes told him that.

'David, do you have to be so argumentative?'

'If the alternative is agreeing with every word you say then, yes, I do. Now, for God's sake tell me about Christmas.' She was bringing Rupert and his mother to share their Christmas lunch. Well, that was all right. They would be a buffer between India and him, and he could probably slope off at some stage and see what was happening at Mellows.

---

Sarah had excused herself from the supper table, and now Max and Catherine, were alone with some of Max's brandy in balloon glasses. It felt oddly right, no trace of embarrassment, and yet they were still strangers. He was talking of the men they cared for. 'I'd done some keloidal work before the war – motoring accidents, industrial, that sort of thing.'

She knew a little about keloid tissue, areas of contracted scar tissue that formed where the skin was drawn over prominent bony areas. It took several months for them to form, and sometimes they would come on the flap edge of a graft.

'The funny thing is, the burns cases do better if they land in the sea. There's more chance of the epidermal adrexal recovering.'

She was out of her depth now, and he noticed it and laughed. 'I'm boring you.'

'No, no.' She sat up in her chair. 'Anything but. It's just that I'm not very knowledgeable.'

'And I'm blinding you with science. Let's change the subject. And let me refill your glass.' He was bending over her, and she could smell him, a warm, soapy, man smell, this time not tainted with the whiff of the hospital.

'Thank you.' She watched the brandy flowing into the glass and wished it would go on forever, so that he would never move away and they could stay like this. He was straightening up, putting the bottle down with his good hand. For some reason she stood up, too. They were face to face, chest to chest. He didn't move away.

'This is crazy,' she said. 'Isn't it?' He kissed her, a long kiss, and then answered her question.

'No. It's war, Catherine. It's war – and we are nothing more than leaves, blown this way and that.'

His mouth was warm and gentle, his arms around her comforting beyond belief. 'Do you want to make love to me?' she asked.

'Very much. But I'm not sure it's fair.'

'None of it is fair, Max. But it's all we have.'

≈

If David had had his way, he would have saddled his mare and ridden until horse and man dropped. but it wouldn't be fair to the animal. Besides, and he smiled wryly at this, he might run into a stray Home Guard patrol and be arrested for his pains. Instead he went into the library, a glass of whisky in his hand. He had not sat here to read for years, not since he was a child. Then it had been Kipling's *Just So Stories* and *Stalky and Co* and John Buchan. Now he took down a slim, suede-covered volume of the poetry of A. E. Housman. He riffled through the pages, reading a line here and there, until he came to one poem that held him. He read it, and then read it again.

> *Into my heart an air that kills*
> *From yon far country blows.*

*What are those blue, remembered hills,*
*What spires, what farms are those?*
*That is the land of Lost Content,*
*I see it shining plain.*
*The happy highways where I went*
*And cannot come again.*

He repeated the last line to himself. He had lost Catherine – not that she had ever been his to lose, but still, he had lost her. He had known it the moment she opened the door and looked at the American on the step. It was there in her face. He had been a fool to ever imagine it could be different, so why, now, could he not bear it?

Tomorrow would be the anniversary of Henry's death. He had loved Henry, missed him every day; but after he had died, in some small part of him a hope had sprung up. A hope that one day . . . But now –

A clock chimed in the hall. It had chimed on the night they heard Henry had died. David had not noticed it then but he remembered it now. And there had been carol singers, 'O Little Town of Bethlehem', and the three of them staring at one another, and no one quite able to take it in.

But even then, even at that moment, he had looked at Catherine and hoped . . . his brother's death just come upon him, and even then . . . Now he grieved, for his brother, for Christmas, and most of all for that happy pre-war highway where he could never come again.

---

They had made love three times. Once savagely, and then once gently, neither of them fully believing it was possible so soon afterwards. And then a third time, after waking in the dark and reaching for each other. Max had cursed his bandaged hand, but wooed her body with the other in a way that thrilled her. So this is love,' she thought, and then again, 'So *this* is love.' Afterwards they slept. It was half-light when she woke again, and stretched out her arm towards him, but the bed was empty. She raised herself on her elbow and saw that he was standing by the window.

'What is it? What's wrong?'

He didn't answer, and she slipped from the bed, pulling on a wrapper and going to his side. 'You're cold. Come back to bed.' She put her arms around him, trying to shield him with her own warmth.

'I didn't intend this. It was wrong, Catherine, wrong of me.' She was shaking her head, but he continued, 'I love Miriam. We were never in love, but I love her. It was a good Jewish marriage. It is a good Jewish marriage. I love my children. I have to go back. When this war is over I must go home. I can't offer you anything.'

'Is that all? I know that. I've always known it. This moment, this little piece of time, is all we have. It's like you said – we're leaves blown by the wind. But we're together in this moment. That's all I expect, all I want.'

He kissed her then, and took her back to bed, where they lay tenderly in one another's arms until the light strengthened and drove the shadows from the room.

# BOOK 3

# Chapter Twenty Four

## April 1942

THE SUN CAME IN THROUGH the split in the curtains just as it did on an ordinary day. Sarah could hear the normal birdsong outside the window, and on the other side of the room her son lay sleeping. But today was different. Today was her wedding day. She lay for a while, contemplating the wonder of it all. Little more than two years ago she had been a girl in her father's house. Now she was a widow, a mother, and soon to be a bride again. How had it happened?

But as she asked the question, her mind supplied the answer. It was war. Without the war she and Gerard would have had a long, tranquil courtship, waited for a house to come up, then married. They would have tried, as far as they were able, not to have a child until they had something to offer it. But war had intervened, telescoped their plans, and ultimately broken their lives in two. Now she was to marry – again, because of the war. Without conflict, Hamish would have served in the Army but never been posted to a hastily built camp in County Durham. Their paths would never have crossed. War had brought him to a foreign place, brought her into his life, and wounded him so that he would bear the scars forever. 'It's up to me,' Sarah thought now. 'I must make it come right for him. And for Gerard's son.'

Eyes tight shut she made her vow, opening them only when Catherine knocked on her door and entered, bearing a tray.

'You shouldn't have bothered.' Sarah struggled up on to the pillows. There was tea on the tray, and toast, and a boiled egg in a cosy.

'Eat up,' Catherine said. 'It's going to be a long day.'

They sat together as she ate, pausing sometimes to admire the blue crêpe dress that hung on the wardrobe. From the moment news of her wedding had got out, her father's door had been busy. '*We hear your Sarah's getting wed. She'll likely need a dress. There's two clothing coupons. It's not much, but it all helps.*' The coupons had come in, in ones and twos until 'the help' had not only covered a dress, but a skirt and blouse, and a blue satin nightdress with lace over the bust. And, to top it all Catherine had given her a tan suede bag and shoes, and a hat, a silly little thing of ruched crêpe to match the dress. It had a veil that came down as far as her nose and made her want to sneeze, but it was the smartest thing she had ever possessed.

'I wonder how Hamish feels now?' Catherine was holding her cup in two hands, and gazing into it. 'He seemed at home with your father and the boys. They'll see to him.'

Last night they had installed the bridegroom in a room at Hannah Chaffey's, just two doors from Sarah's old home.

'Yes,' Sarah said, sinking back on her pillows, 'Dad'll see to him.'

---

'Honestly!'

India lowered her paper in disgust. 'It says here that the Board of Trade is banning embroidery and appliqué on underwear. And lace! How that's helping the war effort I do not know.'

David shrugged, and went on reading his own paper.

German U-boats were wreaking havoc on world shipping. More than 800,000 tons of shipping had been sunk in March, and figures for the current month were predicted to be worse. Oil tankers were suffering most: more than half of the sinkings had been of tankers. How long could it go on without serious interruption to the war effort?

'I hear the Graham-Poole girl has joined the ATS?' India's eyebrows were raised in mock horror.

'Yes,' David said, 'she has, and I think it's marvellous.' He waited for India to say it was a terrible idea, and that Valerie would be forever besmirched, but she said nothing. In fact, her expression seemed one of quiet satisfaction.

'You'll have to eat alone tonight,' she said suddenly. 'Rupert is taking me to the County for dinner.'

'The flesh-pots,' David said wryly. 'No sticking to the five-shilling rule there.'

Hotels were supposed to serve only one-sixth of an ounce of butter with each meal, and one-seventh of an ounce of sugar – two lumps – and no meal was to cost more than five shillings; but these rules were easily got round. A sumptuous meal provided by the black market would cost the legal five shillings, but the accompanying drinks several pounds.

'Anyway, I won't be in for dinner, either,' he said.

'Oh?' India's eyebrows indicated polite interest.

'I'll be at a wedding.'

'Not the Foxton girl? Catherine's caretaker, or whatever she is?'

'She's a housekeeper, India, and yes, she's getting married, and I am invited. In fact, if it interests you, I have an important role: I'm co-ordinating transport.'

'You mean you're running after everyone and using valuable petrol . . . which, I might add, is given you for war purposes.'

'Yes,' he said. He tried not to speak with gusto. 'Yes, I am going to run after bride, groom, cook and bottlewasher, and all against the rules. You could report me, India. You never know, I might be shot for treason – and all over a gallon of petrol.'

'Don't be silly,' she said, but it was a weak response. She had reported others for less, in her role as self-appointed *gauleiter* of the district, David thought, as he returned to his paper, and tried to concentrate on news of the King's award of the George Cross to the island of Malta.

---

Max Detweiler had visited Europe as a student in the years before the war, his life stretching before him like a bright, if pre-dictable, fairy-tale. Now he watched from the train window as wartime Britain unrolled. In stations he saw mostly khaki, interspersed with Air Force blue and the occasional darker blue of naval personnel. Where there were women in mufti, their colours were subdued. When he had left New York, life there was going on much as usual. It still was, if Miriam was to be believed.

He thought of her last letter. '*Aaron is excited about going to his grandparents. "Will Dada be there?" he asked. He can't seem to work out where you are. I tell him, I show him on the globe, but he expects you to be around every corner, down every street. As I do, dear husband. I think I see you in the mart, the park . . . I look up and my heart leaps at the sight of some man. And then I remember. You are not here, on this con-tinent, you are on the other side of the world. And sometimes I cry.*'

That was why he had left the letter behind in his bedside cabinet – because he was betraying the woman who had written it. He was on his way to be with another woman. Tonight he would share her bed, and kiss her mouth, and banish thought of his wife, her children at her knee, who looked for him in parks and shopping marts. 'It's the war,' he told himself. 'It isn't me, it's war.' Not for a second did he believe the excuse, but, equally, he knew himself powerless to invent a better one.

———

'There now. It looks fine.' Pamela stood back to look at her mother. They had washed and pressed her Moygashel suit, and it had come up as good as new. She put her head on one side. 'It needs something. A brooch, perhaps?'

They added a brooch of pink and white brilliants, and her mother sighed with satisfaction. 'That's one good thing about rationing. Remember when we had to have something new for special occasions, and everyone trying to outdo everyone else?'

'It seems like a lifetime ago.'

'Dolly Herbert was the worst,' her mother said. 'Quite vicious, she could be, if anyone wore something twice. And now she's wearing black. Poor Dolly.'

Dolly Herbert's son had been killed in Singapore, and for her the joy had gone out of competing. 'All the same,' her mother was continuing, 'we've never heard from them since . . .' She halted.

'Since Daddy's money went.' Pamela had heard this before. Many times. Most of her parents' friends had been the fair-weather kind, vanishing at the first sign of need. How false that world had been.

'Today we're going to enjoy ourselves,' she said firmly. 'We haven't been to a wedding in ages, and there's sure to be something decent to eat. You know Catherine – she'll have come up with something. So powder your nose while I see to dad. Cathy needs us today.'

'Catherine, dear. Cathy is so . . .'

'Common? That's me now, Mummy. Common as muck. Now get a move on. I want to be there when they all set off.'

They had dressed little Joe in a white romper suit and covered it with a bib in case of accidents. Sarah sat in the new cami-knickers Catherine had just given her. 'I've never had anything like this,' she said wonderingly, fingering the butterflies appliquéd on the hem. 'It's a sin to cover them up.'

'They'll still be there tonight when you undress.' Catherine clipped the last curler into Sarah's hair, and sank back into her chair. 'We're on schedule. In fact, we're ahead of ourselves. Can you believe it?'

Sarah was silent for a while, and when she spoke she sounded quite serious. 'You've been good to me, Cathy. Like a sister. Better than many a sister. Was it because of our Joe?'

It was out now, the question that had hung between them for so long. For a moment Catherine wavered. She could lie. Sarah would not raise the matter again if she quashed it now. But the time had come for truth.

'Partly,' she said. 'I've always liked you, from the beginning, that day I saw you in church. But, yes, I do see Joe in you, and he meant a lot to me.' It all came out, then, the story of that first meeting and how love had grown.

'Would you have wed our Joe, if he'd come back?'

'Yes.' Catherine spoke vehemently. 'Yes. The war would have swept away all the things that kept us apart – silly things.'

Sarah was lost in thought. 'You married Henry Callingham straight after. Joe was hardly gone.' Her voice had hardened.

'I had to,' Catherine said. 'I was carrying Joe's baby. Henry was a kind man. He was going away, and he wanted – needed – to leave someone behind.'

For a moment Sarah was speechless, and then she spoke. 'Did he know?'

'No. I let him think the baby was his. I would have told him, when he came back. When it was over.'

'But he didn't come back. Like Joe. Like Gerard.'

'Yes,' Catherine said.

There was a pause, and then Sarah held out her arms. 'I'm glad you told me, Cathy. It wasn't your fault. None of us are to blame for any of this. I'm getting wed today, and for the life of me I don't know if I'm doing what Gerard would want.'

Afterwards, as she moved around the kitchen, Catherine felt a sense of relief. At last she had told someone, and the load felt lighter. But the relief was short-lived. Somehow, in the telling, the enormity of what she had done had been revealed to her. She had always felt a degree of guilt, assuaged by the idea that no one need ever know what she had done, so no one had been hurt. But two people, her husband and her baby, had died to buy her that immunity. She had escaped punishment, but she would never completely escape the guilt.

Her thoughts were interrupted when the doorbell pealed. She went to answer it. When she returned she was accompanied by Max Detweiler.

'Sarah!' He was moving towards Sarah, who had pulled a dressing-gown over her underwear, but she still blushed and fingered the wretched curlers.

'I'm glad you could come, Doctor.'

He was leaning to brush her cheek with his lips. 'Max. Call me Max. Would I have missed your wedding day?' Sarah accepted the embrace, but when her eyes met Catherine's it was clear what she was thinking: '*He is nice but he is married. Where will this end?*'

And then Catherine's parents and sister were crowding into the room, and introductions were interspersed with greetings, and Sarah could scurry upstairs to don the blue crêpe dress.

David had collected Max Detweiler from the station and deliv-

ered him to Mellows. Now he turned the car in the direction of
Belgate. His next mission was to pick up the bridegroom and
deliver him to the church. He had met Carlyle the night before,
and had found him an amiable enough fellow, though more in
the grip of alcohol than he would have thought wise on a
wedding eve.

Sarah's brothers had been with Hamish, fine enough young
men but unsure of how to handle themselves in the presence of
their employer. David had shared a beer with them, and done
his best, but the wall between them, polite though it was, had
stayed solid. Today he found them solemn-faced, above stiff
white collars and the dark suits that saw Belgate men through
weddings and funerals alike, and quite often served them from
puberty to the grave. A van was transporting the Maguire clan
to the church, but Jim, who was to act as best man, ushered
Hamish into the front passenger seat and climbed into the back.

The Scot seemed composed, even jovial. He was, he
announced as they left the village, glad his war was over. Soon
he would be invalided out on a pension, and he and Sarah could
return to Scotland and make a start on their life together. 'And
lick the wee-un into shape,' he said.

David took his eyes off the road for a second. The Scotsman
was staring straight ahead and there was no hint of a smile on
his lips. How old was Sarah's boy? About eighteen months,
David guessed inexpertly. How could a babe still in arms be
'licked into shape'? Or, more pertinently, how could a baby be
out of shape to need licking?

'I don't think I like you, Carlyle,' he said to himself. And
then the spire of St. Mary's was looming up, and it was time for
his passengers to disembark.

It was a relief when at last Catherine could slip into a pew, little

Joe in her arms, and gaze at the altar before which soon Sarah would stand. Why had she told her? Would it have been better left unsaid? Yet it had felt as though a weight had been lifted from her. Ahead, the window shimmered, red and blue and gold. If Henry had lived, come home, seen a child too far advanced to be his, what would he have done? The sheer enormity of what might have been dried her mouth.

'All right?' Max was looking down at her, his eyes anxious.

'Yes,' she said. 'Yes, I'm fine.' And then the organ was pealing, and Hamish and Jim were rising and turning to look down the aisle. Catherine turned, too, and saw Sarah, on her father's arm, looking every inch the bride, enfolded in that special magic all brides acquire. 'Let them be happy!' Catherine had spoken half-aloud. The baby was looking at her, its eyes round, and Max's hand was on her arm, warm and reassuring.

'It's going to be all right,' she thought then. 'At least, for Sarah it will be all right.'

———

'It's a pity about the cake.' The woman next to Catherine was gazing at the offending item. 'I'm Mrs Chaffey, Sarah's Dad's neighbour. They've done their best, but you can't beat a bit of icening, can you?'

White icing sugar had been forbidden since 1940. Today's cake was small – never enough to go round, Pamela thought – and covered in mock marzipan. The coating was yellow, but that was about the only resemblance it bore to the real thing.

'Never mind,' Pamela said aloud. 'She's a lovely bride, and he seems nice.'

'Hmm,' Mrs Chaffey pursed her lips and hugged her handbag to her bosom. 'Nice is as nice does. He's Scottish.'

Pamela tried to keep her face straight. 'Better than being German,' she said.

Hannah was not to be outdone. 'Not much. I could tell you tales . . .'

For the next 20 minutes Pamela let tales run in one ear and out the other while she thought about Michael. In his last letter he had talked about the conversations he had with fellow pilots. '*Some of them wonder how they'll take to a humdrum, respectable existence after what we're doing now. Johnnie Randall says he's going to set up an air circus, do stunts and that sort of thing for money. I know what I want to do, Pammie. Apart from marrying you, which I hope to do before this bloody war ends, I want to be a schoolmaster. I'll have to train – three years, they say, but I'll get a grant, and I'll work hard. We'll be happy, Pam. Torchie Lord, the New Zealander I told you about, says he's not keen on going home when the war's over, so he doesn't care how long it lasts. But I can't wait to come home to you. To lead an ordinary life again.*'

' . . . so I told her, wipe that grin off your face. Have you ever heard the like?'

'No,' Pamela said hastily. 'No, I've never heard anything like it.' She could have added, 'I've never heard a word of it,' but she smiled as Hannah leaned forward.

'I'll say this for you, you're nothing like I expected. Toffee-nosed bitch, I had you down for, but you're all right. Ordinary.'

'Yes,' Pamela said, 'that's me. Ordinary. An ordinary life: that'll do me.'

David had watched Catherine moving among the guests, making sure everything was running smoothly. 'She has done Sarah proud,' he said to Max.

'Were they friends from childhood?'

David shook his head. 'No. As far as I know they met when Sarah's brother was killed in France. His was the first death in the village. Sadly, not the last. Catherine went to offer sympathy, and she's done what she could for the family since.'

Max was silent, then, and David thought over what he had just said. Was it only three years since England had been at peace? Iron barriers had separated the classes, then. He had not known the men and women who served his family. He had driven through Belgate, that was all.

Catherine had lived in the no-man's land between the upper and lower classes. The Dene, home to traders and the professionals. He had not usually mixed with people from the Dene either – would never have known the Allertons if it had not been for Henry's passion for tennis.

And now he went in and out of homes in Belgate, he was here with the Maguires and the Foxtons and the Allertons, and for the life of him he couldn't see any difference between them. In fact, he felt a greater kinship with them than he felt even with his own sister. The war had not been all bad. It had broken lives, but it had broken those barriers, too, and that was to be applauded.

He glanced at his watch. In an hour he would take bride and groom into Durham, to the guest-house where they would spend their three days of honeymoon. And Catherine and Max would go back to Mellows and climb the stairs . . . He realised he was clenching his hands, and tried to unwind. That was how it was, and he couldn't even blame the war, as everyone did for everything nowadays. If war had not brought Max Detweiler into their lives, he would have had to see Catherine with Henry instead. Together through the years, making love, having children, sharing everything.

Suddenly she was there in front of him. 'David, I haven't had a chance to thank you. You've been a brick today. But then you always are.' And she was reaching up, and her lips were against his cheek and all he could do was stand and mutter, 'Not at all. Not at all.'

'They say Douglas Fairbanks has enlisted.'

Around them the restaurant sparkled, their bottle of wine jutted from ice in the bucket beside them.

India smiled. 'Has he really? Or is it a stunt? You know what film stars are like.'

'No.' Rupert looked earnest. 'No, I think he means it. He was thick with Ribbentrop and Ciano before the war. In London.'

'London?'

Again Rupert nodded. 'Yes, Ribbentrop was here as Ambassador, of course. And Ciano, who is Mussolini's son-in-law, was probably running backwards and forwards as a messenger.'

'So Fairbanks was friendly to the Axis.'

'No, never. Always keen on America weighing in on our side. And now he's a naval lieutenant, so no more film roles for a while.' He lifted a hand to a waiter, and the man hurried to pour more wine. When he had gone, Rupert raised his glass.

'I've been thinking, well, wondering . . . we get on really well, India, we're the same class. Will you marry me?'

She was tempted to point out that they were not quite the same class, but this was not the proper time. She lifted her glass in a mock salute.

'I think I just might do that, Rupert. Once I've got over the shock.'

Max carried the sleeping child upstairs and laid him in his cot. Catherine watched him. He had done this before. His hands were deft, and certain of what was needed. 'He's thinking of his own children,' she realised, and was suddenly afraid.

After they'd left the room, he turned and took her by the elbows, tilting his head back to gaze at her face.

'Well done,' he said. 'I was proud of you today.'

'Did it go off all right?'

'More than all right. It was a triumph.'

'In spite of the cake?'

'I didn't get any, and nor did most people. But yes, in spite of the cake.'

They walked along the landing together, and into her bedroom. She stood as he unbuttoned her dress until it slid to lie in a pool around her feet. He kissed her throat, while his hands reached to unfasten her brassière. When it too fell away, he kissed her breasts, dwelling on the nipples until she felt desire rise within her. Her hands were in his hair, tugging at it until he had struggled free of his own clothes, and they could come together, both hungry, both needing fulfilment, but trying desperately to hold it back in order that they could enjoy it more.

Sarah had hoped they could sit quietly in the lounge when they got to the guest-house, but Hamish would have none of it. 'Let's get to bed,' he said, so loudly that Sarah looked apprehensively at the landlady in case she had heard.

Once in the room, he cast off his jacket and shirt, and she winced as she saw the scars on his body. He still limped from his leg wound, but it was the scar on his forehead that seemed to have darkened as the day wore on.

'Come on,' he said. And then, as she hesitated, 'I'm going to the lavatory. Don't be long.'

He means me to get undressed, she thought. It made sense to undress while he was away, so she did it, slipping on the new nightdress and covering it with the Chinese robe, another gift of Catherine's.

When he came back he advanced on her until she could smell the beer on her breath. 'We don't need this.' The silk robe was removed, and he was reaching down to pull the nightdress up and over her head.

'Put the light out,' she said but he ignored her. 'Come on,' he said, urging her towards the bed. Suddenly and desperately she wanted her baby, so much that a whimper came to her throat. But he was on her, then, and over her, and inside her, and all she could do was accept the grunting and thrashing until it was over, and he rolled away. She lay for a while until his breathing turned to snoring, and then she made her way along the landing to the lavatory.

She sat there, in the dark, and thought of the years ahead. Hamish had smiled at her in the church, he had been good with the baby at the reception, he had been all right, in fact, until the drink had taken him. But it had been his wedding day, after all. And he was still on pills for his wounds – they would have made it worse. No, he would be sorry in the morning and they would start again.

'It's going to be all right,' she said aloud, before she unlocked the door and made her way back to bed.

## Chapter Twenty One

December 1941

'DEPRESSING!' MAX THREW DOWN THE paper in disgust.

'Eat your toast,' Catherine said abstractedly. She was trying to work out how she could make a meal tonight without meat or eggs or fish. The cupboard was well and truly bare. Living in Max's flat would have been perfect if it had not been for the worries of housekeeping. That, and the secrecy. They tried to be discreet, never leaving the hospital together, being completely formal to one another on the ward, and going out together in public as little as possible, but sometimes she wondered why they bothered. The war had changed people's way of thinking. Society was less judgemental – and, after all, Max's other life was on the far side of an ocean. For her own name, she cared not a fig. Tonight other couples could go to a restaurant, taste decent food for a change, if decent food still existed, but for them it wouldn't do.

She looked up to see Max smiling at her. 'What?' she said.

'I should be asking you that question. I tell you Burma is falling to the Japanese, the Germans are mowing down the Russian army, the US have surrendered in Corregidor, and you tell me to eat my toast. What is pre-occupying that British head of yours?'

'Where I can get hold of the only thing not on coupons –

fish,' she said desperately. 'Or we won't eat tonight.'

<hr>

David had retreated to his office as soon as he could decently leave the breakfast table. Normally, he took refuge behind his newspaper, but the headlines today were so depressing that he had skipped whole pages. Without the newspaper, however, he had been forced to watch India admiring the ring Rupert had given her. She had always been obsessed with her hands. Now, with a huge diamond flanked by emeralds adorning her left hand, the obsession had become uncomfortable viewing. David made his excuses and ran for cover in his study.

He was not left in peace for long. 'David,' she was advancing towards his desk and perching on the corner. 'We need to talk.'

'What now, India? I'm rather busy.'

'Rupert and I have been talking.'

'Since you intend to marry him, that sounds like a good idea.'

'Don't be facetious, this is serious. Rupert feels – well, I feel . . . He has offered to take over some of the burden of the estate. The colliery, too, if it helps.'

David felt rage rising within him and tried to control his breathing. 'So Rupert's offered!' he said at last. 'If I thought Rupert really had offered, I might be tempted to go after him with a whip. I suspect, however, that you have prodded the poor fool into this "offer" – if indeed he knows a damn thing about it.'

'David . . .'

'No, don't speak just listen. I am running the estate. I own the estate. I own this house in which I permit you to live. Got that, India? *I* permit . . . *my* house. Now get out of here before I forget we're related and lift my hand to you.'

He saw she was opening her mouth to speak, so he fired his

bombshell. 'And while you're here, I have long wondered how you, an able-bodied young woman, have managed to avoid conscription. Why aren't you in one of the services, or in a factory doing something useful? I said I've wondered, but I'm pretty sure you've done it by something illegal – one of your friends in high places. . .'

She butted in as he drew breath. 'I've got an important job. I co-ordinate . . .'

'Co-ordinate? You mean bully. You bully a lot of utterly decent, well-meaning women into doing your bidding. Oh, the work is useful, and it does need co-ordination, but any one of those women, wives and mothers, even pensioners, could do that co-ordination and free you to do a real job. As Catherine and Valerie are doing. So don't tempt me, India. One more mention of you or your paramour usurping my role here at Kynaston, and I will ask the authorities to look into how you avoided the draft. Please, please, believe I mean what I say.'

For a moment there was silence, and then, without speaking, she straightened up and walked out of the room.

'So they're going to start the grafting soon. It'll be slow. They do an area, then let it rest before they start again. You'll see a face emerge bit by bit, and when it's all there, you'll go home.' She saw a tear form in the twisted socket that was the boy's eye. 'You're half-way there, Spender. Remember when you couldn't see, couldn't close your eyes? You have eyelids now. It's already begun. You heard what Mr Detweiler said: he's going to let you face the world again.'

She stood there, trying to cheer Spender, all the time remembering the state he had been in on admission. His arms, ending in his charred hands, had been propped up in front of him, the fingers half-curved like witch's claws. Every three hours she had

269

injected him with morphine, and then fed him with liquid through a tube. When at last he had spoken, it was to ask for ginger beer. Ginger beer! She had laughed out loud at the incongruity of the request, and from then on there had been a bond between them.

'I'm proud of you, Spender. You're my star patient, so no more doom and gloom.'

When she got back to the desk, the Staff Nurse, Sheila Hodgson, shook her head. 'I wonder if he'll stand the pace?' She was a pretty girl, red-headed and freckled, and Catherine liked her.

'Why do you say that?'

'No reason. Well, he keeps talking about his girlfriend. Joyce this and Joyce that. Doesn't he realise that if she hasn't come by now she never will? We've seen it before. They're either here as soon as we'll let them in, or they vanish.'

All Catherine could do was nod. 'He does seem to be pinning his hopes on her. But there'll be other girls.'

'Do you remember that boy who came in to see Mayhew? Jimmy Pennington was his name, I think. You had a date with him. You borrowed Tilly's coat, I remember. Poor Tilly. Well, Jimmy's died. He was shot down in the Channel.'

'Pendleton,' Catherine said. 'His name was Pendleton. Who told you?'

'Mayhew. He told me just before he was discharged, while you were at that wedding.'

Long after she had gone to prepare the elevenses trolley, Catherine was remembering Jimmy Pendleton's words: '*And then the next day they're not there in the mess, being loud and throwing their weight about, and you think, "It'll be me one day, wiped off the board" – that's what they do when you buy it – everyone saying "Good old Jimmy" and then never mentioning you again.*' But not everyone would forget, Catherine thought. She would remember the feel of him in her arms, and his tears on her cheek when he had confessed to being afraid. She had held him tightly, then. Now, just for a little while, she felt proud of what she had done.

———

The view from the cottage was beautiful. From the door, the ground sloped down to a loch, Loch Earn. Mountains were all around, and there was a wonderful feeling of space. But Sarah had not bargained for the total isolation of the place. It had been quiet at Mellows, but there had been cars passing on the road, or the occasional caller. Here there was only silence.

Today Hamish had gone to Callander to visit old friends, and Joe was sound asleep in the armchair. 'Poor little boy,' she thought, looking down on him, 'you're worn out.' He had not settled in his new home, and their nights had been disturbed because Hamish had banished him from their bedroom and refused to allow her to go to him when he cried.

She would have liked to talk to a priest, and it was troubling her that she had not been to mass since she came here, but the nearest Catholic Church was miles away, and Hamish had told her curtly, when she asked about other Catholics in the area, that the Popish religion was not popular hereabouts and the sooner she forgot it the better. She realised she was wringing her hands and put them down at her sides. Sometimes he was quite loving. He had brought her some wild flowers yesterday, and placed them in a jar. If she kept calm, if she took things a step at a time, it would all come right.

Something between a laugh and a sob bubbled up inside her, but she quelled it. She had made her bed. Now she must lie on it.

———

The woman in front of her looked strained and anxious. 'Not

up to the job,' India thought, and tried not to let her irritation show on her face. 'The rules are quite straightforward,' she said. 'Tell them they can claim at the end of the war, and not before.'

The rules were simple enough. Even a moron like this should understand them. Insurance companies had declined to insure against war damages as soon as war appeared likely. So the War Damage Commission had been set up to make payments for bombed buildings, in order that they could be repaired. But property, goods and chattels, would be paid for only after the cessation of hostilities. At market value 'at the date of damage'. India quoted these exact words now, for she knew them by heart, but the silly woman went on looking hopeless.

'But they need things now,' the woman said. 'All of them. It was a bad raid, and there are 17 families in the rest centre.'

India drummed on her desk with her fingernails. 'Well, I don't care. If their income exceeds £400 per annum, we can't help.'

'Some of them are pensioners. I don't suppose they have that sort of income.'

'Then find out! Don't come in here bleating to me, do some checking. And if they give you trouble, tell them they'll get nothing at all.'

When the woman had gone, India sighed and tilted back her chair. Only the sight of the light glancing off her ring lifted her mood. They really were splendid emeralds. Emeralds could differ horribly, but these were perfect. However, even her ring couldn't completely lift her mood. If there were 17 families in the rest centre, the likelihood was they'd need rehousing. Unoccupied homes could be requisitioned, or she could billet them on people. She had the authority.

Suddenly, she thought of Mellows, standing empty since the Foxton woman had gone. It would serve Catherine Allerton right if India arranged for it to be requisitioned. She reached for writing paper. All of a sudden the day was turning out not quite as badly as she'd feared.

≈

When David approached Mellows, he saw that the front door stood open. Strange! He was climbing out of the driving-seat when a figure emerged. A small part of him had seen the open door and hoped against hope that it was Catherine, returned unexpectedly. But it was Mrs Chaffey, the woman Catherine had hired to clean occasionally, staggering under the weight of a rug.

'Mr Callingham. Ooh. . .' She clapped a hand to her mouth. 'Sir Callingham. No . . .' The rug was threatening to engulf her.

'Call me David,' he said and took the rug from her. 'Where do you want this?'

'On the grass, if you don't mind. I'm bottoming that hall – but I could make you a cup of tea.'

It was hot, and David was tired. 'Why not?' he said.

Half an hour later, he was regretting that. The tea was good, but the stream of conversation which accompanied it rolled over him like lava in full flow. They had disembowelled Sarah's wedding-cake, which had had to be made without any of the proper ingredients. Mrs Chaffey made the lack of candied peel and glacé cherries sound like war crimes. As for white icening sugar . . .' He kept itching to correct her, and say 'icing', but she wouldn't have heard him, so ceaseless was her talk. 'There's rabbits when you can get them, but two shillings apiece? Scandalous, when they're teeming round your doors. Fish one and four a pound! And if I never see another herring, it'll be too soon. And then there's everything else . . .' She paused for a sip of tea and he seized his chance.

'Yes, it's difficult for women nowadays.' He was rising to his feet, but the mention of women had primed the pump.

'Not just women! Where's your razor blades and cigarettes? Down the pit all day and can't have a smoke. I tell you, Hitler's got a lot to answer for!' Her words followed him down the steps. 'If you hear from Catherine before I do, tell her I've got everything ship-shape here, mind.'

David promised to give Mrs Chaffey a glowing reference when he spoke to his sister-in-law, and breathed a sigh of relief as he gunned the car down the drive. She had done him one favour, however – given him an excuse to ring Catherine and tell her all was well. He pursed his lips and began to whistle a Noel Coward song, or was it Ivor Novello? *'I'll see you again, whenever spring breaks through again . . .'*

---

Staff Nurse Hodgson filled two mugs, and pushed one towards Catherine. 'Drink up. We've got half an hour before Queenie gets back.'

'She's not so bad,' Catherine said. 'She was lovely to that boy yesterday'

'Nineteen,' Hodgson said into her mug, 'only 19. He'd done no living at all. It was his air passages, and the effects of the searing flames. Queenie never left him till he was gone. His mouth was dry after the anaesthetic, and she just sat there putting ice to his mouth and whispering to him. She's a right cow, but, by gum, she knows her stuff.'

Catherine nodded, and she was seeking for something to say when Hodgson spoke again. 'At least my George has had a life.'

'He's all right, though?' Catherine's voice showed alarm. The Staff Nurse had spoken as though George were dead.

Hodgson threw back her head and laughed. 'He's OK. Nine lives, that one. He was torpedoed first few months of the war, picked up by the Jerries – well, that was lucky, for a start, because some German captains machine-gun survivors in the water. Anyway, he was on a Jerry ship, battened under hatches, when it docked in Norway. Norway wasn't in the war then, and the Norwegian dockers got them out. Then he was on a tanker, in a convoy, and the U-boats got the ships before him and behind. How's that for jammy? I tell him third time catchy-time, and he just laughs.

'He's leaving the sea after the war. He wants to be a bookie. A bookie! Still, as long as he's OK.'

'Will you wait till then to get married?'

The red head shook until the white cap threatened to tumble. 'I'm having him down the aisle next leave. Before someone else snaps him up.'

Outside there was the sound of heels on the tiled corridor. 'Stand by your beds, everyone. Here comes Queenie.'

The QA was not alone. Max was just behind her as she swept on to the ward. He followed her, but not before he had whispered to Catherine, 'I've got sausages for tonight – and don't ask how or where.'

<hr/>

Her mother had pulled out all the stops for dinner. There was cheese and leek pie, with nice veg., and a delicious apple concoction with custard. 'I tried for some meat, sausage, anything,' she had whispered in the kitchen. 'I told them we had a pilot staying. He offered me two kidneys. What can you do with kidney if you've no steak?'

'It was lovely, Mum. You've done him proud.'

Her mother was holding the teapot, turning it round so that hot water warmed it before she made the tea. 'He looks tired, Pamela. Worn out.'

Michael did look tired. He had been given unexpected leave because half his flight had been shot down. She had noticed his hands shaking slightly over supper, but he would be all right now, now that she had him home. 'I've put him in your room,' her mother said. 'And I've laid out towels. I thought you'd like that. I've made up the bed in the spare room for you.'

'Thanks,' Pamela said. A thought struck her: not so long ago she had thrown a tantrum because her parents had not let her have Catherine's room when she married Henry. As if it mattered where you slept, as long as you were alive. Tonight when the house was silent, she would tiptoe along the landing to climb into Michael's bed, and love him till the strain and fear of war was banished.

≈

Outside the window, the London traffic continued unabated, in spite of the lateness of the hour. Carefully, so as not to wake Catherine, Max raised himself on an elbow, and craned to see the bedside clock. Two a. m. Back home, Miriam would be feeding his children, trying to slow things down so they would be ready for bed.. He thought of Aaron, but it was hard to summon up the boy's face – he had not seen him for two years, now. He would have grown. His daughter had been a baby when he left the States. Would she even remember him? '*I talk to them about you, my darling, and tell them you are doing this for them. So that they will be safe and grow up free.*' That was what Miriam had written, trying to comfort him.

There was still no news of her family in France. There had been no news of them for more than a year now. Tonight he had read about Jews in France and the Netherlands being forced to wear a yellow star. In Poland a new camp had been set up, in woods near the river. Called Sobibor, it was near a railway line, to make for easier transport. Jews were not being taken there as forced labour – there were no factories within miles. They were being taken there to be exterminated, as was already happening at Belzec and Mazdenek and Treblinka and Auschwitz. 'They mean to wipe us out,' Max thought, and felt fear in his belly.

On his closed eyelids he pictured Shabbat, Miriam's face rapt above the candles as she cared for her family. If the impossible happened, and the Allies failed, they would take his family and burn them like *drek*.

Beside him, Catherine stirred, turned on her side and slept again. He couldn't sleep for tormenting thoughts. He loved his wife, but he loved Catherine too, a situation he would have thought impossible. 'God help me,' he thought. But God had not helped the Jews of Poland. Perhaps there was no God? That was a possibility he could not bear to contemplate.

He turned on his side until he fitted against the warm body next to him, and slipped his arm over her. There was comfort in closeness, sometimes the only comfort you could get.

# Chapter Twenty Six

## November 1942

SARAH WAS AWAKE LONG BEFORE dawn, listening to the birds singing their hearts out in total darkness. She would have liked to ease from the bed and go to check on her son, but if she moved Hamish might wake. She thought of last night, the mood black upon him. His rage had been directed at everything – at his body which was refusing to heal, his inability to return to Army service or get other work, the lack of understanding on the part of authority, his neighbours, almost anyone – but especially at her and little Joe. 'Can't you stop that child crying?' he had shouted, and had taken the child's terrified response as defiance.

She watched the light creep stealthily through the thin curtains. Things would be better today. His pension was due; someone might offer him work; she would cook something to tickle his palate; little Joe would be an angel. And if the mood in the house was good, peaceful, she might tell him about that other baby, growing now inside her. His son or daughter. That might be all he needed. Something of his own to cherish.

And soon it would be Christmas. There was holly aplenty in the woods around. And Christmas trees everywhere. Food was more plentiful in Scotland. They would have a bird, and plum pudding – or as near as you could get without cherries and fruit. Hannah Chaffey had used carrot last Christmas, and her pudding had tasted almost real. What had Catherine said in her last letter? '*I think of you often, up there in such a lovely setting, in your little house, the three of you together, safe and sound.*' She let a tear escape her clenched lid, and felt it progress down her cheek, around her nose and down. And then she turned her face into the pillow, and tried not to think about the coming day.

Tilly had been dead for almost a year now, Catherine thought, as they cleared the breakfast trays. Her place had been taken by a new VAD, a girl from Northern Ireland who had been strictly brought up and was in constant fear of Divine retribution. 'Tilly was fearless,' Catherine remembered. She would have approved of Catherine's moving in with Max. '*You go for it,*' she would have said. '*You only live once.*'

But the mood of the war was changing now. No longer did people say 'if' the Allies won. They talked of 'when'. And when the war did end, her relationship with Max would end, too. She finished stacking the trolley for the porter who would return it to the kitchen, and went off in search of something to occupy her mind.

She was sitting at the desk entering case notes when a figure loomed up. It was Stephen Baker, almost the first of the pilots she had nursed. The vividness of his scars had faded, and there was a new light in his eyes, which was explained by the pretty girl at his side.

'Hello, Nurse. Wondered if you'd still be here.'

'I'm still here, Baker. But look at you . . .' She turned to the girl. 'Has he told you what a bad patient he was?' She was smiling as she said it, but the girl looked up at Baker and nodded.

'No, but I can imagine.' She put a proprietary hand on his arm and Catherine saw the small, winking diamond on her ring finger.

'This is Daphne, my fiancée.' Catherine was moved by the pride in his voice. 'I want to see Johnny Spender, if he's still here. I don't know him, but his sister was at school with my sister. She asked me to look him up.'

'I'm delighted for you both. Of course you can see Spender, but –'

'– if Queenie comes back, we have to hide under the bed. I know the drill,' Baker said, and then, turning to his fiancée, 'Queenie is the Wing-Co and a dragon.'

Catherine saw them settled at Spender's bedside, and then sat down again. But the case notes no longer held her attention. She had just witnessed a happy ending. If they happened for other people, perhaps there could be one for her?

———

'So I'm sorry, India, I'm afraid they're not interested. It's too big for individual civilian use, and not big enough for anything else.'

'I see,' India said, trying not to sound disappointed. 'Well, I thought it was worth suggesting. An empty house, and people in need of accommodation. Still . . .' She mouthed platitudes until the man rang off and she could replace the receiver and let out her irritation.

She had put Mellows forward for requisition, but they it had been turned down. It would have served Catherine Allerton right, pretending to nurse in London, keeping David hanging on her every word. She should never have been given Mellows outright. When the war was over and Kynaston restored to greatness and fully staffed, the estate would need such houses.

Still, no point in brooding. She drew the folder marked

'Wedding' from a desk drawer, and tried to lose herself in planning.

———

'I tell you, it was bloody marvellous.' The speaker spooned sorbet into his mouth and savoured it. 'The old man standing there, looking like a Buddha – you know, that cherubic but inscrutable look. Everyone hanging on his words, and the words just rolled out. No notes, or none I could see.'

Rommel, the Desert Fox, was in retreat at last. He was said to be short of fuel, and had only a fraction of the number of tanks possessed by his adversary. Now his Afrika Korps was withdrawing, as General Montgomery's Eighth Army surged forward at El Alamein. Churchill was overjoyed, and the nation was rejoicing with him.

'He'd spoken in the House earlier, hadn't he?' David asked. Around them, the murmur of conversation in their club seemed to have a new note. Optimism, perhaps.

His lunch companion was nodding vigorously. 'He said he'd offered nothing but blood, toil and sweat – you remember that speech in 1940 – and then he said: 'Now, however, the bright gleam has caught the helmets of our soldiers and warmed and cheered all our hearts.'

'You've got it off by heart,' David said, laughing indulgently.

'Too bloody right, my friend. If they could bottle the great man's words, I'd drink them. But the best bit came at Mansion House, the Lord Mayor's luncheon after the House. "Now this is not the end. It is not even the beginning of the end, but it is, perhaps, the end of the beginning." He put the last spoon of dessert into his mouth, and then wiped his lips with his napkin.'I tell you, he's worth a battalion, two battalions, every time he opens his mouth.

'Anyway, enough about Churchill. What brings you up to town?'

'Business,' David said. 'Odds and ends, you know.' He sipped his claret then, unwilling to say more. In fact he had come to London with one purpose only, to see Catherine. Tonight he would sit opposite her in a dimly lit restaurant, and already expectation was drying his mouth.

＝＝＝

'Yes,' Max said, straightening up from the bed, 'healing nicely. And you, my friend, seem very chipper. News from home?'

The boy's eyes gleamed in their scarred sockets. 'Baker came in yesterday. You remember Baker? He said you would.'

'Indeed I do. Worse patient than you, Spender, and that is saying a lot.'

'Well, he's engaged. How about that? A lovely girl, Daphne something. And his face – well, you've always said scars would fade, and I could see it on him. Actually see it.'

'So he looked OK?'

'He did indeed look OK. You're a great man, sir!'

'Don't speak to soon. I plan on giving you a Schnozzle Durante nose.' They competed with one another to imitate the Durante drawl and parted laughing. There are times, Max thought, as he left the ward, when I know why I make the effort'. He would tell Catherine tonight and she would be pleased.

＝＝＝

Pamela read the letter a second time, drinking in the words.

*'I love you, Pam. I think I always will. You can tell the boys who have someone they care about; they're different from the unattached men. Calmer, I suppose. More secure. Not that we ever talk about it. We don't talk about anything much. Not the war or the peace, come to that. No one mentions the war's end*

*although we must all be thinking about it, and I know where I want to be then. With you. We never discuss how we hope the world will be after the war, or what will happen to Europe, or who we'll vote for when an election comes. We don't talk about our women, either. Not if they're important to us. Well, not much. There's a lot of ribaldry from the unattached, all trying to seem a greater rake than anyone else – but it's all bravado. Anything to stop us thinking about the night's op, and wondering who'll come back and who won't. We just talk about nothing really – the canteen and the weather and who beat who at cards. And then we get a red alert and it's all systems go. We don't talk about changing the world, Pammy. We just concentrate on staying alive.'*

The letter ended with '*All my love, darling*' and a row of kisses. Did they really talk about nothing when they knew each conversation could be their last?

She folded the flimsy writing paper and tucked it back under her pillow. Tomorrow she would hide it in her undie drawer with all the others, but tonight it was still too precious to put away.

Downstairs her mother was wide-eyed at the contents of her *Woman and Home*. 'It says here they're soaking engineers' blueprints so the paper will dissolve and the linen can be used for blouses and shirts.'

'But it'll be practically see-through then,' Pamela said.

'Well, you'd think so, but that Lux advert said you could use the best bits of old lace curtains to make brassières. Said it would look really French.'

Pamela wrinkled her nose at the prospect of a lace bra. 'I want to get hold of some parachute silk, if I can. It's like gold dust, but some folks manage.'

'Black market.' That was her father. 'You can get anything on the black market. The papers are full of it. Spivs, they're called. A spiv can get you anything.'

'Well, if you meet one, get me some parachute silk.'

'How much?' he said, and chuckled when she threatened to lob a cushion his way.

'Now, now,' her mother reproved them, from deep in her magazine. 'It says candlewick bedspreads can make dressing-gowns – and you can re-gusset knickers with old tea-towels.'

'That's disgusting,' Pamela said, but her mother ploughed on. 'Apparently you can get two pairs of boy's trousers or a skirt out of one set of plus fours!' She looked up at her husband. 'Daddy?'

Her father didn't raise his eyes from the book he was reading. 'No,' he said emphatically. 'Definitely not. I'm keeping them. They're Harris tweed – and the last time I counted we didn't have any boys.'

'We're all right now,' Pamela thought. 'We're a family again. One day Catherine will come home, and I'll be with Michael, but we'll still be a family.' The cut on her left palm where a sliver of metal at her machine had caught her was stinging, but it seemed not to matter.

She thought of the letter upstairs – '*I love you, Pam. I think I always will*' – and was happy. Until she remembered that tonight, as on most nights, Michael would be high in the heavens, trying to avoid being silhouetted against the moon, and thereby becoming an easy target for another plane or the searchlights down below.

---

The steaks were tiny compared with pre-war ones, but were still delicious. Around them Darlesden society ate and drank, for all the world as though the war were over. She could see Felicity Tarleton with a man who wore the red tabs of a brigadier, and the Graham-Pooles were in an alcove, mother and father with silly Valerie, who was supposed to be a soldier but still pursued

David like a love-sick cow whenever she was on leave.

'How is David?' Rupert asked suddenly.

Still being David,' she said. 'Flapping around pretending to be busy while the estate crumbles. I only hope we keep afloat until the end of the war, when we get an agent back. I daren't ask about the colliery.'

'The pits will go at the end of the war.' Rupert said it as a statement of fact, and it shook her.

'You mean they'll close down?'

'Nationalisation. The Labour Party is pledged to bring it about.'

'But Churchill would never countenance that. Public ownership? Surely that's Communism?'

'I very much doubt whether Churchill will have any say in it, India. There's a new mood abroad. Men who would never have set foot outside their villages have travelled the world courtesy of Herr Hitler. They won't come back and be grateful for what they can get: they'll want more. Women, too. You would never have held down a job as you do now, if it hadn't been for the war. Don't you feel stirred?'

Inside India resentment grew. She didn't feel in the least bit stirred. She felt as though the pattern of her life had been violated. She glanced at her hands, seeking reassurance before she replied, 'I suppose I do. See a need for change, I mean. All the same – nationalisation! That's a step too far.'

<hr/>

'Where do they get the food from? I hear such tales from Mummy and Pamela, who say they're literally starving, and we've just dined like kings.'

'Black market, I suppose.' David reached for the wine, a good Sauvignon, and refilled her glass. 'India goes on and on about it. According to her, County Durham is a hotbed of villains, haunting the side roads in unmarked vans, poaching, raiding houses. As for pigs, that really drives her mad – the thought of someone getting some illicit bacon.'

'Is she in control of food, too?'

'Food, billeting, war damage, breathing . . .' They were both laughing now. 'You think I'm joking, but I'll have you know she would say "Breathe in, breathe out" if she could.'

'Hasn't love mellowed her?'

'Nothing will change my sister. A mere man make her alter her ways? Please! She is inordinately fond of her ring, though. It's big, Kynaston standard. Everything must be Kynaston standard for India.'

'And I never was.'

The note of regret in her voice emboldened David. He put out a hand, and covered hers where it lay on the table. 'You were good enough for my brother. Never forget that.'

'Thank you.'

'Now, how is the good doctor? And is he good to you?'

'Very. We have a flat together – don't tell anyone at home, but it made sense. Does make sense. We don't go out much, but he's introduced me to music. He loves music.'

'Classical or dance?'

'Classical. He loves Tchaikovsky and Mahler and Debussy. There's a haunting thing by Debussy . . .'

'*Claire de Lune*?'

'That's it. I like that, and a thing he calls *Andante Cantabile*.'

'Tchaikovsky?'

'Yes. That makes me feel peaceful. Max laughs about that, and calls it my sleep-inducer, because I get so relaxed when I listen to it that my eyelids droop.'

Her face had softened, and it seared David's soul. She and Max together in some flat, music on the gramophone, her eyes closing, their bodies entwining –

'Let me tell you about Churchill,' he said brusquely. 'I

lunched at my club today, and the talk was all about his speech at the Mansion House.'

He rolled off her at last, and within a minute he was snoring. Sarah lay quietly, willing herself not to move in case she woke him. Tonight she had seen a mark on her son's leg. A red mark. A hand print. She had heard little Joe crying as she pegged out washing, and she'd hurried to use the last pegs and get in to console him. But the crying had ceased abruptly, and when she came into the house he was quiet except for a hiccup now and then. But undressing him tonight she had seen the mark – a weal, that was what it was. She had raised it with Hamish, who had flown into a rage. Was that what she thought of him, that he would strike a child?

She had backed down, then, because she was afraid, and had kept herself to herself until it was time for bed, but it was useless. He had been at her as soon as she slipped between the sheets. Through the uncurtained window she could see the sky. The stars were more visible here than at home, but it was the same sky. In her father's house they would be settling for the night, murmuring goodnights, stoking the fire and covering it with ash to slow its burning so that it lasted through the night.

Tears flowed freely over her cheeks, and she tried not to sniffle. Soon there would be another baby, a child Hamish could call his own. It would be all right then. He was a good man, really. It was just the war.

# Chapter Twenty Seven

January 1943

Catherine had dreaded the time that Max would be away in the United States, but in fact it had flown by. At Christmas, she had worked on the wards, so she had had no sense of abandonment, just a huge desire to provide the men with as good a Christmas as could be managed. Now she cleared away her breakfast dishes, glanced round to make sure everything was ready for Max's return, and donned her great-coat and hat for the bus journey to the hospital.

She squeezed into a window seat, leaned her face against the glass, and couldn't repress a frisson of fear. Would he come back a changed man? Would Miriam have won him over, so that he put her, Catherine, away? And what about his children? As she got up to alight, a terrible thought struck her. What if he hadn't come back at all? His chance to go home for a visit had come out of the blue. '*They can get me on a flight that goes out tonight. I'll be back in a week – ten days, tops. It's an embassy flight. They knew I hadn't been home for so long.*'

His eyes had been pleading, so she had packed his case, and wished him bon voyage, all the time feeling as though her heart would break. It was not Miriam she feared, it was what the sight of his children might do to him. She hurried off the bus, putting anxiety to the back of her mind in her determination to do a good day's work.

As soon as she hit the ward, she knew something was wrong. Even Queenie looked forlorn, and slightly dishevelled, although Catherine could not put her finger on an actual error in her appearance. It was the ward-maid who told her what was wrong.

'Poor Staff Nurse, word's just come – a ship's gone down in the Barents sea. Her man wouldn't last for a minute in those temperatures. Probably just as well.'

A convoy bound for Murmansk had been scattered by heavy gales, and a German U-boat had seized its chance. 'Where is she?' Catherine asked, thinking of Hodgson with her red hair and freckles and ready smile. The day after that boy had died, she had said: '*He's got nine lives, my George.*' She put up a hand to her mouth to still her anguish, but Queenie was recovering herself and swooping down on them.

'None of your business where she is, Nurse. We're shorthanded, so stop asking questions and get on with it.'

There was one bit of good news, however. Spender had had a letter from his sweetheart. 'Never!' Catherine said, and was assured by a fellow VAD that it was true.

'Says she couldn't trace him – a likely story. Anyway, she's found him now, and she says she's going to visit. I only hope she means what she says.'

---

Even inside worn slippers, David's feet felt the chill of sodden fields. All night his patrol troop had ploughed up and down, going through the motions of being a fighting force. He had felt water penetrate his boots, and been astonished. Was nothing made to last any more? He would have to be more generous with the dubbing, that was all he could do. Now he sat down at the breakfast table, and took up his paper. But if he hoped for uplift, he was in for a disappointment.

A few weeks before, in the House of Commons, Anthony Eden had condemned the Nazis' systematic extermination of Europe's Jews, and promised retribution after the war. The declaration had been broadcast across Europe by the BBC, but much good it had done to the Jews walled up in the Warsaw Ghetto. Now they had sent a warning that they were poised on the brink of annihilation. '*We notify you of the greatest crime of all times, about the murder of millions of Jews . . . respond, at least, in the last days of our life.*'

He closed the paper and pushed it away from him. There was nothing to be done, he accepted that, but the scream in these words still rang in his ears. He was pondering how slight a problem cold, damp feet really were when Mrs Earnshaw brought in the post, and his heart leaped at the sight of a letter from Catherine. It was not the only surprise.

'There's a lady asking for you, Sir David, a young lady. A Miss Graham-Poole.'

───

'You can button up now.' The doctor removed the stethoscope from his ears and went back to his notes. 'You have a wee boy already?'

Sarah nodded. 'He's two and a half.'

'Well, it looks like he'll have a wee brother or sister. Your breasts are engorged and you've missed your monthlies, but we'll leave an internal examination for a while yet. Let's get you some extra vitamins'. She knew about that: pregnant women and children had extra milk and eggs. Being under five, little Joe already got orange juice, rosehip syrup, and cod-liver oil, but only half the meat ration. She was about to say 'Thank you,' when the doctor cleared his throat. 'You've a bruise or two, on your arms and chest.'

'Yes,' Sarah said. The button at her neck would not do up, no matter how hard she struggled.

'Aye – it's easily done. Women bruise easily.'

'Yes,' Sarah said again. All she wanted now was to escape from this man and reclaim little Joe from the receptionist.

'Hamish OK?' She nodded and the doctor smiled. 'War does strange things to men, upsets them. But with patience . . .'

He knows, Sarah thought. He knows, but he doesn't intend to do anything about it. Last night, Hamish had taken her by the arms and then by the throat. 'Why are you making me do this?' he had said. And then again, 'Why do you make me do this?'

He had asked it again and again until he got the right answer. 'I don't know,' she had said at last, and he had hit her across the mouth to signal it was over.

~~~~~~~

There was a picture on the front page of the morning paper of Roosevelt and Churchill together at Casablanca. The name 'Casablanca' seemed to be on everyone's lips lately, as Ingrid Bergman and Humphrey Bogart were starring in a film set there. India had never seen Bogart as a screen lover. He looked coarse, although they said he came from a good background. And the other male lead, Paul Henreid, was presentable enough but foreign. Where were the good British leading men?

There was some other lunacy in the paper about the TUC wanting women to receive equal compensation with men for war injuries. They would be asking for equal pay next. And worst of all, the heads of the women's services were supporting it. The war had a lot to answer for!

She put the paper aside in disgust, and went back to wrestling with the accommodation folder. Everyone, or so it sometimes seemed, wanted to be somewhere else. If she had been able to get her hands on Mellows – well, she would try again, but not for a week or two. It didn't do to look as though you were defying decisions.

She sat back for a moment, considering how good she was at managing unreasonable people. Petty little people, with too much power in their hands. It was war, of course; it scrambled everything so that substandard people were suddenly brought to the top, rather like earthworms forked up by the digger and wriggling in the unaccustomed light.

Pleased with such a clever analogy, she went back to the accommodation file with renewed vigour.

---

Around Pamela, the machines whirred and clattered. The news from North Africa had had a good effect on everyone. 'The tide is turning,' she thought. When the buzzer went for break, they sipped their tea and talked of peace-time plans – mostly of the houses they would have, but sometimes about the meals they would make, meals laden with meat and butter and all the delicacies so long denied them. It was food today.

'I'm going to eat sugar with a spoon,' one girl said defiantly. 'Never mind in bloody tea, I'm going to make a meal of it.'

'Golden syrup,' another said.

'And chocolate spread, and butter icing.'

There was a chorus of 'Shut up!' when longing became too much to bear.

'Do you think they talk about food?' one woman said. 'Men, I mean?'

'Sex.' The woman in the orange turban spoke flatly. 'They talk about sex. Kinky sex. All the stuff they've seen abroad. God help us when they get back – we'll be doing it upside down and sideways, mark my words.'

There was general laughter, but Pamela did not join in. Another girl was also suddenly thoughtful. 'There's bound to be change, isn't there? We can't just pick up where we left off, as though none of it has happened.'

Pamela was remembering what Michael had told her in his last letter: '*No one mentions the war's end, although we must all be thinking about it. We don't talk about changing the world, we just concentrate on staying alive.*'

'Penny for 'em, Pammy?' The orange-turbaned woman was leaning towards her.

'Not worth a penny, Gracie. I was wondering if I can afford a new dress for Christmas. Coupons, I mean. I've forgotten what it's like to dress up.'

The conversation moved safely on to coupons, then, and the level of hem lines. It stayed there till the buzzer went, and it was time to go back to the bench.

———

Catherine had given Spender his medication and changed his dressings, all the time listening to his plans for the future. They centred on this Joyce, who was assuming Betty Grable proportions in Catherine's mind's eye. She murmured 'wonderful' and 'marvellous' in between 'sorry', when she knew she was causing him pain. But today he seemed impervious to the pain.

'That's wonderful,' she said again, but he seemed not to hear. The face with its patchwork of grafts and burned skin remained oddly immobile, though emotion poured forth in his voice. 'I knew she'd come. She's really a splendid girl. And funny! That's why I liked her, right from the first time she came to the mess. She could always make everyone laugh. I will be all right by then, won't I? She says a week or two?'

'Of course you will, but if you don't settle down and get some rest, I won't let her into the ward.'

'You wouldn't do that, you haven't got it in you.' But he was settling back on the pillows, allowing her to smooth the sheets over him so that his hands, still clawlike, could rest there.

'Please let it be all right for Spender,' Catherine thought as she walked away. 'And let it be all right for me tonight. Let Max come home.'

The dining-room of the Grand Hotel was dimly lit, as befitted war-time, but otherwise it looked very much as it had always done. Silverware gleamed on a vast buffet-sideboard, waiters moved about like black-and-white penguins, the air was heavy with the smell of food. Opposite David, Valerie Graham-Poole picked at her food and responded shyly to his attempts at conversation. Yes, she was glad Christmas was over. Certainly she had enjoyed it. Yes, she was enjoying her Army service. In a pre-war world she would never have worked at all, David thought, simply bided her time until she married. Now she was in the ATS, in spite of her parents' reservations about the rough and tumble of service life.

David thought he detected a note of wistfulness in her voice, then, and pursued it. She had wanted to join the Wrens. Had always wanted to go to sea. But Daddy had said only a certain type of women joined the services, and she was better off serving her country at home. By the time she had had the courage to defy him, it had been too late to pick and choose.

David thought of Catherine's letter, full of detail about her patients and the success they were having with war wounds. 'Did you consider nursing?'

Valerie shook her head. 'I'm not brave enough, I'm afraid. Is it awful to say that?' Her blue eyes were clouded by doubt, her mouth looked about to tremble.

He put out a consoling hand. 'Not at all. Not everyone has that kind of bravery. And if you're attached to an Ack-Ack battery, I suspect you have to be very brave indeed.'

Mention of Catherine had caused his mind to wander. Catherine was brave. Brave and determined. He felt the familiar ache in his heart, and tried to subdue it. 'Have you seen any good films lately? They tell me *In Which We Serve* is damn good. Noel Coward and John Mills, I believe – it's all about Louis Mountbatten's ship. You'd like that.'

Hamish had enjoyed his meal, so the mood was good. Sarah sat opposite him, on the other side of the stove. He had removed his boots, and now his wet socks steamed gently in the fire's glow. 'I saw the doctor today, Hamish.'

He looked up, brows coming down in a frown. 'What for? You didn't say . . .?'

'No, I went because –' she was trembling over her words in an effort to keep him sweet, '– I've fallen wrong, Hamish. Well, not wrong, it's a baby. Are you pleased?'

Suddenly he was down on his knees, his head in her lap. 'Thank you. Thank you.' His face, when he raised it, was alight. 'Are you sure?'

She nodded. 'Quite sure.' Under her hand his hair was thick and curly. 'It's going to be all right,' she thought. 'A baby, his baby, will make a difference.'

They sat on like that, two souls in harmony, until a cry came from the far-off room where little Joe slept. She began to extricate herself so she could go and soothe him before he was too far awake, but the man at her knee resisted her movement.

'No,' he said, 'let him cry.'

And when she struggled, he pinned her arms till she cried out. Although why she cried out, she couldn't imagine. There was no one to hear.

295

'Let me get in!' Max was flicking snow from his mac, taking off his peaked cap to shake it free of flakes.

'I'm so glad to see you back.' His cheek was cold to the touch, but the familiar smell of him was there. 'I've missed you so much.'

He didn't answer her, except with a kiss. Catherine had intended to ply him with food, draw him to the fire, tell him hospital news, and only then to take him to bed. The reality was different. Their mouths clung together like limpets, while they feverishly shed clothes, helping one another with buttons or straps, all the while moving backwards towards the bedroom and the bed. 'I love you, Catherine.' He was over her, and in her, and she gave herself up to the sweetness of it, begging him not to stop, urging him on, feeling the elusive climax coming, coming – until it washed over them together, and they could collapse apart, gasping and exulting with the same breaths.

Afterwards, after the bathing and eating and sharing news, they spoke of other things – of Hodgson's bereavement, of Pamela's engagement, of India's summer wedding. Never of the wife and children who were not for a second out of the forefront of their thoughts. But, 'We heard from the Red Cross,' he said at last. 'Miriam's parents died in Belsen.'

# Chapter Twenty Eight

## April 1943

CATHERINE WOKE TO AN EMPTY bed. So Max had not come home. He had telephoned her at 11 o'clock: '*Go to bed darling. I'll be in theatre for another hour at least. Two pilots . . . I'll fill you in later. Not much hope for them, I'm afraid, but we're doing what we can with a man down.*'

They were short of medical staff to deal with incoming casualties. Normally Max would not have been involved till a later stage, but at present it was all hands to the wheel. So she had set her clock and gone to sleep, confidently expecting to find him by her side when she woke.

She was clearing her breakfast tray when he arrived, pale and drawn, his chin stubbled, an air of defeat about him. 'We lost one of them,' he said. She didn't speak. She simply held him in her arms until he straightened his head and kissed her forehead. She ran him a bath, laid out clean pyjamas, and whipped up scrambled eggs. 'Breakfast on the table,' she said as he emerged from the bathroom, towelling his head. 'Only dried egg, I'm afraid, but there's a tiny knob of butter in there. See you tonight. I love you.'

Max smiled at her. 'The feeling is entirely mutual.'

Sarah had hoped for an uplift in Hamish's spirits when his final discharge came through. Now, though, with the papers lying on the table in front of him, he seemed bitterer than ever. Her back was aching, her swollen belly got in the way, and his voice in her head was like a drill. 'Nine years I gave them. Nine years, and cast off with coppers now. Bloody useless, and no thanks.'

'I thought you had enjoyed it,' she ventured, 'before . . .' She got no further.

'Enjoyed? I loathed it. Loathed every bloody minute of it – orders, orders, bullshit, bullshit, nothing ever good enough for them. Being marched everywhere – meals, games, prayers. Prayers! As if there was any point in praying. Do you know what I saw, Sarah. I saw a woman lying dead in a shattered house, a bairn dead still pulling on her tit. Killed as she suckled him. Nobody told me I'd see that when I signed on. No one said I'd see a man separated from his legs and still screaming.

'Don't stand there looking shocked. Do you know what shock did to me, Sarah? It put a scream in my head, a blood-curdling bloody scream that I couldn't let out. I thought it would go, when you came. I thought you'd drive it out. Give me peace. But all I got was more screaming, a child that cries day and night. Night and day.'

He was rocking backwards and forwards, and she wanted to go to him – but most of all she wanted to go to her son and make sure he made no noise.

Staff Nurse Hodgson was back from compassionate leave. 'She doesn't want anyone to sympathise,' the QA told them. 'Just behave as though nothing has happened. That's best.'

Hodgson laughed and joked with the patients, heard news of Spender's letter and the imminent visit of his girlfriend as though it was the best news in the world. But it was not the same. 'It's as though a light has gone out in her,' Catherine thought, and felt ashamed. She had not felt like that when Henry died. She had felt, instead, as though her life could really begin. And even with Joe's death, though there had been pain, she had never been hollow-eyed as Hodgson was. No one had been able to tell that she had lost the man whose child she was carrying. 'Perhaps I am cold,' she thought. 'Feelingless.'

But she had feelings for Max. Tonight she would cook for him, something special. The sheer improbability of finding something special on her way home from work occupied her for the next hour. She was still thinking about it when Hodgson appeared at the door of the sluice.

'You're wanted, Nurse. In the office.'

'What've I done?'

'How do I know? Straighten your cap and pull yourself together. It's probably nothing.'

The QA was seated at her desk. 'Come in, Nurse,' she said. 'I don't normally allow telephone calls, but . . .' She smiled one of her rare smiles. 'Your brother-in-law, Sir David, is a persuasive man.'

She waved a hand at the telephone receiver lying on the desk, and Catherine picked it up gingerly. 'David?'

'Catherine, thank God I've got through to you. I have bad news. One of the McGuire boys has been killed in the pit. I'm trying to get a message to Sarah, but her family have only a postal address. I thought you might have a telephone number.'

'Which boy is it?' Catherine asked.

'The young one, Terry. It was a fall of stone. Nothing could be done. Do you have a number for Sarah?'

'They haven't a phone. She has my number, both here and at Mellows, but she's never used either of them.' So Terry was dead. Terry who had worn a borrowed suit for his sister's wedding, whose bony wrists had protruded a good two inches from the cuff, who, in a sane world, should still have been at school, not down a hole in the ground.

'Don't worry,' David was saying. 'In that case, I'll ring the police, and get them to pass on a message.'

'Ask Sarah to ring me,' Catherine said, urgently, because she could see Queenie's patience wearing thin. She put down the phone, stammered her thanks, and went back to her duties.

---

'Yes.' India turned this way and that in front of the cheval mirror. 'Yes. It's coming on.' Her wedding dress was being made by Darlesden's leading dressmaker. The material was Brussels lace, a bolt bought by her mother in the far-off days when she had been a leader of fashion. The neckline was a deep V with a Byronesque collar and sleeves to set it off. 'Quite regal,' India thought, but kept it to herself.

The seamstress was on her knees, her mouth full of pins as she adjusted the hem. 'You were lucky with the fabric.'

India pursed her lips. The material backing the lace was not what she would have liked, but beggars couldn't be choosers in a war.

When at last the dress was back on the dummy and she had donned her uniform again, they talked about the bridesmaid's dress. Her old school friend, Loelia, had never been a beauty. Her dress was to be eau-de-nil, which would do nothing for her complexion, but would look good in tinted photographs. The caterers had promised to do all they could with what was available, there would be game of some sort from the estate, and the Kynaston cellars still had wine and champagne in plenty. A pleasurable glow grew inside India. In spite of shortages, it was going to be a wedding of note.

---

Max woke sweating from a dream – or a nightmare – so real that he put up a hand to see if his yarmulke, worn only at home in New York, was in place on his head. Miriam had been there, laying the Sabbath table, covering the snow-white cloth with poppy-seeded *challahs*, and wine, and an abundance of food: blintzes and strudel and *lokshen kugl*, gefilte fish with *kichl*, the *hamanlasken* of the Purim festival and the bitter-sweet *charoset* that was for Passover, stuffed cabbage leaves and chick peas – all muddled together until the feast became an orgy of conflicting flavours and reasons. And Miriam, gentle Miriam, was urging him to eat, to stuff himself.

Now, broad awake, his gorge rose at the thought of so much excess. But in his dream Miriam had been stern-faced, her eyes hostile. When she had first been suggested to him as a wife he had liked what he saw. '*She is gentle*,' he had thought, '*and that is good*.' That was what had drawn him to Catherine – that quality almost of serenity, even amid the blood and turmoil of the casualties of war.

'I love them both,' he thought now. 'God help me, I love them both.' In the end, he rose from the bed and fetched his tallis and tefillin, unused since he came to Britain. As he draped the fringed prayer shawl around his shoulders and strapped the tefillin to his forehead, he prayed for forgiveness for the hurt he must cause at least one of the women he loved.

———

Pamela had to strap-hang on the bus on her way home, but she didn't care. In two days' time, Michael would be home on leave. Two days to get ready, hair, clothes, hands – she would have to do something with her hands. She was adept at operating her lathe now, but cuts and scrapes were still inevitable, and they showed.

It would be a relief to have him home, even if only for five days. Bomber Command was stepping up its attacks on Germany now, as the BBC made clear in every news broadcast. Michael's fighter squadron was flying above the bombers, trying to protect them from enemy fighters, but none of the planes could escape the searchlights raking the night skies, or the Ack-Ack units down below.

'I'm home,' Pamela called as she let herself into the house. No one answered, but her father appeared in the doorway of the living-room.

'Dad?' His expression was sombre, stricken even. 'Dad? What's the matter? Say something. You're frightening me!'

Her mother appeared then, standing behind him as he spoke. 'It's bad news, Pamela. Michael's father telephoned. Michael is missing. His plane was shot down over – well, we don't know exactly where.'

Inside her, a little howl began but her lips stayed firmly closed.

'That doesn't mean he's dead,' her mother was saying. 'He's missing, that's all.'

Pamela untied her headscarf and dropped her shoulder bag on to the hallstand. 'I'm going upstairs,' she said. 'Just for a little while. I'll be down in a moment.'

'He's only missing,' her mother repeated helplessly.

'I know, Mummy. I know.' She said it to console, but she knew in her heart what 'missing' usually meant. It meant 'gone forever'.

———

The room was silent, except for the fire spitting in the grate. David cleared his throat. 'I came to see if there was anything I could do. I've arranged for some money to be . . .'

But Terry's father was holding up a hand. 'We can look after our own, thank you. I know you mean to be kind, but there's no need.'

The other brother, still in his pit clothes, was stirring in his chair. 'You could get word to our Sarah. She's in Scotland.'

'I've already done that,' David said. 'This morning I telephoned Catherine Callingham. I thought she'd be in touch with your sister, as they were friends. Apparently there's no phone where Sarah is, so I took the liberty of telephoning the local police. They've promised to contact her, and ask her to ring Catherine. She has that number, apparently. I hope that contact has already been made, and that Sarah will be making arrangements to come. I'll speak again to Catherine, and make sure Sarah has everything she needs to travel. We can meet her train at Durham.'

Mr Maguire was rising to his feet and holding out a hand. 'Thank you,' was all he said, but the tone was friendly.

'I'm being dismissed,' David thought, as he walked from the house. But he understood their need to separate their grief from someone who represented a coal industry that had robbed one man of a son and another of a brother. 'The price of coal,' David thought, as he put the car into gear. 'The price of coal – blood and tears.'

‒‒‒‒‒

'Cathy?' The voice was hesitant and tearful.

'Sarah! Yes, it's me. Where are you?'

'I'm at the police station. They brought me here in a car. It's our Terry, isn't it? They say a brother, but I know it's him – I've been thinking about him since yesterday.'

'Yes, it's Terry. It was a fall of stone. They say he didn't suffer.' Catherine heard a sob at the other end, and ploughed on. 'When are you coming? David says he'll meet you at Durham, and will pay for everything. Do you have enough money to get home?'

'I can't come, Cathy.'

'Why not? Are you ill?'

'No. No, I'm not ill, but I can't come. I can't explain, not now. I'll write. Tell Dad and Jim – tell them – tell them I'm sorry.'

There was a click and then the dialling tone. Catherine put down the receiver, uncertain what to do for the best. Max was in the kitchen, and she went through to him. 'That was Sarah. She says she's not coming – well, can't come.'

'She's pregnant, Catherine. Maybe that's the reason.'

'No, it wasn't that. Something's wrong, Max. I know Sarah. Nothing would normally stop her coming to her family.'

He put down the spoon he was stirring with, and took her in his arms. 'There's nothing you can do about it, my love. She's a married woman. She knows her own mind. Now, this soup smells good. Come eat.'

They sat on either side of the table, making an effort to continue conversation. She told him about Spender's coming visit, and saw that it pleased him. He commiserated with her about the change in Staff Nurse Hodgson. But there was something missing. 'It's that I'm upset,' Catherine told herself – but it was more than that. Max looked – subdued. Sad.

When they were in bed and the lights turned out, he kissed her tenderly, but he did not reach for her, and in the end he turned away from her and settled himself for sleep.

＝＝

India had felt good ever since her visit to the dressmaker. Watching her across the dinner table, David wondered quite what she was up to. India malevolent he was used to. India full of sweetness and light was worrying.

'What sort of a day have you had?' she asked as they forked some kind of mince and potato dish around their plates.

'Bloody!' David said. 'Well, you did ask. There was a death in the pit, a young boy.'

'It happens,' India said with a sigh of regret so palpably dishonest that he felt his hackles rise.

'Is that all you can say, India? I'm far from certain that it was inevitable. I think they were cutting corners.'

'They're being harassed to produce more coal. That dreadful Bevin man. What else do you expect?'

'We can hardly blame a death in one of our pits on Ernest Bevin.'

'Oh, I can. I can blame anything on those Labour men. What they're doing in Churchill's government, I do not know.'

'Saving his neck,' David said gleefully. 'When his own party would have dumped him, it was Attlee and Bevin who stood firm. So don't be so quick to dismiss them.'

'They mean to nationalise the coal mines, I hope you realise that?'

'I wish they'd already done it! I wish heartily that that boy's death was on their conscience, not mine.'

'You're very foolish if you take responsibility for something you had no control over. If you want to worry about something, worry about the Budget. The Chancellor intends to turn the screw on us, and everything's going to cost more. A shilling a bottle on wine!'

Suddenly David felt weary. Half the world was dying or starving or facing extinction in gas chambers, and they were discussing the price of wine. He thought of the McGuire boy's body as he had seen it today, his face seemingly untouched, and yet every bone in his body smashed. It had been the face of a child.

'Excuse me,' he said, flinging down his napkin. 'I've had enough. I think I need some fresh air.'

# Chapter Twenty Nine

June 1943

A N ANCIENT TAXI CARRIED HER away from the cottage and on to the road to Stirling, where she would board the London train. The driver was obviously intrigued by her visit to 'yon Hamish', but Catherine answered only in monosyllables. She was glad to get away from what was clearly an unhappy house, but sorry she was leaving Sarah and little Joe behind. The visit had been a disaster from start to finish.

She had written as soon as Terry's funeral was over, saying that she was going to take leave and come up to visit them. Sarah's reply had been disjointed and totally unlike her, but the message had been plain: *Don't come.* That had only served to make Catherine more determined. She had talked with the Maguire men, and seen the incomprehension on their faces that Terry could die and Sarah would not come home. 'If you *can* go –' Mr Maguire had said. Jim had beseeched only with his eyes, his wife's hand patting his shoulder meanwhile.

So Catherine had rung the policeman whose name David had given her, got the name of a bed-and-breakfast establishment from him, and caught the Aberdeen train as soon as she could get leave.

That Sarah had been pleased to see her was not in doubt, and little Joe, dashing around, was a delight. Hamish had been polite enough, but the jovial face of the wedding day was gone, and there was a terrible feeling of tension in the house. Sarah was heavily pregnant and unwieldy. Catherine would have liked to spend time alone with her, but Hamish had never left their side. Until the third and last day, when she had walked over and found Sarah and Joe alone.

'He'll be back soon,' Sarah had said. It was a warning that meant, '*Don't let him catch us talking.*' When she spoke aloud, her eyes filled with tears. 'Do they know I would have come if he'd've let me?'

Catherine nodded, and seized her chance. She had put two £20 notes into a small purse the night before. Now she pressed it into Sarah's hand. 'Put this away. Hide it. I won't ask questions now, but I want you to know you can come home whenever you want to. To me, or to your father. This money will get you home, and you can have more. So promise me –'

The sentence was never finished. The door creaked, and Sarah began to babble about the shops in nearby Callander. After that it had been farewells, and watching the road for the taxi that was bringing her bags and taking her away.

Catherine looked out at the towns and cities passing by as she travelled south. If she had had more time, she would have stopped off and visited her family. Pamela must be despairing now, with Michael missing for seven weeks. She would go and see them soon. Perhaps Max would come with her. She put her head against the back of the seat, and closed her eyes for a snooze.

～～～

The breakfast-room in Rupert's house was pleasant enough, but India yearned for Kynaston's height and space. Still, this house would do until the day she could return to her true home. She enjoyed breakfast-time, largely because of relief that the night was ended, and Rupert's clumsy invasions of her body were over for at least 18 hours.

She had always wondered why sexual relations seemed so important to people, and now she was even more perplexed. The first night had not only been agony, it had been undignified. The moment when her hymen had ruptured and she realised it was nearly over came as such a relief that it brought tears of joy to her eyes. Now she submitted to his efforts which, considering his age, seemed surprisingly juvenile. But she had banned a repeat performance in the morning. That had been a surprise to her, an unwelcome surprise – that men could even contemplate sex at the start of a working day.

However, all things considered, it was going well, and the wedding had been a triumph. She was bound to be pregnant before long, and then sex would cease until such time as another child was necessary. And at least Rupert looked like a consort. This morning, as every morning, he was correctly dressed, with that newly washed and brushed air she liked.

'Anything in the papers?' she asked.

'A scuffle between black and white GIs. In Cornwall.'

'I knew there'd be trouble when we were flooded with Americans. Any fool could see what would happen if they sent negroes here.'

'We were glad enough to have them, India. Jolly glad to have America enter on our side.'

'You're sounding like my brother now. He's always lauding them.'

'No, I'm not lauding them, but we have to be fair. We needed their Forces and their technology. But it's complicated, I agree.'

'Complicated is putting it mildly.' India was into her stride now. 'You know what they call the buses that take English girls to their barracks for so-called dances? They call them passion-wagons. What does that tell you? And it's causing unrest with our own boys. The Yanks have cigarettes, chocolate, and the new aphrodisiac – nylon stockings! And their uniforms are tailored to quite a disgusting degree. Women have lost their heads over them.'

'Isn't that a myth put about by Lord Haw-Haw in his broadcasts? *"British troops, your women are with American soldiers while you fight."* That sort of thing?'

'It's not a myth, it's all too real. There'll be bastard children by the thousand, the war will end, the Americans'll go home, and we'll be left with the problem. And if the children are half-caste . . . well, the mind boggles. And VD is rocketing up.'

'Please.' Rupert shook out his paper. 'Not at the breakfast table.'

'We can't pretend it isn't happening. However if all the stories of blacks and whites fighting one another are true, they'll wipe one another out. Or land in jail.'

'They have black days and white days in some places. Passes are issued to white troops on Mondays, blacks on Tuesdays, and so on.'

'That makes sense. The authorities have talked to me about establishing some kind of hospitality for Americans here, but fortunately the nearest US camp was out of my zone. I'd have refused anyway. But enough of awful Yanks. I must go and change. What have you got planned for today? A woman's work is never done – not this woman's, anyway.'

<hr/>

'I don't mind telling you, I'm worried.'

David sat back in his seat, and tried to look attentive. He had a host of things on his mind, not least Catherine's expedition to the wilds of Scotland, but the summons from Home Guard headquarters had brooked no refusal. The Commander was a retired brigadier, and had an almost religious belief in the role of his men. 'We were raised as a force to fight a German invasion, David. We've drilled and trained until we are just that, a fighting force. I can tell you there are those who think we should be sent to supplement the troops when the counter-invasion begins.'

David nodded gravely. Privately he was reviewing the rows of largely elderly, or at best middle-aged, men who comprised his unit. Stalwart in defence of their own territory they would be, but liberating France and Belgium?

'Anyway, there are rumblings. Polls are indicating that Home Guard duty is increasingly seen as unnecessary. I tell you, David, the powers that be think the Axis is a spent force, but they could be in for a nasty shock. The trade unions are against us, too – they say we've been used in disputes. I said that was a mistake. We're not police.'

There had been intervention by Home Guards in labour disputes in Scotland, and in Middlesex. David had privately vowed his troop would never be used in such a way, but the damage had been done, and *The Daily Worker* had accused employers of using the Home Guard against organised trade-unionism.

The Commander was continuing: 'Anyway, to cut a long story short, I understand they want to stop our free uniforms, and make us surrender coupons. The War Office is fighting this tooth and nail, on the grounds that morale will slump. But the clothing ration of civil defence has already been cut, and it could be our turn next. I'm relying on Churchill.'

'Yes,' David said. 'The old man won't see us done down.'

He promised to do all he could to influence anyone with clout, and made a grateful exit. He had more things on his mind than clothing coupons, however valuable they might be. Life at Kynaston was peaceful, now that India had gone off to her new life, but he also felt isolated alone in the echoing vastness of his home. No wife, no children . . . but he was day-dreaming, and he knew what the end of that could be.

He switched on the engine of his car and took the Kynaston road.

It was a relief when Catherine's taxi cab was lost to sight, but it left Sarah with a wrenching fear in her gut. All the time she had been here, Sarah had been afraid and ashamed. Afraid that Catherine would say or do something to bring on one of Hamish's rages; ashamed of the mess she had made of her life. 'I am lost now,' she acknowledged to herself. 'I am lost and my child – my children – are lost as well.'

Now that she was far into her pregnancy, sex had become more difficult, but to refuse Hamish was to bring on a torrent of abuse, some of it directed at her, most of it directed at an establishment he saw as ruining his life. She had tried to point out that the war had been no one's fault but Hitler's, but when Hamish was in a black mood there was no reasoning with him. The purse, which she knew contained money, was safe inside her blouse, and she would find somewhere to put it later. One day she might be able to give it back to Sarah untouched. If Hamish found work, if the doctor found a way to help him . . .

But in her heart, now, she knew these things would not happen. She turned back into the house and heard Hamish's grunt of satisfaction. 'She's away, then, with her fancy ways?'

'Yes,' Sarah said. She would have liked to defend her friend, but it didn't do to argue.

Max knew there was something amiss by the tone of voice. QAs did not do panic, but this one was precious near it. 'I'm coming!' he said. As he pushed open the swing doors to the ward, he saw a student nurse, her shoulders heaving with sobs.

'Mr Detweiler!' The QA had regained her composure, but only just. 'It's – he's – Can you come to the sluice?'

Max saw blood on the floor as he went through the doorway. Red, glistening, seeming to ripple in the draught from the door. The body was slumped between two sinks, and a scalpel lay on the floor where it had fallen from the man's hand. The ugly gash that was his throat gaped wide. No need to check for a pulse. Spender was dead.

'What happened?' he asked, with difficulty.

'I don't know. I was with Matron when Staff Nurse called me. We're trying to find out where he got the scalpel from. He seemed all right when I spoke to him at breakfast time.'

'It was this,' the Staff Nurse said, holding out a blue envelope. 'It came with the post.'

Max opened up the folded sheet.

'*Dear Johnny,*' he read. '*I think it's only fair to be honest with you. It was good to see you the other day, and I'm glad you're getting treatment, but I think I have to tell you now that my feelings have changed. There'll be someone someday for you, I'm sure, but I'm not up to it.*' More excuses followed, and then it ended with, '*Very best wishes, Joyce*'. And, the final irony: a cross to represent a kiss.

The train was passing through Peterborough, now. Someone who'd got out at Doncaster had left a paper behind. Catherine retrieved it, and leafed through the pages. The actor Leslie Howard was dead – well, missing, believed killed. His plane had disappeared over the Bay of Biscay, and its last message had been '*Enemy aircraft attacking us.*' She had loved Leslie Howard's film *The First of the Few*, which she had seen with Henry. Henry. Had she really been married to him? At times he seemed almost a figment of her imagination, although she could remember him next to her in the darkened cinema. She had difficulty summoning up Joe's face now, and once she had loved him so.

In the paper, there was a piece about concern over morals. The number of illegitimate births in the United Kingdom had almost doubled since the beginning of the war, and syphilis and gonorrhoea were on the rise. She turned the page over swiftly, but there was nothing else to grip her attention.

It was getting dark, and she looked out of the window at lights leaping up here and there. It would be good to be home to Max and the flat. Good, even, to get back to the ward and catch up with everyone. Spender had been so jubilant when she left. She would be sad to see him go when he was healed, but if he was going to be happy that was all that mattered.

---

Pamela seldom put her curlers in, nowadays. There seemed no point, when she covered her hair with a turban, anyway. She should have got a bath, but it would have to wait until tomorrow. She was tired. She was always tired nowadays. The factory seemed oppressive, and the other girls talked all the time about their men. She felt tears prick her eyes and blinked them away.

She slipped off her dressing-gown and put out the light, and then she heard the telephone ringing below. The illuminated face of her alarm clock said half-past nine. Who would ring at that time of night?

There was a pounding of feet on the stairs, and then her father was switching on the light. 'Come down, Pamela. Come quickly! Michael is alive. The Resistance have him in France, and he's fine! It's his father ringing!'

---

Max was waiting on the platform. Catherine saw him as the train drew slowly in. 'Max! Max!' She was out and running, her case bumping against her legs. He held her close, and kissed her. But she felt tension in him. 'What is it?'

'Nothing. I've had a hard day, that's all. Give me that bag. Let's get you home.'

But in the taxi she could contain herself no longer. 'Something's wrong Max, I know it. Have you been recalled, are you going home?'

He was shaking his head. 'It's not me, Catherine. I meant not to tell you this until the morning, but I'm afraid Spender is dead. He committed suicide.'

Dead? Catherine heard him, but she didn't believe her ears. Not dead now, when life was beginning again for him? When she said goodbye he had said, '*Hurry back, Nurse. I'll be out of here and gone if you don't hurry. And I want that goodbye kiss you've promised me!*'

---

David ate alone in the dining-room, serving himself from the heated tray on the sideboard. Now that he was alone, there seemed little point in keeping servants out of their homes at night. When he had finished, he cleared the plates to the sideboard for collection in the morning, snuffed out the candles in the hot tray, and whistled up the dogs. The sky to the west was still rosy, the stars pale above him. Catherine would be back from Scotland now, safe with Max. He smiled to himself, remembering the girl she had been in those halcyon days before the war, remembering all the golden girls and the equally golden boys. 'We all knew where we were going,' he thought. 'Our lives stretched out before us, straight as furrows.' Now, they were all dead or scattered. War was a river, men and women simply leaves dropped into the current and carried who knew where.

Behind him, the bulk of Kynaston Hall loomed against the pale sky. Would he end his days alone in that dark and brooding house? Fanciful thought overtook him. When the war ended, he could emigrate to Australia, Africa even. He could take to the roads in a caravan and eke a living from nature. Perhaps he should become a sybarite, enjoying the fleshpots on the Riviera? Or join a monastery, and brew a new and potent liqueur?

He chuckled, thinking of India licking her lips as she repossessed Kynaston. Well, she was welcome to it. But, as the dogs snuffled around him, he knew that, no matter where he went, he would not find happiness unless Catherine was part – a small part would do – of his life.

# BOOK 4

Chapter Thirty

September 1943

INDIA KNEW BEFORE SHE EXAMINED her underwear that she was having a period. She had been so sure that she was pregnant, had felt it in her breasts, and even thought her belly looked somehow rounder. But she had been wrong, the red stain told her so.

She was unbelievably healthy, careful with her nutrition, getting the right amount of sleep. It must be Rupert's failure, not hers. A sudden fear that she might never have a son, an heir to Kynaston, swept over her and was instantly extinguished. She had never failed at anything in her life. She would not fail at this.

Max had left her post on the neatly set breakfast table, along with a note. *'Sleep well, darling. I love you.'* Catherine stood, unpinning her hat and loosening her coat, a foolish grin on her face. She hated night shifts because it meant they slept apart, she in the day, he in the night. But his notes were a boost. Different wording every morning, but always the same message

She couldn't be bothered to eat, but she brewed tea and opened her post as she drank it. A letter from her father, and another from Pamela. Michael was still in France, but he was expected home imminently. According to Pamela, there was a sophisticated network for hiding and eventually repatriating Allied pilots. No one could say whether he would be smuggled out by sea or over the border into neutral Spain, but getting him home was a priority. 'So that he can fly again,' Catherine thought, and shivered at the prospect.

There was nothing from Sarah. It was eight weeks now since the brief note telling of Alexander's birth. Catherine had replied by return, and then sent a baby gift, but as yet there had been no response. She rested a weary head on her hands for a moment before deciding she would worry about it tomorrow. They had lost a patient in the night. She had helped to lay out the scarred body, and done her best to make the burned face presentable for his family. Now all she wanted to do was sleep.

---

'There you are, Maxie – and you owe me.'

What Charles Cohn had pushed across the desk was a cornucopia: tinned ham, peaches, chocolate, pretzels, and best of all, a tin of gefilte fish.

'I do owe you, Chuck, big time. Wait till –' He was about to say, 'Wait till Catherine sees this lot,' but checked himself in time. No one at the Embassy knew about Catherine.

Charles Cohn was a long-time friend, but he would bridle at the thought of Miriam's being betrayed. He had been a guest at their wedding, and at the celebrations when the children were born. Max felt shame colour his face and tried to change the subject.

'So, why the summons? Incidentally, security is tight here. I thought they weren't going to let me through.'

They were high above Grosvenor Square, in a room in the US Embassy, where Charles was a liaison officer.

'It's not an official summons.' Charles put his hands flat on the desk, a sign of strain, and Max wondered what was coming next. 'But I hear on the grapevine that they think its time you re-located.'

'Back home?'

'Not necessarily. The emphasis of the war will shift before long. Germany has its back to the wall. The counter-invasion will happen soon, and then we'll turn on the Japs. I know we're holding our own in the Far East, but Europe is top priority. When that's done, you'll be needed elsewhere. They like it that you've worked with McIndoe, but now – well, you're a maestro too.'

Max shook a deprecating head. 'I wouldn't say that. Are we talking weeks, here?'

'There'll be no invasion of Europe before the spring. When it comes, we'll be the major force, and US casualties will be high. You'll probably be transferred to more general duties for that stage, but you'll be necessary here for a while. I just thought you might need some warning.' He was staring at his hands as he spoke.

'He knows,' Max thought suddenly, and again felt shame. But of course he would know: it was his business to know everything that crawled which might affect his countrymen.

'I see,' he said at last.

Charles was opening a folder. 'If you've ever wondered whether the fight is worth while, Max, I got this report yesterday. It's from the Polish Interior Ministry in exile. German doctors are using healthy prisoners in the camps for experimental surgery. Removing bone and muscle to see if it will regenerate. You can imagine what happens if it doesn't. They are infecting healthy men and women with tetanus or TB to see how long they take to die. They're wiping out our race, Max. We need to stop them.'

Outside in Grosvenor Square, an autumn sun was shining. But it was not strong enough to dry Max's tear-stained cheeks as he walked in search of a cab.

David called in at Mellows on his way into Belgate. He needed to pay Hannah Chaffey a month's wages for her cleaning work. At first Catherine had sent her cheques, but Hannah had protested at the stress of getting them cashed. Now Catherine sent him a quarterly cheque and he passed on the money.

Hannah was in good form. 'You've heard about the trouble at the pit? Well, of course you have, you're the coal owner.' Their monthly chats always took place over a cup of tea, and Hannah obviously regarded David as a friend.

'Yes,' he said. 'But it's worse in other parts of the country, isn't it?'

Nine thousand engineers were striking at Vickers Armstrong in Barrow-in-Furness, in spite of their union's disapproval. The local strike leaders were demanding to speak directly to Ernest Bevin, the Minister of Labour, but he was a stickler for protocol and would only talk to the AEU officials.

'No one thinks more of pitmen than me, but this is wrong,' Hannah said stoutly.

Striking had been made illegal in 1940 – but how could you send 9,000 men to prison, David thought. Last year miners in Kent had struck. A thousand of them had been fined, and had refused to pay. Bevin had held the fines in abeyance and the men had returned to work; but disputes lingered on. Now 7,000 Scottish miners were striking in Scotland. Bevin was blaming Trotskyites, but were Trotskyites to blame for the 16,000 men threatening to come out at Rolls-Royce? Unwilling to commit himself, he made soothing noises.

'Well, I don't hold with striking during a war,' Hannah said again. She held her mug in both hands and gazed at it mournfully. 'Sugarless tea. Who'd've thought we'd be reduced to that?'

'It won't be for much longer,' David said, glad of the sudden change of subject. 'Mussolini's defeated. The Russians are doing well. You'll have your sugar soon.'

'Ooh!' Hannah was shaking her head. 'Sugar comes from the Far East. Sugar cane. We'll never get the Japs out.'

David wondered if he should explain about sugar beet, but decided against it. Hannah needed a little gloom in life. Why deprive her?

≈

She had felt elated when she boarded the train, but as the North East fell away a curious flatness overtook her. The call had come the day before yesterday.

'Pammy? It's me!'

She had cried and laughed, and tried to form sensible questions, but it had been useless. Michael had had to keep repeating that he was in England and reunited with his best friend, Chalky White. 'He's with me now, Pammy. Say hello to him.' She had stammered out a few words to his friend, all the while wishing he would get out of the way and let her talk to Michael. When he was back on the line he told her he was getting checked out and de-briefed, and would then get leave – a week, at least. She had just written to Catherine promising his safe return, and, as if by magic, it had happened.

Now she was on her way to his mother's house, and soon she and Michael would be together. She would find him changed. For all the bravado of his phone call, he had sounded shaky, and older. How long had it been? Little more than five months. You couldn't age in that time, surely? She knew the exact moment when she had moved from spoilt girl into womanhood, but Michael had gone away already a man. What would he be when he returned?

She turned her face to the window and tried to concentrate on the passing scenery.

Catherine was calling it a meat pie, but it would be mostly vegetables. She was rolling the pastry when the telephone rang.

'Cathy? It's me, Sarah.'

'Sarah. Oh, I'm so relieved. Are you all right? And the baby? And little Joe?' She remembered to add Hamish to her list of solicitations, but only just.

They were all fine, the baby was lusty and feeding well, and little Joe had taken to him.

'Where are you ringing from?'

A phone had been recently installed in the village shop. 'No need to mention it in letters,' Sarah said, when Catherine expressed delight at the innovation. So Hamish did not know about the phone call. Furthermore, he read Sarah's letters. She would need to be careful.

They talked of family, then. Jim's boy was thriving, and forward for his age, according to letters Sarah had received. Hannah Chaffey had been fined for supplying eggs to the black market, and Father Lavery was moving to a parish in Scotland.

'Will you get home before he goes?' Catherine asked. Sarah was fond of the priest who had commemorated her dead husband, christened her baby and married her.

'Maybe,' Sarah said. 'Maybe.' But the resignation in her voice told Catherine there would be no visit home.

He had made excuses for weeks, but this time David had had to submit and agree to dine with India and Rupert. 'We dress,' India had said in tones that suggested he had cast off all civilised habits. 'Of course,' he had answered urbanely, in the hope of annoying her.

In truth, he had no room for such fripperies now. Every day

he heard reports of men dead in one war zone or another. Half the women in Belgate seemed to be wearing black for husbands or sons. Yesterday he had heard that two of his contemporaries at school had died in the battle to retake the Dodecanese island of Kos. They had both enlisted in 11th Paras. He had had a drink with them the last time he had been in London, and now they were dead.

'Sherry?' Rupert was a good host. David accepted the pale liquid and sipped appreciatively.

'Good?' Rupert was raising his glass.

'Very' David said. 'I haven't had a good dry sherry since – well, in years.'

'A friend had a cellarful, fortunately. He threw me a bottle or two as a favour.'

'Lucky you,' David said, thinking of what Hannah Chaffey had said today when speaking of the unrest at the pit. *'It's the shortage of beer and fags – well, that's my opinion. What does a working man want at the end of a hard day? A drink and a smoke.'* Perhaps he should see if Rupert's friend could spare a bottle or two for the miners?

Opposite him, India was fidgeting. 'I hear there's unrest in the pits. Not in Belgate, surely?'

'We're not on strike,' David said. 'But I gather there are rumblings.'

'Well, I would shoot them,' India said. 'Striking in wartime is treason, nothing less.'

'I wouldn't go that far.' Rupert was standing with his backside to the open fire. 'It's quite a backside,' David thought, 'India must be feeding him.'

She was swinging her foot now, a sure sign of trouble. 'That's it, Rupert, contradict me. Well, I'm sorry. I'm giving every ounce of effort I can to this war and I won't tolerate shirkers. Those people breed like rabbits, and then do nothing for the war effort.'

This from a woman who had shirked taking an active role in the war effort and had opted to skulk at home, David thought, but he kept his thoughts to himself. Ten million women had already registered for war work. Now the authorities were registering women up to the age of 50, which the press had decried as 'registering grandmothers'. India was still a young woman, and a strong one. Other women were working on the railways, and as welders in shipyards, but his young and fit sister preferred to ride around in a car ordering people about. 'Always in command,' he thought. It was a relief when the time came to go in to dinner.

There was a good smell as Max opened the door of the flat.

'Mmm,' he said, pretending to look past Catherine towards the kitchen. In reality he was noticing the shadows under her eyes, the pallor of her skin. Night shift did that to nurses. They worked a ten-hour stretch, and then slept for half that time. Any more, and there would be no time for life.

'Sorry I'm late,' he said when she had relieved him of the uniform trench-coat and peaked cap which he had worn since his country entered the war. 'We had late admissions.'

'Never mind.' She was drawing him towards his chair, putting a glass into his hand. 'It's the last of the gin, so enjoy it.'

Max sipped appreciatively, and then glanced at the clock. Seven-thirty. In little more than an hour it would be time for her to go to work.

'Come here,' he ordered, but she shook her head.

'I need to see to the pie,' she protested.

'To hell with the pie.' Max put down his glass and took her in his arms.

Sarah had feared questioning when she came back from making her telephone call at the shop, but Hamish accepted that she had simply been for milk. He was nursing Alexander, gazing fondly at his son from time to time, and humming softly under his breath. 'The house is peaceful,' Sarah thought and gave thanks.

She had washed little Joe's hands and face, had given him his supper and was preparing to take him to his bed when Hamish spoke. 'He's old enough to be away to his bed on his own.'

Apprehension fluttered in Sarah's chest, but she stood her ground. 'He's only three,' she said. 'Time yet for him to go to bed on his own.'

She was shepherding her son towards the back bedroom when she heard a movement behind her. Hamish had laid the baby in his crib and was turning to follow her.

'I said he goes alone.'

She shook her head. 'We'll talk about it later.' She relaxed a little as she and Joe went through the doorway and Hamish made no move to intervene. But as she was helping little Joe into his bed, she realised he was trembling. 'There, there,' she said, tucking him in. 'Everything's all right. Mammy's here.' His thumb went up to his mouth, and the sucking was compulsive. 'He's afraid,' she thought. 'And so am I.'

She stayed with Joe for a while, but the need to see to Alexander forced her out at last. It was time for his feed, the tension in her breasts told her that. She turned down the lamp, kissed him once more, and went back to the room. The blow caught her as she came through the door.

'Defy me, would you? Think I'm no more use?'

She said nothing, but the silence seemed to rouse him further, so at last she spoke. 'You know that's not true.'

'So I'm a liar then? Am I? Am I? Am I a liar? Don't look at me like that, you whey-faced bitch. Am I a liar?' His words were punctuated with blows. In the end she no longer felt them. She sank to her knees and would have stayed there if he had not lifted her by her hair. And then, suddenly, he was crying. 'Why do you do this? Why do you always do this?'

There was a dull pain in her cheekbone and she could feel blood in her mouth.

'I went through hell, and you don't care. Where's the sympathy for my suffering? For what they did to me? They killed me, Sarah. They killed me out there, and now you do this.' He was asking God to forgive her, but there was no God. For all the years she had believed in cross and candle, now she knew the truth. There was no God in Heaven. Only hell on earth.

———

'So they moved me to a little village called Buerges, near the Channel coast. I was hidden in a bakery for a while, and then a church. But the Germans were active there, near to the coast, so I was taken inland.'

'Were you frightened?'

Michael pulled her into the shelter of his arm. 'Terrified. All those beautiful French girls lusting after me . . .'

'Michael! How can you be so beastly when I –'

He shut off her protests with his mouth, and she gave herself up to the sweetness of his body, the male smell of his naked flesh, the feeling of him in her and above her, and the knowledge that, together, they made a whole so perfect she never wanted it to end.

Afterwards, tiptoeing back to the guest room in his parents' house, she wondered what would happen if she became pregnant. She would just have to deal with that, as she had dealt with everything else. 'I could manage,' she thought. 'I could manage anything, as long as he comes safely back to me.'

# Chapter Thirty One

### December 1943

SARAH ALWAYS ENJOYED THE WALK back to the cottage from the village shop.

The new telephone nestling in the far corner was a comfort, a link with home. The thought of the money Catherine had left for emergencies was a comfort, too. Please God, she would never need to spend it, but it was there, that was what mattered. Her purchases completed, she had loaded them into the pram, taken Joe by the hand, and set out on the road again.

Today one of her neighbours had been in the shop – although it seemed strange to call her a neighbour when their houses were so far apart. But their paths followed the same road. After she was served, she had lingered, and had fallen in beside Sarah as she set out for home.

'You'll likely be settling in?' she said.

Sarah turned to smile at the woman, whose face was full of curiosity. 'Yes,' she said. 'This is a beautiful place. Good clean air.'

'Different to your own place.' It was not a question, it was a statement. What had she been told?

'I don't know. Durham is beautiful, too. But I do like it here.' As she spoke, she knew it wasn't true – but what else could she say?

'Aye. Hamish said you came from Durham. A pit village, wasn't it?'

'There is a pit there, but the countryside is very near.'

'Aye.' The woman said it tones of polite disbelief. There was a pause and then she continued: 'Yon Hamish has suffered, hasn't he?'

Again Sarah agreed, but she quickened her pace, anxious to shorten the walk.

'He was a fine man before the war. Never a wrong word for anyone. Never lifted a hand to anyone, man or beast. And a good man to his mother before she went.'

'She can't know!' Sarah thought. It was almost a quarter of a mile from Hamish's cottage to the woman's dwelling. But the pitying look the woman gave her as they parted left her in no doubt: she knew everything there was to know about the state of her marriage to Hamish.

He was sitting by the stove when she came into the room that served as both kitchen and living-room. Today he was in a peaceful mood. He expressed pleasure at the news that she had some fresh herring, and got up to help her unload the pram, taking care not to wake the sleeping child. When they had done, he took her hand in his. 'I'm sorry, Sarah.'

'For what?' She felt embarrassed.

'For bringing you to this. If I could get work . . . '

'You will, when you're over your wounds. And we're managing, aren't we?' His lips on her forehead were gentle. It's going to be all right, she thought.

———

There was a new patient today, a boy of 22. At least, he had been a boy. As Catherine approached the bed, a hand – or what had been a hand – came up. 'Is that you, Nurse? What have they done to me? Am I blind?'

'We don't know. Probably not. We've put tannic acid on your burns – that's the hard black stuff you can probably feel on your skin. And your eyes have been coated with gentian violet. We've covered them loosely to protect them from the light.' How did you tell a man his eyelids had been half-burned away? 'I'm going to give you a drink now. Let me put this tube into your mouth.' No need to mention that the lips had gone.

She soothed him then, promising him that his parents were on their way, and would be here before long. Then she smoothed his bed as best she could. His body was held up by straps so that the burned flesh cleared the mattress. She leaned close to him.

'We're going to get you better. It will take a while but we will.'

'Will I fly again?' The words were a whisper.

'If you're silly enough to climb in an aeroplane, I expect you will.'

By the time she finished her shift, Catherine knew he would be dead before morning.

'Chuck! Over here.' They had arranged to meet in a pub not far from the Embassy. Max had ordered two G and T's, so Charles Cohn sank straight into the booth.

'I can't stay long, but it's good to see you. Miriam OK?'

Miriam was fine, and the children too. Max admired the latest picture of Charles's sons and then, the proprieties over, they both settled back.

'Things are heating up.' Charles was staring into his glass as he spoke.

Max nodded. 'Yes. A Second Front by the summer.'

'There'll certainly be a Second Front. As to the timing –'

'You wouldn't expect them to signal it.'

'There's a lot to sort out. Who will command it, for one thing.'

'Anyone in the frame?'

Charles shrugged. 'It will be one of ours, that's for sure. Dwight Eisenhower, probably. He handled the campaigns in North Africa and Italy well. But you can never be sure. There'll be lobbying behind the scenes. Best not say too much here.'

Around them the pub seethed with smoke and laughter. Military personnel, workmen, a few women in groups, looking faintly self-conscious about their surroundings. Surely none of them were eavesdropping enemy agents? Before the war you had seldom seen an unaccompanied woman in a British pub. Not a respectable woman, certainly. The world was changing.

'We lost a lot of men in the Gilberts,' he said.

Charles nodded. 'Over 1,000 Marines dead, and 2,000 wounded. Most of the Japs committed hara-kiri. All for a piece of rock the length of your New York street.'

'How much longer?' Max tried to keep his tone light, but he knew time was running out, and it was difficult to be insouciant about it.

'Eighteen months? Two years, tops. But you will be on your way long before that. They want you to move now, Max.'

———

There were curious stares as David drove into the pit yard. He did not visit often; usually the manager came to him. But today he wanted to see things for himself. The manager's secretary brought them tea on a metal tray, and he accepted a cup.

'I used to prefer coffee for elevenses,' the manager said. 'Funny the things you miss.'

'Yes,' David said. 'Still, it looks as though the tide has turned. Now, about these conscripted men . . . '

Ernest Bevin had announced in the Commons that 30,000

men of 25 or under were to be chosen by ballot from the call-up, and those chosen would be directed into the mines. 'One recruit in every team,' the manager concluded.

David whistled softly. 'Conscripts. How will that go down?'

'Not well. Bevin says it's "urgent national necessity", but the men are not convinced.'

'I knew coal production was down, but this sounds like a desperate measure. What have the miners got against it?'

'Safety issues, mostly. Untrained men working alongside them, stuff like that. Although the recruits won't go underground without first being trained. I think the miners are closing ranks, really. They don't want strangers, they don't want "townees". But we've got to get the men from somewhere. They've already recalled miners from the Army, but the trouble with that was that there weren't that many trained miners in there. Plenty of lads from a mining background, but they'd joined as regulars rather than go down the hole. They won't come back to the pits if they can help it.'

'So we may have trouble?' David asked.

'I expect their sense of humour will come to the rescue. I heard one yesterday saying his piece about "over his dead body" would strangers come in. Another man said he had a lad in the Army, and if more coal would shorten the war he'd welcome "Bevin boys" – over the other miner's dead body if need be. He said it with some heat, and I stood by for a blow-up, but the first man just cocked his head and said, "By lad, thou's a gobby bugger!"'

<hr />

The women worked with a different zeal, now. Once they had turned out munitions because they were afraid. Now they scented victory. They still worked hard, but the mood was lighter. Background music played from loudspeakers, but it did not drown out conversation. The women were jubilant about the way RAF Lancasters were pounding Berlin.

'Night after night,' a woman said, almost salivating at the thought. 'They started it but, by gum, we're finishing it.'

'Bomber Harris says he'll send in the RAF till the heart of Germany stops beating.'

'Who says the buggers have a heart?'

There followed a dissection of the morals and habits of Nazis in terms that would have made a navvy blanch. Pamela grinned to herself. If her mother were here she'd be laid out by now, or needing sal volatile. Or would she? There was less talk from her mother about the conventions now, no sense of having to keep up appearances, less fretting over things – unless it was shortage of food. Losing everything because of the war had hurt their pride, but they had more peace of mind now.

A tide of love for her parents flooded over her. 'I'll do something nice for them tonight,' she thought. And Catherine, too. She found she was smiling foolishly, remembering how they used to fight, and turned her attention back to her workmates.

The conversation on the shop floor was switching to turkeys. That was one of the things Pamela loved about her workmates: they never harped on about any one thing for too long. Apparently there would be no turkeys for Christmas, or precious few. 'Who could afford them anyway?' a woman said bitterly. 'We were glad of a bit of pork, pre-war.'

'Pork!' There was a general sighing over crackling and onion gravy, and then the conversation switched again. Churchill was ill with pneumonia. He had been taken ill in the Persian city of Tehran, where he had been meeting with Roosevelt and Stalin.

'He'll come round,' Pamela said. 'He's been ill before.'

'And if the worst came to the worst we could manage without him now.' The speaker was an older woman who had a quiet authority. 'It would've been different in 1940, but he's seen us through.'

There was general agreement that Winston was a good'un, as far as a Tory could ever be called good, and then they were on to music. Glenn Miller. 'In the Mood' was declared the best tune ever, though a large minority favoured 'Moonlight Serenade'. Pamela closed her eyes, remembering the time Michael had taken her to a dance hall. They had danced cheek to cheek to the sound of 'Moonlight Serenade' and she had known then that they would be together for the rest of time.

---

Once more India had met with disappointment. There had been a pain in her groin, and she had known then that a menstrual flow would follow. It wasn't fair. For a moment tears pricked her eyes, but they were tears of rage. How dared life treat her in this way! All around her women were getting pregnant, stupid, slatternly women with bellies like gourds, great gourds full of life. It had always been the same: she had been disadvantaged. Fate had given her a man's brain and drive in a woman's body, but why was that body not responding as it should? 'It isn't fair,' she said. 'It isn't fair!'

---

Catherine had used their entire meal ration on two small chops. They had looked seductive in the butcher's shop, but in the pan, they looked pathetic. Still, meat was meat. She had cooked Brussels sprouts, and used a precious lump of butter in the mash. Best of all she had a bottle of beer, gift of a patient's grateful father.

'A feast,' Max said when he sat down to the table. They ate slowly, anxious to make the most of it. 'Wonderful,' he said when he had finished. She brought in blancmange and he declared his cup was running over as they carried their coffee to the settee, and settled companionably side by side.

'Catherine,' he said slowly.

Within her, nerve endings sprang alert.

'I'm going to be moved to the South Coast,' he went on quietly, 'as soon as the holiday is over.'

'Where will you live?'

'I'll live in at the hospital at first, I expect. Afterwards I may get a place. I'll play it by ear.'

Use of the word 'I' told her everything. He had not said, 'We'll get a place.'

'Will I see you still?'

He put down his cup. 'Of course you'll see me,' he said. 'How can you even ask that?'

But the time would come when she wouldn't be able to see him, and they both knew it. 'He is easing me into it,' she thought. Even though it made sense for him to move to a casualty reception area, he was preparing her for the moment when they must part for good.

They made love that night, slowly and tenderly, as though each stroke, each thrust was to be savoured, because it would not come again.

Pamela had paid for her mother to go to see *Stage Door Canteen*. She would have taken her father, too, but he had declined. Before the war, her parents had loved the cinema, had gone every week. Now they hardly ever crossed the doors. 'Their lives ended in 1940,' Pamela thought, and in a way it was true. They had lost everything then; but there was still laughter in the home sometimes, and mutual affection, and that was something.

Above them on the screen, Joan Crawford and Bette Davis were doing their bit by dancing with GIs. 'Bette Davis jitterbugging,' her mother whispered. 'I never thought I'd see that.'

Pamela preferred her films to be a bit more realistic. Lately she had seen films so real they almost leaped from the screen. She had tasted the sand in *Desert Victory*, and no wonder: seven cameramen had been killed or were missing in its making, and four more taken prisoner. That was real war; and *Millions Like Us*, a film about factory workers, had made her thrill with pride.

But on the way home arm in arm, she could tell that her mother had loved the picture. 'We'll go again soon,' she promised, 'p'raps when our Catherine comes on leave.'

For days Sarah had thought about the woman's remark: '*He was a fine man before the war.*' It was true. Hamish had protected her in the pub that night when she had first taken notice of him.

Now they sat by the stove with mugs of hot milk. Milk straight from the cow, which tasted richer and creamier than the milk back home. Sarah watched as he rattled the stove, sending ash down the pan, and causing the flames to shoot up. When he settled back in his chair, she put out a hand and covered his.

'Don't worry,' she said. 'We'll get by. You'll get work before long, and until then I can work. The woman in the shop –'

She got no further. The blow knocked her sideways from her chair. Instinctively she put her hands to her face to protect it.

'Why?' he was yelling, 'why do you shame me? Why do you remind me I'm a useless hulk?' His face was dark red, his features contorted. He hit her again, and she closed her eyes. She could shut out the sight of his face but she could not shut out his words. 'You do this. Whore! Slut! Bitch! You make a show of me to my neighbours! Why? Why?'

They had covered several miles, keeping to the hedgerows, filtering round corners, for all the world as though there were Germans lurking behind every tree. Now David was tired. His gammy leg throbbed and he wanted a drink. First, though, he sank into a chair and undid his boots. He had given up on the regulation boots and had a pair hand-made for him. Not only were they watertight, they incorporated the lift that compensated for his shortened leg. It had made marching easier.

When he had rid himself of boots and paraphernalia, he went in search of a drink. Crossing the hall, he was struck again by how beautiful it was. Moonlight was coming through the long window on the landing. It was uncurtained, which was why he had not switched on the light. But moonlight cast a ghostly glow on the stairs, and reflected off the polished wood of the floor. The corner beside the stairs was in darkness. In childhood, Henry had convinced him that a ghost lurked in the stairwell. Now he smiled at the memory of his brother's teasing. Henry! What he would give to have Henry by his side.

Suddenly he thought of the tree he had put up for Henry's leave that last Christmas, when he was killed. Catherine had helped him decorate it. Where would she be this Christmas? With Max, no doubt. He himself was taking Valerie Graham-Poole to the carol service in the cathedral. Or rather, she was taking him: it had been her invitation, and her tickets.

He collected a whisky from the library, and came back into the hall. The light fell differently from this angle, illuminating the stairs. Once they had pretended the stairs were Camelot. Henry had been King Arthur, defending his castle against all comers. '*Never fear, Sir Lancelot, my trusty knight. . .*' David had not understood what 'trusty knight' meant but he had known it was a good thing to be.

Now he lifted the whisky glass to his lips with shaking hands and felt the fiery liquid burn his throat. 'I want it back,' he thought. 'I want to be a boy again, with Henry my senior to take the strain. I want Catherine to come in in tennis whites, to have Hutch on the gramophone, Papa in his study, and no one looking to me for answers.' But no one was listening. No one was watching.

# Chapter Thirty Two

### March 1944

As soon as Catherine opened her eyes she remembered. Max was coming home. Only for 24 hours, but after an absence of five weeks that seemed like a miracle.

She listened to the morning news as she ate her toast. Someone in Parliament was complaining about female crooners, saying they reminded him of the caterwauling of an inebriated cockatoo and would depress the troops. Vera Lynn wouldn't be pleased about that. Unless they meant Ann Shelton? Actually, she herself rather liked them both, and probably so did the troops.

She had two plaice fillets in the larder, and new potatoes and peas, enough for a feast. The pleasure this gave her suddenly struck her as absurd. It was only fish, quite a small fish, and two veg., and yet she was as thrilled as if it had been caviar and truffles. Before the war they had taken food for granted. She thought of the groaning buffets at parties, and remembering pre-war parties reminded of her of David. His last letter had said the house was empty with India gone. He did not say he missed India or wanted her back, but he had sounded lonely all the same. She would write to him, soon, even go up for a weekend, or suggest he came down.

She glanced at her watch. Six-fifteen already. If she didn't get a move on she'd be late, and Queenie in a bate. Not that that mattered on such a day. Max would be home tonight, and all was right with the world.

≈≈≈

Hamish had been working for a week, now, and already Sarah felt a lightening of spirit. Once the wee-uns were up, dressed and fed, the day stretched ahead of her, gloriously empty. The work of the house was easily accomplished, and then she could either take to the open air with the pram, or put the baby in his playpen, set Joe to crayoning, and settle herself to the radio. She liked *Workers' Playtime* best, endless music designed to lift the spirits and keep Britain working.

That was something she missed, having someone to pass the time of day with, but the memory of the blow to her head when she had mentioned working still smarted. He had not hit her since, and she did not intend to provoke him again. She had the bairns, and she had Vera Lynn, and, no matter what the wireless had said this morning, when Vera sang it reminded her of Gerard. Lately she had tried to give thanks for a roof over her head and healthy bairns and a man who had triumphed over his wounds and was willing to work for her and her children.

She was beginning to love this place too, the mountains studded with sheep and patterned by clouds, the little rivulets that sprang up here and there in the rocks, and the clean, cold air. All in all, she could be a lot worse off.

Today she kept thinking about Catherine, down there with bombs and all the dangers of the big city. She would likely be at her job now, and not on the other end of her phone. And when Catherine was at home at night the shop was shut and Hamish was watchful. One day, perhaps, she would try telephoning. Catherine must have days off sometimes. For today she would stay by the stove and watch spring approaching outside the window.

⸺

Max's new hospital was near Folkestone, a great, sprawling, prefabricated place built for the thousands of casualties they were obviously expecting when the Second Front got under way. The words 'Second Front' were on everyone's lips. Newspapers speculated about it endlessly. He was pretty certain Catherine's first request when he reached her tonight would be for news. As if he were any more likely to know Eisenhower's intentions than anyone else! Even Chuck seemed short of information.

Now Max moved from bed to bed, inspecting wounds, altering medication, cheering up the depressed, and joking with the men on their way to recovery and in high spirits. The man in the corner bed was blind. They had got him too late to save his sight. His wife sat beside him as he began to learn Braille. Max watched them for a moment, seeing the two heads bent together. When she had first come to visit him, he had been a helpless hulk in the bed. She had not even been able to reach out and touch his burned hand. She had stood there, fighting back tears, and said, 'My goodness, what have you been doing?' in tones so full of love that Max had felt his own eyes smart. That was what marriage meant: for better, for worse. That man would be all right. The woman beside him would make it so.

Once more Max's conscience smote him. Damn the war that scattered people and left them in turmoil.

⸺

David pricked up his ears at the mention of Monte Cassino. For weeks now Allied troops had been fighting for every inch of the Liri valley below the ancient monastery of St Benedict. It had been essential to break through to relieve the Allied divisions under attack at Anzio. Last month they had bombed the monastery where it stood on the high ground of Monte Cassino, being used as an observation post for the German artillery. But the troops who went in after the bombing were repulsed by paratroopers, and the conflict had continued. He was hoping to hear that it had been resolved, but he was disappointed. The fighting and the bloodshed on both sides were continuing.

He pushed aside his plate and began to sort his post. There was a letter from Catherine, and he tore it open. She was fine, and hoping to see him before long. Max Detweiler had moved to work on the South Coast.

Monte Cassino or not, as David got ready to start his day he was humming softly under his breath.

---

India wove her way in and out of the traffic, anxious to get home. Work had gone well today, and yesterday the Lord Lieutenant had hinted at recognition of what she was doing. It would be only fair, but it would also be very pleasant. An investiture, her photograph in *The Tatler*, letters of congratulation. The sad thing was that they would all give her her married name. Still, everyone knew she was a Callingham of Kynaston.

Thinking about Kynaston reminded her of the importance of securing its future. Militancy was abroad now, all the fault of this foolish war. Still, that was almost over. Every day she received dossiers came – about resettlement, rebuilding, the part the WVS would play in creating the brave new world everyone was expecting. All nonsense, but not, thank God, anything to do with her.

The minute the war was over she would consider herself free. Then she would attend to Kynaston: re-staff the place, refurbish it, repair the neglect of the last few years. And put some backbone into David so that he fought for their joint heritage. Churchill would never countenance the coal industry passing out of private hands, but it would do no harm, meanwhile, to bring pressure to bear on individual MPs.

She had not given up hope of a child of her own, a boy. But if the worst came to the worst, David would have to do his duty. The only woman he had ever shown interest in was the Graham-Poole girl, but she was in the ATS and everyone knew what that meant, from a point of view of morals. So she was out of the question.

India changed gear for the junction, and made up her mind. She would give herself another year, and then she would draw up a shortlist of suitable breeding-stock, and make sure David chose someone fit to be mistress of Kynaston and mother to its heir.

≈

As Catherine walked along the ward corridor she heard sobbing in the sluice. The girl was a VAD too, an Irish girl from Cork who had volunteered earlier in the war.

'What is it, Bridget? Has someone upset you?' The girl put her hand inside the top of her apron and drew out a newspaper cutting, and Catherine spread it out to read it. Britain had sealed off the Irish Republic because Dublin had refused to expel Axis diplomats. No travel was permitted either way. According to the paper, the 250,000 Irish citizens working in Britain would not be allowed to return home, and neither would the 164,000 serving with the British armed forces.

'That isn't fair,' Catherine said. 'You're helping us, surely they can see that? Were you wanting to go home soon?'

The nurse was shaking her head. 'No. But I knew I could if I wanted. Now I can't.'

'Never mind,' Catherine said. 'We'll see if Queenie can do anything about it. She knows the right people. Now, how about a nice cup of tea?'

Max had been withdrawn lately. She couldn't put her finger on it but when they were together there was a subtle difference. She had been worrying about it, and it would do her good to worry about someone else's troubles for a change.

Sarah loved the way night fell, here. In Belgate, streetlamps had sprung to life while it was still daylight. Here the light lingered, and when darkness fell the sky was spangled with stars, paling in the west where the sun hung on as though reluctant to let go. Tonight she had told little Joe to sit in the window and watch for Hamish coming home. She had wanted to say, 'Watch for your Dada,' but somehow the words wouldn't come, and Joe did not seem keen to watch, anyway. Hamish was right – she would have to stop thinking of, and referring to him as, 'little Joe'. He was nearly four years old and tall for his age. He was going to be like his real Dada, a big man.

She closed her eyes, then, remembering Gerard and his gentle love-making. Nowadays her body ached from Hamish's clumsy sex. She could not refer to it as love, because it wasn't. Sometimes she thought he was punishing her for something – for the pain in his leg, for the loss of his profession of soldiering, for being, as he had told her more than once, a millstone round his neck. But there was no point in thinking like that now. He would be here soon, and if his meal was not on the table . . . Haste made her clumsy. She dropped a spoon and then a knife, cut her finger as she peeled and chopped. What had Hannah Chaffey often said? You made your bed in this life and then you had to lie on it.

Suddenly she ached for Hannah to walk through the door. At home she had dreaded the noise of the woman's voice. '*Anybody in?*' she would call as she breezed through the door, and Sarah would raise her eyes to heaven before she called, '*Come in.*' But Hannah was 200 miles away and in the back room Alexander was wailing. She dried her hands on a tea-towel, brushed one hand across her eyes, and went to comfort her baby.

———

David had invited Valerie to dinner on the last night but one of her leave, reasoning that she would want to spend the last evening with her parents. She looked smart, but oddly childlike in uniform. Tonight, though, she wore a dark-red velvet dress with a little bolero jacket whose collar framed her face. 'She is pretty,' he thought, as they settled either side of a table in the Grand Hotel's dining-room.

But her first remark was not feminine at all. 'I see Orde Wingate has been killed.'

'Yes.' David leaned back as the waiter filled his glass. The Chindit leader had been a legend, his operations behind enemy lines to harry the Japanese in Burma causing Churchill to hail him as a genius. And now he was dead in a plane crash. 'Yes,' he said again, 'he'll be a loss.'

They ordered something called *mouton purèe*. 'Old sheep,' Valerie mouthed at him from behind her menu, making him laugh. It came with mounds of vegetables and something that resembled a dumpling. 'Do you remember chops?' David said as they ate. 'Sometimes I yearn for chops.'

'Fillet steak,' Valerie said.

'Pork crackling!'

'Anything but fish!' They laughed, with David pretending to drool.

'I enjoy her company,' he thought. 'I admire her principles, and her straightforwardness.' But he couldn't imagine going to bed with her. With Catherine . . . with Catherine . . . his daydreaming suddenly found him sweating and ashamed. 'Why is life unfair?' he asked suddenly, and realised with shock that he had spoken aloud.

'Who knows?' Valerie said, appearing to see nothing odd in the question and continuing to eat her meal.

They talked of war, and life in the ATS.

'I didn't choose it, but I like it now, and it pleases Daddy. He was a military man, so if it's good enough for him . . .' She grinned suddenly. 'I know what you're thinking. You're thinking what I used to think – that the WAAFs and the Wrens are much "nicer".'

'I wasn't,' he said, and then, overtaken by honesty, 'Well, perhaps a little.'

'The Army is good enough for Mary Churchill, too.'

'*Touché*,' David said. 'You're with an Ack-Ack battery, aren't you?'

'I was. In the beginning they thought our voices wouldn't carry above the noise of gunfire, but they can. You should hear me shout "Fire!" But I've operated searchlights, driven officers, even repaired three-ton trucks and gun limbers! We're wizard at vehicle maintenance – you should see me strip down an engine. There are more than 200,000 of us women now, and they say 80 per cent of the Army's driving is done by us. Since my commission came through, I've been mostly in welfare. We have a lot of girls in out-of-the-way places who need support. But I loved my time with a mixed battery. When we downed a Jerry plane, it was a huge thrill.'

She was silent for a moment. 'You tended not to think it was someone's son, someone's brother, you just blasted them out of the sky.'

'That's war,' David said, and knew that, like him, she was

remembering how Henry had died.

$$\approx$$

They had gone to a pub, and now they sat in a smoky booth, hardly able to take their eyes from one another's faces. 'Will you miss flying, when it's all over?'

'I thought about that through all those days and nights in France, with nothing to do but wait. Of course, I wanted – I want – to come home to you, for everything to be normal again. But I worry sometimes that, after this, nothing can quite measure up. I look at the other chaps, living for danger, some of them. How will they take to peace?'

'Do you mean they'll miss the excitement?'

Michael shook his head. 'No, not exactly. I think I mean the sense that what you are doing matters. It's nonsense, of course, but – '

'It does matter, you know that.' She covered his hand with her own. 'I'm so proud of you.'

Again he shook his head. 'I'm not as brave as you think I am.' He told her, then, about being afraid, not only for himself but for the men and women who hid him and gradually eased his path to freedom. 'They were just kids, some of them, or old men. And women. I was kept in the back room of an old widow for a while. Ninety if she was a day. I told her I felt guilty at the risk she was taking, and she said if I got back to England and killed a Boche for her, it would be worth every moment of risk.' He laughed. 'She really wanted blood.'

He looked down at his glass, then. 'I'm going to enjoy these few days' leave with you, but then I want to get back to flying. Get the job done, once and for all.'

She smiled at him, trying to ignore what she had read in last week's papers – that 72 aircraft had been lost over Berlin in one raid alone; that many airmen had been shot down on their first operation; that the rest had just a 50-50 chance of completing their tour of 30 ops. How many of his nine lives had Michael already used?

Afterwards they walked hand-in-hand through the dark streets, feeling a kind of exaltation at being united. 'It won't be long now,' Michael said as they neared his home, and she knew he did not mean their homeward journey.

Later, when they had drunk cocoa with his parents and made their separate goodnights, she tiptoed along the landing and found him waiting for her. Their loving was frenzied at first, born out of need, but at last it was gentle. He kissed and marvelled at every inch of her body, allowing his lips to linger when he sensed a need in her for more. And at last they climaxed, unable to quell the release of emotion that made them cry out.

'They must have heard that,' Pamela whispered, ashamed.

'I should think they heard it out at sea,' Michael said. They subsided into laughter, muffled laughter that was almost as sweet as what had gone before.

———

Catherine had set a beautiful table, added logs to the fire, chilled the wine. Now, even though everything was turned off, she hovered over pans and stove like an anxious parent; but when Max came through the door she forgot everything except how very much she had missed him. Their lips met and were glued even as each of them struggled free of clothes, and then he was carrying her towards the bed.

It was only afterwards that she remembered the fish that she had queued for and had poached to perfection, for serving at eight-fifteen. She turned her head slightly to see the glowing face of the clock. It was twenty past ten. 'What a waste,' she thought and closed her eyes for sleep.

# Chapter Thirty Three

June 1944

IT TOOK CATHERINE A MOMENT to realise where she was. There was no sound of London traffic on the road outside, so she was at home in Mellows. And then she remembered her promise and threw back the covers. The clock showed five past eight. She had slept in. At nine the Maguire family was arriving, and at nine-fifteen Sarah would be on the other end of the telephone line. They had arranged it all by letter, and Catherine had checked with the Maguires last night. They were all agog to hear Sarah's voice.

She didn't switch on the wireless as she usually did, in case the phone rang early and she didn't hear it. She bathed and dressed, and was cramming toast into her mouth when they arrived, sheepishly trooping in: Sarah's father, her brother Jim and his wife, Molly, child in arms, Aunty Jessie, and, bringing up the rear, Hannah Chaffey. 'I might have guessed it,' Catherine thought.

She made them tea and put out biscuits, and they made desultory conversation, but there was only one thing on everyone's mind. When would the phone ring?

'She might have forgotten?' Hannah offered when it got to twemty past nine. Catherine shook her head, but doubt was nagging her. Had Hamish found out about the telephone in the village store? Found out, and stopped Sarah using it? And then, magically, it was ringing.

'Sarah? Yes, they're here, they're all here.' She turned to pass the phone to Sarah's father, but his cheeks were wet with tears and when he spoke to his daughter, his voice was choked. 'It was a good idea,' Catherine thought. 'I'm glad I did it because it's going to work.'

David was carrying a tray through to the breakfast-room when he heard the distant mention of 'beaches'. He quickened his step. He had switched the wireless on earlier when he set the table, but he had not paid attention to it. Now, though, there was something in the announcer's voice. He reached the table, put down the tray, and listened. '*Here is a special bulletin read by John Snagge.*'

And then another voice: '*D-Day has come. Early this morning the Allies began the assault on the north-west face of Hitler's European fortress. The first official news came just after half-past nine, when Supreme Headquarters of the Allied Expeditionary Force issued Communique No. 1. That said: "Under the command of General Eisenhower, Allied Naval Forces began landing Allied forces on the northern coast of France.*'

The voice was dry and unsensational, but David felt his skin prickle. The Second Front had begun at last.

When she put down the phone, Sarah felt overcome. Why had she ever left them? The sound of her father's voice, croaking as though he had a cold; Jim not knowing what to say and calling her 'our littl'un' as he had done when she was growing up;

Molly, shy at first and then full of chat about the baby; Hannah, spurting out news as usual. She found she was laughing as she walked back from the shop, but the laughter was not far from tears. When would she see them again? Before she rang off, Catherine had promised there would be other such calls, but it was still not the same as seeing them.

Still. Hamish's job at the tannery had done wonders for him. Things would get better . . . were already getting better. She let herself into the house, and when she had settled the children she switched on the wireless. She was unbuttoning her coat when she heard the excited voice of a commentator.

*'This is the greatest seaborne invasion in history. The sea is teeming with ships. Fast-moving torpedo boats, warships, merchantmen, minesweepers, landing craft and barges. This an armada, and up above them the RAF are protecting the ships. History is being made this day.'*

So it had happened. All morning Max had stayed glued to a wireless set, drinking in details. He was listening to an on-the-spot report when his phone rang. It was Chuck Cohn. 'You heard, then? This is it, Max. I hope you're ready for casualties – men are dropping like flies. Still, not for much longer. Our troops have gained a foothold.'

For an hour or more, Max had been reflecting on the sheer courage of the young men splashing ashore to face a German army dug in behind fortified bunkers. So they were dropping like flies, were they? 'We're ready,' he said.

Before ringing off, Chuck told him something of Operation Overlord. 'The British went in first, the 6th Airborne Division. Gliders. But the wind scattered part of the force. We put the 82nd and 101st Airborne into Utah –'

'Utah?' Max was puzzled.

'Sorry. Utah Beach. There are five beaches, Utah, Omaha, Gold, Juno and Sword. The bloodiest battle is at Omaha, apparently. We lost men in the water, and there was mortar and machine-gun fire. It's bad.'

'How long before the first casualties reach us?'

'I don't know. At the moment the emphasis is on pouring men in – but they'll reach you soon enough. Good luck.'

When Chuck had rung off, Max slumped in his chair. It was over – or, at least, the liberation had begun. Hope would be alive again in Europe, especially in the camps. Suddenly he thought of Miriam. She would know all this, too. He smiled to himself, knowing just what she would do – what she always did at moments of high drama. She would put on an apron and bake. And bake, and bake. And she would be remembering her parents who had died in Belsen, and wishing that they had been alive to see this day.

⸻

They were all clustered round one desk where someone had plugged in a wireless. 'What's all this?' India said. Six voices answered at once: 'D-Day has come!'

'Not before time,' India said. 'But can we all get back to work now?' They had made the same ridiculous fuss when Rome fell two days ago. As if that hadn't been a foregone conclusion. Everyone knew what Italians were like. Pusillanimous.

She sat at her desk, signing letters, and trying not to think about the way everyone would go on and on now. Every little detail. For weeks! Still, there would be compensations: freedom from all this dreary office work; better food – and, better still, the return of staff. It would be a relief have them in the home she shared with Rupert, but, more importantly, Kynaston would come alive again. The estate would be properly run, instead of being run into the ground as it was now. The problem of an heir would remain, however.

She must have a child! Rupert would have to be checked: it couldn't be her. She clenched her inner muscles, glorying in their strength. Nothing wrong with her! Her period was due tomorrow. With luck, it might not come.

Work had ceased in the factory as soon as the news came. The lathes had fallen silent one by one as it was passed from mouth to mouth, and for once the foreman had not played war. They had been wondering quite how to celebrate, when the works manager had appeared. He couldn't close the factory, he explained, because, believe it or not, there was still a war on. But in view of the occasion there would be a longer dinner-break, and the drinks would be on him.

The drinks were crates of light ale or orangeade. There were paper cups and miraculously, the canteen served up chips in paper packets.

'Three cheers for the gaffer,' Joyce said, raising a cup.

'And Winnie!' came several voices.

'And Eisenhower – and Roosevelt –' They were on to minor members of the wartime Cabinet when someone remembered the King. 'God bless the King,' the foreman said. 'And the Queen!' For some reason that made one girl cry, and the tears spread, like a virus, till they were all sobbing, quite why they could not tell.

And then a voice started up, quavery at first, but getting firmer: '*Land of hope and glory, Mother of the free. . .*' Shoulders straightened, tears were dried, as one by one they joined in. They sang on until the end, and then went quietly back to their workbenches.

'So it's come, then,' Sarah said, as Hamish came stooping through the doorway.

'What?'

'D-Day! The Second Front.'

He was shrugging off his coat, bending to unlace his boots. 'Aye. I heard.'

She shifted the baby to her other arm. He was angry about something. She thanked her stars that Joe was playing with his blocks in the back bedroom. 'Are you ready for your meal?'

He didn't answer, just shook his head.

'Is something wrong?' She moved to the pram and laid Alexander in it. If there was going to be trouble he would be better there.

'What's wrong?' she said again.

His shoulders were shaking. She knew that sign. 'Wrong?' When he was angry his accent thickened until she could hardly understand him. He was on his feet now, turning towards her. 'They've let me go. I'm not wanted. All for speaking out, that's all. I earned the right to speak out, didn't I? I suffered for those bastards with their safe jobs. I should have died. I'd've been better off dead.'

He was crying now, working himself up 'You're all against me, even you. Especially you, standing there gloating. Yes, I've been cast adrift again – surplus to requirements – and it's not –' she flinched as the blow landed, 'not –' This one rocked her back against the dresser. '– not my fault – not my fucking fault!' She saw the bedroom door open and a little face appear in the crack.

'Go back!' she cried. 'Go back, pet!' And then her mouth was full of something, saliva maybe – even blood. And there were lights flashing on her closed eyelids, for all the world like gunfire flashes far away in France.

It had begun in the early afternoon. Landing craft full of wounded and dying were towed into the dockyard, the men conscious mostly, but not talking much, though with eyes which told of bloody conflict. Lorries brought them up to the hospital. 'There are German soldiers there, too – I'm not touching Jerries!' a young nurse said, as they were helping to unload. But before Max could intervene, a sister turned on her: 'They're not "Jerries", Nurse. They're wounded. Remember your profession.'

Max worked on, sweat clouding his eyes, until his body threatened to betray him and his legs give way. He rested for a moment in the cool of the sluice, and then he went back in to the theatre. What seemed like a thousand men had been cleaned up, wounds were dressed and beds were full, but the casualties kept on coming.

'What shall we do?' a nurse asked, despairingly.

'Manage,' another said grimly. 'Just manage'.

'Where are you from, son?' Max asked one boy in theatre.

'Missouri, sir.' And then, as the anaesthetic began to take hold, 'Will I see it again, sir?'

'You will if I have my way,' Max said, and began the debridement of the boy's wounds.

'I'm sorry we have to serve ourselves.' In the Kynaston dining-room there was food on the sideboard in chafing dishes, and they stood side by side to fill their plates.

'Don't apologise,' Catherine said, 'I like it better this way.'

She sat down on the right-hand side of the table, near to the head where David would sit. 'I was over-awed when I first came to Kynaston. It was all so grand.'

'I suppose it was. I can't say I miss it. Still, tell me what's happening to you.'

'Max is near Portsmouth now. They moved him from Folkestone to where the casualties from France will go first. Afterwards they'll be transferred if they need specialist treatment, but he's at a sort of forward station. He's a specialist, as you know, but I think it's all hands to the wheel at first. Which is why I'm going back to work tomorrow. I wouldn't have left, if I'd known it was all going to happen today, but we've been talking about it for so long that I suppose I thought it would never be real.'

'So you're on your own in the flat?' David tried not to let the satisfaction show in his voice.

'Yes. I have been for months. Max comes up to town when he can, and I've been down to visit him once. The hospital is amazing. It's newly built, single storey, and the wards are long, low huts, each with 20 beds and things like theatres and dispensaries in what they call blisters. Very utilitarian but very efficient. They're ready for whatever comes – well, what I suppose is already coming.'

They talked on through their sausage casserole and sponge and custard, and then David looked at his watch. 'Ten minutes to nine,' he said. 'You go into the library, I'll bring the coffee.'

'Better hurry,' Catherine said. 'He's on at nine o'clock.'

They sat in companionable silence until the faltering tones of the King came through the wireless.

'If I could,' David thought as he listened, 'I would keep this moment forever. Just as it is. Catherine there, opposite me, and this sense of the triumph of right.'

≈≈≈

She was lying in the dark, wondering, when the telephone call came.

'Pamela, get up – get up! It's Michael, for you.'

She followed her father downstairs and took the receiver from her mother's hand.

'I'm back on the ground, Pammy. I knew you'd worry so that's why I rang. It was wonderful – men pouring up the beaches as though they were going to a football match. They were all brave, our lot and the Yanks. They took a terrible thrashing on Omaha apparently. Do you know what that is?'

'Yes,' she said, 'I know about the beaches. It was on the wireless.'

'I went down low to see what I could see. The men didn't have any cover, except where a shell had landed and there was a sand mound. But they kept on pushing forward – even when the men beside them fell, they just pushed on. There were ships as far as the horizon, and the sky was black too . . . planes towing gliders, our chaps harrying the Germans. Not much opposition up above, though. They say the Luftwaffe is a busted flush, and we had Spitfires, Typhoons and Thunderbolts up there. I had a new Spit – Mark V, with gyroscopic gun-sights. Two kills I got! Saw them going down, so I banked and then came in again to make sure.'

'Don't,' she said, 'You're scaring me.'

'I had it easy, Pammy, up there in the clean air. Out of the smoke and confusion down below. We lost a lot of men today, brave men. Still, *c'est la* bloody *guerre*, as Chalky says. We've got to go off again, after some kip. I love you, Pammy. Sleep tight!'

Then he was gone.

## Chapter Thirty Four

### October 1944

Max caught an early train into London. He was travelling light now, many of his possessions having already been shipped out. He would be reunited with them when he got home to New York. Home? He had come to think of London as home, even when he was in Portsmouth, because that was where Catherine was. But this would be their last couple of days together.

He sat there, incredulous. How could he leave her? How should he leave her? With tears? With a cheery farewell? He had thought about buying her a gift, a huge gift, and then rejected the idea. It would smack of a pay-off, and that would be a travesty. 'I love her,' he thought. 'She is the love of my life and always will be. But I love Miriam, too, and she is the mother of my children.'

He sat for a while, wondering why he did not feel more guilt. He had betrayed Miriam – something that five years ago he would have sworn was impossible. But five years ago he had seen his life stretching ahead, rich, certainly, as long as men and women were vain, a little boring but filled with the love of family. And yet he had become another woman's lover, and now he was hurting her, too. He had seen it in her eyes for weeks.

'It's war,' he thought, and then felt ashamed that he was

shifting blame.

≡≡≡

'So will you wear white?' a woman asked.

'Course she won't. Our Pamela's not a hypocrite.' There was a roar of raucous laughter at that.

'Wish I was a virgin,' a woman said plaintively. 'You give it away, and then it's too late.'

'You should have kept it on a bit of elastic, Maisie. Then you could've pulled it back.'

'Well, at least I can remember who I lost it to, Jenny. Not like some.'

'Hey up.' As usual it was Joyce who stopped things getting nasty. 'The war's not over yet so don't get demob happy.'

'No, it's bloody not over. My brother's in a Jap. camp. Everyone goes on about Rome and bloody Paris, but that's not the end of it, not by a long chalk.'

'Did you see that about them suicides, in the paper a bit ago?'

'D'you mean the Japs?' Voices were subdued now.

'That's right. Eight thousand of them killed themselves rather than be taken prisoner. On some island, I can't remember the name.'

'It was in the Pacific. I know that because they tossed themselves into the sea, some of them. They won't give up. It'll take years to finish them.'

The mood had turned sombre now. For weeks everyone had been euphoric, but reality was setting in. No one was thinking of weddings.

'They're evacuating London again. V-1s are falling day and night, killing hundreds. Now V-2s. My man's sister's down there, and her bairns.'

'Let's get back to work,' Joyce said. There was a stubbing

out of cigarettes, and a final swig of cups, before they went back to their lathes.

―――――

The V bombs that fell night and day had brought back unhappy memories of that other bombing for Catherine. They had been talking about it at break, and now she couldn't get it out of her mind. The weight of the rubble on her, the inability to move, and then the sight of Tilly's anklet glinting in the glare of the lights. She felt her eyes prick at the memory and blinked fiercely. No use looking back.

Or forward. Tomorrow would be her last whole day with Max, and she would have to interrupt it to have lunch with David. That had been arranged before she realised it would be Max's last day, and she couldn't disappoint David when he came up to town so rarely. But she was counting hours now – could she spare even two?

She couldn't bear to think about it, so instead she checked on the young pilot she had prepped for going down to theatre. She had sterilised the area of skin to be used for the Thiersch graft, and shaved off the surrounding hair. The skin they would take, thin as cigarette paper, was to make him a new eyelid. She checked the loose bandage covering the graft area, and squeezed his hand. 'You'll be fine,' she whispered. 'They'll give you your injection in a moment, and the next thing you know it will be over.'

'Do you have to go now?' he pleaded.

She straightened his sheet and patted him gently. 'Yes. But I'll be back. You'll be sitting up and eating by then.'

'I couldn't have a cig before you go, could I?'

She looked around. 'Two puffs, and even then I'll be shot.' She lit a cigarette, let him draw on it for a moment, then nipped it out and put it carefully in the packet she kept for moments like this. 'Be good,' she said.

The burned mouth puckered in what was supposed to be a grin. 'I don't want to be good when you're around, Nurse.'

Catherine drew in a theatrical breath. 'What are you suggesting?'

'Wait till I get out of this bed and I'll show you.'

It was her turn to grin. Flirting with them was part of the healing process, a reminder that they were still sexual beings. 'Behave yourself, then, and you'll get better quicker. Don't keep me waiting'. On an impulse she bent and put her lips against the scarred and leathery cheek. 'Now, do behave or we'll both be in trouble'.'

---

Opposite David, the colliery manager was pessimistic. 'If the unions get their hands on the pits, coal-mining is finished. They think it'll be so simple. When we lost that man in the fall of stone last month, an overman said to me: "There'll be no deaths in the pit when they're in public ownership." They really think it'll be that easy.'

'What will you do if it does come to nationalisation?'

'Stay, I suppose. If they want me, that is. They may line managers up against a wall, for all I know.'

'They'll still need expertise,' David said. 'To be honest, I'm not sure how I'd feel. I ought to care – the family's fortune, such as it is, grew out of one of my forebears' grubbing coal from the earth with his bare hands – or that's how my father used to describe it. He was rather proud of it; my sister less so.'

'Yes,' the manager said laconically, 'I can imagine that.'

As David drove away from the pit, he looked at the fields, many of them already harvested. The landscape of Britain had changed with the war. In 1939 about 17 million acres had been grassland used for livestock; 12 million acres had been arable and crop-growing. The U-boat blockade had changed all that. More food had had to be produced at home, so chalk downs had been ploughed up, to the disadvantage of wildlife. Hedgerows had been removed to facilitate the passage of tractors. 'We've made the land work for us,' David thought, 'but it will never be the same again. Unless we work now to restore it.'

Suddenly he realised how much he loved this land. He had never wanted it, had hated the fact that Henry's death had forced it on him. But now he loved it with all his heart. The feeling of elation lasted until he remembered he was having lunch with Rupert and India. She would play hell if he was late. He put down his foot, and a few minutes later he was slipping into his seat at the immaculate table.

'They say the V bombs have caused a bigger evacuation than 39-40.' Rupert was toying with his smoked mackerel. 'Half a million mothers and children were shipped out, and half a million elderly and homeless.'

'Thank God they didn't send any of them here,' India said. 'And why don't they shoot those rocket things down? Honestly, they just need to get some organisation!'

'You could go down there and do it for them, India. Make a plan, delegate a little.' David saw alarm flare up in Rupert's eyes. Not fair to get India in a bate when poor Rupert had to go home with her. 'Anyway,' he said conciliatingly, 'I'm off to London myself tomorrow.'

'Why go down there if it's dangerous?' She sounded really distressed, David thought. Perhaps she did care about him a little?

'I'll be careful,' he said. 'Anyway, they say you get a warning. The engine cuts out, and then it just drops, but you have time to take cover.'

'That was the V-1. Apparently these new things, the V-2s, just dive straight down,' Rupert put in.

'Why are you going?' India aligned her knife and fork and fixed her gaze on him.

'Oh, odds and ends. The club, a theatre maybe.'

'With Catherine Allerton, I suppose.'

'With Catherine Callingham, you mean.' Again Rupert shifted uneasily, but this time David wasn't backing off. 'She married our brother, remember? In a half-way decent society, she'd own Kynaston now.'

'Don't be silly! She has no right to it.' She stopped herself and drew breath. 'Anyway, will you still think she's a Callingham when she marries her Jew-boy?' There was triumph in her eyes as her dart went home.

'Who told you they were marrying?' David asked.

There was a moment's pause before she replied, 'She did, when she was here. As soon as the war ends, she said. Then she's off to America.'

David wanted to tell her that they couldn't marry because Max already had a wife, but he wouldn't betray Catherine's confidence. Though even as he gave himself a noble motive for his silence, he recognised the truth: he couldn't be sure that Catherine wouldn't marry Max. Max could get a divorce – or they could simply co-habit. They were doing that already.

———

Sarah swayed with relief when she saw the blood. Thank God! Thank Mother Mary! She could not face another pregnancy, not with the way things were. She had her hands full protecting the two she had. Now that Hamish was at home all the time she had to be constantly vigilant.

Hamish had nightmares, too, screaming nightmares that woke the children, and left him lying in a pool of sweat, seemingly unaware of what was happening. He had had to go to Glasgow to see an Army doctor – something to do with his wounds and his pension. She had asked him what the doctor had said, and he had muttered something that began with 'post'. She had not understood the rest.

But he had been calmer since that visit to Glasgow, so maybe they were helping him. He had not wanted his rights as often, either, which was a blessing. But even once could be enough for a baby. Still, she was safe for another month. She picked up the laundry basket and went out into the sunshine to peg out her washing.

The journey was dragging, now, so Max opened his paper and tried to concentrate. The new V-2s were knocking hell out of London – Chuck had told him that over the telephone when they had arranged to meet today. In the paper, a columnist was advancing the theory that Washington was changing its commitment to the 'Hitler first' strategy that had been agreed by Allied leaders. Chuck had told him last time that Washington considered the war in Europe virtually won. There was some argument between Eisenhower and Montgomery over how to finish it, but that would be easily settled.

The emphasis then must shift towards the war in the East. As the Allies moved into Europe, they were setting up field hospitals, and gradually the need to send any but the most serious cases back to England would cease. Admiral Nimitz would advance, then, across the central Pacific, and MacArthur would come from New Guinea to the Philippines. It looked as though that was already happening. The large Japanese forces in the South Pacific Islands would be isolated by airpower. 'And I'll be needed there,' he thought as the train came into Waterloo.

He went straight to the taxi rank and climbed into a waiting cab. 'Where to, Yank?' the cabbie asked.

'The Lamb and Flag,' Max said, and settled back in his seat.

He looked at his watch. He was fifteen minutes late, but Chuck would wait. He was laid back about time. He was actually relaxed about most things, except for love of his country and his race, and his detestation of those who would do harm to either. 'He's been a good friend to me,' Max thought. 'And he'll keep what he knows about Catherine and me to himself.'

The pub was in a one-way street, so he paid off the cab at the corner and began to walk. The Woolworths store next but one to the pub was crowded with shoppers: if rockets were a regular occurrence, they were clearly not frightening the populace. A wind had got up, and the pub sign was swinging in the breeze.

Max was almost there when everything seemed to explode around him. The noise deafened him, and he felt himself blown sideways. The bang was followed by a giant sucking sound; there was smoke everywhere; and out of the corner of his eye he saw a flicker of flame. Things were falling out of the sky, whirling like pieces of paper but landing with a thud. He could hear screaming, and also a terrible animal sound. A horse was half on the road, half on the pavement – its flanks were twitching but its head was almost blown away. It gave one last shudder and was still.

That was when he saw the pram, twisted and buckled. The woman who had been pushing it lay in a heap half under the wheels. He reeled towards it. Her eyes stared up at him, her mouth open in astonishment. He pushed aside the blankets and saw that the baby was dead, too.

He straightened up then, and looked towards the pub. There was nothing left of it, just piles of rubble and bricks.

⸻

The obstetrician ushered them to seats and sat down facing them. 'Well,' he said.

India tried not to let her irritation show. Why wouldn't he get on with it? And if he did that ridiculous thing of putting left and right finger tips together as he usually did, she would scream.

'Well,' he said again, 'I'm happy to tell you that the tests we did on you, Rupert, show perfectly healthy sperm. No problem.'

'So it's not my fault?' Rupert said.

'It isn't anyone's fault,' the doctor said smoothly, 'unless you blame Mother Nature.'

'Mother Nature!' India couldn't help but erupt. 'If we're both so revoltingly healthy, why am I not pregnant? And if you can't provide an explanation, at least tell us what to do next.'

To her amazement, she heard Rupert chuckle. She was turning to wither him when he spoke. 'I suppose we just have to keep trying. Well, that's not too hard.'

The doctor was laughing with him now in the way that men always clung together. It had been a mistake coming to a man who was a member of Rupert's club, she'd said that at the time. Now, like Henry and David had done through all those years, they were shutting her out. As David and Rupert had also done at lunchtime. Making her feel the outsider who would never, ever be allowed inside the charmed circle. 'It's happening again,' she thought.

'I can't see anything really wrong,' the obstetrician repeated. 'Your organs are fine. You're ovulating regularly. There's no mechanical reason why you shouldn't conceive.'

'Then why don't I?'

He pulled a face. 'It could be a dozen reasons, including simple bad luck.'

India gathered up her dignity. Bad luck, indeed! You didn't pay doctors outrageous fees to be told you had bad luck.

Max had stayed around to see if he could help, but rescue workers had been quick on the scene. 'I'm a doctor,' he had said when one would have elbowed him aside.

'You're a casualty, mate, from the look of you.'

He knew the man was right. He must look a spectacle. There was dust in his mouth, he had lost his cap, and there was blood on his hand – whose blood he did not know. He shook his head at offers of an ambulance, and made his way to the next street. There was a pub there, and he went in. It was strangely silent. 'Brandy,' he said. 'If you've got it.'

'I have for you, sir,' the barman said, diving under the bar counter. 'Caught in that lot, were you?'

'I was meeting a friend – in the Lamb and Flag.'

'Did it catch any of it?'

'It's gone,' Max said. He was fumbling for money to pay but the barman shook his head.

'On the house' he said. 'And another later on if you need it.'

After an hour or so in a corner booth, Max sought out a telephone box and rang the Embassy.

'Charles Cohn,' he said. 'Have you heard from him?'

'No, sir.'

'I think he may have been caught in a V-2 raid.' He gave the details, and was about to ring off when the man checked him.

'Actually, sir, we were trying to contact you. Your flight on Thursday has been cancelled but we're trying to get you on another. Can you keep in touch?'

⸺⸺

It was sunny today, which was nice, but Sarah preferred the evenings. There was so much space here that the moon seemed brighter with no smoke to obscure it. Sometimes in the night she would tiptoe to the window and watch the moonlight on the loch. At times it made a roadway that looked solid enough to walk on. She would dream of walking along it, on and on until it petered out somewhere. But she could never leave her bairns.

Tonight it would not grow dark before bedtime. Which meant that Hamish would not go to sleep when his head touched the pillow. She sighed and went back to her chores, but she had hardly begun her peeling when she heard a cry. She turned and saw Hamish stepping back from where Joe had been playing. The man looked suddenly sheepish but the child's eyes were wild with shock.

'Come here, Joe.' Sarah tried to keep her voice calm but the child stood, transfixed, the red mark on his cheek already deepening. She moved towards him, not caring now that Hamish stood between them. He was silent, had been so since he had struck the child. She drew level with him and met him, eye to eye. At the same time she reached out with her hand and sought for her son. She touched his hair. If she reached for his shoulder or tried to grasp his jersey she would have to bend and that would mean she would have to take her gaze from Hamish's face. She couldn't risk that so she tugged gently at the little boy's hair.

'Come to Mammy, Joe. Here, by me.' Would he obey her without her making eye contact? She felt him move and then suddenly he was against her, burying his face in her skirt. So far, so good.

'Now,' she said, her eyes never wavering, 'listen to me and listen hard. If you ever, ever again, lay a hand on my child, on either of my children – I will kill you!

≈≈≈

There were candles on the table, and a chrysanthemum head floating in a bowl. But as he sat in the dimly lit room listening to Catherine in the kitchen, finishing cooking the meal, Max was thinking of other candles, flickering in the synagogue as the *chayan* sang the *baruch habo*, the blessing of the bride and bridegroom. Chuck had been there as he had slipped a ring on to Miriam's ring finger and said: 'Behold, thou art consecrated unto me by this ring, according to the law of Moses and of Israel.' And then had come the *ketuba*, the marriage contract, and the crushing of the wine glass under his foot. 'I am Jewish,' he thought, 'and I cannot escape it.'

Over dinner Catherine told him about her mother's letter. 'Daddy has a job, in a garage. Some kind of book-keeping, but it's getting him out of the house, and the money will be a huge help.'

'You've helped them with money?'

'A little, and I think Mummy was grateful for it. But I don't think Daddy felt comfortable about it, so having his own money again will be wonderful.'

She was remembering how the light had gone out of her father when his business had gone. Truly the war had a lot to answer for.

They had peaches and tinned cream for pudding. 'How do you do it?' she asked, then, 'No, don't tell me – Americans are resourceful!' They had coffee, too, real coffee, courtesy of the mysterious Chuck, whom she had never met. 'Lovely!' she said as the smell assailed her nostrils.

Max smiled but he didn't speak. She realised then that he had hardly spoken all evening. 'What's up?' she said. 'You're very quiet.'

He told her about the bomb.

'So Chuck is dead?' He nodded. 'I'm so sorry, Max. I know what a good friend he was.' She rose from her seat and went to take him in her arms. Afterwards they sat quietly, neither of them saying much, nor referring to the fact that soon they would part forever. Catherine was surprised at her own calmness. Perhaps that was how you felt when your world ended – quite flat and unemotional.

'Do you know what time your flight is?' she asked at last.

He shook his head as he reached for her hand. 'I don't want to leave you, Catherine, but I must. I always told . . .'

She held up a hand to stay his words. 'I know. You have always been honest. You'll go home, and I will wish you well, Max. Because I love you.'

When he would have spoken, she held up her hand again. 'Don't say anything. Just take me to bed and make love to me. We mustn't waste a minute we have together. Not a single minute.'

He took her in his arms, and she closed her eyes, and tried to blot out everything but the moment. Anyway, who knew the future?

But if he went, would she be able to remember him? She had loved Joe, but she now couldn't remember his face properly. She put up a hand and ran her fingers gently over Max's face, tracing cheek and eye and nose and lips.

'What are you doing?' He was smiling down at her.

'Remembering,' she said. 'Just remembering.'

In the bathroom, she took out the Volpar Gels, held them in her hand for a moment and then put them back, unused. Max and she were in the hands of Fate. Why interfere?

# Chapter Thirty Five

## October 1944

Max lay quite still, listening to her breathing. He wanted to make love to her again, but there had been lines of fatigue around her eyes last night. God knows they were all tired now, tired of the relentless toll of torn and mutilated bodies coming out of France. Still, it would not be long before Europe was free. After that, only the Japanese would remain.

He closed his eyes, remembering Europe before the war. His grandfather had come to meet him from the plane when he landed in Poland, eyes round at the sight of an airport. His gentle grandfather whose eyes had seldom left a book, wiped out in a single savage act. He winced now, remembering the jubilation he had felt on D-Day, as though it were all over. Four days later, SS troops had descended on a French village, Oradour-sur Glane, had shot the men, and driven the women and children into the church, which they had then set on fire. Those who broke out through the flames had been machine-gunned. A whole community wiped out, as it had been also at Bydgoszcz. Had it been the SS Einsatzgruppen in Oradour, too?

A few weeks ago, London newspapers had reported the Red Army's liberation of Majdanek. If it could be called liberation. The place was filled with corpses, for more than half a million people, mainly Jews, had been gassed and incinerated there.

The final horror – their charred bones and ash had been pulverized, tinned, and shipped to Germany to fertilise the farmers' fields. How would Miriam justify her God when she heard that? He no longer could.

The flying bombs were now falling thick and fast on London, launched indiscriminately from the Pas de Calais with no attempt to target them. Maybe he and Catherine would die today, which would be a solution of sorts.

Beside him, she stirred. He raised himself on his elbow and looked down at her. Dark lashes fanned her cheeks, the dark hair curled around her face, a child's face. How could he leave her? But how could he stay?

---

November was a bleak month altogether, David thought as he looked from the train. The train had been almost at Doncaster before the first glimmer of day appeared in the east. October still had an autumnal glow, December had festivities, February brought hints of spring, but November and January had nothing to recommend them.

He shook open his *Telegraph*. Nothing in the papers about Hitler's secret weapon, the V-2 although their existence was common knowledge and had been since the first one hit Chiswick in September. He turned the page. Olivier was being hailed as the finest actor of his generation for his performance in *Richard the Third*. How did people sit in theatres knowing that silent death might be approaching overhead?

'Never mind,' David thought, returning to the view from the train. In less than three hours he would be with Catherine.

---

Pamela's head was aching, whether from factory noise or

anxiety she couldn't be sure. Night shift always had that effect on her, and thought Michael's last letter had been jubilant, it had filled her with terror. '*We're patrolling the Channel most of the time, gunning doodlebugs. You can get close enough to just catch their wing tips and tip them over so they go down into the sea. We're getting quite good at it, but you have to watch out for the Hun coming up behind you. I heard Rayburn on his radio whooping because he'd just scored, and then a Hun came out of the sun above and behind him, and that was that.*'

That was that! He had seen a friend killed, and that was that? Would he expect her to say, 'That was that' if he went down? Pamela looked at the passengers on the bus, afraid she'd been expressing her anger aloud. But everyone was wrapped up in their own affairs, so it was all right.

She tried to calm herself. Everyone said the war couldn't last much longer. Then he would be home, and she need never worry again.

There was a good smell when she let herself into the house. 'Come in,' her mother said, appearing from the kitchen. 'I've done you a rasher of bacon'. She paused for effect. 'And an egg! What do you think of that? And I've got the same for Daddy. An English breakfast! I feel like a queen.'

As she went upstairs to get out of her work clothes, Pamela felt calm grow inside her. Two years ago, or not much less, she had thought her parents finished. And now they were whole again.

———

'You look well,' David said, but it was hard to say it with conviction. Catherine had lost weight, there were shadows under her eyes, and, although she smiled as readily as before, there was something infinitely sad about her.

'How are you?' he asked when they had ordered.

'I'm fine. But I want to hear about you. And India, of course. Are you taking good care of Kynaston?'

David recounted tales of Kynaston and Belgate, anything to bring a smile to her face. A smile, he noticed, that never quite reached her eyes. She perked up at tales of his encounters with Hannah Chaffey. 'She said she'd managed to get some sausages, then she bunched herself up – you know how she does it?'

Catherine nodded, put her arms across her chest and pushed her breasts upwards.

'That's it,' David said. 'Then she said, "What's in sausages now is a mystery, and I hope no one solves it in my lifetime, thank you."'

'Oh David' Catherine said, putting a hand on his arm, 'it is so very, very good to see you again.'

〜〜〜

The woman's shabby raincoat strained over her swollen stomach. India felt saliva flood her mouth and passed a hand across her lips.

'What an earth made you think we could supply things?' She waved the list the woman had given her. 'How many children do you have?'

She was cringing now, which was somewhat satisfying. 'Four – four bairns.'

'Then you surely have these things already?' Most of the things on the list were needed for admission to hospital: night-gown and towels, slippers, toiletries – but what did that matter? These people needed to be brought up short and taught a lesson.

The woman had dropped her gaze. 'They said I should come here,' she mumbled.

'Who said?' India kept her tone sharp.

'The hospital.'

'The hospital? Then they had no right. We're not here to provide every last little thing. Where's your husband? Does he work?'

'He's in hospital. He was wounded in a V-2 raid down south.'

India was tempted to say that letting yourself get wounded was foolish, but she held back.

'Well, I don't know. How long has he been in hospital?' The pregnancy was well advanced, so he couldn't have been there long. She tapped on the desk with her fingers. 'It is his child, I suppose?'

The woman was crying now, which showed some sense of shame.

'Speak up,' India said. And then, when no answer came: 'I suppose he got leave. But neither of you thought ahead, did you? Well, I can't promise but we'll see what we can do.'

When the woman left she sat down. The past five years had been tedious beyond belief, but there were times when she knew she was doing a worthwhile job.

---

Hamish had brought her vegetables, fresh from the fields, and his expression, when he held them out, was contrite. 'I got these for you. Tatties and neeps.' He couldn't meet her eye.

'That's nice,' Sarah said as she took them from him. He was sorry. But then he was always sorry afterwards.

'We could go into Callander the morn,' he said. 'Take the wee-uns. Jock Inskip goes by – he'll give us a lift.'

'That'd be nice,' she said. They both knew it would never happen. The kindnesses of the day would be lost in the violence of the night.

'He can't help himself,' Sarah thought. 'He thinks I can help him – he wants me to help him.'

But she could no more change what was happening than she could stay the ripples on the loch. And that was the sad fact.

~~~~~

'It was the most awful stroke of luck to run into you,' David said as they entered the club. He had spotted Valerie across the width of Piccadilly, trim in her uniform, another servicewoman at her side. Her face had lit up when she turned at his call, and when he suggested dining at his club her response had been instant. She was staying with her friend's aunt and uncle in Bruton Street. He had extended his invitation to the other girl, but she had thanked him and declined, much to his relief. Now they ate salmon with a delicious sauce and asparagus tips with duchesse potatoes.

'You'd never know there was a war on,' Valerie said as he refilled her glass.

'I don't know about that. I heard some tremendous explosions through the day.'

She nodded. 'Yes, V-2s. You get used to them,' she said. 'It's amazing, but you do.'

'She's brave,' David thought. The Graham-Pooles had been loath to let her join a service at all, but she had persisted, and that, too, must have taken courage. 'When will you get leave again?' he asked.

~~~~~

'It's for you.' Pamela heard her father's voice and threw herself towards the stairs.

'Michael?' She sank on to the bottom stair and leaned against the wall. 'Are you OK? When are you coming home? Shall I come to you? Is there anything I can send you?'

'Steady on!' At the other end of the line he was laughing.

'I'm OK. I've got leave next week, and I'm coming home. Now – what else did you ask?'

He chatted on about someone who was getting the DFC, and another school friend who had written to him from hospital, and a sweater his mother had knitted for him into which the whole squadron could fit . . . Pamela listened, but all she could think of was that he was alive and soon he would be coming home.

Sarah had not shared Hamish's bed since the moment when she had defied him over Joe. Each night she crept into bed in the back room, put her arm protectively across her child, and went to sleep. Tonight, though, Hamish had different ideas. 'I want you in my bed,' he said, when she would have gone to the back room.

She shook her head. 'I'm sleeping in the other room.'

'Then I'll come in and drag you out.' He did not sound angry. He sounded cold, and somehow that was more frightening.

'I don't want to sleep with you.'

'You can sleep where you like, but you're in my bed first.'

So that was it. He would rape her, and if she didn't submit he would drag her from the other room and terrify her child. She looked at him.

'All right, she said. 'Let's get it over.'

When Catherine came back into the room, Max waited until she put down the dish she was carrying, and then he took her tenderly into his arms. 'I can't stay tonight, Catherine. I know I said we could have this last night, but they've changed my flight. It leaves at 4 a. m., and I have to get to the airfield. I want you to know this: we will never meet again, but I will love and honour you for the rest of my life.'

They sat down at the table and made a pretence of eating. Catherine felt unreal while she forked food around her plate and sometimes put some of it in her mouth. She was trying hard not to cry, but sometimes a tear would escape and roll down, salty, into her mouth.

'I'm sorry' he said at last, laying down knife and fork.

'Don't be,' she said. 'I had what I wanted, what you promised. And now it's time . . .'

Her voice faltered, then, and Max reached for her hand. They sat silently for a long time, neither of them speaking. At last he got to his feet and moved out of her vision. There was a second, and then she heard it – the *Andante Cantabile*. She sat still, knowing that if she got up and embraced him she could never let him go.

She sat on when he kissed the top of her head. A long, long kiss. She stayed there as the door clicked shut behind him. She was still sitting, the food grown cold on the table, when the record ended and there was only the clicking of the turntable.

## Chapter Thirty Six

### February 1945

SARAH HAD SEATED JOE ON the side of the pushchair for the long walk down to the shop. She had change ready in her pocket to ring Catherine on the hospital number that was only for emergencies, since there would be no possibility of her getting out after dark to ring her at home. Even if Hamish would have let her, she was not sure she could brave the unlit road at night. And yet what could happen to her here, in the open, that did not happen in her own home?

Her body ached, partly because of her bruises and partly, she suspected, because she held herself in a permanent state of tension. Little Joe was doing it, too, now, seeming always in a state of readiness for flight.

She didn't know why she needed to speak to Catherine: Catherine's money was squirreled away in her work-basket, so she had no need of more money if she wanted to leave. But she needed to confide in someone, and there was no one among her neighbours who she felt close enough to trust. Even if they believed her, someone who took it upon themselves to upbraid Hamish would precipitate disaster. With neighbours he was polite, even affable, and although she suspected they knew the truth, they never betrayed their knowledge, appearing to accept him at face value. 'An inside devil and outside saint,' Hannah

Chaffey had called a man once and it was true. You never knew a man until you lived with him. Or a woman, come to that.

Sarah looked around her, trying to find some cheer in the landscape, but there was only bleakness – a leaden sky, frost-withered hedges, and the dull gleam of water in the roadside ditches. She clutched her coat closer to her neck and trudged on.

The shop was crowded. She parked the pram, lifted little Joe down, and carried him inside. There was no one on the telephone, or in the corner where it stood. She could just march over there and dial. Instead, she meekly waited her turn and then asked for a packet of lentils and two onions.

Nowadays Catherine lived for her time on the ward. The flat without Max, with not even the prospect of his coming, was cold and echoing, or it felt like that. There were more general casualties, now, and fewer burns victims, so the mood on the ward was optimistic, even joky.

'They know we're winning,' Queenie had said yesterday. 'As good as an injection, a positive news bulletin.' Bomber Command were pounding Germany night after night. Two days ago they had razed the city of Dresden to the ground. There were rumours of 50,000 dead, which surely couldn't be true?

Catherine tried not to think about death as she glanced round the ward. Queenie sat at her desk, the huge starched cap perched proudly on her head. Once or twice today Catherine had looked up to find the QA's eyes on her. They were not hostile, which was a relief. Neither were they appreciative. 'She's curious,' Catherine thought, and felt a nervous flutter in her stomach.

She was returning from the sluice when the call came. 'Nurse!' So her fears had been well founded. She followed the imposing figure out of the ward and into the inner sanctum,

'Queenie's lair' as the nurses called it.

'Is there anything you want to tell me, Nurse?'

Catherine licked her lips. 'Not really.'

'Then shall I tell you something?'

She was waiting for an answer, and panic overtook Catherine and left her tongue-tied.

'I think you're pregnant. Am I right?'

It was out. 'Yes, Sister, I am. At least I think I am.' She could have added, 'I hope with all my heart I am,' but it was best not to say too much.

She thought of the Volpar Gels she had discarded the night before Max left. 'I'm glad I did it,' she thought, and regarded her superior with a steady gaze. It was done, and now she must accept the consequences.

———

David carried his breakfast through to the library. What sun there was came in at that side of the house, and Kynaston was so cold nowadays that the least little bit of brightness was welcome. He pushed his plate aside when he'd finished his egg on toast, and spread out the newspaper. The RAF was bombing strategic targets all over the place, and the US Air Force was setting Berlin on fire. The RAF had apparently gone after V-2 installations in the Netherlands, but the paper didn't say with what success. Most pages were filled with the conference at Yalta: Roosevelt, Stalin and Churchill no doubt carving up the peace. There was one angry letter about the bombing of Dresden, but the writer had declined to give his or her name. That would bring some comment. If you wanted to criticise the conduct of the war, you should have the grace actually to sign it.

He put the paper aside eventually and contemplated his day. Valerie was on leave, and they were meeting tonight. And he must ring Catherine at some stage and make sure all was well with her. He quite looked forward to seeing Valerie nowadays. They had a lot in common. But she would only ever be a friend. There was room in his heart for one love and that room was already occupied.

Still, they had gone to the cinema to see *Blithe Spirit* the night before, and he had enjoyed her chuckles at Madame Arcati's antics. Where should he take her tonight? David poured himself another cup of tea and settled back to ponder.

≈

'Yes. About ten weeks, if you've given me the right dates. Where do you want to have the baby? I can refer you to someone here.'

'I'm going home,' Catherine said, buttoning her dress. Queenie had packed her off to the MO, and now that it was done she felt relief.

'You'll have to resign, of course, but there won't be a problem. Is the father a serviceman?'

'Yes.' Catherine smiled. 'He's overseas.'

'Well, off you go and tell him the good news. They usually arrange for that sort of thing to get passed along. I'll fill in the necessary forms.'

'*I will keep you in my heart*,' she had told Max the last time they made love. And so she had. She was still smiling when she reached the ward doors.

≈

Pamela put both hands in the small of her back and straightened up.

'Bad back?' Joyce called out.

'Everything's bad. I ache all over.'

'Shouldn't have done it five times last night,' a girl called out.

'She should be so lucky,' Joyce said reprovingly. 'Her lad's operational.'

'That's what I said. He was operational five times last night, and she's paying for it.'

'Don't be coarse, Vera.' That was Virginia who had gone to a boarding school, and liked to think she had standards.

'Ooh, that's you told,' Joyce said. Pamela bent over her lathe again. They were all happy, and the banter was all good-humoured, now. She couldn't remember the last spat on the factory floor. They know it's nearly over, she thought. All Michael had to do was stay alive for a few more months, and then they need never be apart again.

She thought of his last letter: '*Not much longer, Pammy. There is still work to be done in Europe, but we have been told we are unlikely to go the Far East when Europe is free. They are even talking about resettlement plans. Apparently we'll get lectures on possibilities in civilian life. A lot of men want to stay in the service, but not me. I'm a home bird, Pammy, and I can't wait to get back to you for good.*'

She had felt first a flush of delight, and then an aftershock of fear when she read that. He was tempting fate with all this talk of peace-time. It was best to live one day at a time.

If it could be afforded, she would invite most of the women here to her wedding. She would like a bouquet of some sort, something to throw to the girls. But apart from that nothing mattered. Except the ring – that was the only essential. And once upon a time she had wanted all the trimmings! 'I've grown up,' she thought, and felt a little glow of satisfaction.

———

There was post on the mat when Catherine let herself in, and her heart leaped at the sight of an envelope with an overseas franking. 'He's coming back,' her heart said, but the first line told her differently.

'*I hope you are well. I had two weeks at home. The children hardly knew me at first, but time will change that. I have been posted and am scheduled to go East, but I have applied for a posting in Europe. There is much to do there, as they open the camps, and I want to play my part. I will not write again, but if ever you are in need and I can help, you know where to find me. Take care of yourself and God keep you safe. Lechayim, Catherine. Shalom, Max.*'

She wanted a drink desperately, but drinking alcohol was wrong in pregnancy. She tried not to cry too fiercely, because that too was bad; it had said so in the book she had brought at the chemist's. She was trying to stem the tears when the phone rang.

'Catherine?' It was David.

'Yes,' she said, 'it's me.'

'You sound upset.'

'No, not upset. Happy, really. I wasn't going to say anything, but I must tell someone, and you are my dearest friend. I'm going to have a baby.'

It was out, and however much she tried to take it back it wouldn't go.

The news of Catherine's pregnancy had struck David like a blow. He had stammered out congratulations, but all he had wanted to do was put down the phone. Max Detweiler would marry her, of course. There would be a wartime divorce – the papers were full of the surge in divorce rates – they would marry, and go off to the States. A wry smile touched his lips. He used 'the States' as a whip with which to beat India because she hated the expression. 'America,' she would say. 'It's America.'

He tried to take his mind off the subject by thinking ahead

to the evening. Valerie was good company, and Catherine was – always had been – beyond his reach. In life perhaps you had to settle for what you could get.

But an hour or so later, as he drove towards Valerie's home, he felt a leadenness of spirit that would not be dispelled. When they reached the hotel he drank more than usual with each course. and ordered brandy with the coffee. There was no brandy, the waiter apologised, and he thought he saw a look of relief on Valerie's face.

Across the table, out of uniform, she looked the pretty girl she was. Any man would be proud to call her his wife. And she loved him, he knew that from the way she hung on his every word, followed him with her eyes. The wine was still warm in his throat.

'Will you marry me, Valerie?' The look on her face made an answer superfluous.

Catherine regretted telling David as soon as she put down the phone. Why had she done it? Still, he would have to know some time. Everyone would have to know. She lay in the bath and looked at her body. No sign of change in her belly, yet – well, perhaps. But her breasts had changed. For a moment she felt afraid and then, quite suddenly, she felt empowered. She would give this baby everything, and in doing so make up for all the times she had failed in the past.

Had she been selfish? She was bringing a baby into the world who would not know its father, but thousands of women would have to do that because of this war. When she had dried herself and put on her nightgown, she curled up in a chair and re-read Max's last letter, the *Andante Cantabile* playing in the background because it soothed her. The letter was brief and, until the last, almost formal. '*I will love and honour you for the rest of my life,*' he had told her that last night. Was that true, or would he return to home and family after the war, and forget her? Would she forget him?

She smiled at the foolishness of such a thought, then she put the letter under her pillow, climbed into bed, and put out the lamp.

# Chapter Thirty Seven

## May 1945

CATHERINE'S TRAIN JOURNEY HOME HAD been filled with euphoria, but it was other people's jubilation, not her own. The train had been packed with servicemen and women, all celebrating as though they were being demobbed that very day. Beer was circulating, the WAAFs and ATS swigging it down like men, but the whole atmosphere was good-humoured. As soon as they had glimpsed Catherine's bulk a seat had been found for, her baggage stowed. It reminded her of that day – was it only four years ago? – when she had stood on the station platform, awkward in her unaccustomed uniform, and a kindly sergeant had installed her on the train.

This time she had been travelling by sleeper, but as sleep had overtaken her she had heard their distant merrymaking, and been glad for them. They had survived a war, they were entitled to rejoice.

Now, as she settled in the hired car that would take her the rest of the way, she thought about the events of the past two months. She had worked her last day on the ward three weeks ago. 'Be careful,' Queenie had said when she left – and then, throwing her QA stateliness to the winds, she had clasped Catherine to her starched bosom.

She had skulked in the London flat since then, afraid to go

home and face her parents, yet desperate for the comfort only home could bring. Thanks to Henry's money, she could live more or less where she chose, but she had always known she must go home to Mellows to bring up her child. First, however, there was something she must do. She had not heard from Sarah for weeks now. She had written to tell her of the coming baby, and had confidently expected a reply – a phone call, at least. But there had been nothing.

So she had decided: she would make the journey to Scotland to check on Sarah before settling in at Mellows. She wrote to tell Jim McGuire of her intention, but she did not write to Sarah. She was afraid that such a letter would produce a reply begging her not to come. Her increasing girth told her that soon travel would be irksome, so better get it over. Her baby would be born in September. A line from a poem learned at school came into her mind: '*Season of mists and mellow fruitfulness.*' Yes, September was a good month in which to be born.

She looked out at the Scottish countryside, springing to life now as the sun got power. Once she had checked on Sarah, and made sure all was well, she would retreat to Mellows and wait. For a moment she felt almost happy, until she remembered that returning to Durham would mean having to face her parents.

———

David had listened to the wireless since dawn, moving around the wavebands in search of something definite. The war was over, there could be little doubt of that. There had been an orgy of destruction in London towards the end of March, with V-2s raining death from the skies. More than 130 people had been killed in Stepney when a rocket demolished two five-storey blocks of flats, and two days later a housewife had died in Orpington, killed by the blast from a V-2 that landed in her garden. Her name had been Ivy Millichamp, and she had been

34 years old. For some reason she had stuck in David's mind from the moment her death was reported, and newspapers were now claiming that she was the last civilian to be killed in Britain. Which was probably true, because there were reports that German official sources were saying that Germany had surrendered. But there was still no announcement from Churchill.

David brewed yet another pot of tea, but he couldn't eat anything. He had not spoken to Catherine since the phone call in which she had told him of her pregnancy. What was there to say? Tonight he was taking Valerie to see *Brief Encounter* which the local paper was billing as a tale of love heroically suppressed. He had to smile at the irony. He knew all about suppressing love, but had never thought it heroic. Now, apparently he too was a hero – but there would be no cheering for him, because no one would ever know.

India sat in her office and drummed on her desk with her fingernails until they hurt and she had to examine them carefully in case of damage. Why didn't they make the dammed announcement? She had given instructions to the outer office to listen to the wireless and alert her as soon as anything was said, but nothing had come. The minute it was definite, she was packing up her things and going home. They had had almost five years of her life; they weren't getting a second more than she could help.

According to Rupert, the Germans had surrendered in a school building in Rheims at two in the morning. That meant the war was over. That had been on the wireless, so why was there nothing official from London? Perhaps they wouldn't declare an end until Japan was defeated, and that could take years.

At least, though, it would wipe the smiles off the faces she had seen unfurling flags and preparing ghastly street parties as she drove to the office. God, they were awful, those people who would undoubtedly try to take over the peace. The war had let them get above themselves, disturbed the natural order of things, that was the trouble. It would serve them right if they had to sit on their wretched parties. Except that she couldn't tolerate another moment of this boredom – not when there was so much else to be done.

———

Sarah was pinning out washing when she heard the car engine. That was a rarity round here, so she turned, her mouth still holding pegs. She saw the car halt, and the doors open, and then the pegs were dropping unheeded on to the grass and she was running towards the gate.

'Sarah!'

'Cathy!' As Catherine clasped her in her arms, Sarah knew fear for her family. 'What's happened?'

Even when she had been reassured, fear remained, her original dread of what might have happened back home replaced by fear of what Hamish would say about Catherine's arrival.

———

'I nearly didn't turn out when I heard,' Joyce said. 'And then I remembered the Japs, so I dragged meself in.'

There were one or two unattended benches, but the foreman was not looking too displeased. 'Could have been worse,' he muttered as he walked past with the manager. The mood was strangely subdued, considering it was nearly over, Pamela thought, but she didn't say anything.

'You don't need coupons for flags or bunting,' the woman next to her said contentedly. 'I went to Bixby's, and they were nearly sold out. People have been buying for weeks, according

391

to the woman. Have you?'

Pamela shook her head. 'Not me. I don't believe in counting your chickens . . .'

Her companion dropped her voice. 'Have you seen Virginia's scarf? Her father bought it for her in London – pure silk. It's called a Victory Scarf. Twenty-four and six! Scandalous!' There was a moment's pause and then she added, wistfully, 'Posh, though.'

'It would have to be posh for Virginia.'

The two women turned to face one another. 'Cotton!' they exclaimed in unison, and then, in an imitation of Virginia's boarding-school diction, 'Ay nevah wear cotton!' In her first week, Virginia had made that fatal announcement, and it had stuck to her.

They giggled together for a moment, and then Pamela said, 'She's OK though.'

'Shares her tabs, Pammy. That makes her OK by me. If it is Victory Day, will the shops be shut?'

'Thinking of buying a Victory Scarf?' Pamela quipped. The answer was swift.

'Ay nevah wear silk!'

They were still laughing when the foreman approached.

'OK, OK,' Pamela said, but suddenly something in his face told her he was not there to object to their merriment.

'I'm sorry – you're wanted in the office. There's someone on the telephone . . .'

<hr/>

'There's bound to be an announcement soon. Will it be a national holiday?' The estate foreman looked anxious, but David could only shake his head.

'I don't know. It's a strange set-up – the end of a war, and yet not the end of a war.'

'Yes, we're all forgetting the Japanese. But I need something definite, Sir David. If it *is* a holiday, they're all entitled, but the work of the estate can't stop just like that'.

'I can see that. We could offer them a day's pay in lieu – no, we'll do that anyway, an extra day all round. But ask for volunteers to see to the stock and other essentials, and say anyone who works need only put in the necessary hours, not a full day, plus they'll get two days' leave in lieu.'

'That's generous. What if they all opt for it?'

'Then they can all work, William. God knows we're not setting a precedent – there won't be another war's end in your time or mine.'

But as he drove from the estate office David was thinking of what had been said at the end of the Great War, fewer than 30 years ago. That had been called 'the war to end all wars', and yet it had taken only 20 years for people to forget. A verse from Kipling came into his mind.

*As it will be in the future, it was at the birth of Man,*
*There are only four things certain since Social Progress began:*
*That the Dog returns to his Vomit and the Sow returns to her Mire*
*And the burnt Fool's bandaged finger goes wobbling back to the*
    *Fire.*

They had an hour together before Hamish returned, and Catherine made the most of that time. 'You look ill, Sarah. You're so thin – and you don't write or telephone. Tell me what's wrong.' She was holding little Joe on her knee as she spoke. His face was serene, half-smiling, but she could feel the tension in him. 'He's like a coiled spring,' she thought, but did not say it aloud. Sarah was shaking her head as though dazed. 'Is it Hamish? Are you not getting on?'

It was then she noticed the bruise on Sarah's arm, and the way she pulled her sleeve over it when she saw where Catherine's gaze had rested.

'It's not his fault,' Sarah said at last. 'He doesn't mean it – but the war changed him, Cathy. He's a good man, but he can't handle it – and he's in pain with his leg, and he can't get work. We've got his pension, but he wants to work.'

Catherine sighed. 'I know the war's to blame, Sarah, but it's happened. It's happened to all of us. We've all been thrown into confusion and done things we'd never have done . . .' Her words dried for a moment, but then she spoke again, her voice more determined. 'People have died, Sarah, people we loved. They died for the future, and that means for the children. Whatever you decide must be for them. Do you understand?'

Sarah was nodding, but Catherine's heart sank at the lack of conviction in the movement.

'He cannat stand the children's crying, Cathy. It reminds him . . .'

'Does he hit the children, Sarah? You must tell me! I can see what happens to you . . .'

Suddenly Sarah started up in her chair. 'He's coming – I heard the gate. Don't say anything, I beg you, Cathy, please, please . . .'

And then he was stooping through the doorway, and Catherine was rising and extending her hand. 'Hamish, how very good to see you again. Forgive my flying visit but I wanted to tell you both my good news. I'm going to have a baby.'

———

They had opened a bottle of Bollinger by way of celebration. 'Good!' Rupert said appreciatively of the first sip.

India nodded. 'Yes, it will be wonderful when we can have what we want again. I've had enough of being deprived.'

'It won't be quick, though, India. The world's in a mess – half of Europe's starving or displaced, or both.'

'That's surely not our concern. We did our bit for them, holding out in 1940. They'll have to fend for themselves now. Especially the French. I can't bear the sight of that de Gaulle man – who does he think he is?'

'The next President of France probably.' Rupert stretched to riddle the base of the fire, and then refilled their glasses. 'Strange to think it will all be settled now without Roosevelt. To die like that on the brink of victory . . . We owe him a great deal.'

'I never liked him,' India said firmly, 'but he was better than this funny little draper man they have now.'

'Truman? He isn't a draper, is he? Missouri farming stock, surely?'

'Precisely – absolutely unfitted to be in charge of anything except chickens. Don't laugh at me, Rupert, you know I'm right.'

'Always,' Rupert said.

India looked at him sharply. There had been something in his tone . . . but his face, as usual, was bland. 'And boring,' India thought. Her husband was handsome but boring. She looked at her watch, then. 'It's seven-thirty. Put the wireless on – there must be some definite statement by now.'

The statement came at 7.40. A piano recital was interrupted with a stark announcement: '*Tuesday, 8th May 1945, will be treated as Victory in Europe Day, and will be regarded as a holiday.*'

'Is that it?' India was scandalised.

'That's it, my dear. So shall we raise our glasses?'

Sarah knew what would happen as soon as she came back in from showing Cathy to the outside privy.

'Why has she come? What does she want with the likes of

us? You haven't been whining on to her, have you, because by God . . .'

'I haven't said anything. Do you think she'd be so polite to you if I had?' This seemed to placate him but Sarah felt confused. Had she said anything? She was still trying to remember what had been spoken, what left unsaid, when Catherine came back into the room.

'I'm so sorry that I have to go so soon, but I mustn't miss the train. Thank goodness it won't be such a long journey this time. London to Scotland is quite a stretch.'

'Are you no' going back to London?' He was trying to display polite interest, but Sarah knew what he wanted to hear. What would Cathy say?

'Of course. London's home now, but I'm staying in Durham for a day or two, to see my parents and my sister, and my late husband's family. After that, it's back to the London flat.'

A glimmer of a smile crossed Hamish's face. 'I'll take your bag for you.'

Catherine let him precede her out of the house, and then turned to embrace little Joe and kiss the sleeping baby. 'Right,' she said. 'Let's go,' and Sarah followed her obediently. When they emerged, Hamish had reached the hired car and turned to watch them. Sarah felt Catherine's arms come round her and then her friend's voice urgent in her ear. 'In the baby's crib. All written down. Don't let him see.'

And then Catherine was drawing away, walking down the path, reaching to put her lips to Hamish's cheek, and stepping into the car.

She stood with Hamish until the car was lost to view, and he let out a grunt of satisfaction. 'Yon's a crazy woman, spending good money gallivanting up and down. Good riddance.' He turned back to the house. Little Joe was on the step, and Hamish brushed him aside as he entered. The child stumbled and then recovered himself, but Sarah's eyes were on his face.

His eyelids were blinking convulsively, and his shoulders had hunched as though to protect his head.

She bent to kiss him. 'Run outside and play,' she said, and then she walked into the room, went to check on the baby, felt for the package inside the blankets, and slipped it carefully into the hollow between her breasts.

David and Valerie had listened to the announcement together. 'A bit of an anti-climax,' David said. 'Two days off, that's all.'

Valerie was laughing. 'What did you want, David? Cannon?'

'That would have been nice – but only as a start.' He was laughing too. This girl could actually soothe him enough for him to laugh. He felt a sudden surge of gratitude towards her. 'Valerie –'.

'Yes, David.' She was moving towards him, not stopping until her body was touching his, her upturned face raised to his own. He moved away slightly, but only to put down his glass, then he took her in his arms and kissed her, not drawing away until he felt her shaking. With fear? But she was not afraid, she was laughing!

'What is it?'

'Oh David, if it took the end of a war to make you kiss me, what will it take to make you love me properly?'

He smiled, until he saw that her eyes were steady and fixed on his face. 'Do you mean –?'

'Yes, I think I do mean that. I want you to take me to bed.'

Catherine slept for the first part of the journey. The train was due into Durham at eight-thirty in the evening, but her eyes were already heavy when she embarked, and she was soon asleep. She awoke as they pulled into Newcastle, and the crowds surging on to the train were full of excitement. 'What's happened?' she asked, and a dozen voices were ready to tell her that tomorrow was Victory in Europe Day and a national holiday.

She arrived at Mellows to find Hannah Chaffey bustling about. 'No one told me you were coming back. I heard from Jim McGuire when I called in there tonight. I've kept everything right for you, and I've laid in milk and bread – or what they call bread nowadays.

'By, you should see the goings on in Belgate. There may be nothing up here, but they've gone mad down there – flags, bunting, someone was throwing confetti last night, there's trestles up in the street already.' Catherine smiled and nodded as Hannah went on. What had Max called a celebration – a *simcha*, that was it. Wherever he was now, he would be celebrating.

It was a relief when Hannah went and she could relax into a chair. As Max would have said, it had been a helluva few days. She cried a little, thinking of their days together in the flat, the laughter, the shared experience, the love. Especially the love. But the war was over, Max was gone, and she must go on alone.

# Chapter Thirty Eight

## 8 May 1945

Sarah eased her way out from the covers before dawn broke, and began her preparations. Yesterday, after Catherine's departure, she had gone to the privy and taken out the note left in the crib. Two more £20 notes were enclosed in it, and a pasteboard card. The note was brief: '*This is the telephone number of the car firm that brought me here. If you want to come home, ring them to collect you and take you to Stirling for the train. Tell no one. Ring me when you can. I will be at Mellows. Remember what I said, Sarah: it's the children who matter.*'

She had put the note and the money back between her breasts and stood for a long while at the privy window, staring out at the placid landscape. Eventually she had put on her coat, pleaded a shortage of bread, and hurried down to the store. It was empty so there was no one to overhear. She had to dial the number twice because her fingers were suddenly clumsy, but at last she was through and it was done: the car would meet them outside the store at six next morning.

Now the clock on the dresser said four a. m. Silently she packed the pram with the minimum for the journey: food for the children, nappies, water, a few clothes, the money – nothing for herself. She was happy to leave everything behind except the photo of her parents and the boys taken in the days before the war, when nobody had wept.

When she was ready she woke Joe, putting her hand gently over his mouth and whispering in his ear: 'We're going home, lamby, but you must be very, very quiet.' He tried to struggle free of her hand, but it was only to nod his head. When everything was ready, she put the baby in the pram and eased it gently over the step. It was five o'clock, and almost daylight. She paused only to lift Joe on to the pram, and then she set off down the road without a backward glance.

Somehow the thought of a day of leisure did not thrill David. The empty house served only to accentuate the flatness of his mood. If Henry had been here, how they would have exulted together. Henry had always been the leader, the Quixote tilting at windmills, he himself the faithful retainer coming up behind. But it had been the perfect partnership. He had never envied his brother – except in one respect. 'I knew he would marry Catherine,' David thought now, 'and in my heart I begrudged him.'

All for nothing. War had come and swept each person's intention away. Henry was dead, and Max Detweiler had taken his place. Max, whose path would never have crossed with Catherine's if it had not been for the war. She would go to America when her baby was born, and he would be left to marry Valerie, a girl he liked tremendously but did not love.

Contemplating his situation, David he brought his fist down on the table with a thud. Why had he done it? Even if you disregarded his own fate, was it right to marry Valerie knowing he could give her only a percentage of his heart? And yet, after last night, how could he avoid it? Here, at Kynaston, in the room that had been his mother's, with its mirrored walls and two Corots gazing down on them, they had made love. The first time for both of them.

Sitting at the breakfast table he tried to work out how he had felt. 'Embarrassed' was the word that came to mind. But Valerie had put her lips against his ear and whispered, 'I wanted it to be with you, the first time.' He had known she was a virgin from her cry of pain. He had not betrayed his own lack of experience by anything other than an ineptitude she had been too green to recognise. Still, it was done now, and he must live with it. He was sitting head in hands, wondering how he would face her today, when Mrs Earnshaw bustled in.

'I'm right flustered, Sir David. This letter came for you yesterday. I put it in the pocket of my overall and clean forgot to give it you.'

It was from Catherine. '*Dearest David, I'm on my way home to Mellows. For good this time. It was so good to confide in you. You are a true friend and I will have need of friends. I am going to have my baby and that is a cause for rejoicing, but I will never see Max again. He has gone home to his family, as I always knew he would. I'm going to Scotland to see Sarah now, but I expect to be back in Durham later this week . . .*'

He could read no further. If he had had that letter yesterday, last night would never have happened, and he would have had hope again. A vain hope, perhaps, but hope all the same. Now he did not even have that.

≈

Pamela lay in bed. She had been there since she got home yesterday, pausing only to tell her parents what had happened. Once that was done she wanted her bed and the covers pulled up around her face. It was her fault: she had done the fatal thing, counted her chickens, reckoned Michael safe and the war over. And now he was dead.

The manager had said nothing, just handed her the phone.

'It's me, Brian White,' a voice had said. She had stood there trying to think of a Brian she knew and finding none. And then he had gone on: 'It's me, Chalky. I wanted to tell you before you got the telegram. Mike came down in the Channel, no one knows why. They're searching for him – I'm sure he'll be OK, nine lives that one. . .'

Pamela had not listened any more, simply handed over the receiver and gone back to her lathe. Chalky had said they were searching, but she knew what that meant – that there was nothing left of him to find.

She had come home, gone to bed, and slept fitfully but she had not cried. She felt empty, as though nothing mattered any more. She was lying on her back, dry-eyed, when her father erupted into the room.

'For God's sake, do I have to run up and down these stairs all the time? He's on the phone, Pamela – him – Michael!'

And suddenly Michael's voice was in her ear saying something about a fuel line. 'That's all it was apparently, Pammy, a blocked line – at least that's what they think, but it was still a bloody great awful prang. At least Jerry didn't get me. Once I knew I couldn't make it, I got out. I remembered the drill, but about 20 feet above the water I tried to get rid of the chute. . . couldn't . . . bloody thing nearly forced me under till I struggled free. They say the plane would have gone into a spin at 10,000 feet and I probably fell out, but I do have a faint recollection of ejecting.

'I've got a hell of a bump on my head, anyway, but otherwise I'm intact. I was in the water for seven hours! Good job it was nearly summer but my teeth were chattering in the end and there were a lot of gulls. They're coming for me I thought – big buggers, they were. I must've drifted off for a while, and then the next minute someone was hauling me into a boat and I heard them say, "It's one of ours, Mack, and he's breathing." It was the Margate lifeboat, they saw the chute – so much for getting rid of it. Anyway, I'm here, Pammy. You haven't seen the back of me yet.'

She cried in her father's arms when she put the phone down, and then her mother was forcing her to drink revoltingly sweet tea and talking about God's will. All Pamela could think of was that now they could get married. She could stay at home until he was demobbed, and then they would get a place together. A room would do. They would have to be married first, her mother would insist on that, but it could be arranged.

Back in her room she crossed to the dressing-table. Behind it, lace curtains covered the windows. She reached for one and draped it over her head. Through the mesh her eyes still sparkled. She would make Michael a bride to be proud of.

≈

Today India had come in to clear her desk and leave her keys. Yesterday the Deputy District Commander had gushed: 'You'll stay on, of course? You've been wonderful, and we'll be needed more than ever to get things back to normal.' India had not even dignified that with a reply. She had never wanted to be a pillar of the community, not in that way. The other women were dedicated, so it could be left to them – although without her own intelligence and drive, it would probably be the blind leading the blind.

She closed the door of her office for the last time, handed the keys to the caretaker, and left, never to return. They could beg and plead as they liked: her war effort was well and truly over, and they surely wouldn't try to mobilise her now. Soon the troops would come straggling home, expecting to be fêted and kitted out for peace-time. She had reams of paper detailing how it would be done, but it would not be done by her, thank God. It would be someone else's responsibility. She turned for one last look, and then she climbed into her car and turned on the ignition.

She had left the Darlesden road and was driving towards home when she saw Catherine Allerton emerge from the turning that led to St Hilda's church and from there to Mellows. No one had said she was home! And then she saw the swollen belly, the hand protectively on it in the archetypal gesture of the mother for her unborn child. Catherine Allerton was pregnant!

A cry escaped India's lips. Every woman could get pregnant – every woman in the world, except her.

⸻

Sarah had not felt safe until they were on the train and speeding south. The pram was safely stowed in the guard's van, the baby slept contentedly on her knee, and although Joe still looked tense he was not clutching at her skirts as he had done so often lately. Sometimes, looking out at the landscape of Scotland, she felt regret. It was a beautiful country, and she could have been happy here if things had been different. If Hamish had been different. This was his child sleeping in her arms. Had she done right in stealing it away? And then she remembered Catherine's words: '*It's the children who matter*', and knew she had done the only thing possible.

She was feeling almost content as they pulled into Edinburgh station – until she saw the police on the platform, moving from carriage to carriage, peering in. She might have known Hamish would never let her go!

⸻

David had ridden over half the county, at first in a frenzy of doubt and recrimination, then, gradually, with a sense of calm. He would always love Catherine, but he would do right by the girl who had done nothing wrong except love him. Somehow the sight of the land was comforting. He had feared and dreaded the burden the estate would place upon him, but when he had faced up to it he had come to see it as a privilege and not a burden. So it would be with Valerie. He would come to love her in time, and there would be children to draw them together. 'I will make her happy,' he vowed.

But he would see to Catherine's happiness, too. While there was breath in his body, he would protect her and her child. War had dictated the path for all of them. Now they must follow it to the bitter end. He paused on the brow of the hill for one last look around, then he turned the mare for home.

It took all Catherine's courage to face her parents. She walked from Mellows to their house, seeing here and there wood piled in fields ready for Victory bonfires, and houses festooned with flags. Almost every window had some kind of symbol in it – Churchill predominated, but the King was there too, and once or twice the Stars and Stripes.

At last she was at her parents' gate and the moment had come. Her mother opened the door. Her face lit up with surprise and pleasure, and then her eyes travelled down and took in Catherine's altered figure.

'Hello, Mummy,' Catherine said, and walked past her into the hall.

'Catherine?' Her father's reaction mirrored her mother's, and she felt her throat convulse. Best get it over.

'Mummy, Daddy, I have something to tell you. I'm going to have a baby, and I'm going to have to bring it up on my own because the father and I can't be together.' There, it was done.

There was no softening of the faces opposite her. They were still registering shock. And then Pamela was coming down the stairs. Seeing it all and still smiling. Her arm came round her sister in a protective gesture. 'Come on in, Catherine. Welcome home!'

They had gathered round the fireplace in the Graham-Poole drawing-room. Valerie's father had his arm fondly round his daughter, her mother was pouring champagne into curved, shallow glasses.

'To David and Valerie,' Mr Graham-Poole, said when they were all supplied. 'To their long and happy life together.'

Valerie was detaching herself from her father and crossing to David's side. 'Are we supposed to drink to ourselves?' she asked, looking up at him.

'I don't know,' he said teasingly, 'I've never done this before.'

'And never will again, I hope.' They all laughed at the heart-felt note in Valerie's voice.

'We should drink to peace, too,' Valerie said, and they raised their glasses again.

Valerie's father was shaking his head. 'They're going mad in London. There are bonfires in Piccadilly and Cambridge Circus – they had to bring in the AFS to douse them.'

'Douglas Bader was repatriated today,' David added. 'There was a headline this morning "*Legless Ace is back*". It's a fitting moment, isn't it?'

There was a murmur of approval at that particular news, and then Mrs. Graham-Poole spoke. 'Is your sister pleased about your news?'

David shook his head. 'I haven't seen her to tell her, but I know she will be happy for us.'

'You must ring her, my boy. If I know old Rupert, he'll have opened champagne tonight, anyway. Ring them and give them something more to drink to.'

David would have liked to postpone telling India, but they were all looking at him expectantly.

'If I may use the telephone?' he said.

≈

'I think it's a damp squib.' India turned to place her glass on a side table. She was still angry over the sight of Catherine Allerton, but it wouldn't do to admit it. Instead she vented her fury on the muddle she deemed Victory in Europe to be. 'They promised to ring the church bells when the time came, and I don't hear them. They said they'd sound the All Clear – well, I can do without that, thank you. But this – this muddle . . .'

She was in full flow when the telephone rang in the hall. 'It's David,' Rupert said, coming back into the drawing-room. 'For you.'

India sighed. 'What can he want at this hour?' She went into the hall and lifted the receiver. 'David?'

At the other end of the line he was burbling on and she listened with mounting fury. When she came back into the drawing-room her lips were compressed, her eyes glittered.

'Everything all right?' Rupert asked. He was filling his glass as he spoke and she seized the bottle to replenish her own. 'Steady on, old girl!'

'Steady on? How can I "steady on" when my brother has let this day of so-called rejoicing go to his head? He's proposed to the Graham-Poole girl, who has probably been up to heaven knows what, mixing with ATS rabble. How could he let me, let the family, down?'

Her words dried as she saw her husband's expression. 'For God's sake, India,' he said, 'couldn't you, just for once in your miserable life, rejoice?'

≈

On the way back to Mellows, Catherine thought about the past few hours. 'People will talk,' her mother had said. 'But we'll just have to make the best of it.' Before the war, her mother had fretted if a lace curtain was ruffled. Now she could take a child born out of wedlock in her stride. Her father had looked sad, but his embrace had been warm and loving. 'It isn't what I'd have wished for you, Catherine, but we'll manage, the four of us.'

Only Pamela had expressed joy at the thought of a baby, and insisted on sending her home in a taxi. She had even begged her to stay the night but some instinct made Catherine long to get home. 'Pamela's grown up,' Catherine thought now, 'and happiness has made her generous.' She would not get such generosity from everyone, though. She thought of India Callingham's face that afternoon as the car had swept past, eyes twin coals of fury in a white face.

She got out of the taxi, and let herself into the house, feeling a strange satisfaction as she closed the door on the world. It was getting dark now, and she put a match to the fire, and switched on the wireless. This afternoon, in her parents' home, she had heard Churchill make the formal announcement, and she sat now to listen as he spoke to the crowds surrounding Buckingham Palace. '*This is your victory.*' She could hear the crowd roaring, '*No it's yours!*'

There had been a break in the old man's voice as he continued: '*God bless you all. This is your victory! It is the victory of the cause of freedom in every land. In all our long history we have never seen a greater day than this. Everyone, man or woman, has done their best. Everyone has tried. Neither the long years, nor the dangers, nor the fierce attacks of the enemy, have in any way weakened the independent resolve of the British nation. God bless you all.*'

Catherine had moderated her drinking since she became pregnant, but the occasion called for a toast. She poured herself a small brandy and raised her glass. But before she could take a sip, the sky outside the window was illuminated. Somewhere they were sending up rockets! Or fireworks?

She went through the hall, opened the door, and moved on

to the step. She could hear cheering far off, and there was the glow from a bonfire over to the east. Suddenly she felt her baby kick – hard, as though it too wanted to join in the celebration.

It was then that she saw them coming up the drive. A woman with a baby in a pram, a little child dragging on her skirts.

'Sarah!' She was flying across the space between them, scooping the child into her arms, feeling him sag against her in relief. 'I've got you now, Joe,' she said.

'He's tired,' Sarah said quietly. 'He's come a long way.'

Catherine put an arm around her and turned them both to face the light in the east. 'We've all come a long way, Sarah. But listen! They're celebrating. The war is over and we've all come home.'

She laid her cheek against the little boy's head and felt the silky hair against her cheek. Beside them the baby slept on, oblivious of the fact that history was being made.

They stood there for a while as the sky mirrored the rejoicing, and then they turned and went, together, into the house.

# DENISE ROBERTSON

If you've enjoyed this book and would like to find
out more about Denise and her novels, why not
join the **Denise Robertson Book Club**.
Members will receive special offers,
early notification of new titles,
information on author events and lots more.
Membership is free and there is no commitment to buy.

To join, simply send your name and address to
**info@deniserobertsonbooks.co.uk**

or post your details to
The Denise Robertson Book Club
PO Box 58514
Barnes
London
SW13 3AE

# Other books by Denise Robertson:

DENISE ROBERTSON
A Relative Freedom

DENISE ROBERTSON
The Promise

DENISE ROBERTSON
None To Make You Cry

DENISE ROBERTSON
The Second Wife

DENISE ROBERTSON
The Bad Sister

DENISE ROBERTSON
Wait for the Day

DENISE ROBERTSON
The Beloved People

DENISE ROBERTSON
Strength for the Morning

DENISE ROBERTSON
Towards Jerusalem

Available from all good bookshops price £7.99
or order direct from the publisher with FREE postage and
packing by calling the credit card hotline 01903 828503
quoting DR2009.

COMING SOON FROM
# DENISE ROBERTSON
# The Tides of Peace

If you have enjoyed this book and want to know
what happens when peace returns to Britain all
will be revealed in the conclusion to
*The Winds of War*.

Will Max and Cathy meet again?
Will David find true happiness with Valerie or will
India's scheming continue to work against him?
Will Sarah and her children rebuild their lives or
must she flee a vengeful husband? What will
happen to Pamela in a world no longer at war?

Place an order now at the pre-prepublication
discount price of £6.99 including FREE postage
and packing by calling the credit card hotline
01903 828503 quoting DR2009.